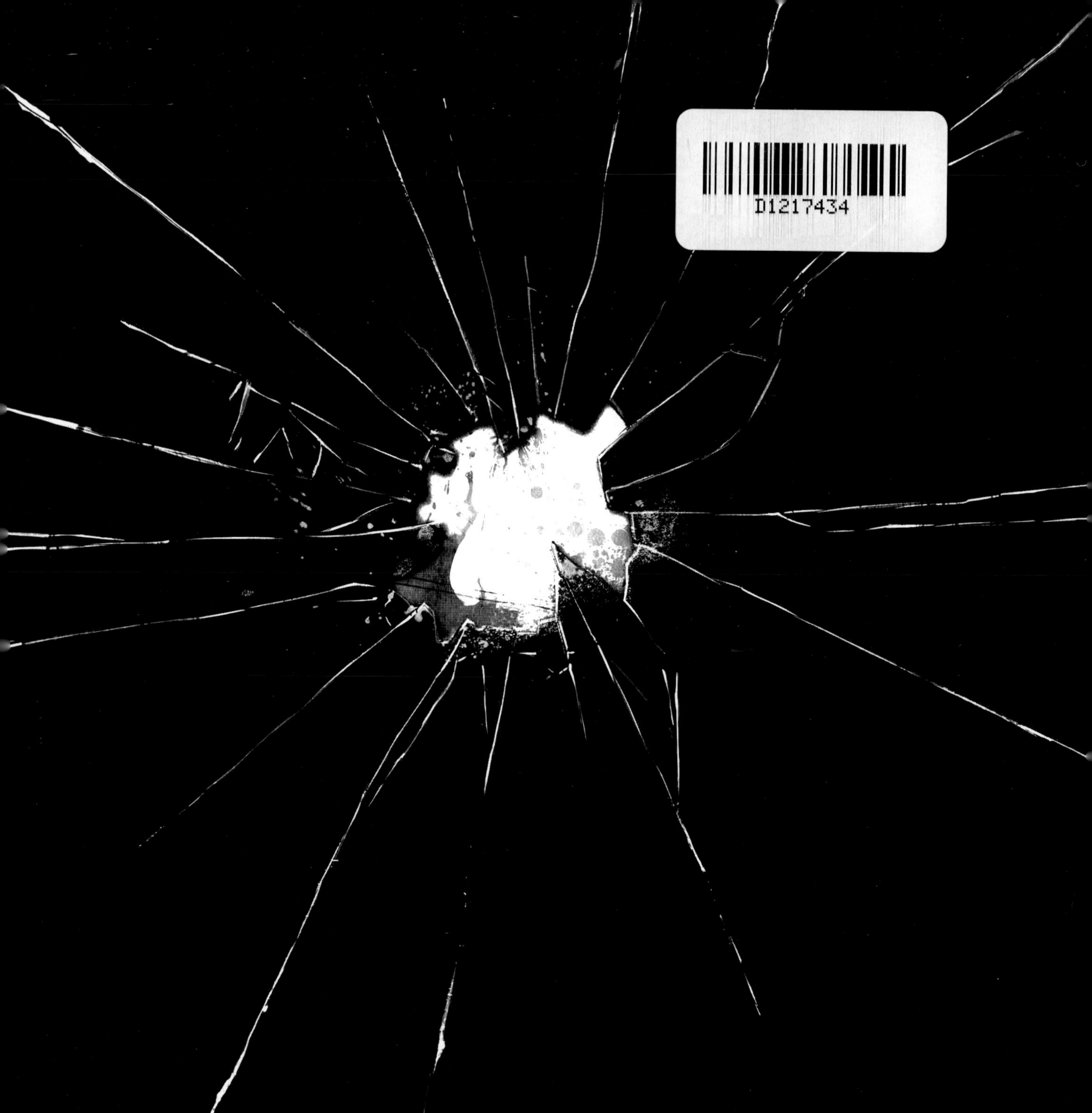

LOWLIFES

IDW

Facebook: **facebook.com/idwpublishing**
Twitter: **@idwpublishing**
YouTube: **youtube.com/idwpublishing**
Tumblr: **tumblr.idwpublishing.com**
Instagram: **instagram.com/idwpublishing**

ISBN: 978-1-68405-376-6   22 21 20 19   1 2 3 4

LETTERING BY
NEIL UYETAKE

EDITORIAL ASSIST
ELIZABETH BREI

SERIES EDITOR
DENTON J. TIPTON

COVER ART
ALEXIS SENTENAC

COLLECTION EDITS BY
JUSTIN EISINGER AND
ALONZO SIMON

COLLECTION DESIGN BY
RON ESTEVEZ

PUBLISHER:
GREG GOLDSTEIN

Special thanks to Olivier Jalabert
of Glénat Editions for his
invaluable assistance.

LOWLIFES. JANUARY 2019. FIRST PRINTING. © 2019 Brian Buccellato. © 2019 Idea and
Design Works, LLC. The IDW logo is registered in the U.S. Patent and Trademark Office. IDW
Publishing, a division of Idea and Design Works, LLC. Editorial offices: 2765 Truxtun Road,
San Diego, CA 92106. Any similarities to persons living or dead are purely coincidental. With
the exception of artwork used for review purposes, none of the contents of this publication
may be reprinted without the permission of Idea and Design Works, LLC. Printed in Korea.
IDW Publishing does not read or accept unsolicited submissions of ideas, stories, or artwork.

Originally published as LOWLIFES issues #1–4.

Greg Goldstein, President and Publisher
John Barber, Editor-In-Chief
Robbie Robbins, EVP/Sr. Art Director
Cara Morrison, Chief Financial Officer
Matt Ruzicka, Chief Accounting Officer
Anita Frazier, SVP of Sales and Marketing
David Hedgecock, Associate Publisher
Jerry Bennington, VP of New Product Development
Lorelei Bunjes, VP of Digital Services
Justin Eisinger, Editorial Director, Graphic Novels & Collections
Eric Moss, Senior Director, Licensing and Business Development

Ted Adams, IDW Founder

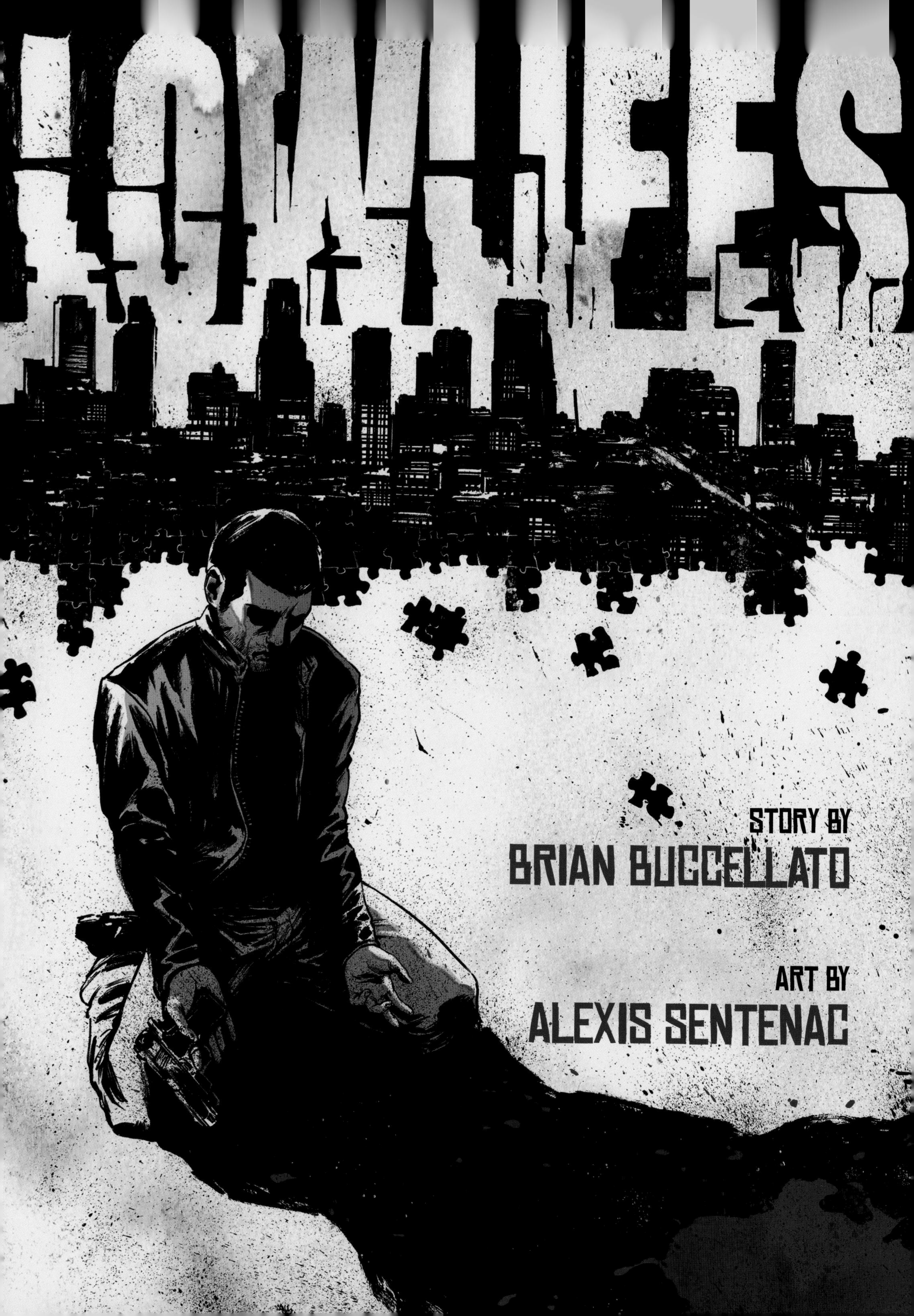
LOWLIFES
STORY BY
BRIAN BUCCELLATO
ART BY
ALEXIS SENTENAC

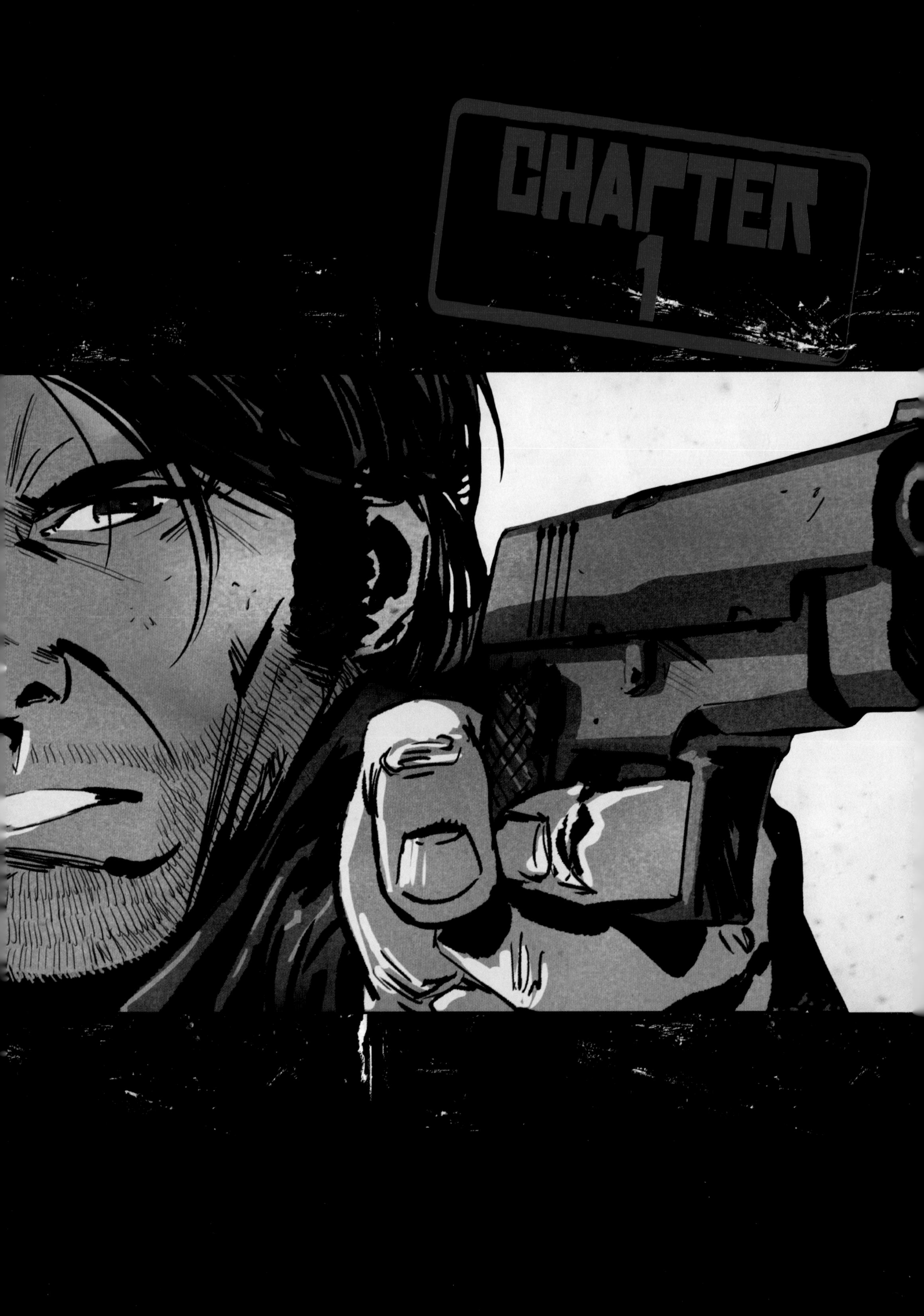
CHAPTER
1

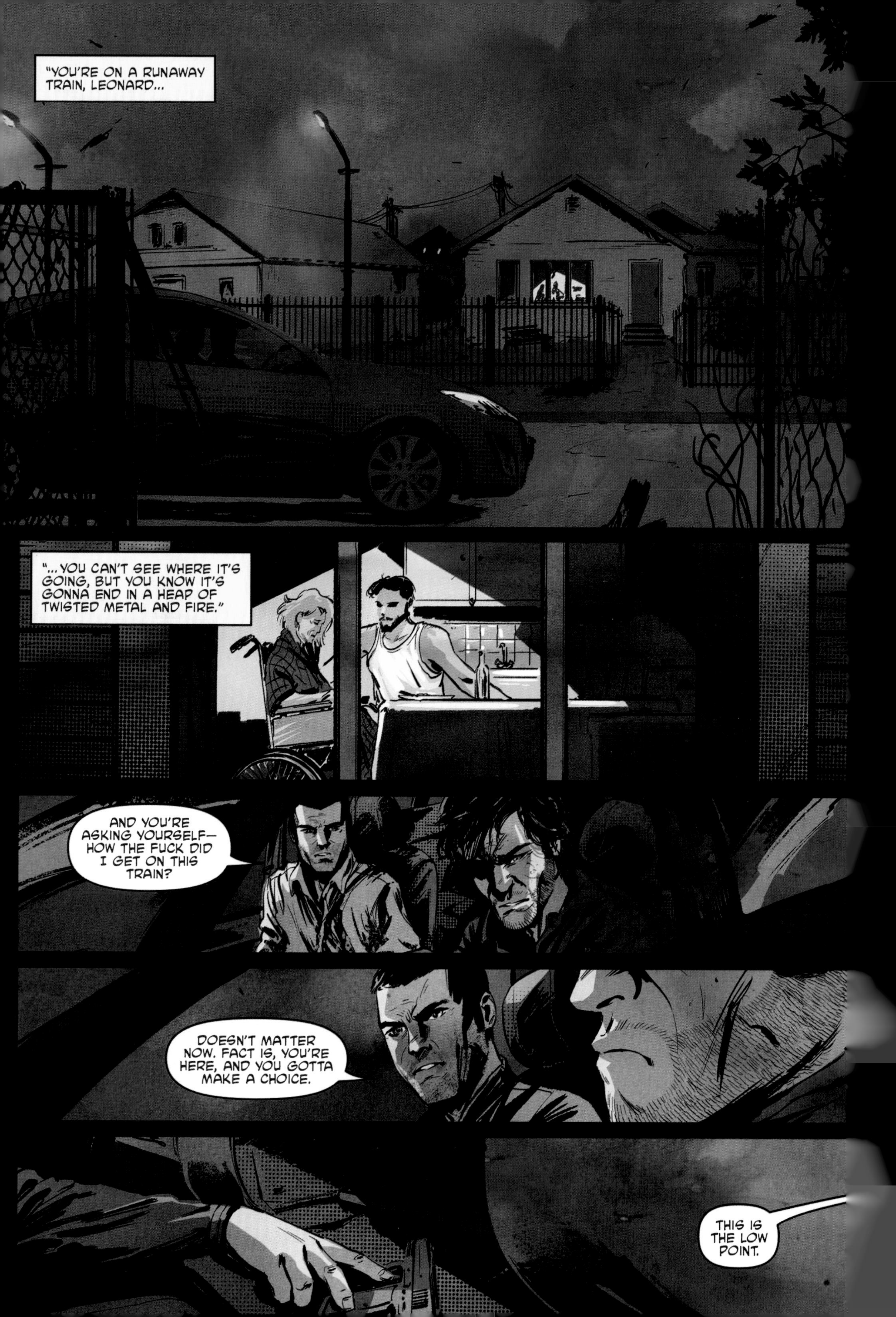
"YOU'RE ON A RUNAWAY TRAIN, LEONARD...
"...YOU CAN'T SEE WHERE IT'S GOING, BUT YOU KNOW IT'S GONNA END IN A HEAP OF TWISTED METAL AND FIRE."
AND YOU'RE ASKING YOURSELF— HOW THE FUCK DID I GET ON THIS TRAIN?
DOESN'T MATTER NOW. FACT IS, YOU'RE HERE, AND YOU GOTTA MAKE A CHOICE.
THIS IS THE LOW POINT.

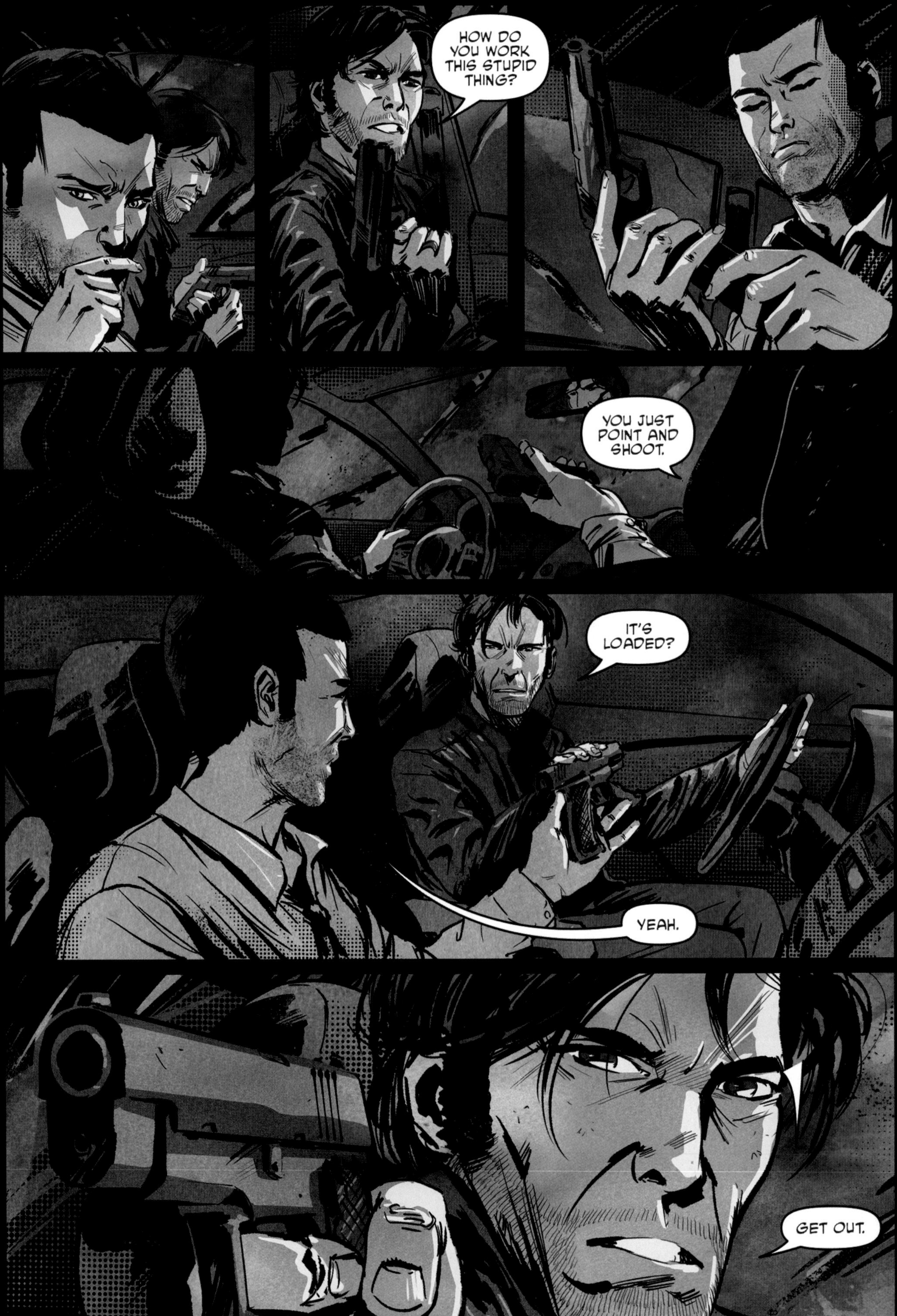
HOW DO YOU WORK THIS STUPID THING?
YOU JUST POINT AND SHOOT.
IT'S LOADED?
YEAH.
GET OUT.

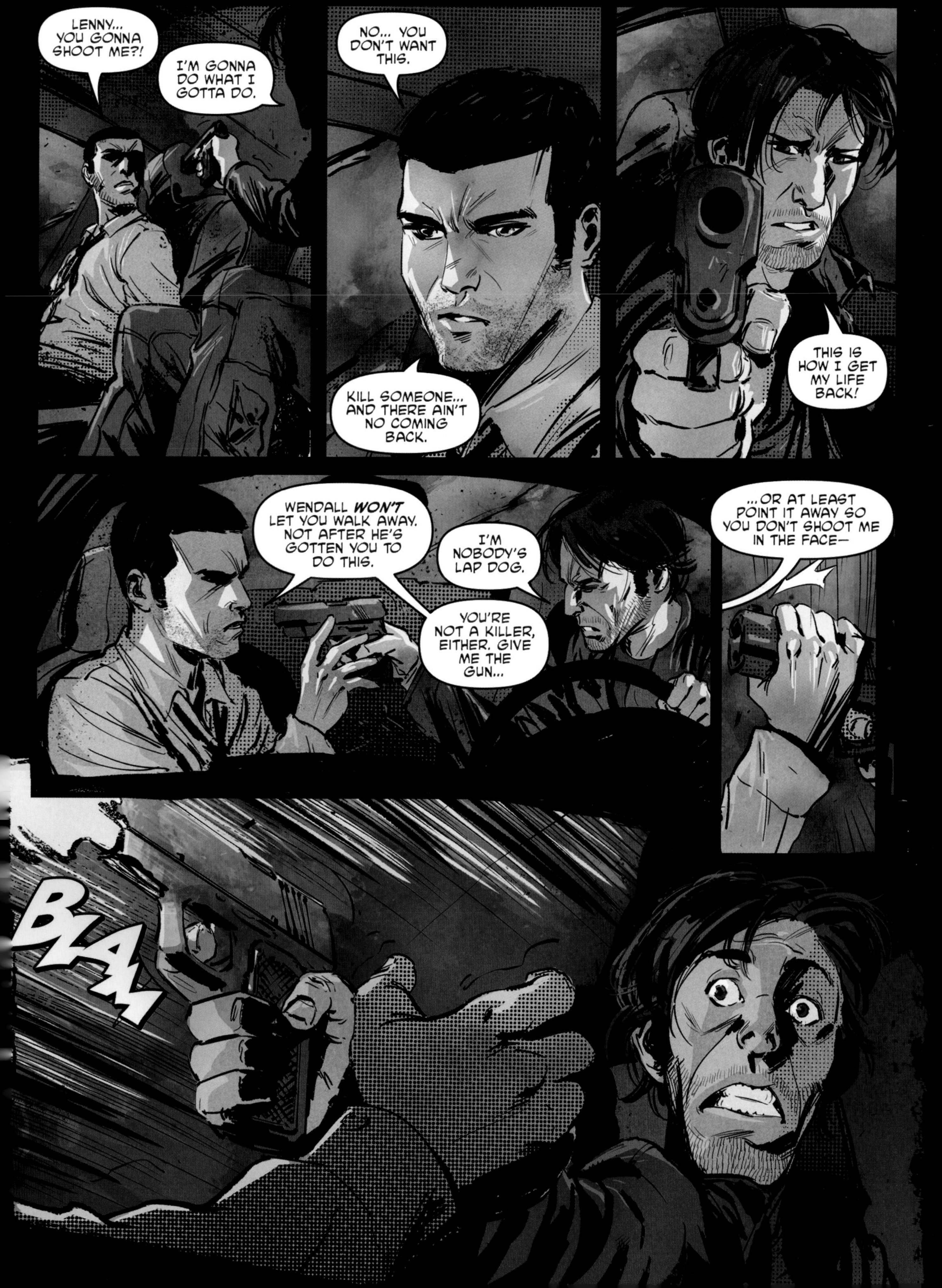
LENNY... YOU GONNA SHOOT ME?!
I'M GONNA DO WHAT I GOTTA DO.
NO... YOU DON'T WANT THIS.
KILL SOMEONE... AND THERE AIN'T NO COMING BACK.
THIS IS HOW I GET MY LIFE BACK!
WENDALL *WON'T* LET YOU WALK AWAY. NOT AFTER HE'S GOTTEN YOU TO DO THIS.
I'M NOBODY'S LAP DOG.
YOU'RE NOT A KILLER, EITHER. GIVE ME THE GUN...
...OR AT LEAST POINT IT AWAY SO YOU DON'T SHOOT ME IN THE FACE—
BLAM

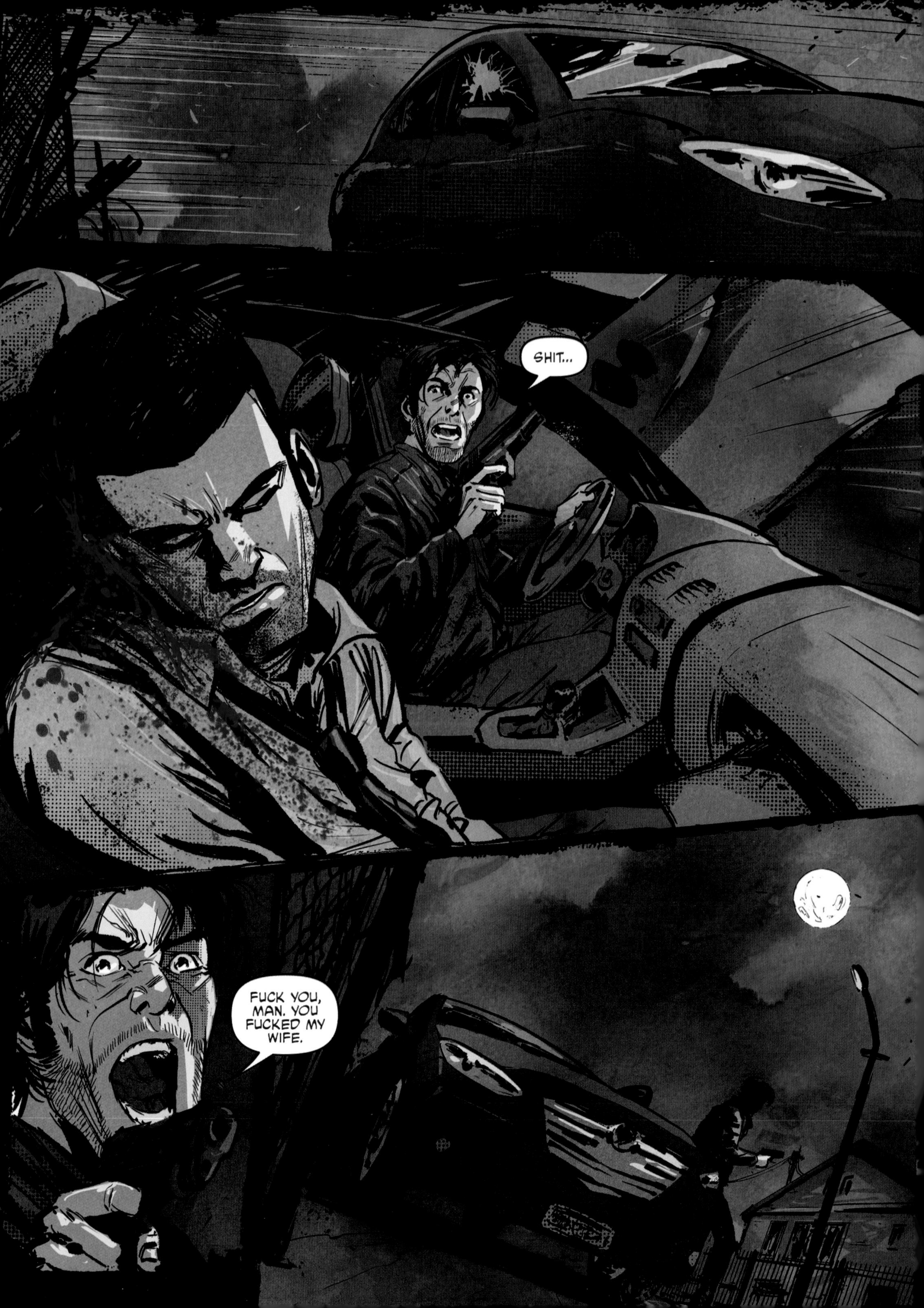
SHIT...
FUCK YOU, MAN. YOU FUCKED MY WIFE.

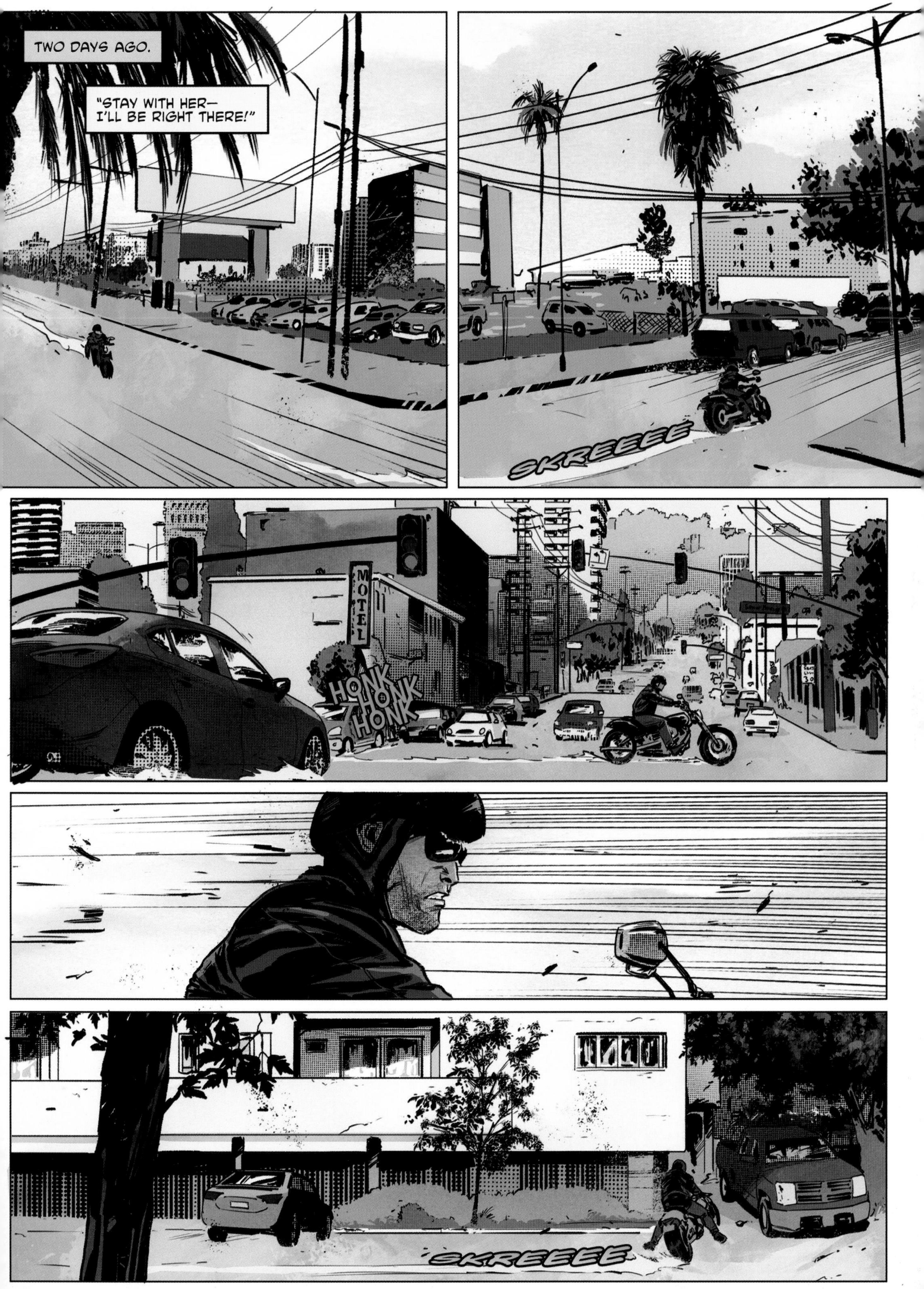
TWO DAYS AGO.
"STAY WITH HER—
I'LL BE RIGHT THERE!"
SKREEEEE
MOTEL
HONK HONK HONK
SKREEEEE

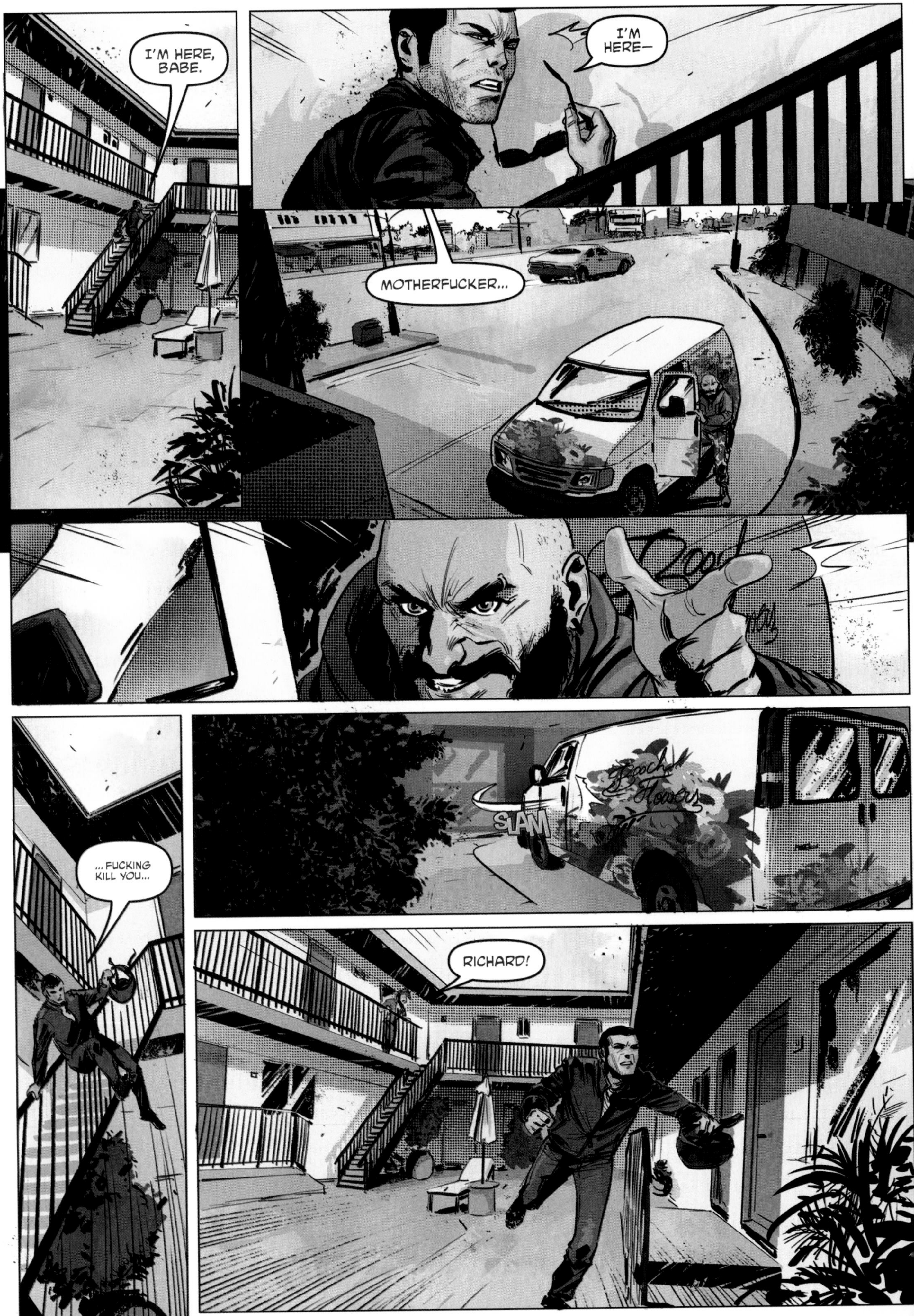
I'M HERE, BABE.
I'M HERE—
MOTHERFUCKER...
SLAM
...FUCKING KILL YOU...
RICHARD!

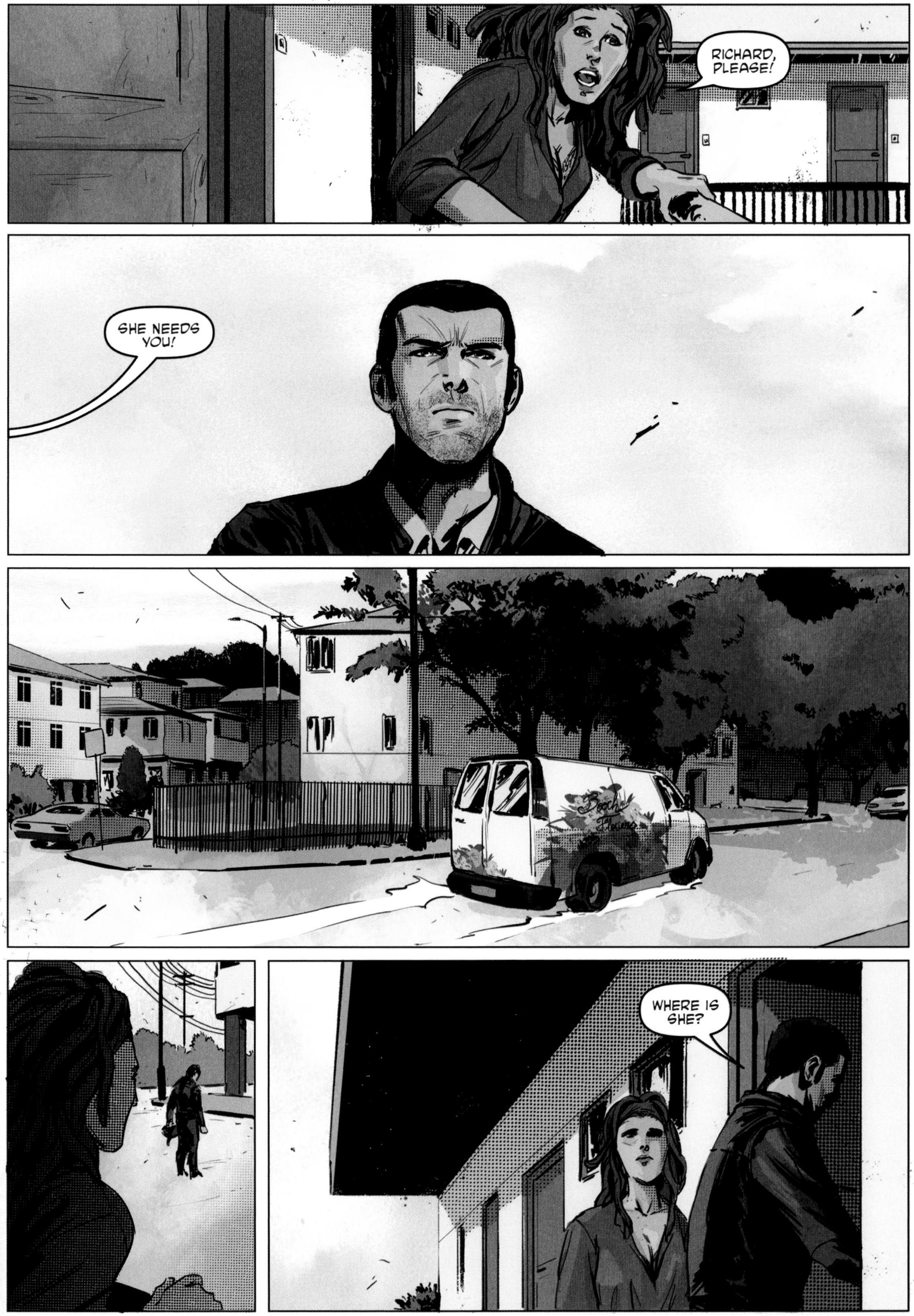
RICHARD, PLEASE!
SHE NEEDS YOU!
WHERE IS SHE?

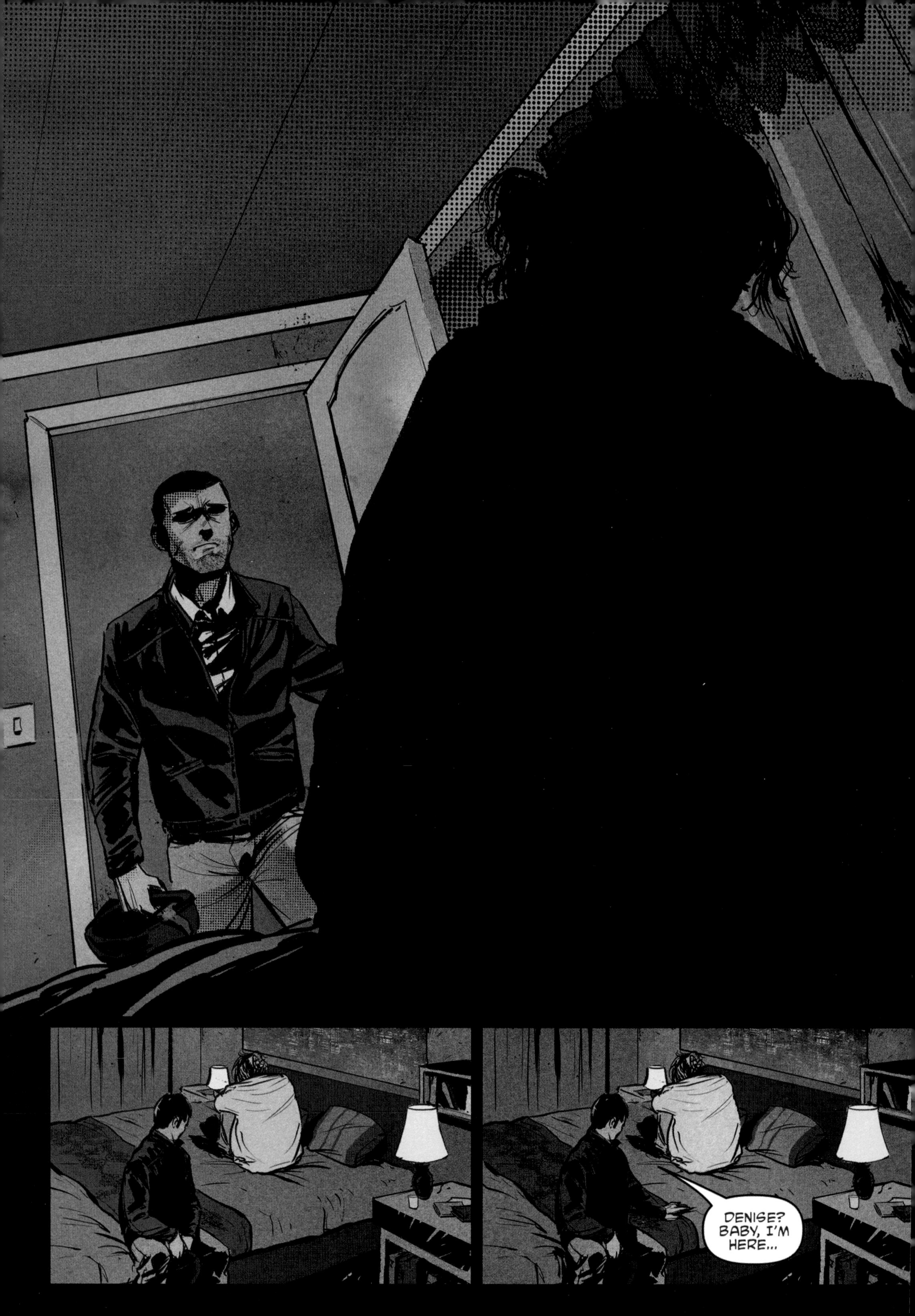
DENISE? BABY, I'M HERE...

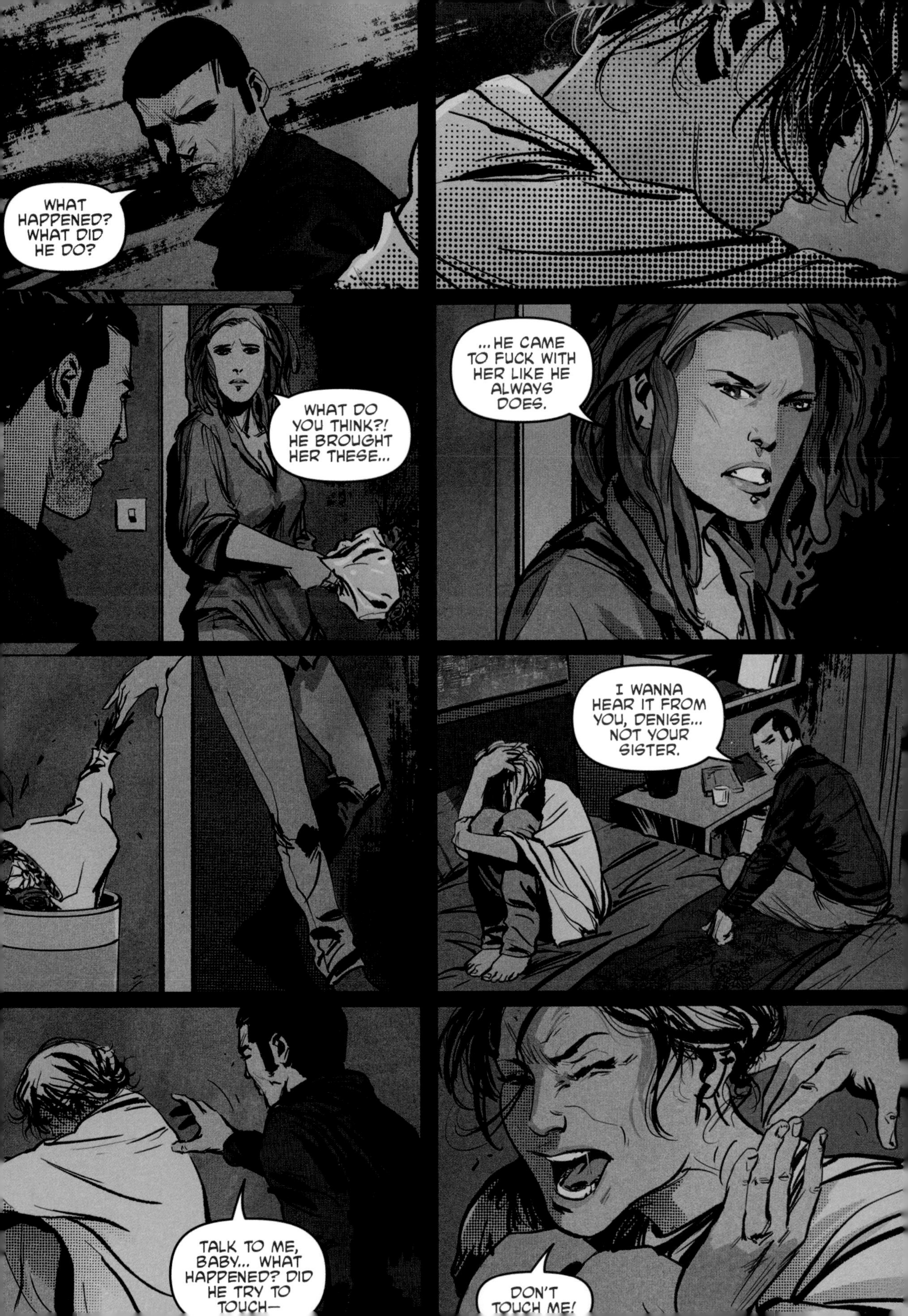
WHAT HAPPENED? WHAT DID HE DO?
WHAT DO YOU THINK?! HE BROUGHT HER THESE...
...HE CAME TO FUCK WITH HER LIKE HE ALWAYS DOES.
I WANNA HEAR IT FROM YOU, DENISE... NOT YOUR SISTER.
TALK TO ME, BABY... WHAT HAPPENED? DID HE TRY TO TOUCH—
DON'T TOUCH ME!

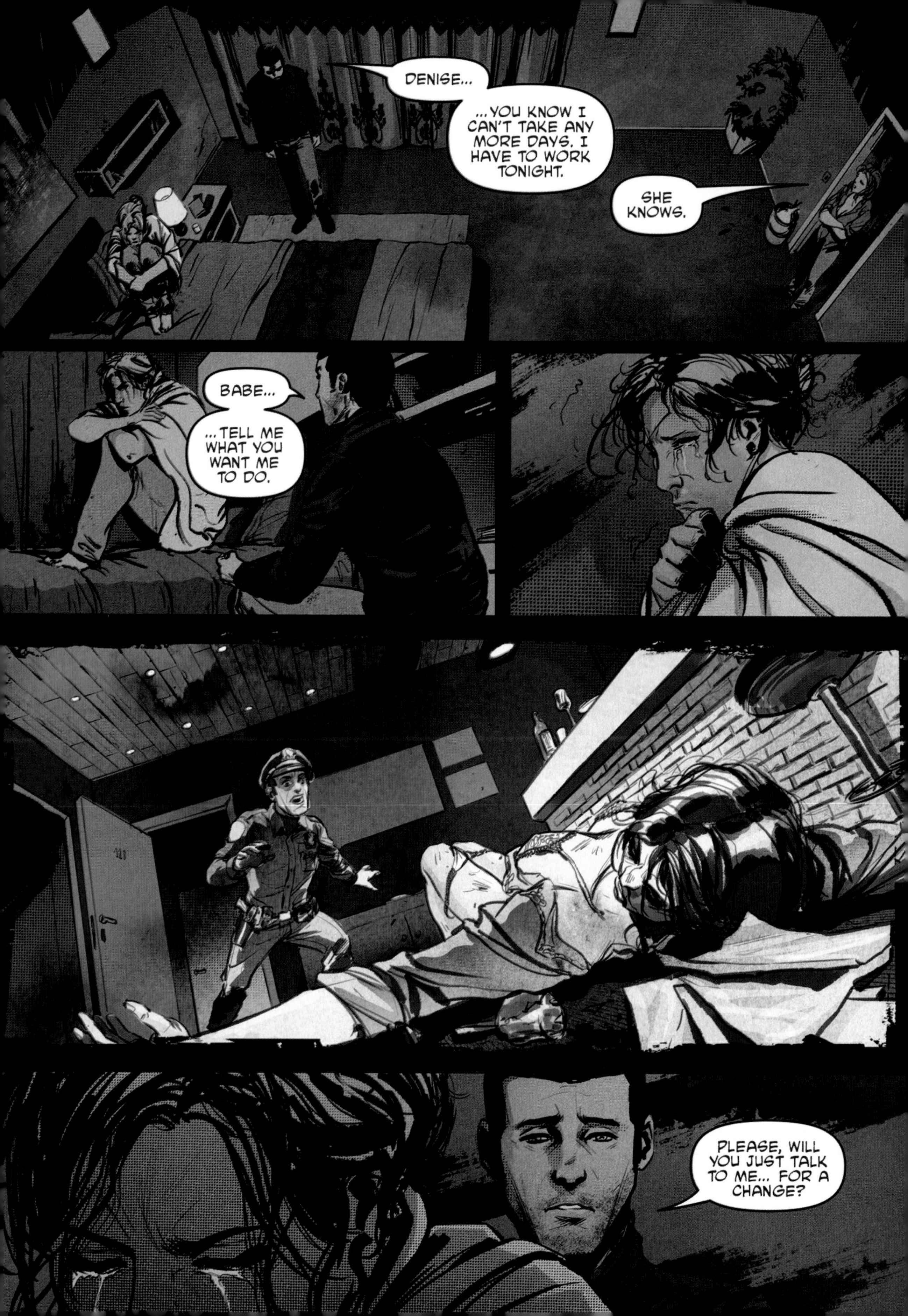
DENISE...
...YOU KNOW I CAN'T TAKE ANY MORE DAYS. I HAVE TO WORK TONIGHT.
SHE KNOWS.
BABE...
...TELL ME WHAT YOU WANT ME TO DO.
PLEASE, WILL YOU JUST TALK TO ME... FOR A CHANGE?

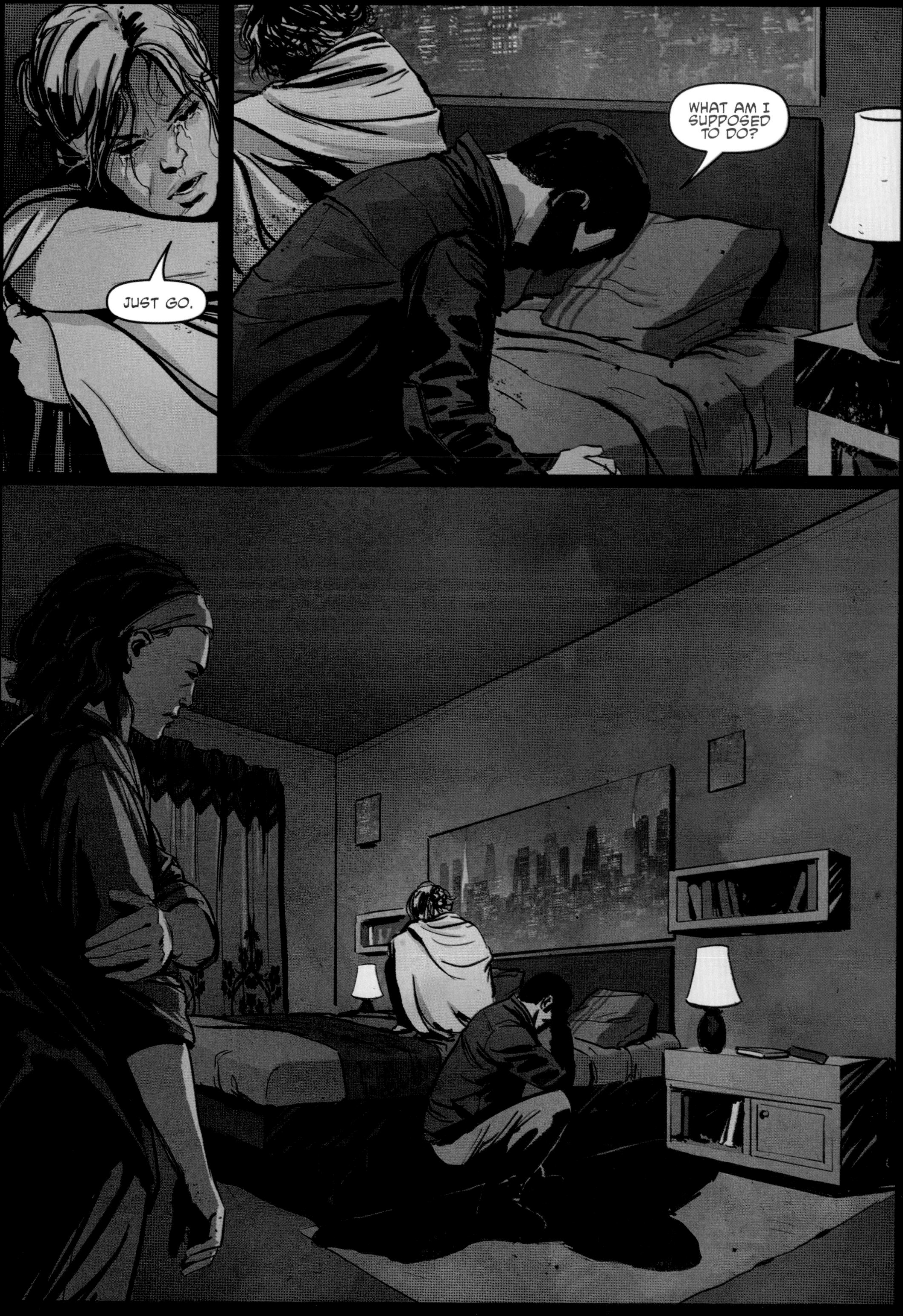
JUST GO.
WHAT AM I SUPPOSED TO DO?

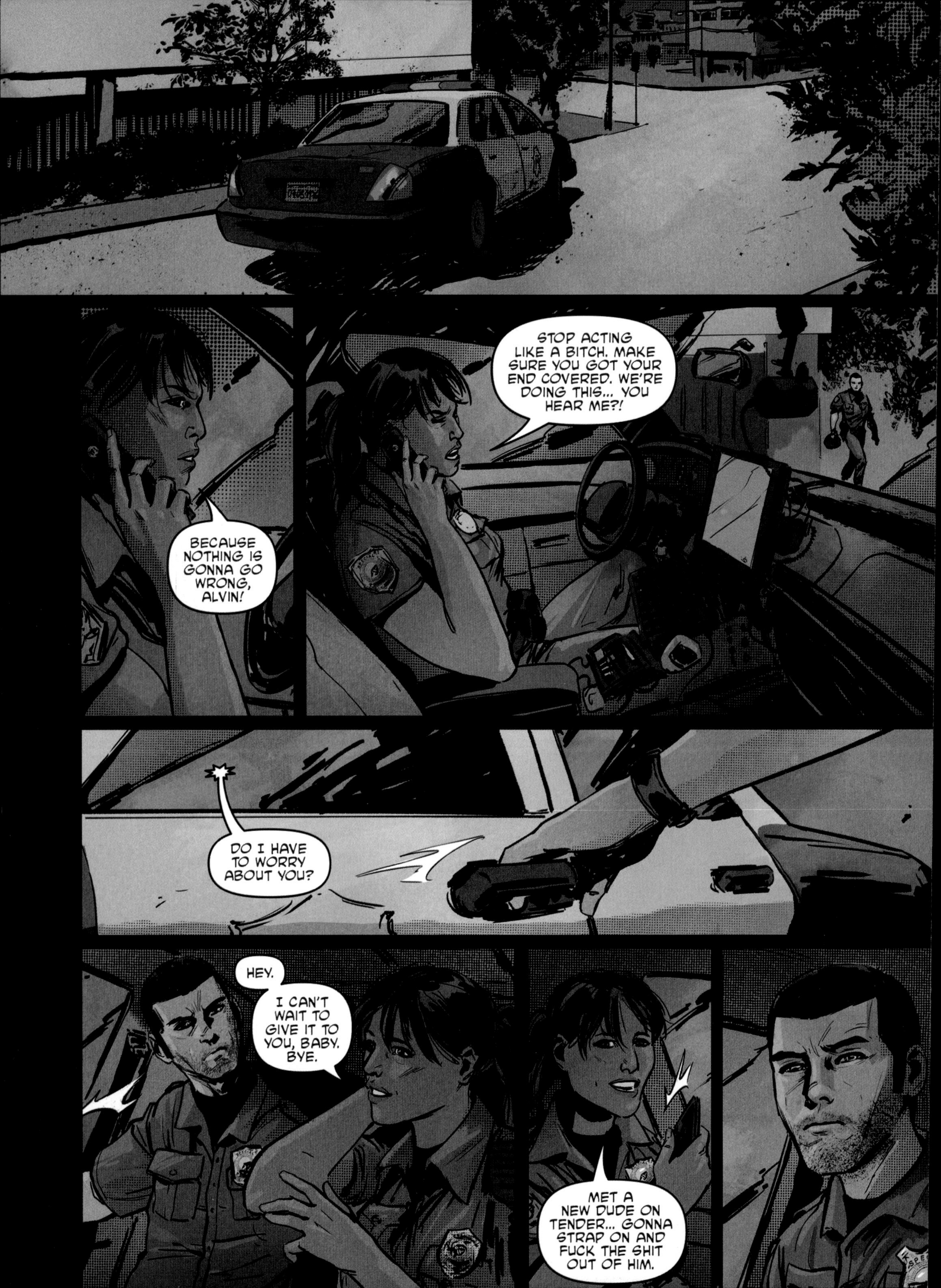
BECAUSE NOTHING IS GONNA GO WRONG, ALVIN!
STOP ACTING LIKE A BITCH. MAKE SURE YOU GOT YOUR END COVERED. WE'RE DOING THIS... YOU HEAR ME?!
DO I HAVE TO WORRY ABOUT YOU?
HEY.
I CAN'T WAIT TO GIVE IT TO YOU, BABY. BYE.
MET A NEW DUDE ON TENDER... GONNA STRAP ON AND FUCK THE SHIT OUT OF HIM.

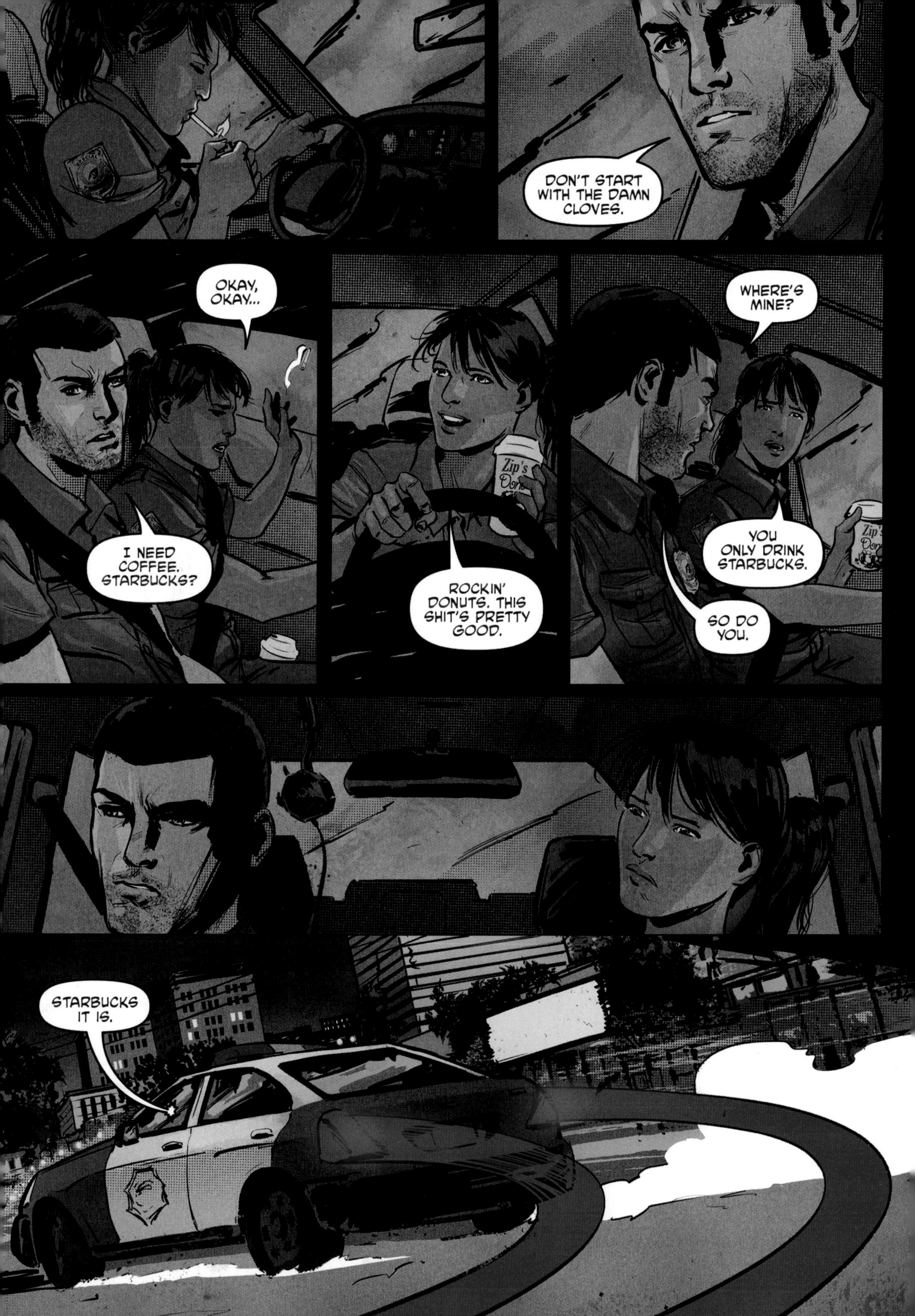
DON'T START WITH THE DAMN CLOVES.
OKAY, OKAY...
I NEED COFFEE. STARBUCKS?
ROCKIN' DONUTS. THIS SHIT'S PRETTY GOOD.
WHERE'S MINE?
YOU ONLY DRINK STARBUCKS.
SO DO YOU.
STARBUCKS IT IS.

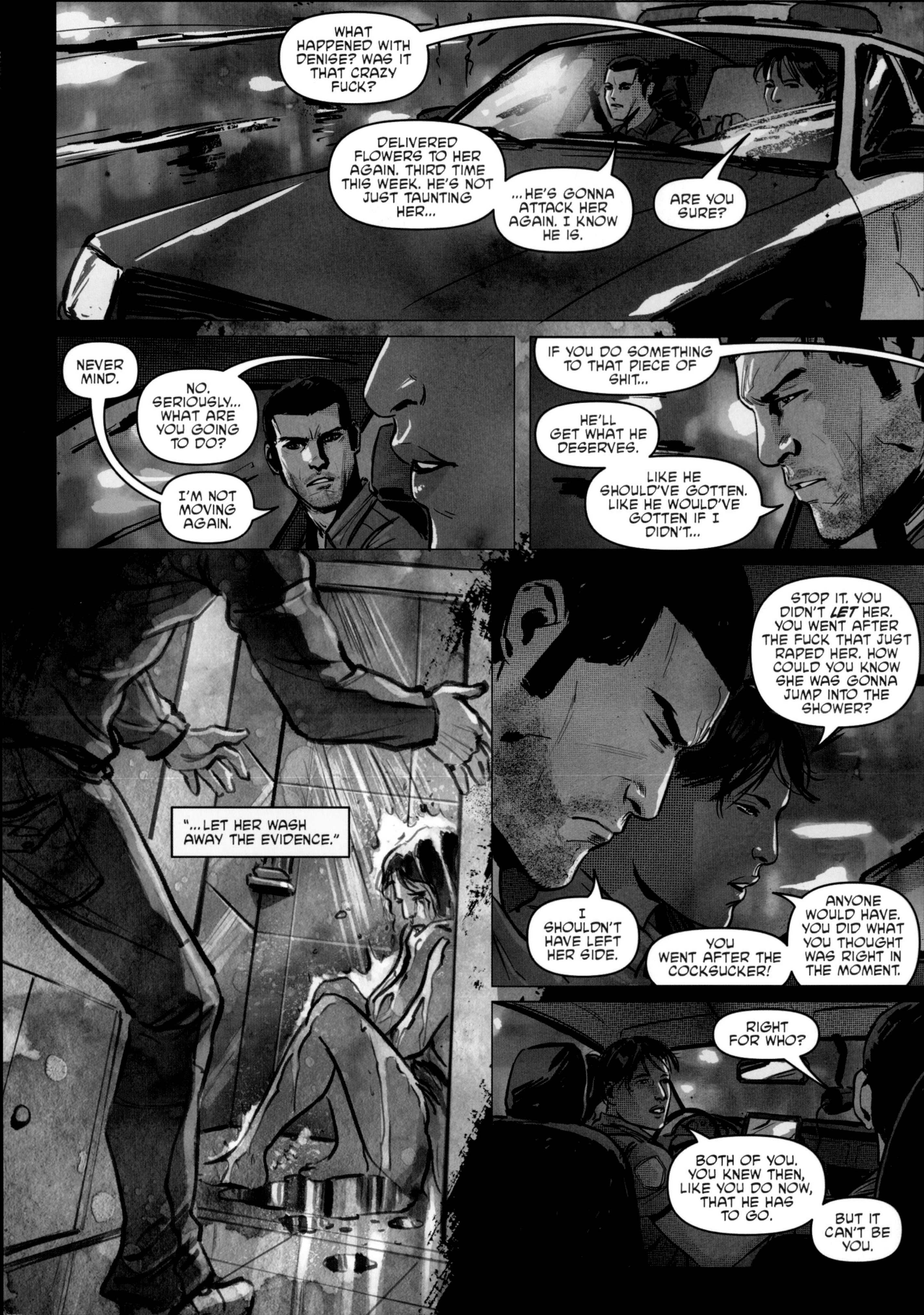
WHAT HAPPENED WITH DENISE? WAS IT THAT CRAZY FUCK?
DELIVERED FLOWERS TO HER AGAIN. THIRD TIME THIS WEEK. HE'S NOT JUST TAUNTING HER...
...HE'S GONNA ATTACK HER AGAIN. I KNOW HE IS.
ARE YOU SURE?
NEVER MIND.
NO. SERIOUSLY... WHAT ARE YOU GOING TO DO?
I'M NOT MOVING AGAIN.
IF YOU DO SOMETHING TO THAT PIECE OF SHIT...
HE'LL GET WHAT HE DESERVES.
LIKE HE SHOULD'VE GOTTEN. LIKE HE WOULD'VE GOTTEN IF I DIDN'T...
"...LET HER WASH AWAY THE EVIDENCE."
STOP IT. YOU DIDN'T LET HER. YOU WENT AFTER THE FUCK THAT JUST RAPED HER. HOW COULD YOU KNOW SHE WAS GONNA JUMP INTO THE SHOWER?
I SHOULDN'T HAVE LEFT HER SIDE.
YOU WENT AFTER THE COCKSUCKER!
ANYONE WOULD HAVE. YOU DID WHAT YOU THOUGHT WAS RIGHT IN THE MOMENT.
RIGHT FOR WHO?
BOTH OF YOU. YOU KNEW THEN, LIKE YOU DO NOW, THAT HE HAS TO GO.
BUT IT CAN'T BE YOU.

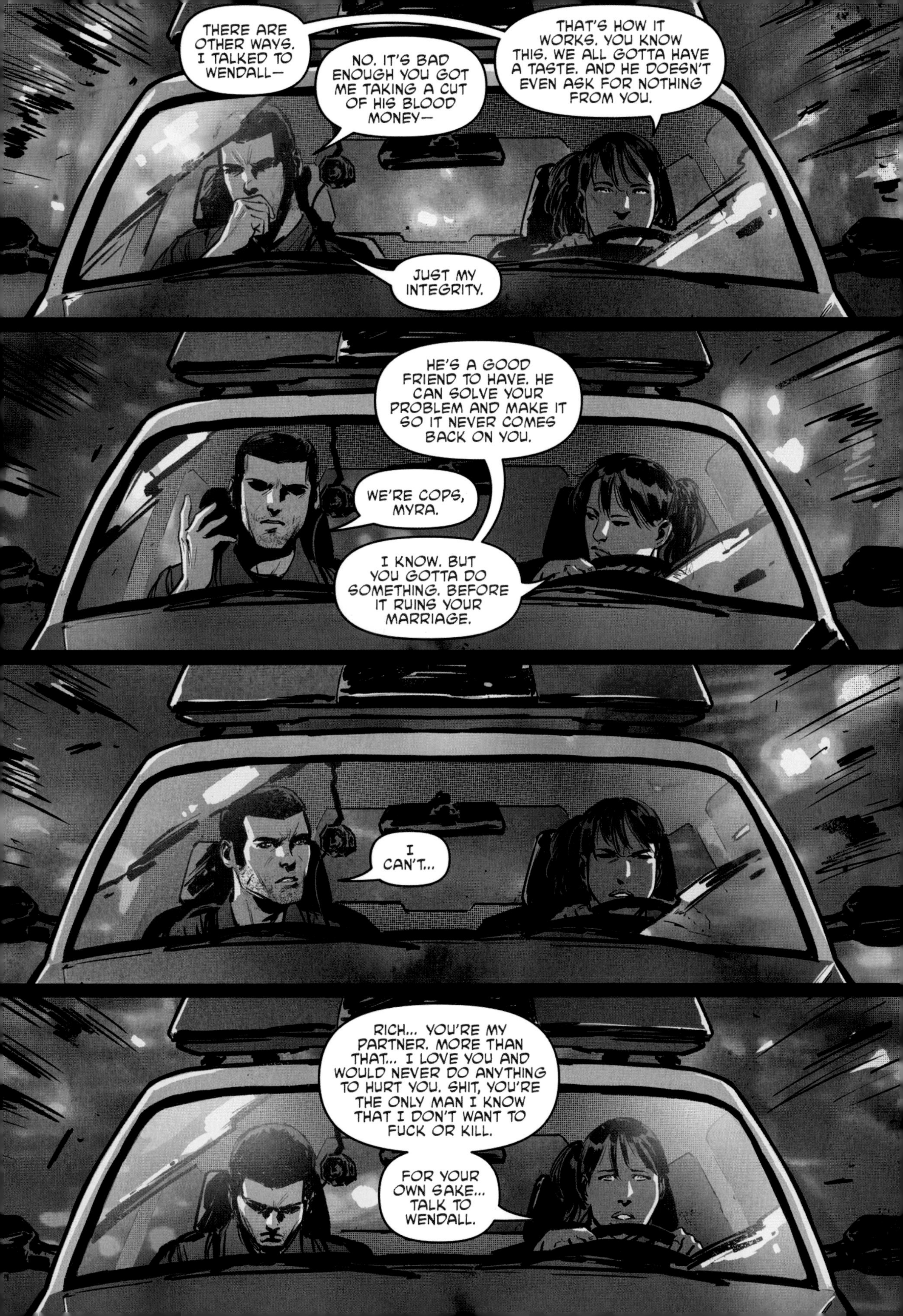

THERE ARE OTHER WAYS. I TALKED TO WENDALL—
NO. IT'S BAD ENOUGH YOU GOT ME TAKING A CUT OF HIS BLOOD MONEY—
THAT'S HOW IT WORKS. YOU KNOW THIS. WE ALL GOTTA HAVE A TASTE. AND HE DOESN'T EVEN ASK FOR NOTHING FROM YOU.
JUST MY INTEGRITY.
HE'S A GOOD FRIEND TO HAVE. HE CAN SOLVE YOUR PROBLEM AND MAKE IT SO IT NEVER COMES BACK ON YOU.
WE'RE COPS, MYRA.
I KNOW. BUT YOU GOTTA DO SOMETHING. BEFORE IT RUINS YOUR MARRIAGE.
I CAN'T...
RICH... YOU'RE MY PARTNER. MORE THAN THAT... I LOVE YOU AND WOULD NEVER DO ANYTHING TO HURT YOU. SHIT, YOU'RE THE ONLY MAN I KNOW THAT I DON'T WANT TO FUCK OR KILL.
FOR YOUR OWN SAKE... TALK TO WENDALL.

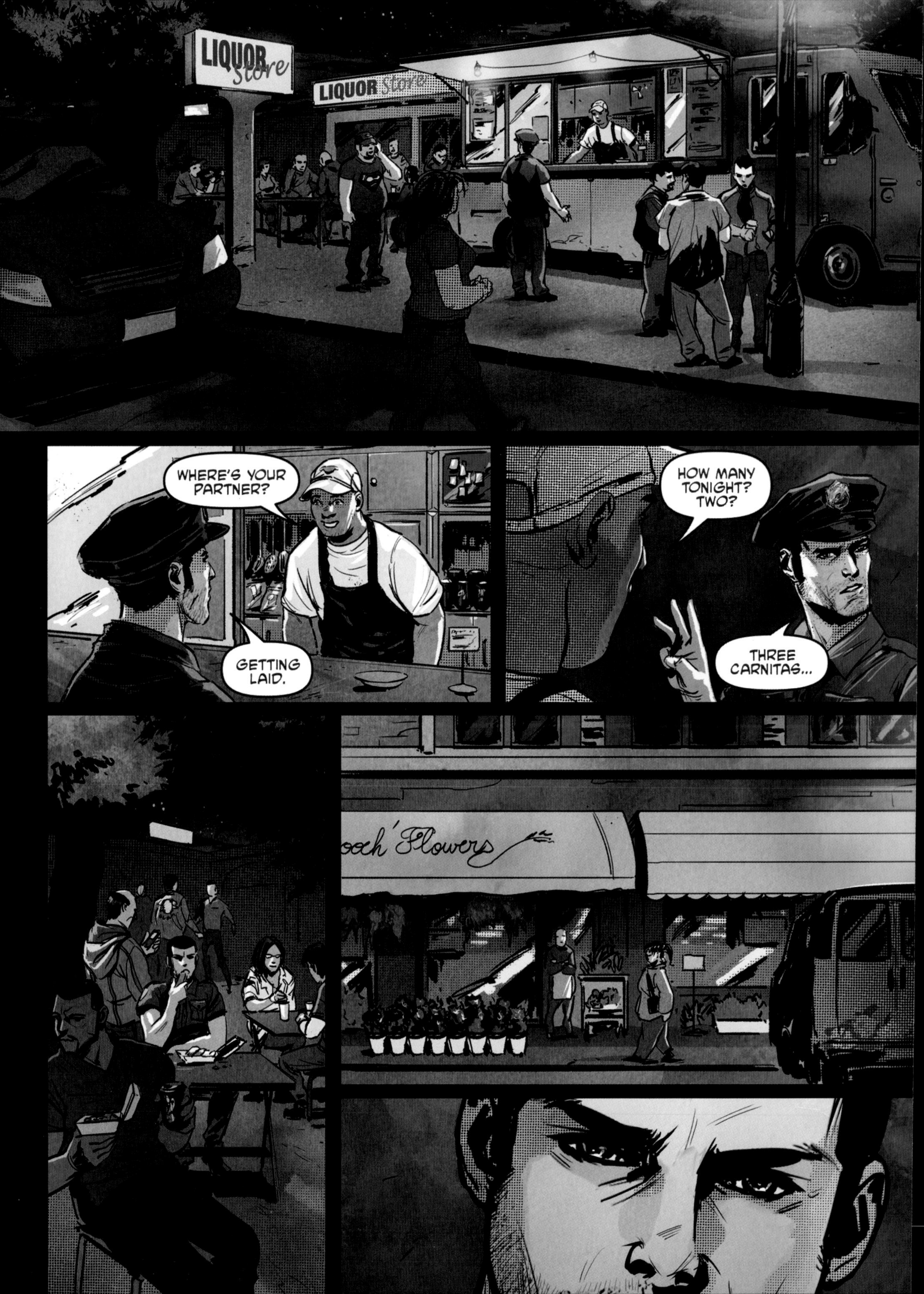
LIQUOR Store
LIQUOR Store
WHERE'S YOUR PARTNER?
GETTING LAID.
HOW MANY TONIGHT? TWO?
THREE CARNITAS...

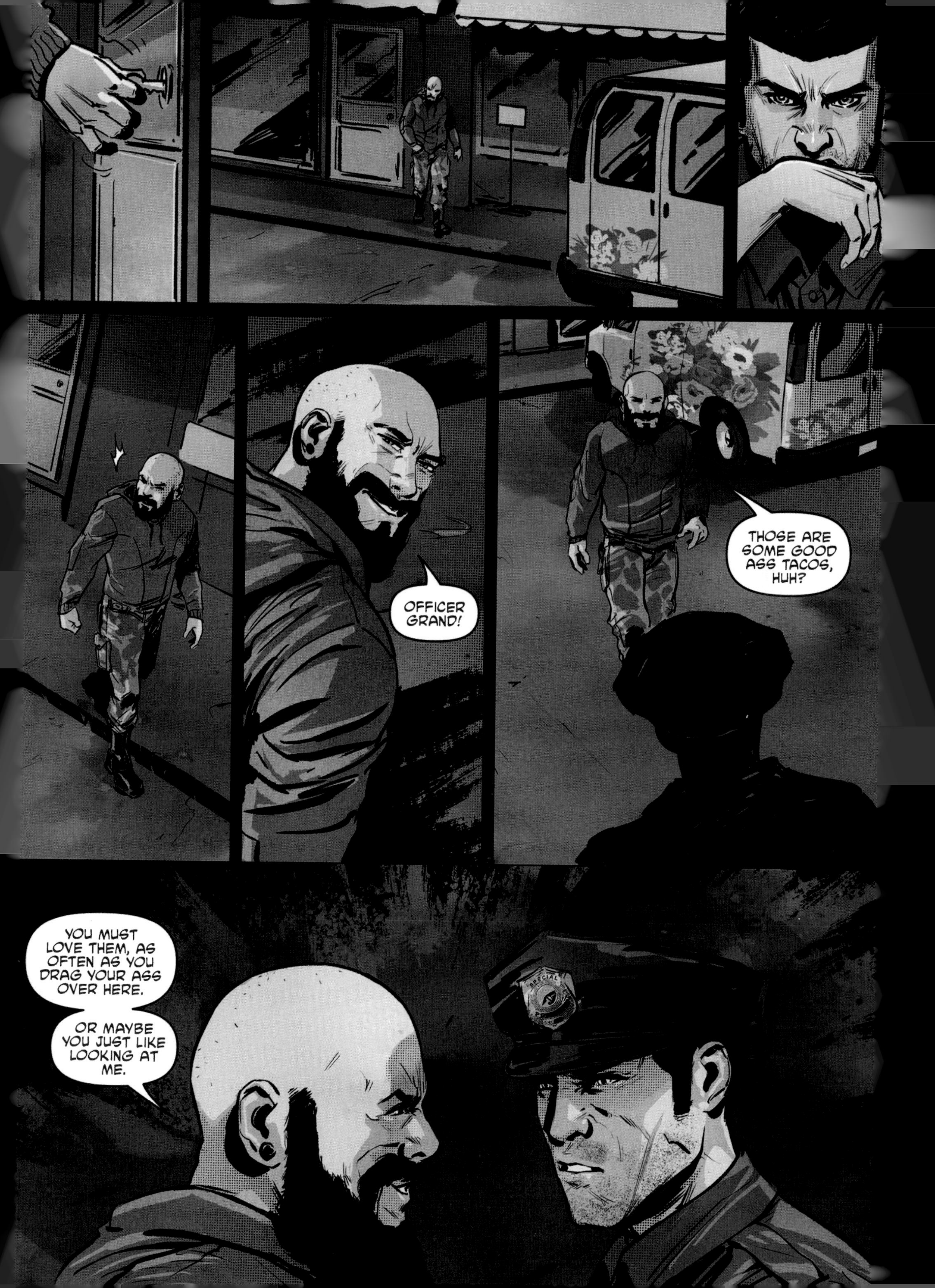
OFFICER GRAND!
THOSE ARE SOME GOOD ASS TACOS, HUH?
YOU MUST LOVE THEM, AS OFTEN AS YOU DRAG YOUR ASS OVER HERE.
OR MAYBE YOU JUST LIKE LOOKING AT ME.

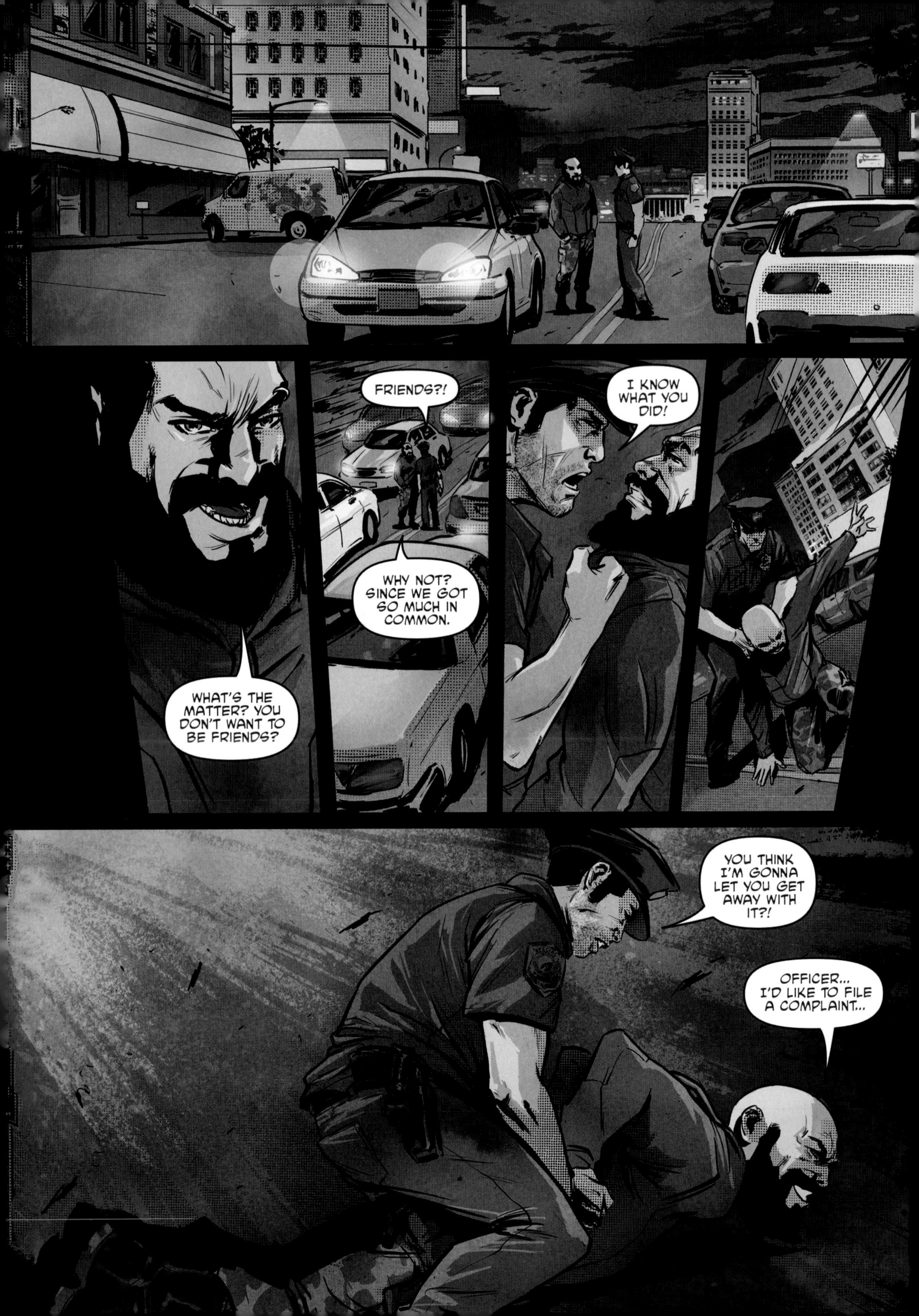
WHAT'S THE MATTER? YOU DON'T WANT TO BE FRIENDS?
FRIENDS?!
WHY NOT? SINCE WE GOT SO MUCH IN COMMON.
I KNOW WHAT YOU DID!
YOU THINK I'M GONNA LET YOU GET AWAY WITH IT?!
OFFICER... I'D LIKE TO FILE A COMPLAINT...

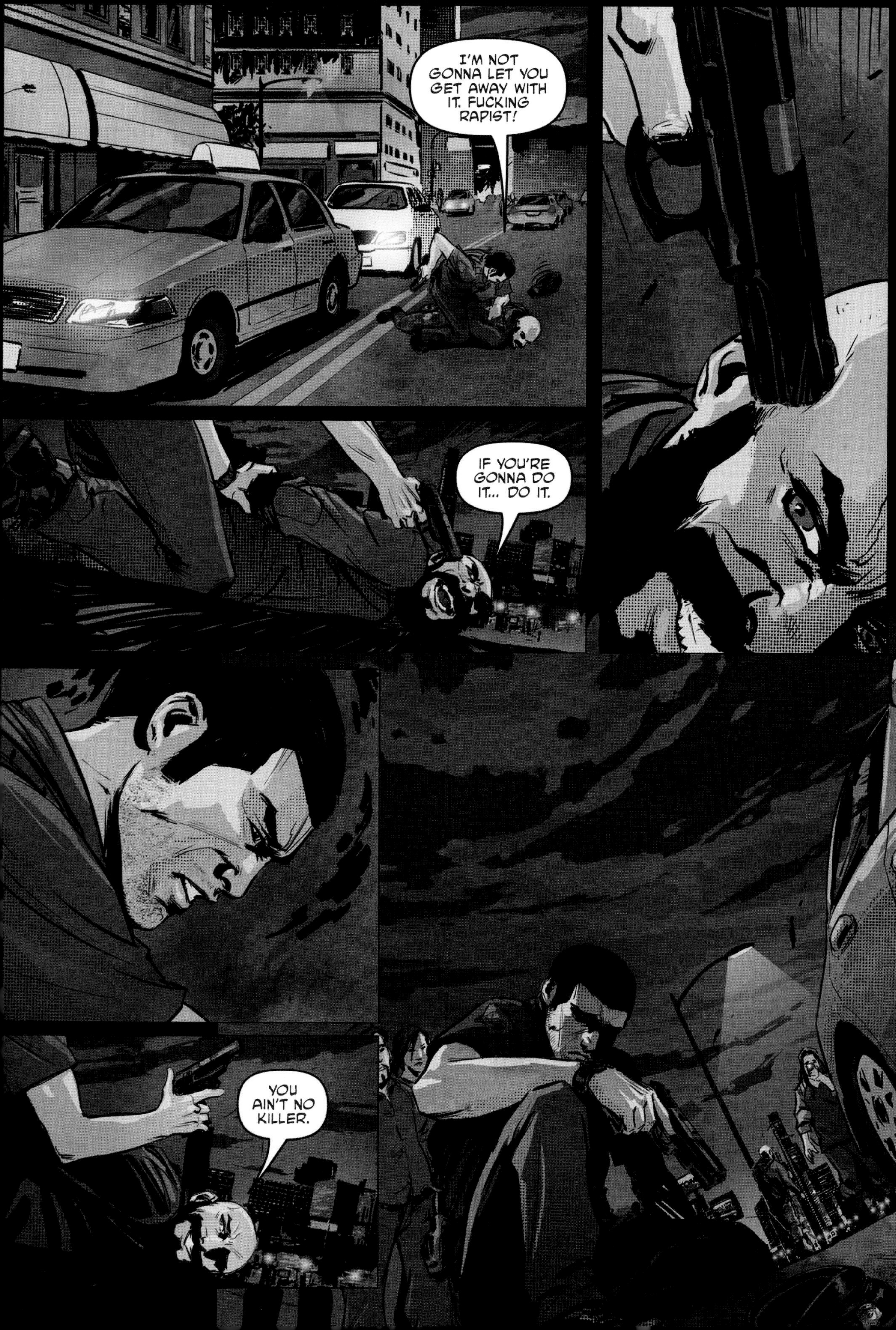
I'M NOT GONNA LET YOU GET AWAY WITH IT. FUCKING RAPIST!
IF YOU'RE GONNA DO IT... DO IT.
YOU AIN'T NO KILLER.

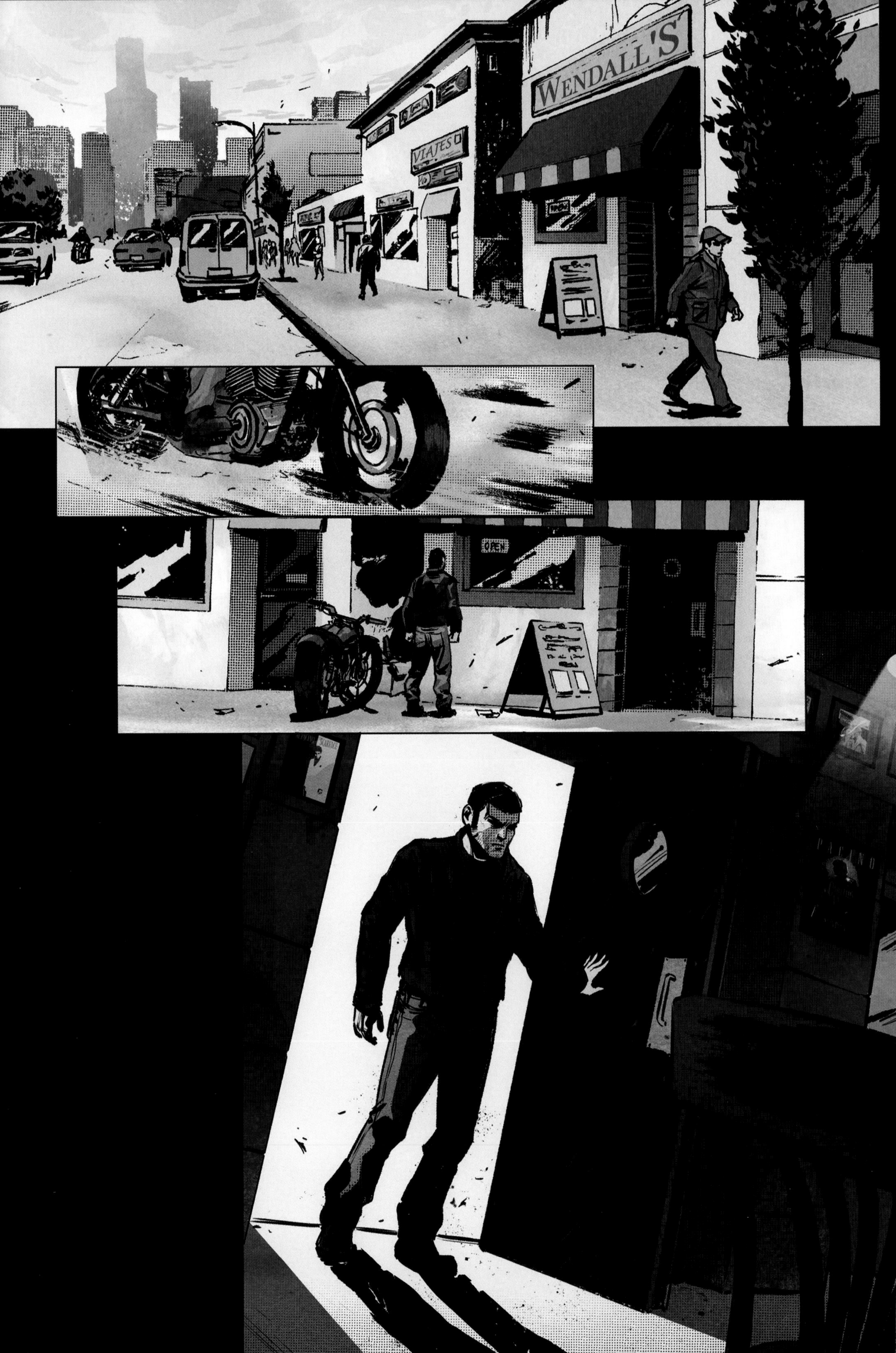
WENDALL'S
VIAJES
OPEN

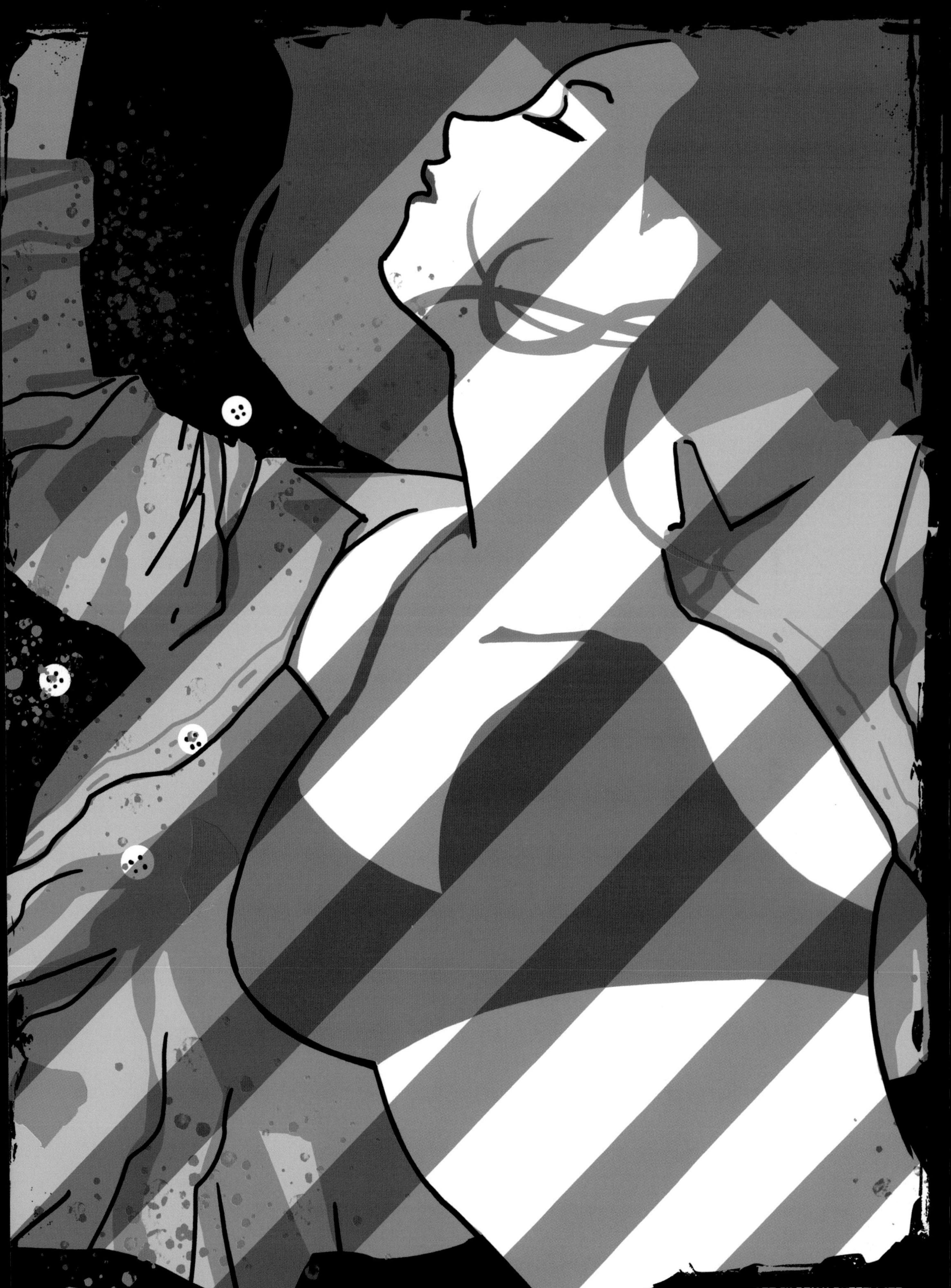

ART BY BRIAN BUCCELLATO

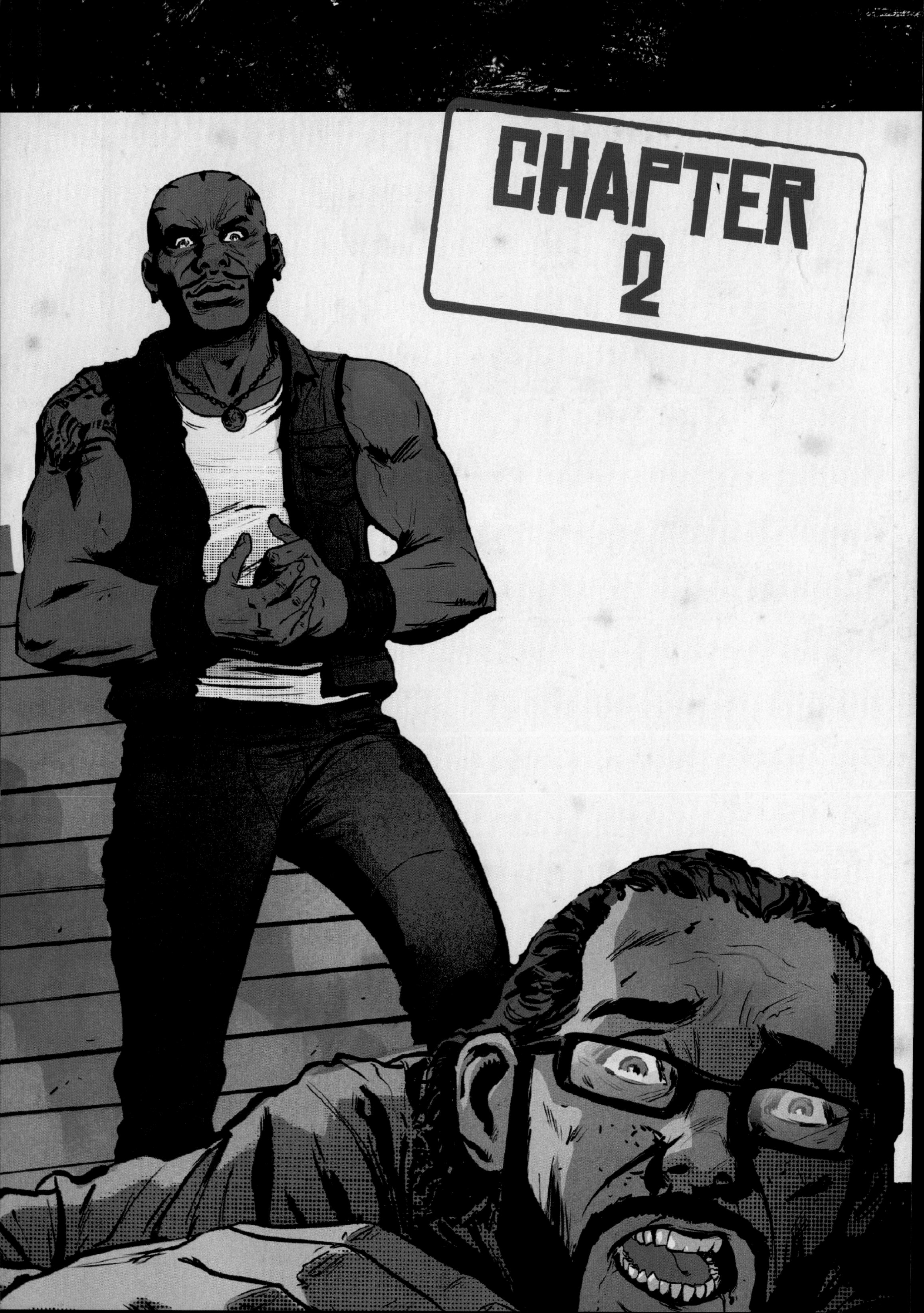
CHAPTER
2

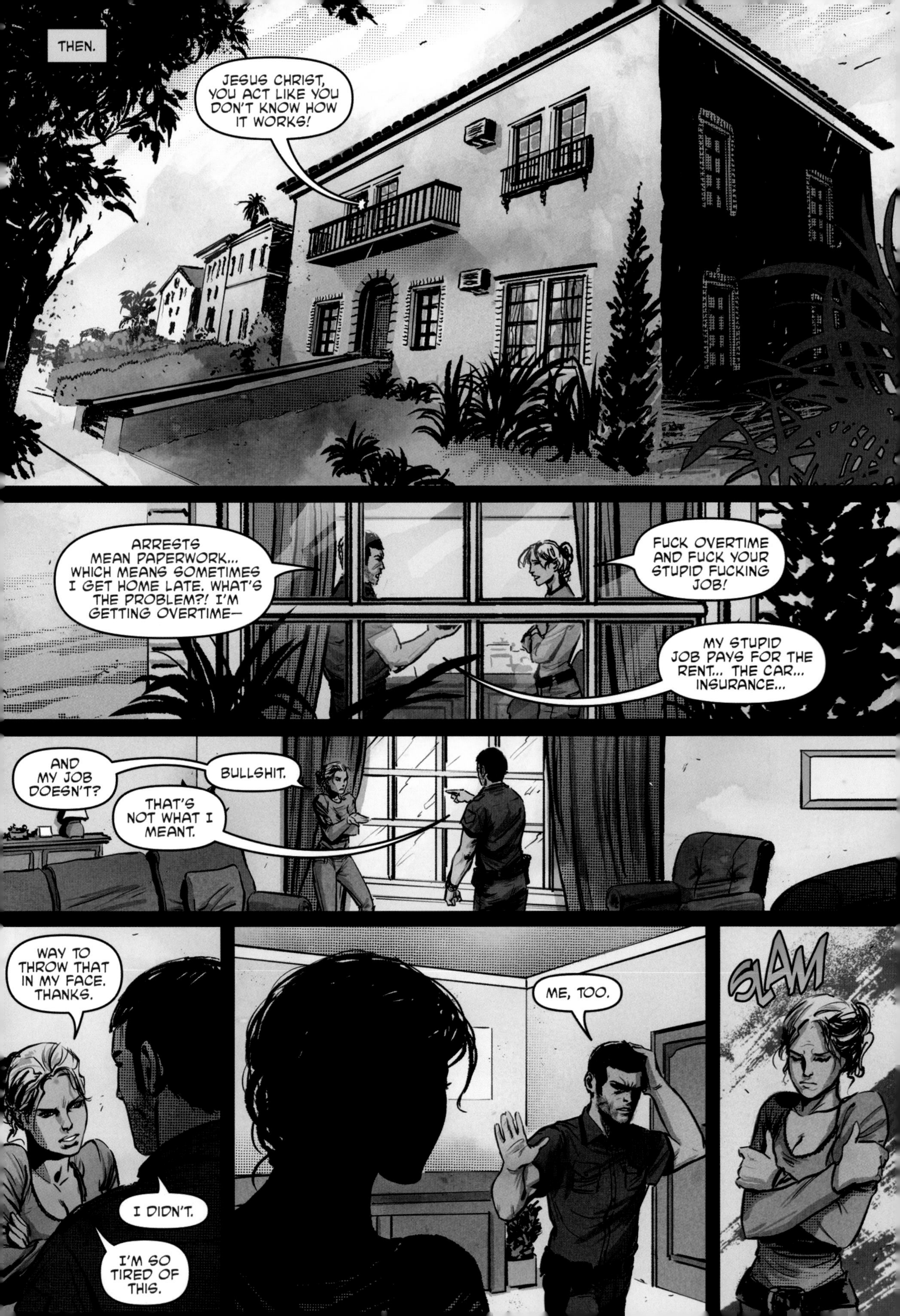
THEN.
JESUS CHRIST, YOU ACT LIKE YOU DON'T KNOW HOW IT WORKS!
ARRESTS MEAN PAPERWORK... WHICH MEANS SOMETIMES I GET HOME LATE. WHAT'S THE PROBLEM?! I'M GETTING OVERTIME—
FUCK OVERTIME AND FUCK YOUR STUPID FUCKING JOB!
MY STUPID JOB PAYS FOR THE RENT... THE CAR... INSURANCE...
AND MY JOB DOESN'T?
BULLSHIT.
THAT'S NOT WHAT I MEANT.
WAY TO THROW THAT IN MY FACE. THANKS.
I DIDN'T.
I'M SO TIRED OF THIS.
ME, TOO.
SLAM

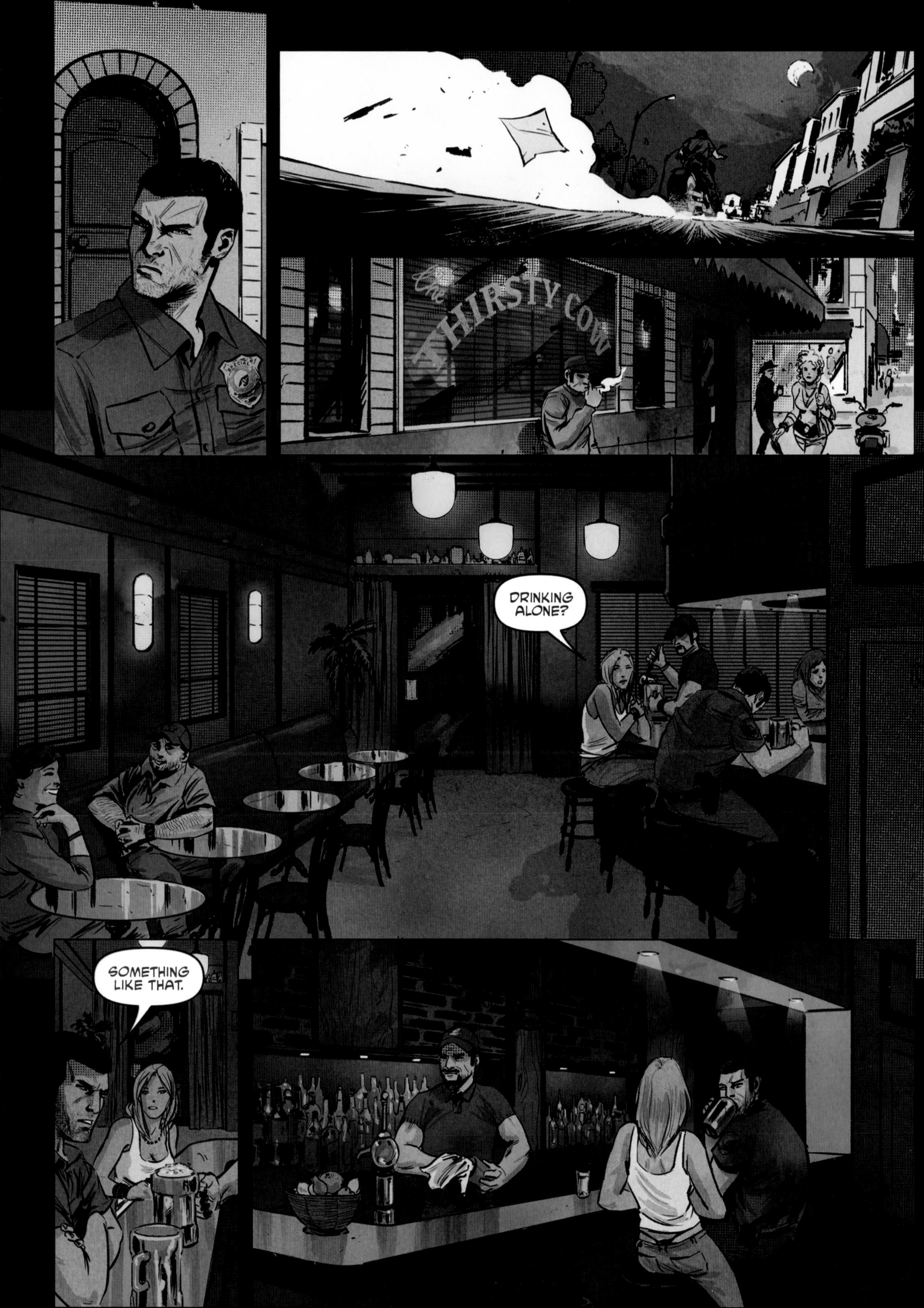
The THIRSTY COW
DRINKING ALONE?
SOMETHING LIKE THAT.

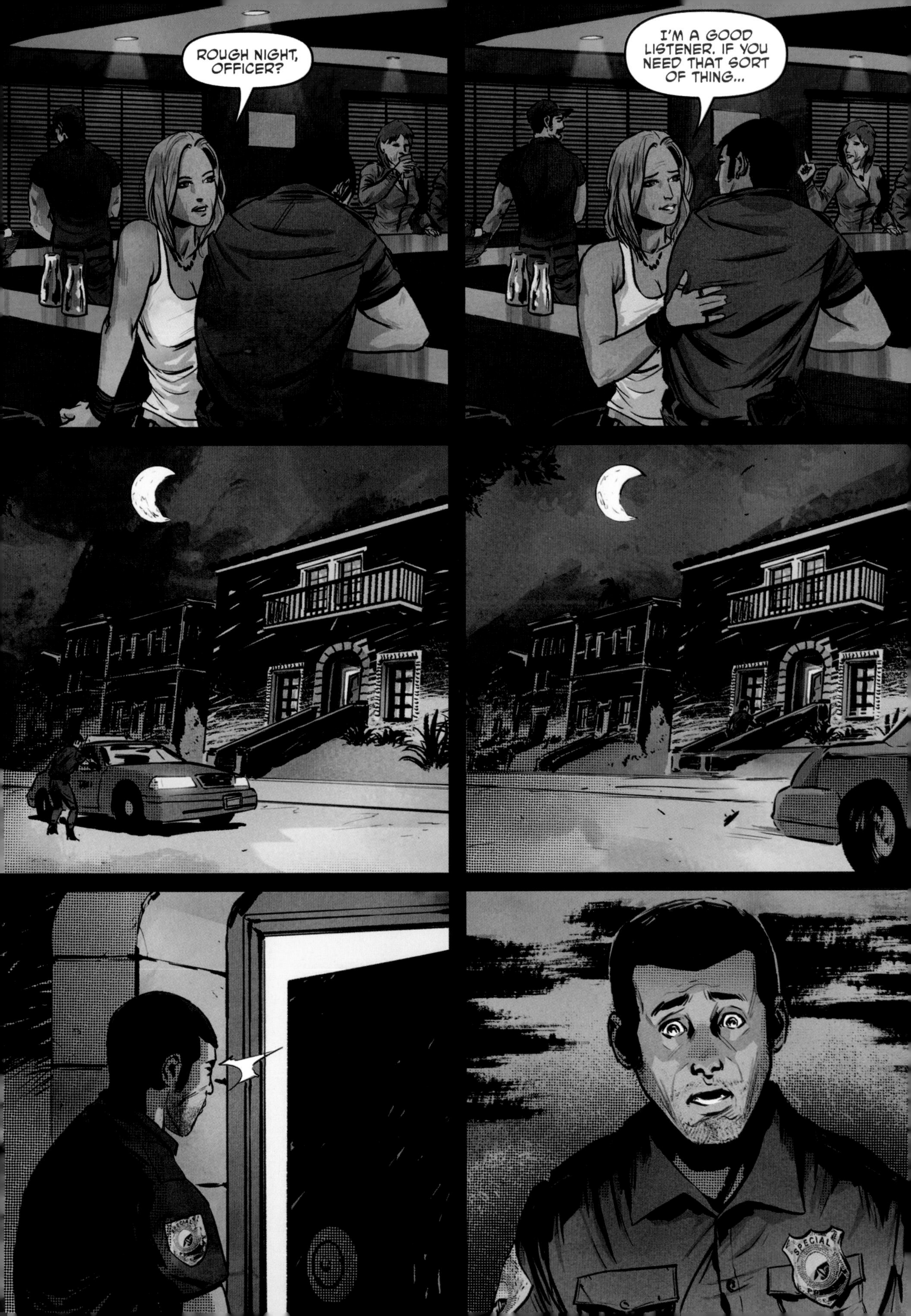
ROUGH NIGHT, OFFICER?
I'M A GOOD LISTENER. IF YOU NEED THAT SORT OF THING...

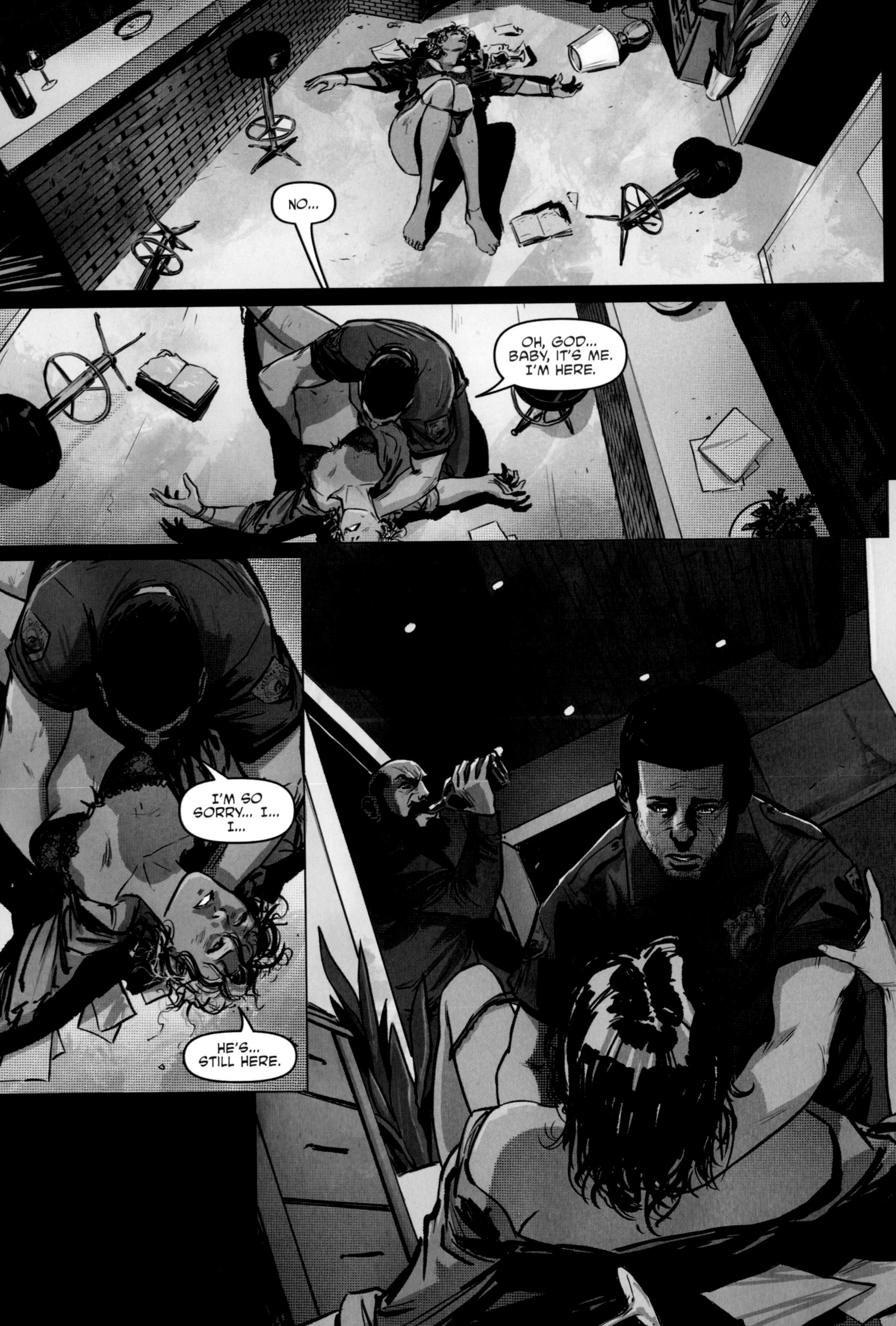
NO...
OH, GOD... BABY, IT'S ME. I'M HERE.
I'M SO SORRY... I... I...
HE'S... STILL HERE.

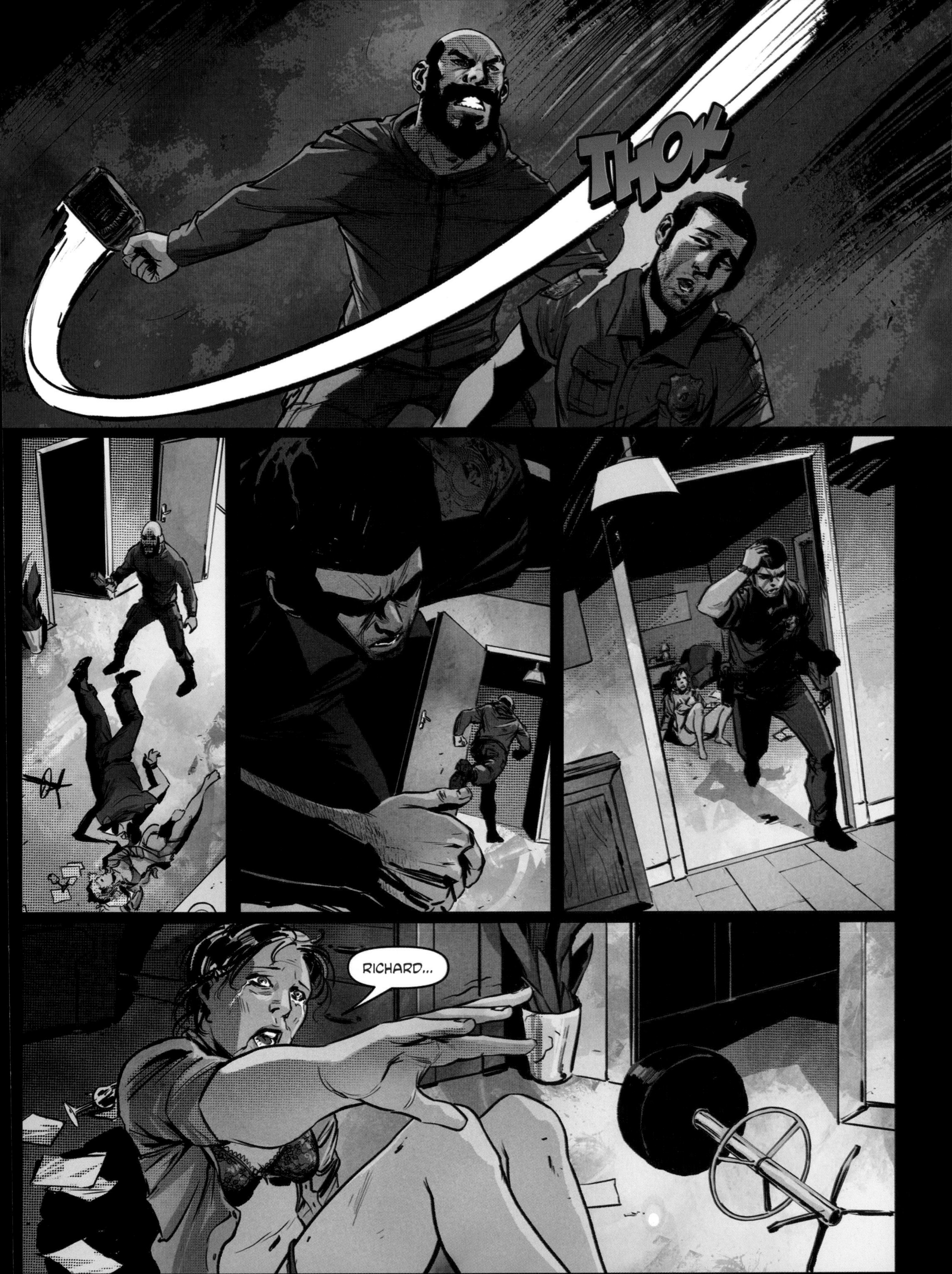
THOK
RICHARD...

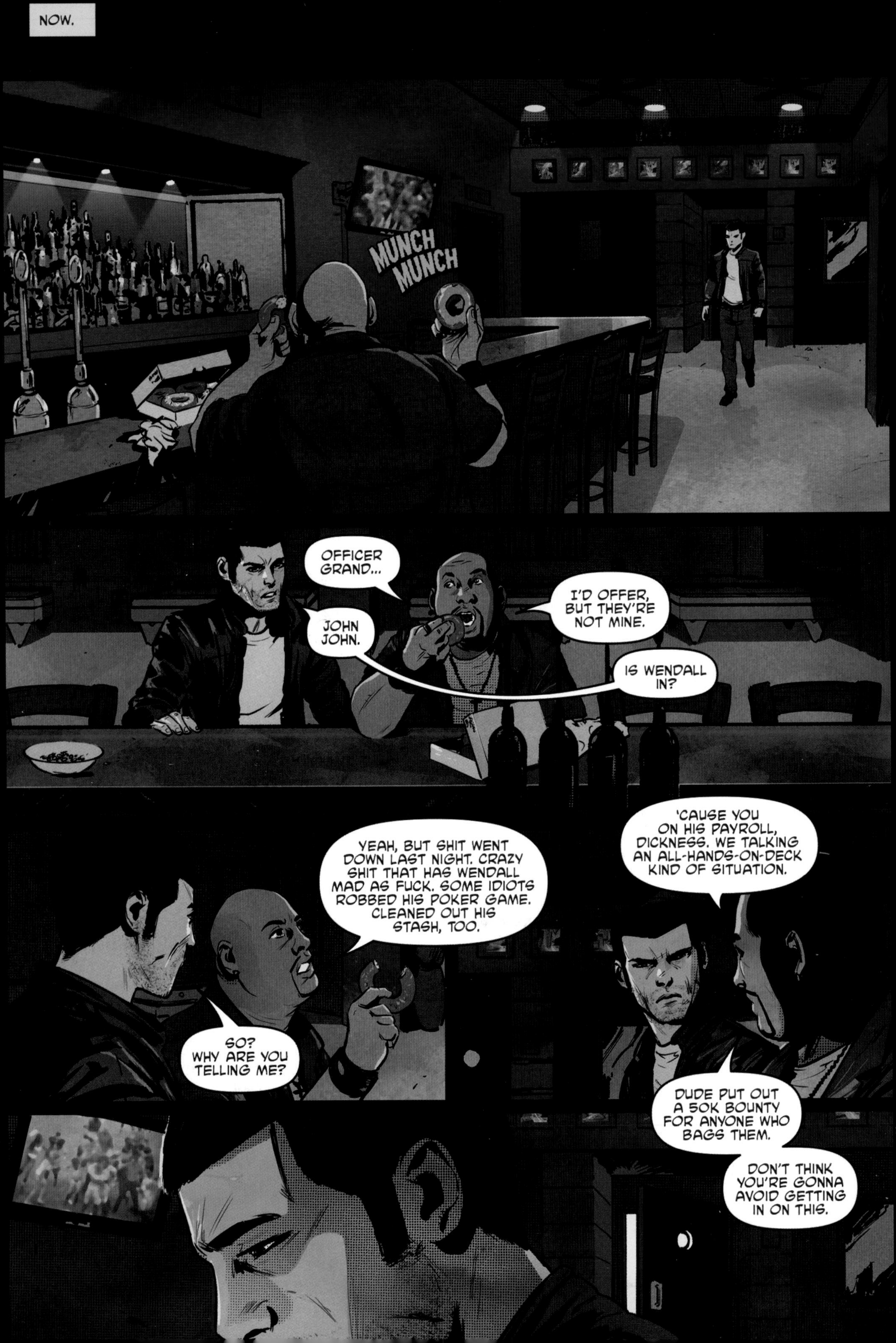
NOW.
MUNCH MUNCH
OFFICER GRAND...
JOHN JOHN.
I'D OFFER, BUT THEY'RE NOT MINE.
IS WENDALL IN?
YEAH, BUT SHIT WENT DOWN LAST NIGHT. CRAZY SHIT THAT HAS WENDALL MAD AS FUCK. SOME IDIOTS ROBBED HIS POKER GAME. CLEANED OUT HIS STASH, TOO.
SO? WHY ARE YOU TELLING ME?
'CAUSE YOU ON HIS PAYROLL, DICKNESS. WE TALKING AN ALL-HANDS-ON-DECK KIND OF SITUATION.
DUDE PUT OUT A 50K BOUNTY FOR ANYONE WHO BAGS THEM.
DON'T THINK YOU'RE GONNA AVOID GETTING IN ON THIS.

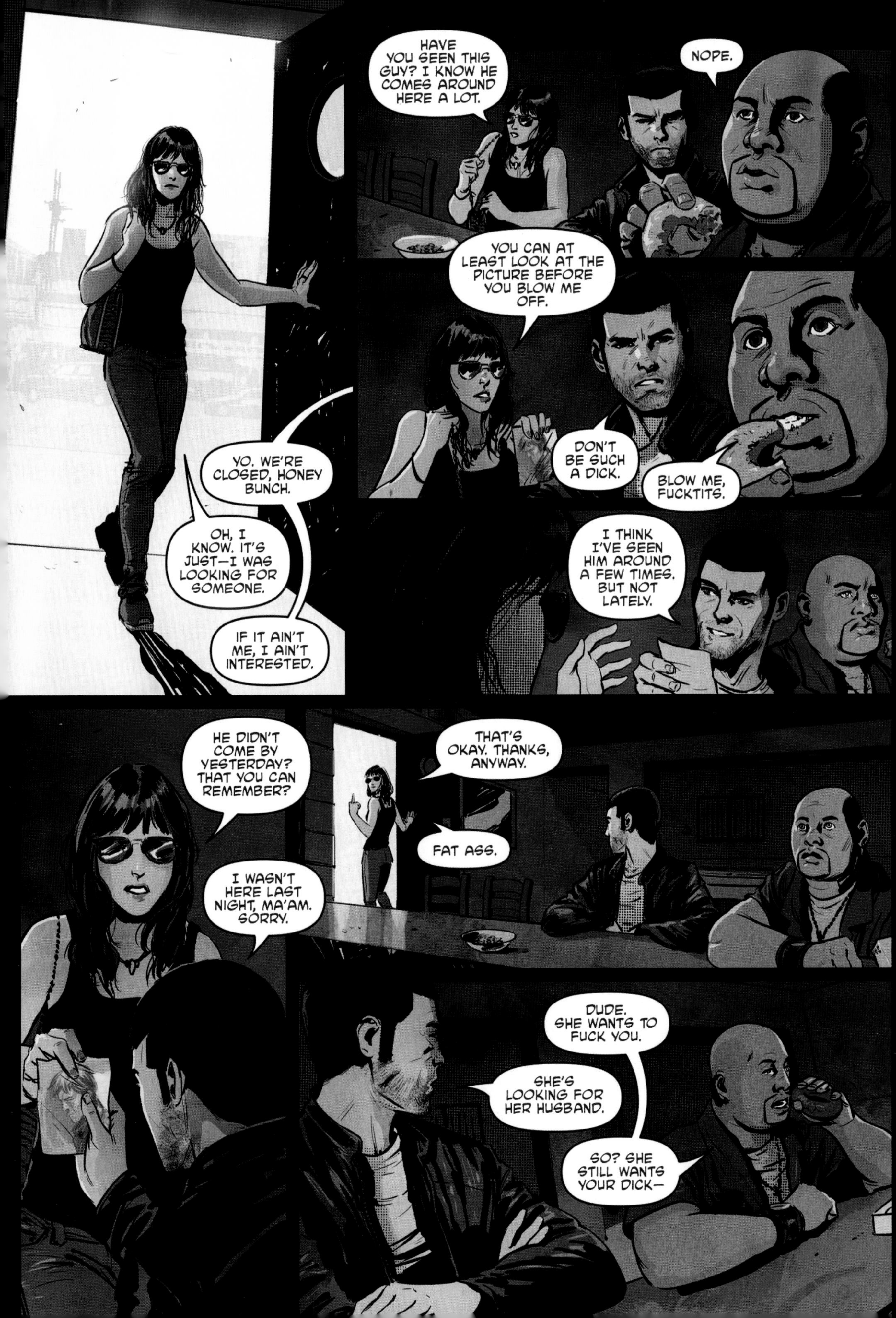
YO. WE'RE CLOSED, HONEY BUNCH.
OH, I KNOW. IT'S JUST—I WAS LOOKING FOR SOMEONE.
IF IT AIN'T ME, I AIN'T INTERESTED.
HAVE YOU SEEN THIS GUY? I KNOW HE COMES AROUND HERE A LOT.
NOPE.
YOU CAN AT LEAST LOOK AT THE PICTURE BEFORE YOU BLOW ME OFF.
DON'T BE SUCH A DICK.
BLOW ME, FUCKTITS.
I THINK I'VE SEEN HIM AROUND A FEW TIMES. BUT NOT LATELY.
HE DIDN'T COME BY YESTERDAY? THAT YOU CAN REMEMBER?
I WASN'T HERE LAST NIGHT, MA'AM. SORRY.
THAT'S OKAY. THANKS, ANYWAY.
FAT ASS.
DUDE. SHE WANTS TO FUCK YOU.
SHE'S LOOKING FOR HER HUSBAND.
SO? SHE STILL WANTS YOUR DICK—

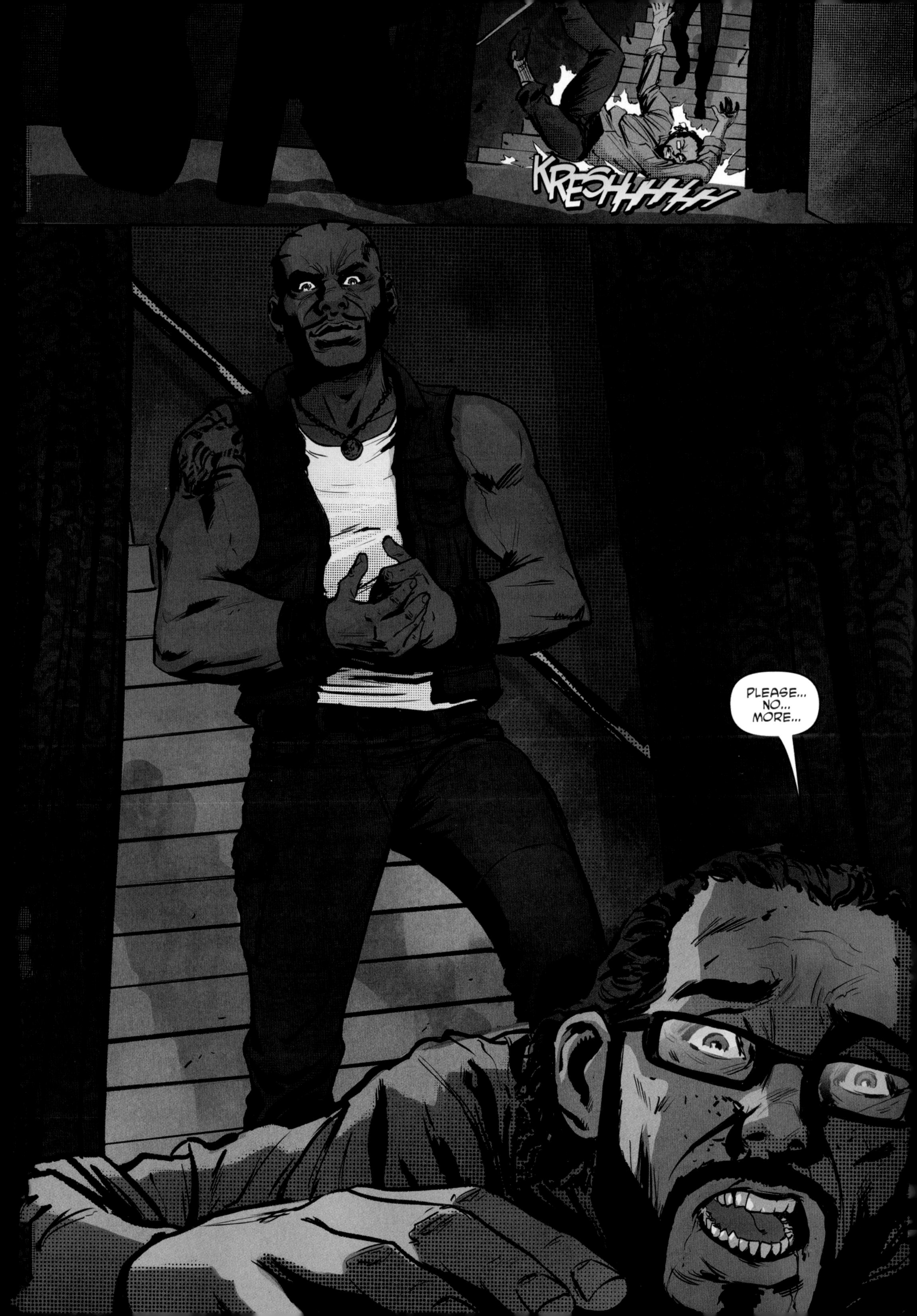
KRESHHHHHH
PLEASE... NO... MORE...

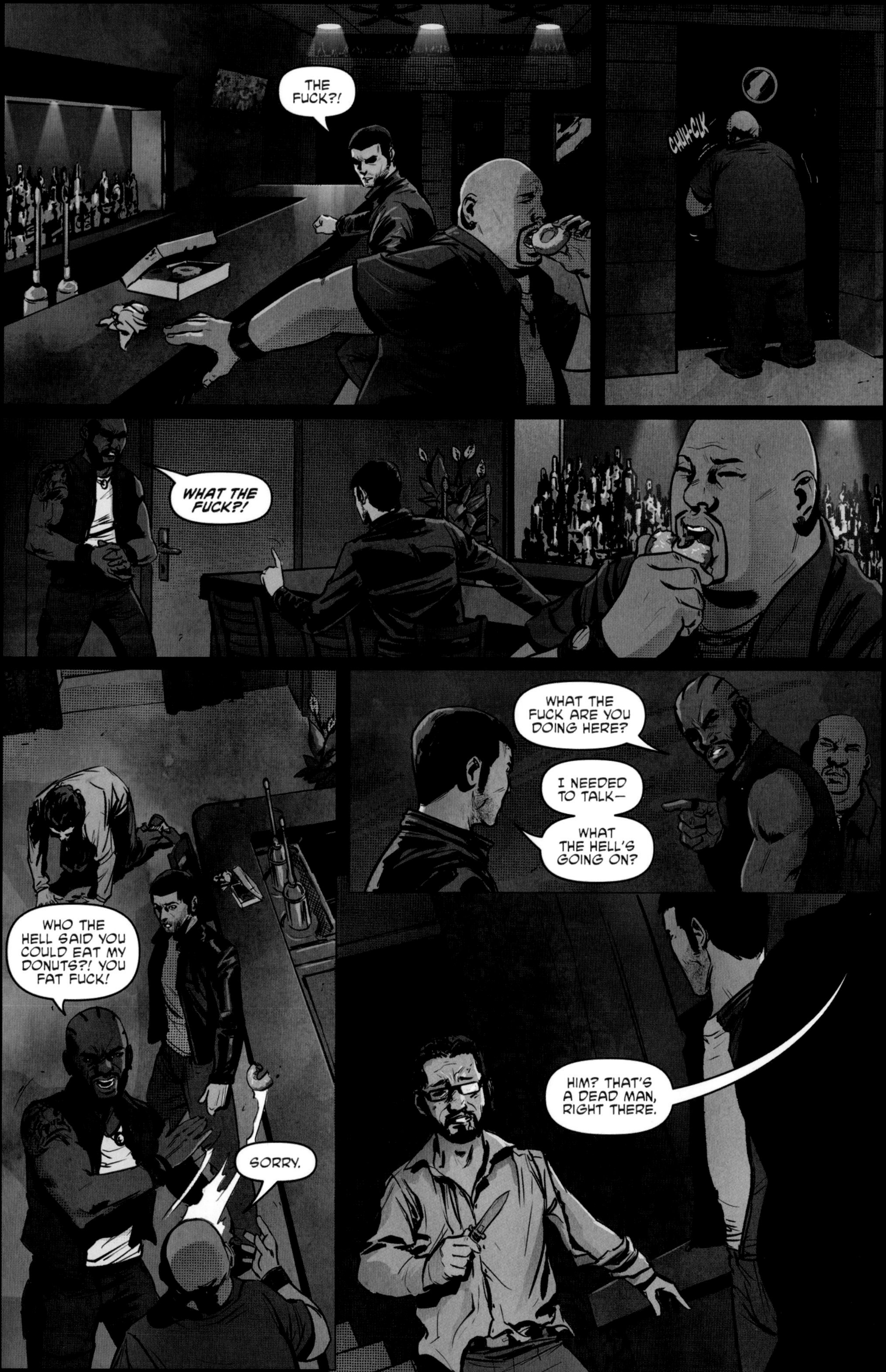
THE FUCK?!
CHUH-CLK
WHAT THE FUCK?!
WHAT THE FUCK ARE YOU DOING HERE?
I NEEDED TO TALK—
WHAT THE HELL'S GOING ON?
WHO THE HELL SAID YOU COULD EAT MY DONUTS?! YOU FAT FUCK!
SORRY.
HIM? THAT'S A DEAD MAN, RIGHT THERE.

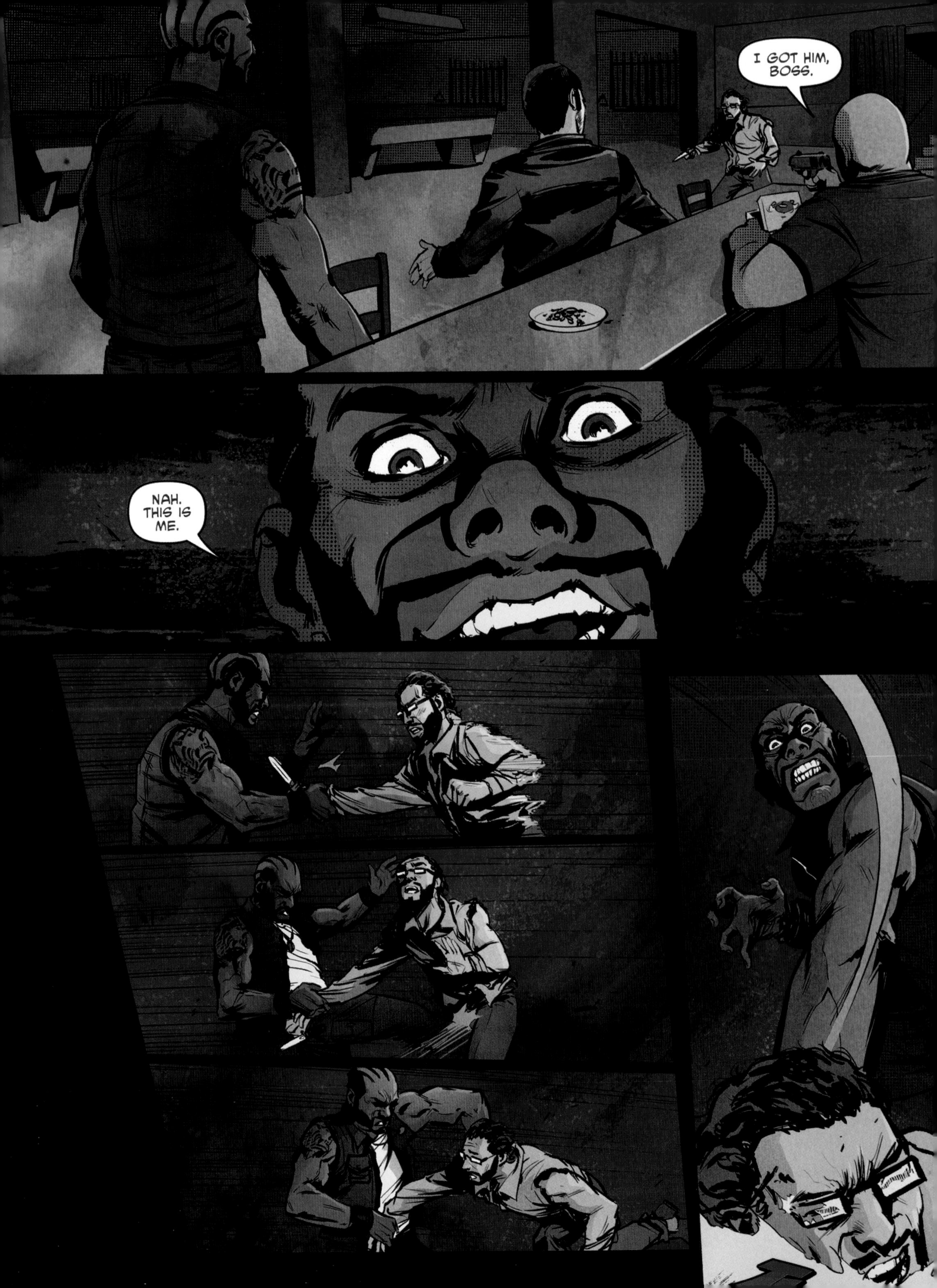
I GOT HIM, BOSS.
NAH. THIS IS ME.

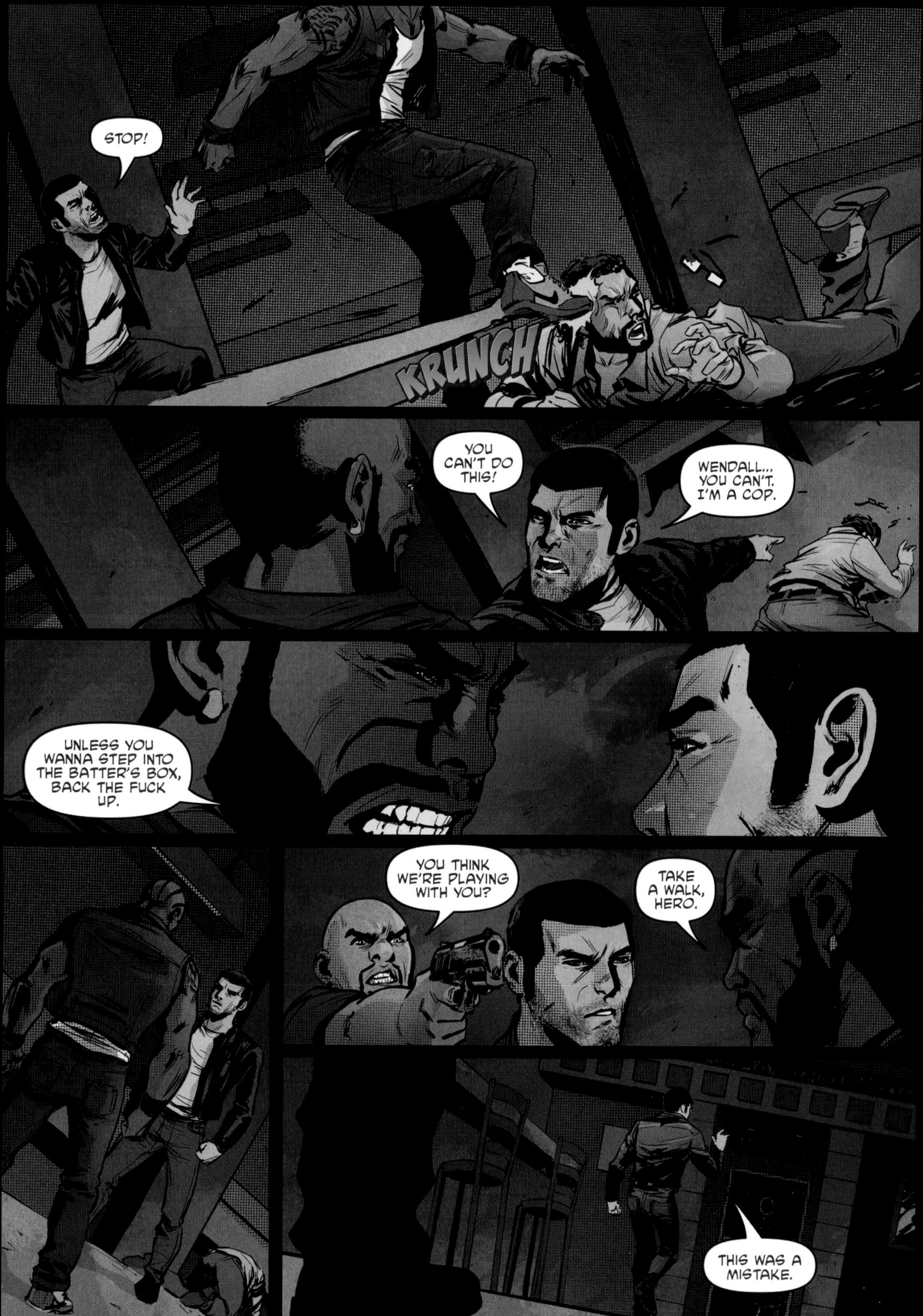
STOP!
KRUNCH
YOU CAN'T DO THIS!
WENDALL... YOU CAN'T. I'M A COP.
UNLESS YOU WANNA STEP INTO THE BATTER'S BOX, BACK THE FUCK UP.
YOU THINK WE'RE PLAYING WITH YOU?
TAKE A WALK, HERO.
THIS WAS A MISTAKE.

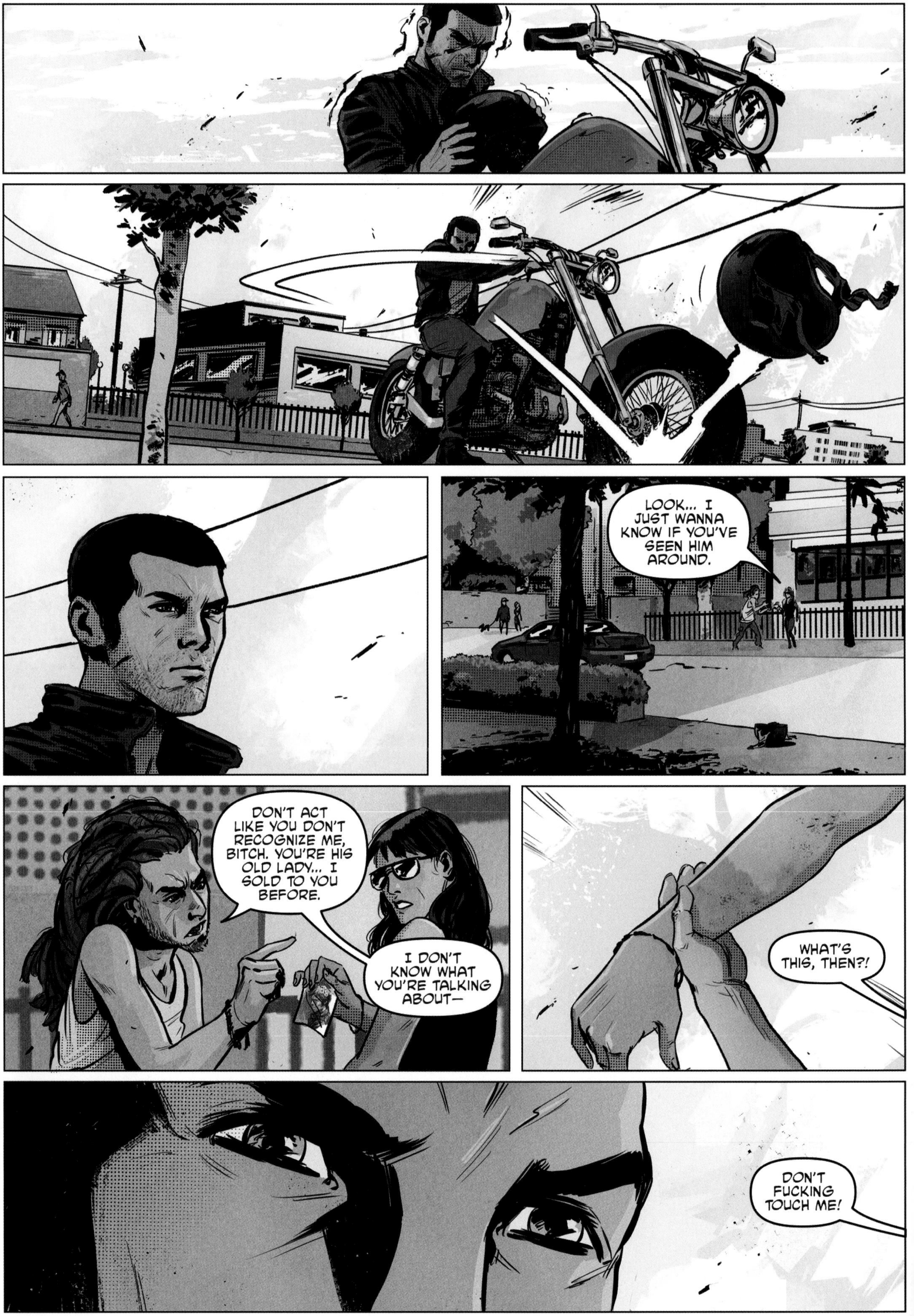

LOOK... I JUST WANNA KNOW IF YOU'VE SEEN HIM AROUND.
DON'T ACT LIKE YOU DON'T RECOGNIZE ME, BITCH. YOU'RE HIS OLD LADY... I SOLD TO YOU BEFORE.
I DON'T KNOW WHAT YOU'RE TALKING ABOUT—
WHAT'S THIS, THEN?!
DON'T FUCKING TOUCH ME!

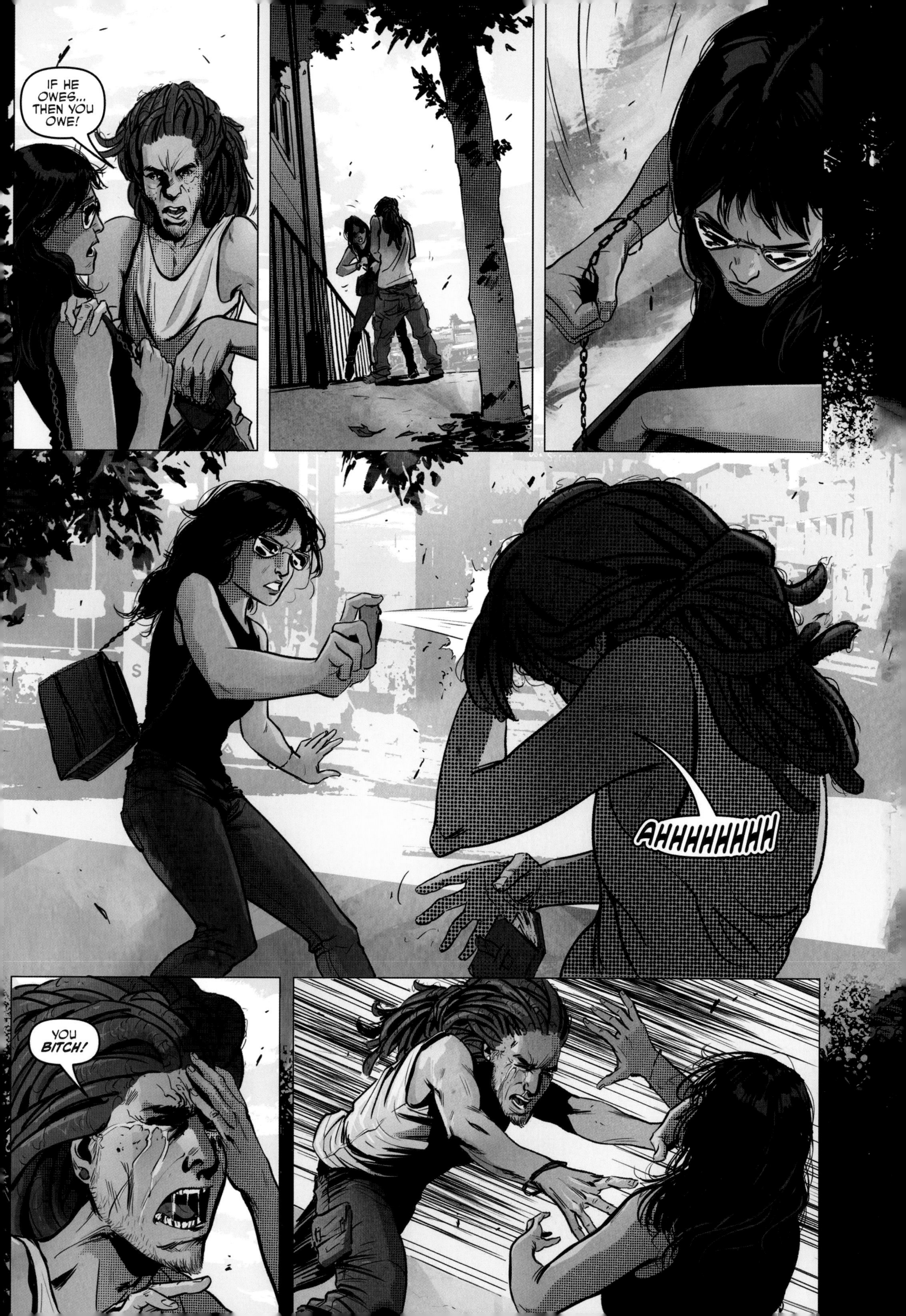
IF HE OWES... THEN YOU OWE!
AHHHHHHHH
YOU *BITCH!*

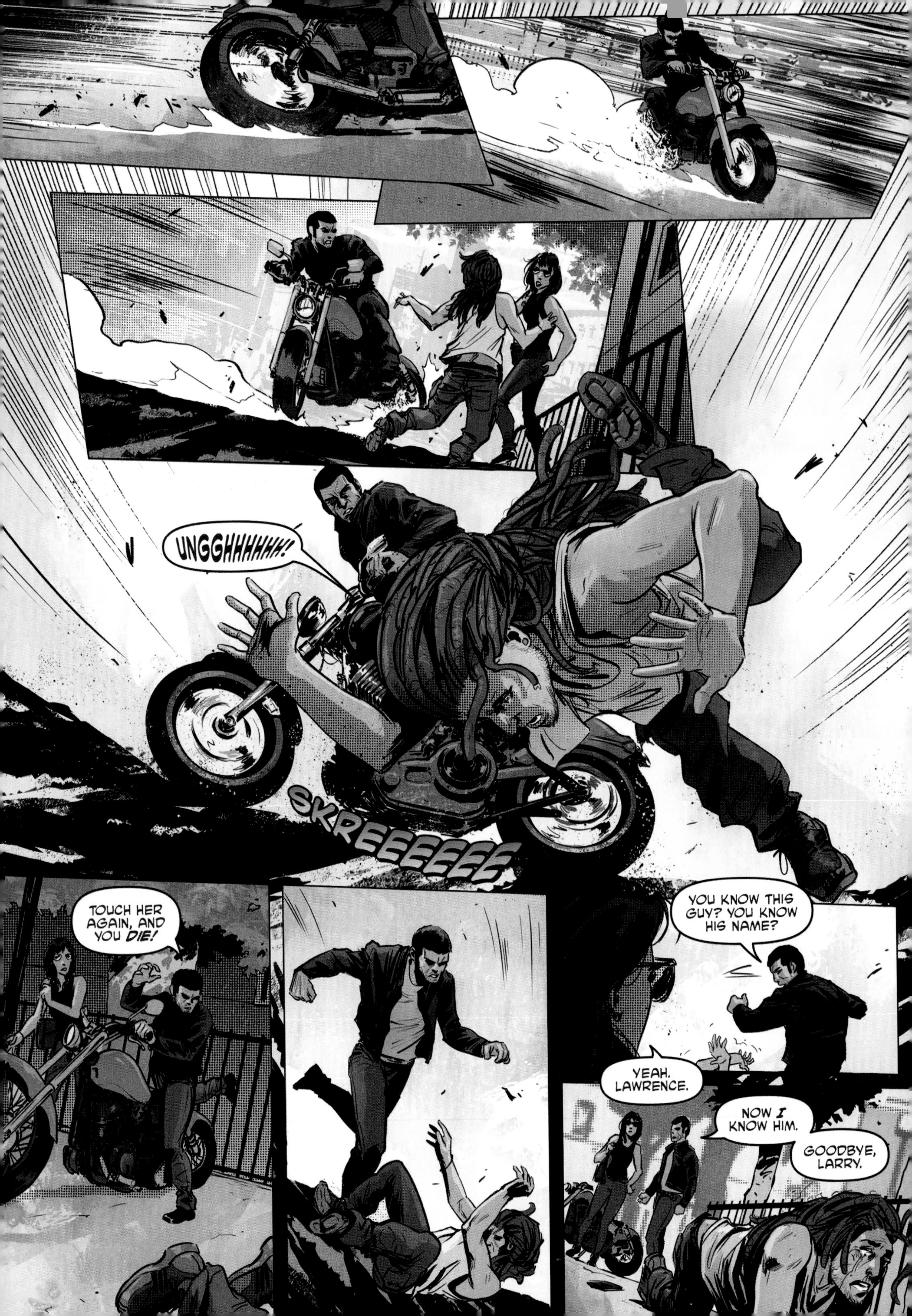
UNGGHHHHH!
SKREEEEEEE
TOUCH HER AGAIN, AND YOU *DIE!*
YOU KNOW THIS GUY? YOU KNOW HIS NAME?
YEAH. LAWRENCE.
NOW *I* KNOW HIM.
GOODBYE, LARRY.

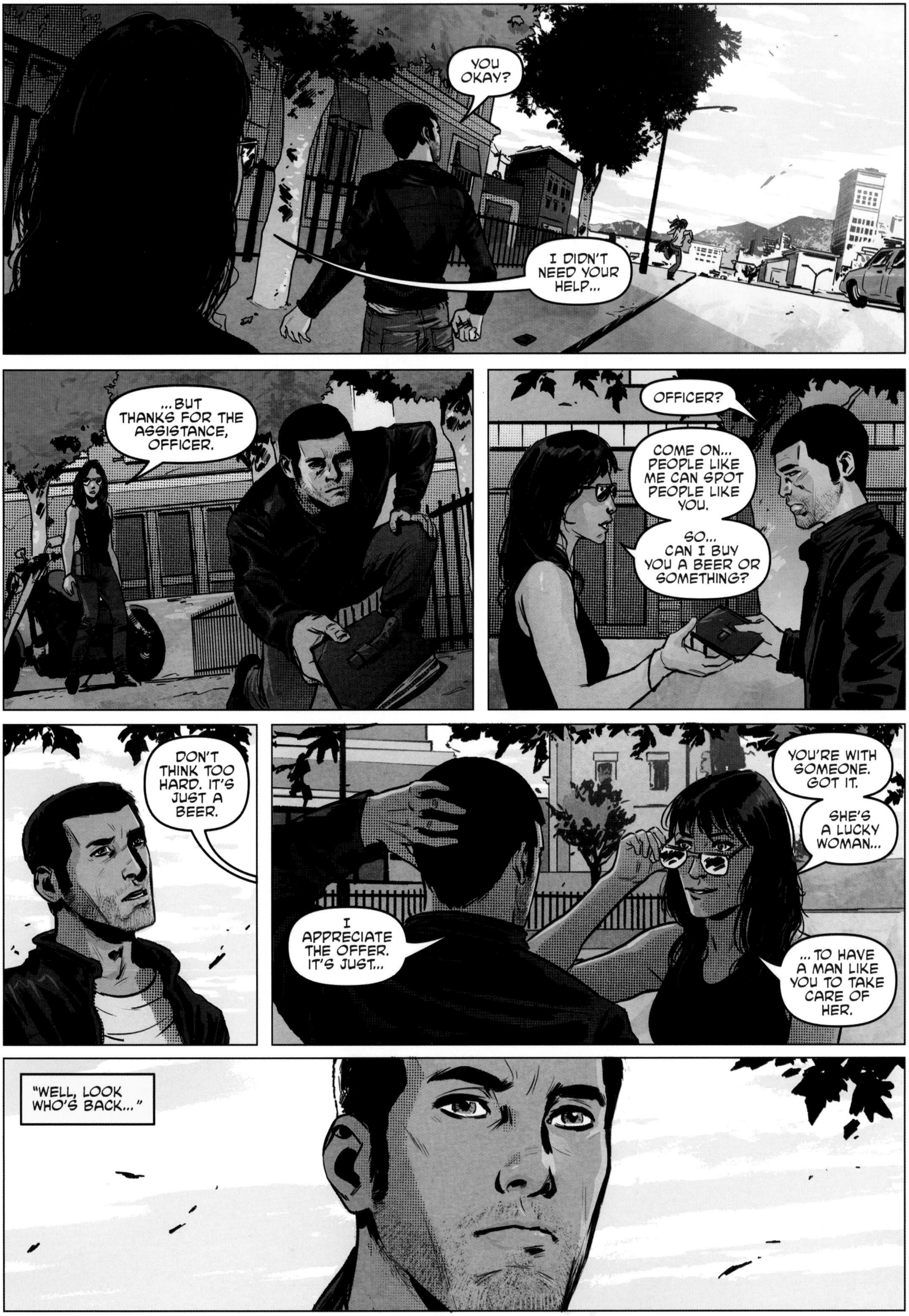
YOU OKAY?
I DIDN'T NEED YOUR HELP...
...BUT THANKS FOR THE ASSISTANCE, OFFICER.
OFFICER?
COME ON... PEOPLE LIKE ME CAN SPOT PEOPLE LIKE YOU.
SO... CAN I BUY YOU A BEER OR SOMETHING?
DON'T THINK TOO HARD. IT'S JUST A BEER.
I APPRECIATE THE OFFER. IT'S JUST...
YOU'RE WITH SOMEONE. GOT IT.
SHE'S A LUCKY WOMAN...
...TO HAVE A MAN LIKE YOU TO TAKE CARE OF HER.
"WELL, LOOK WHO'S BACK..."

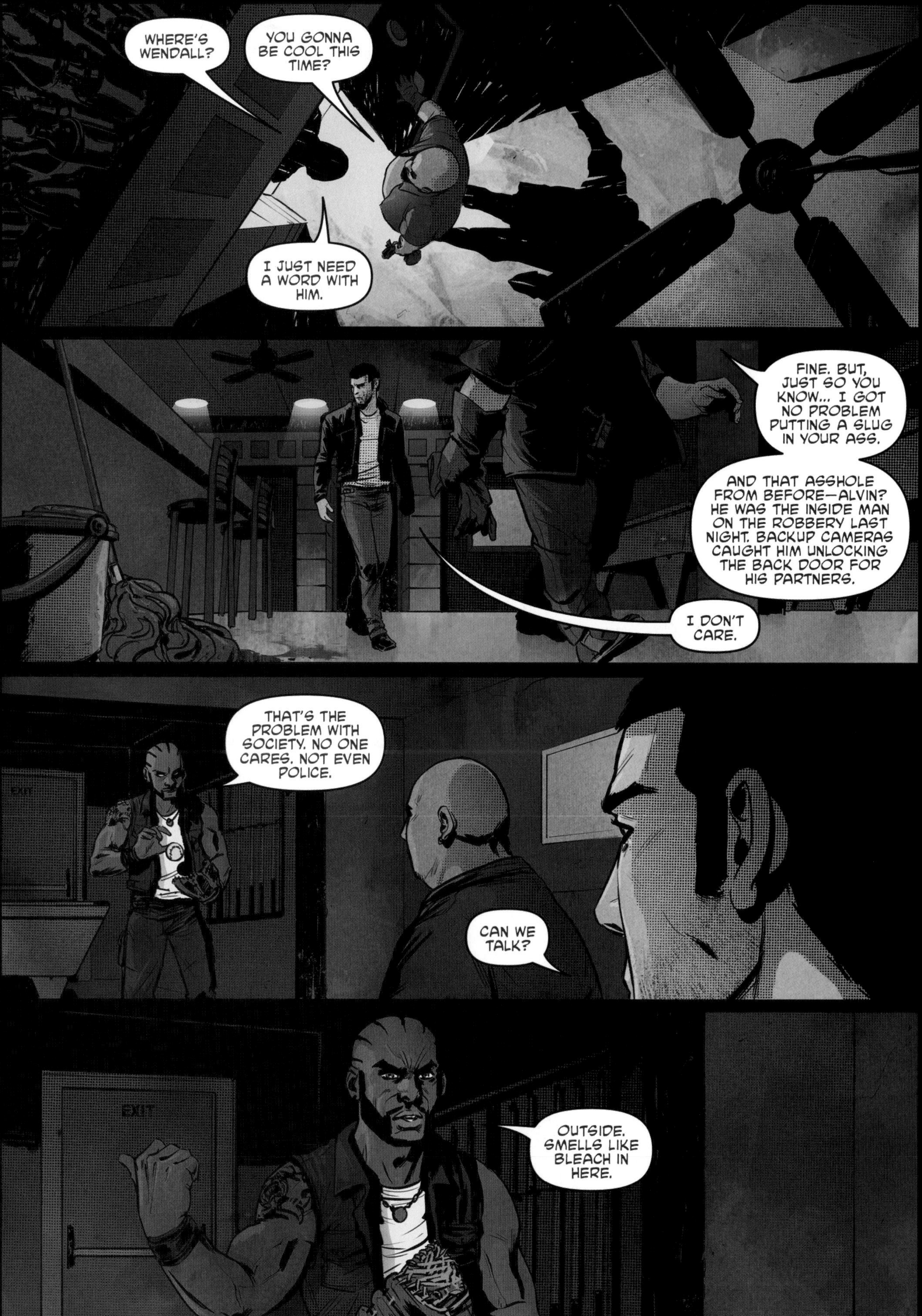
WHERE'S WENDALL?
YOU GONNA BE COOL THIS TIME?
I JUST NEED A WORD WITH HIM.
FINE. BUT, JUST SO YOU KNOW... I GOT NO PROBLEM PUTTING A SLUG IN YOUR ASS.
AND THAT ASSHOLE FROM BEFORE—ALVIN? HE WAS THE INSIDE MAN ON THE ROBBERY LAST NIGHT. BACKUP CAMERAS CAUGHT HIM UNLOCKING THE BACK DOOR FOR HIS PARTNERS.
I DON'T CARE.
THAT'S THE PROBLEM WITH SOCIETY. NO ONE CARES. NOT EVEN POLICE.
CAN WE TALK?
OUTSIDE. SMELLS LIKE BLEACH IN HERE.
EXIT
EXIT

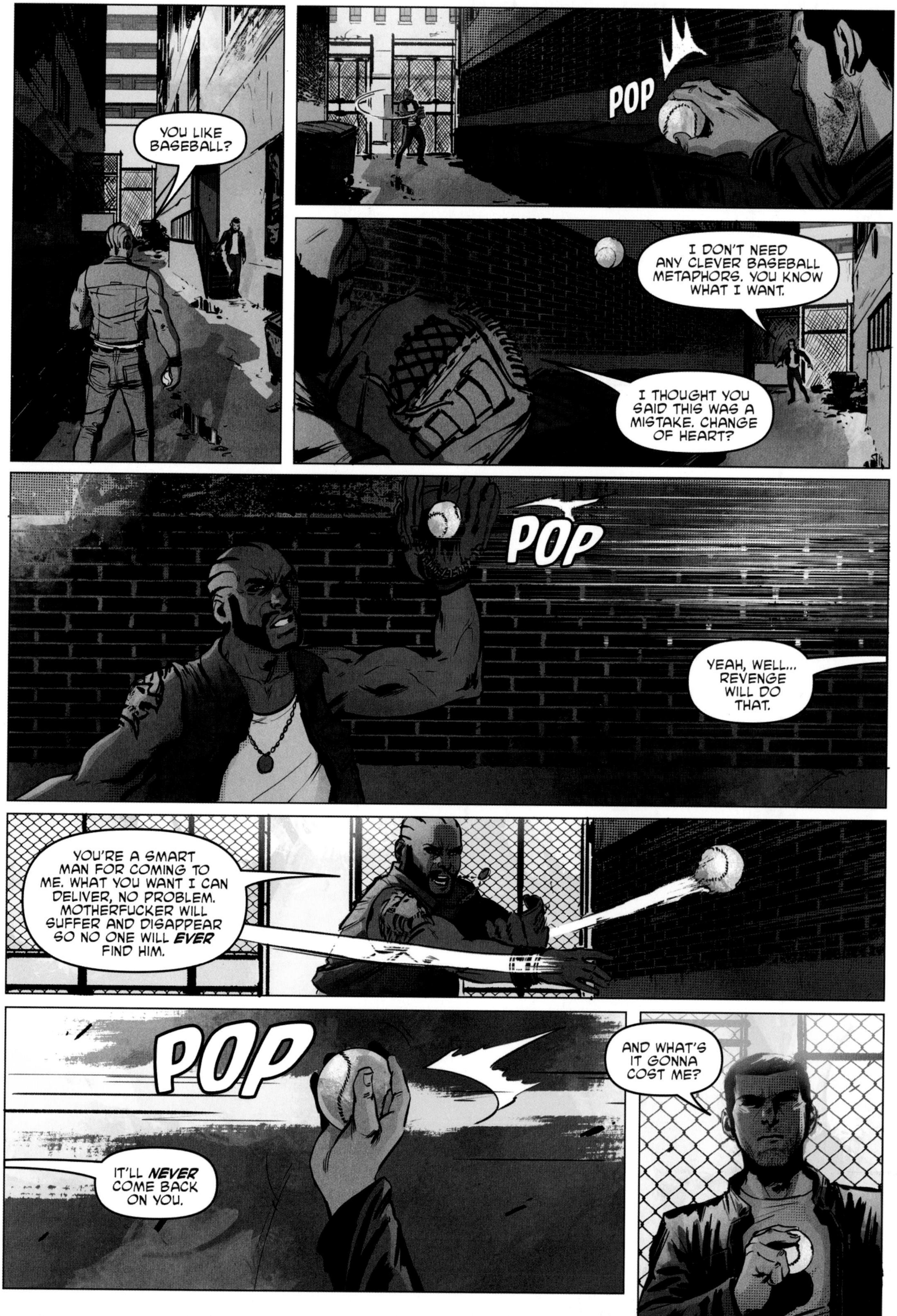
YOU LIKE BASEBALL?
POP
I DON'T NEED ANY CLEVER BASEBALL METAPHORS. YOU KNOW WHAT I WANT.
I THOUGHT YOU SAID THIS WAS A MISTAKE. CHANGE OF HEART?
POP
YEAH, WELL... REVENGE WILL DO THAT.
YOU'RE A SMART MAN FOR COMING TO ME. WHAT YOU WANT I CAN DELIVER, NO PROBLEM. MOTHERFUCKER WILL SUFFER AND DISAPPEAR SO NO ONE WILL *EVER* FIND HIM.
POP
IT'LL *NEVER* COME BACK ON YOU.
AND WHAT'S IT GONNA COST ME?

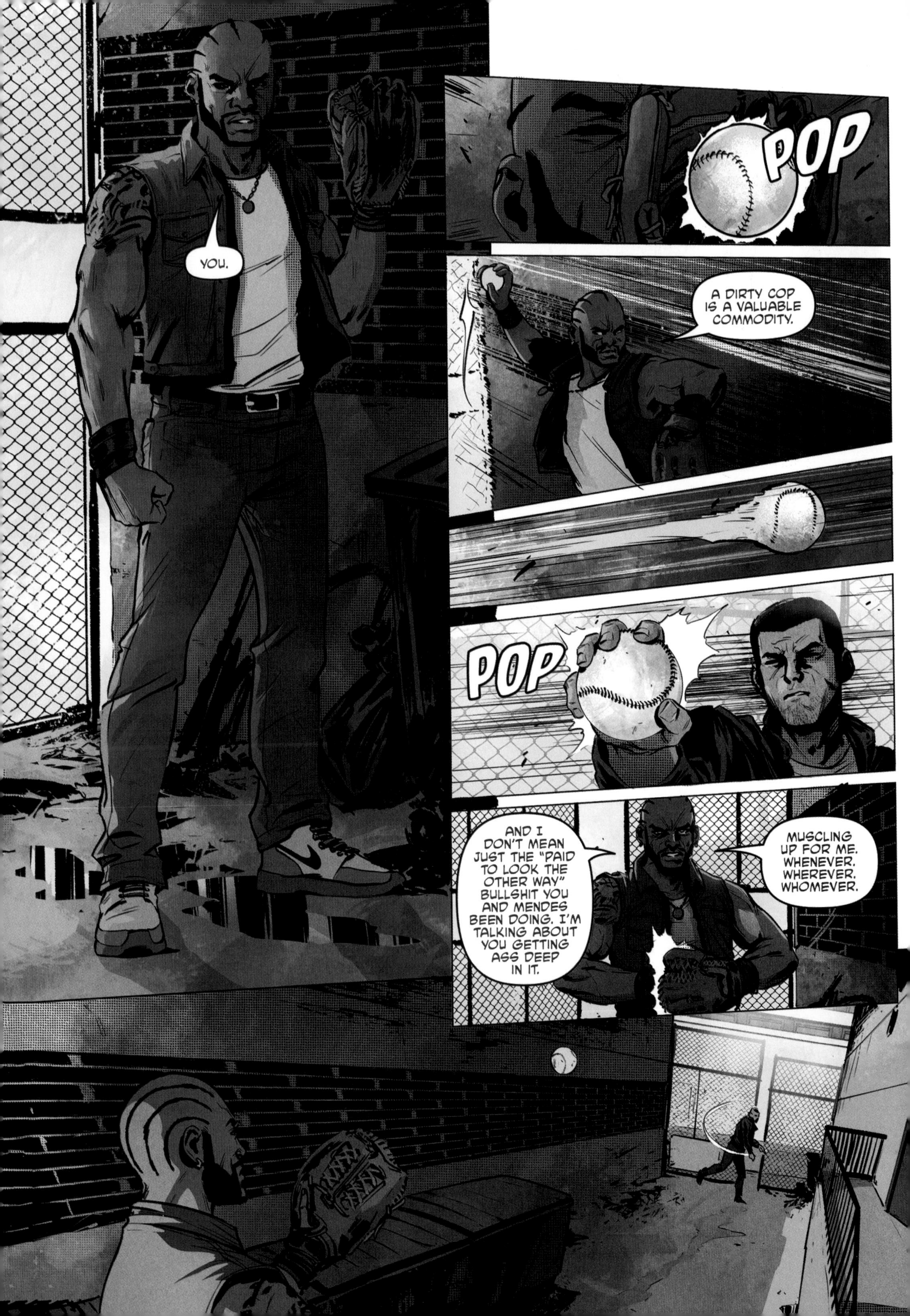
YOU.
POP
A DIRTY COP IS A VALUABLE COMMODITY.
POP
AND I DON'T MEAN JUST THE "PAID TO LOOK THE OTHER WAY" BULLSHIT YOU AND MENDES BEEN DOING. I'M TALKING ABOUT YOU GETTING ASS DEEP IN IT.
MUSCLING UP FOR ME. WHENEVER. WHEREVER. WHOMEVER.

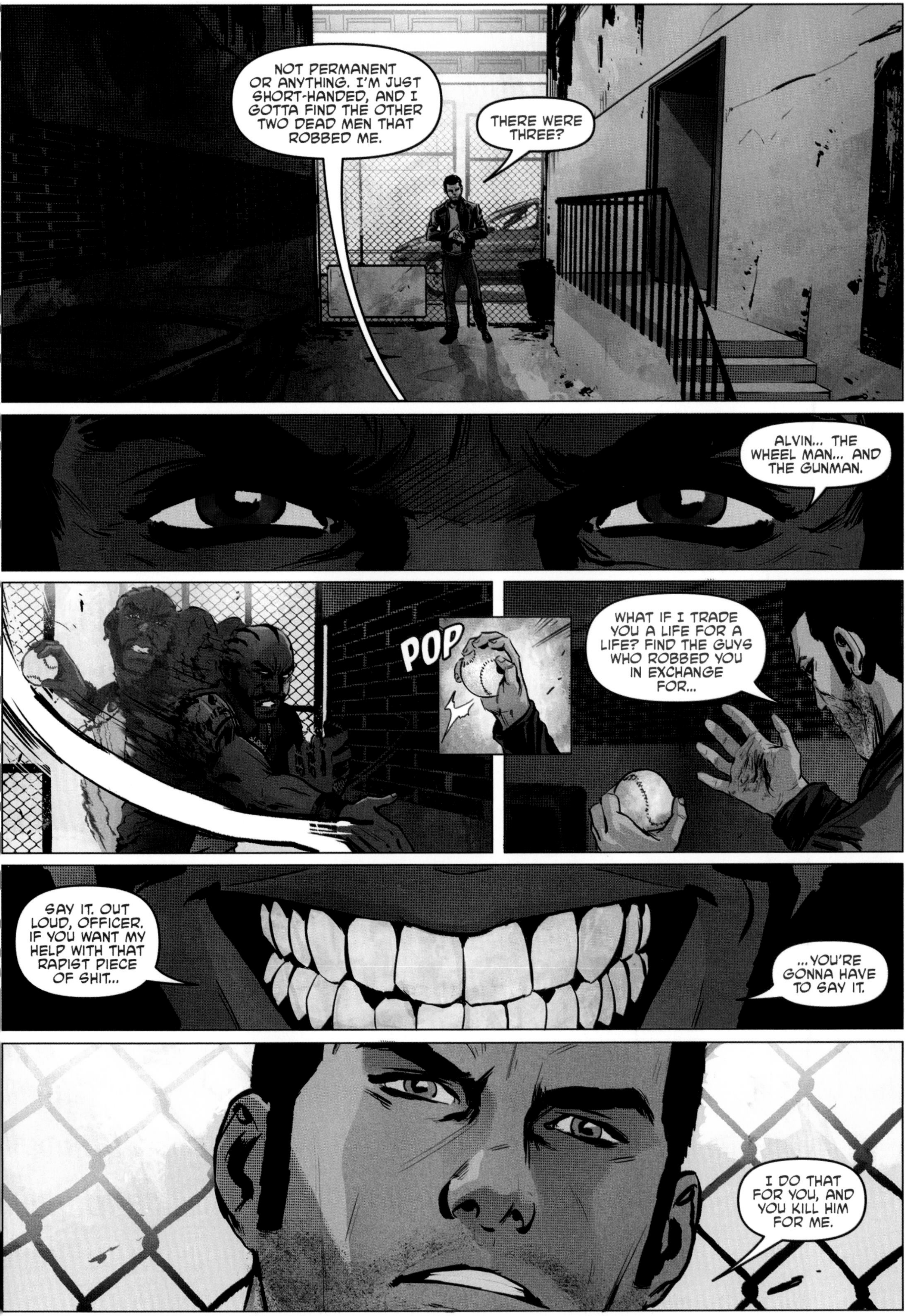
NOT PERMANENT OR ANYTHING. I'M JUST SHORT-HANDED, AND I GOTTA FIND THE OTHER TWO DEAD MEN THAT ROBBED ME.
THERE WERE THREE?
ALVIN... THE WHEEL MAN... AND THE GUNMAN.
POP
WHAT IF I TRADE YOU A LIFE FOR A LIFE? FIND THE GUYS WHO ROBBED YOU IN EXCHANGE FOR...
SAY IT. OUT LOUD, OFFICER. IF YOU WANT MY HELP WITH THAT RAPIST PIECE OF SHIT...
...YOU'RE GONNA HAVE TO SAY IT.
I DO THAT FOR YOU, AND YOU KILL HIM FOR ME.

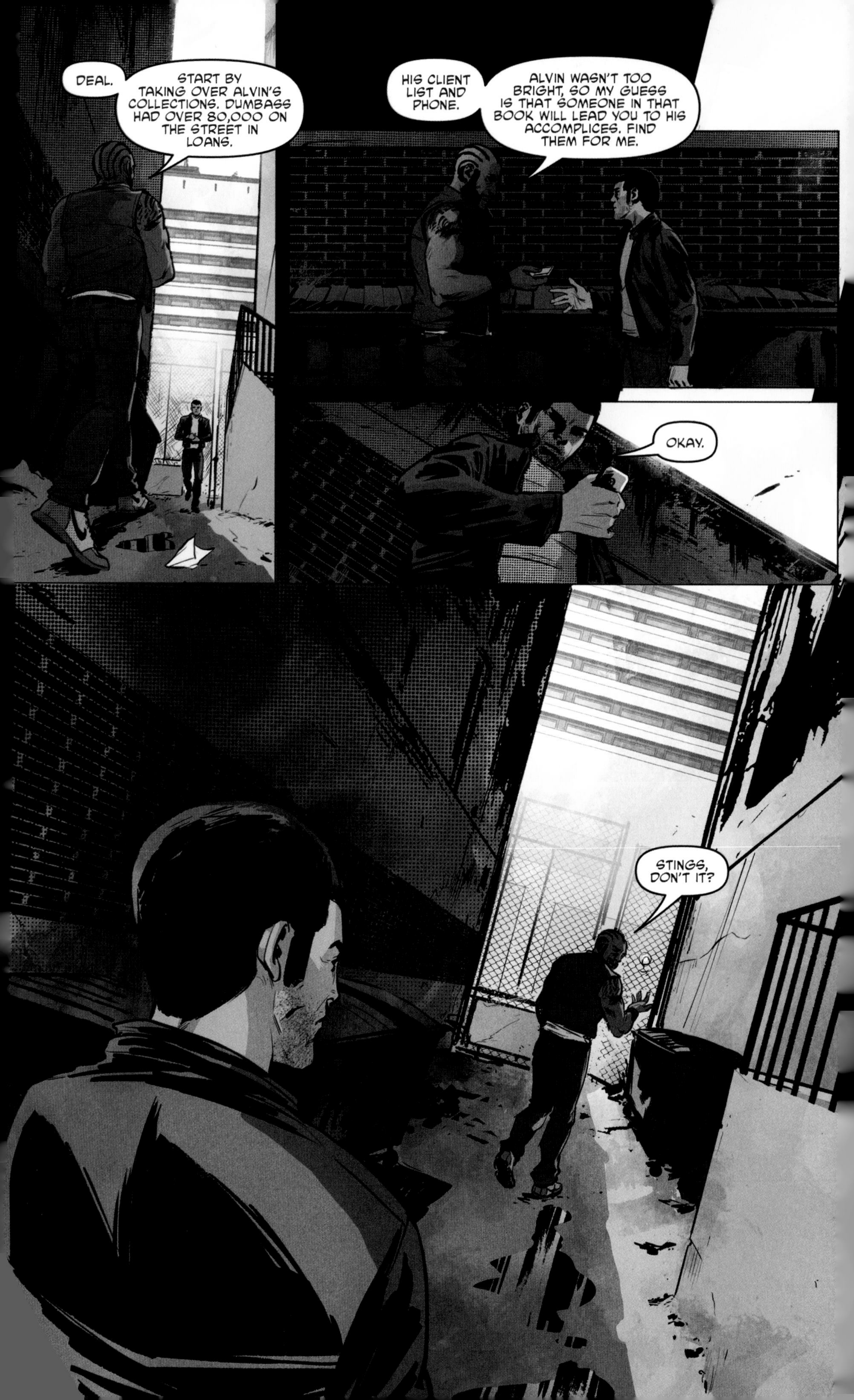
DEAL.
START BY TAKING OVER ALVIN'S COLLECTIONS. DUMBASS HAD OVER 80,000 ON THE STREET IN LOANS.
HIS CLIENT LIST AND PHONE.
ALVIN WASN'T TOO BRIGHT, SO MY GUESS IS THAT SOMEONE IN THAT BOOK WILL LEAD YOU TO HIS ACCOMPLICES. FIND THEM FOR ME.
OKAY.
STINGS, DON'T IT?

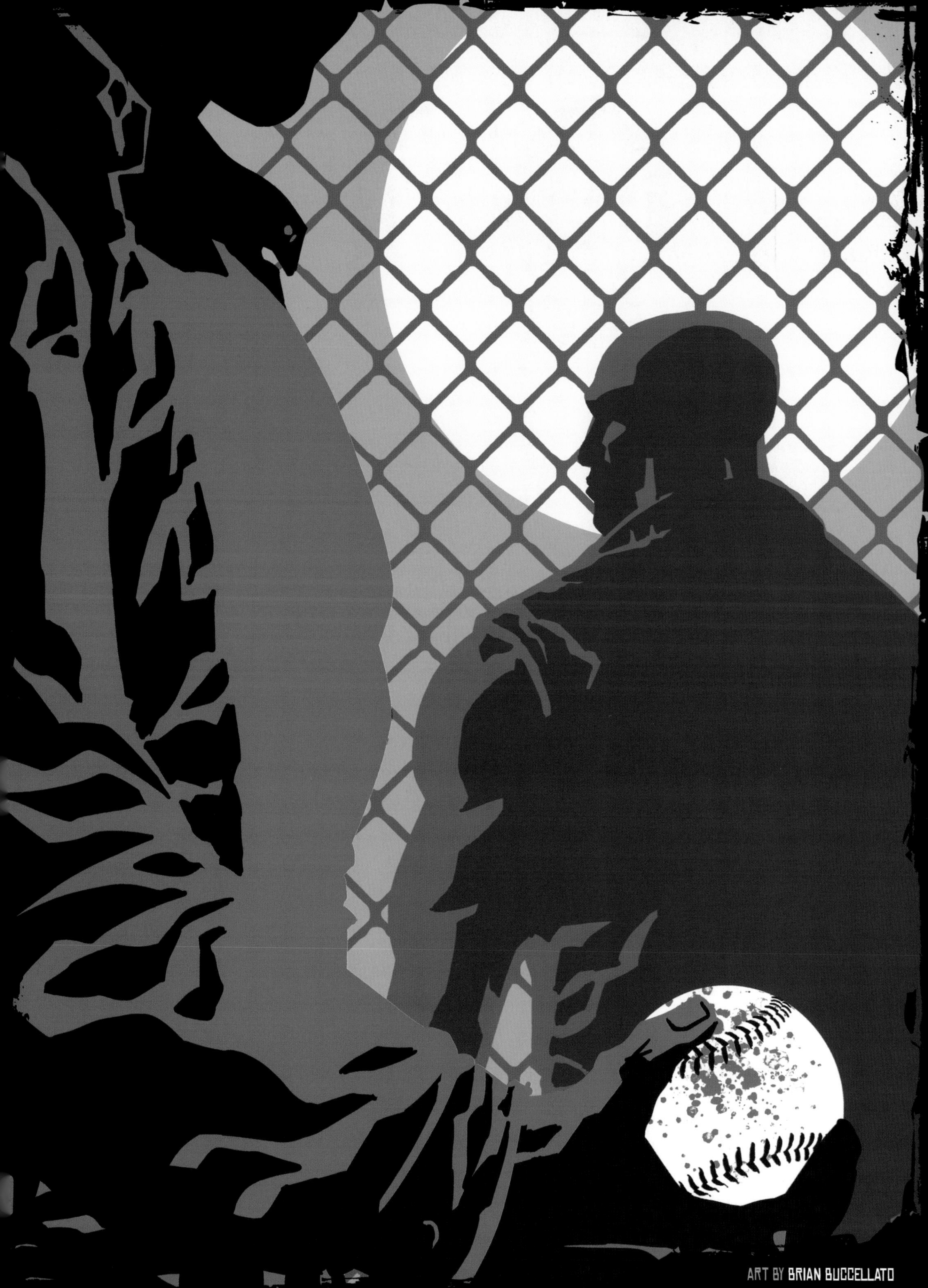

ART BY BRIAN BUCCELLATO

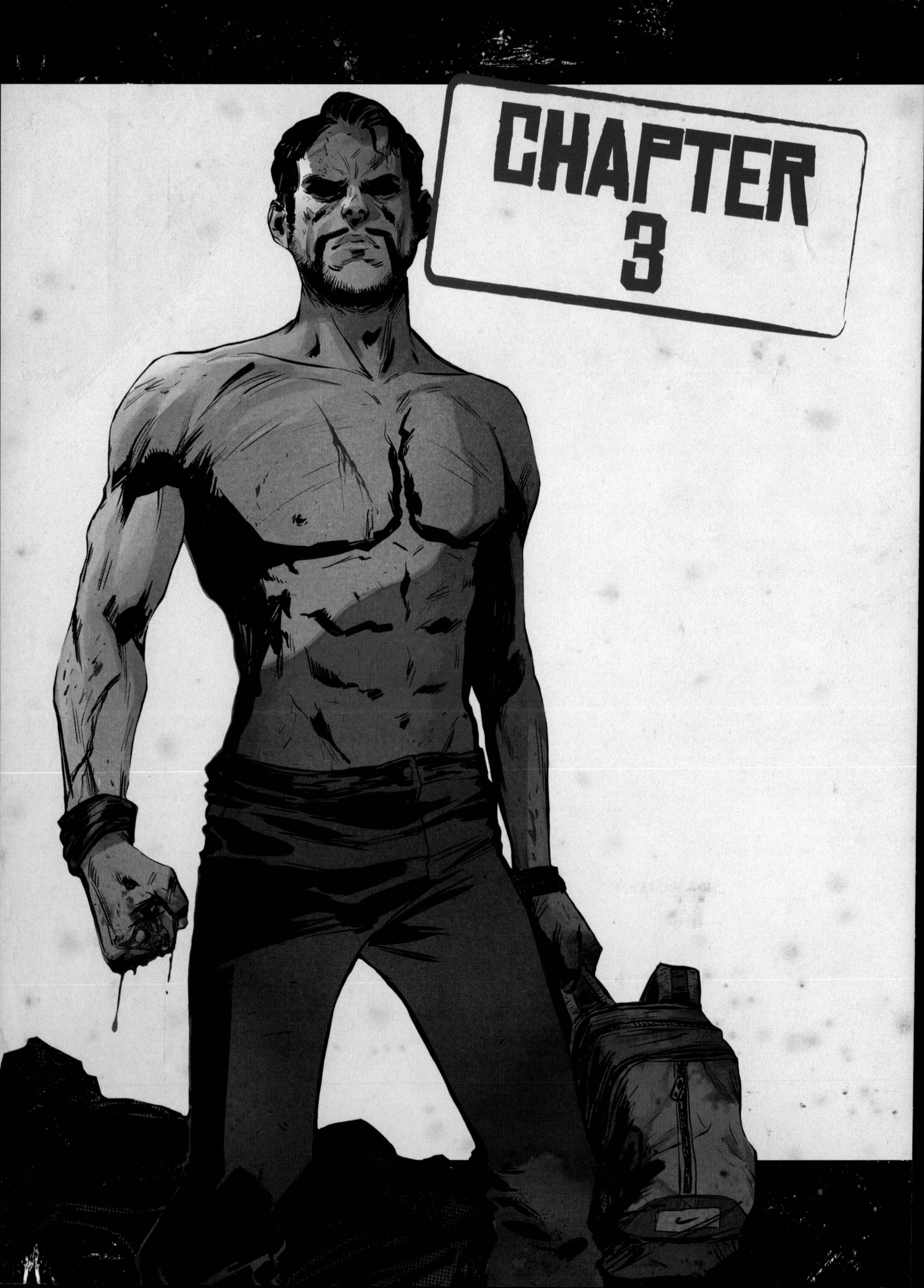
CHAPTER
3

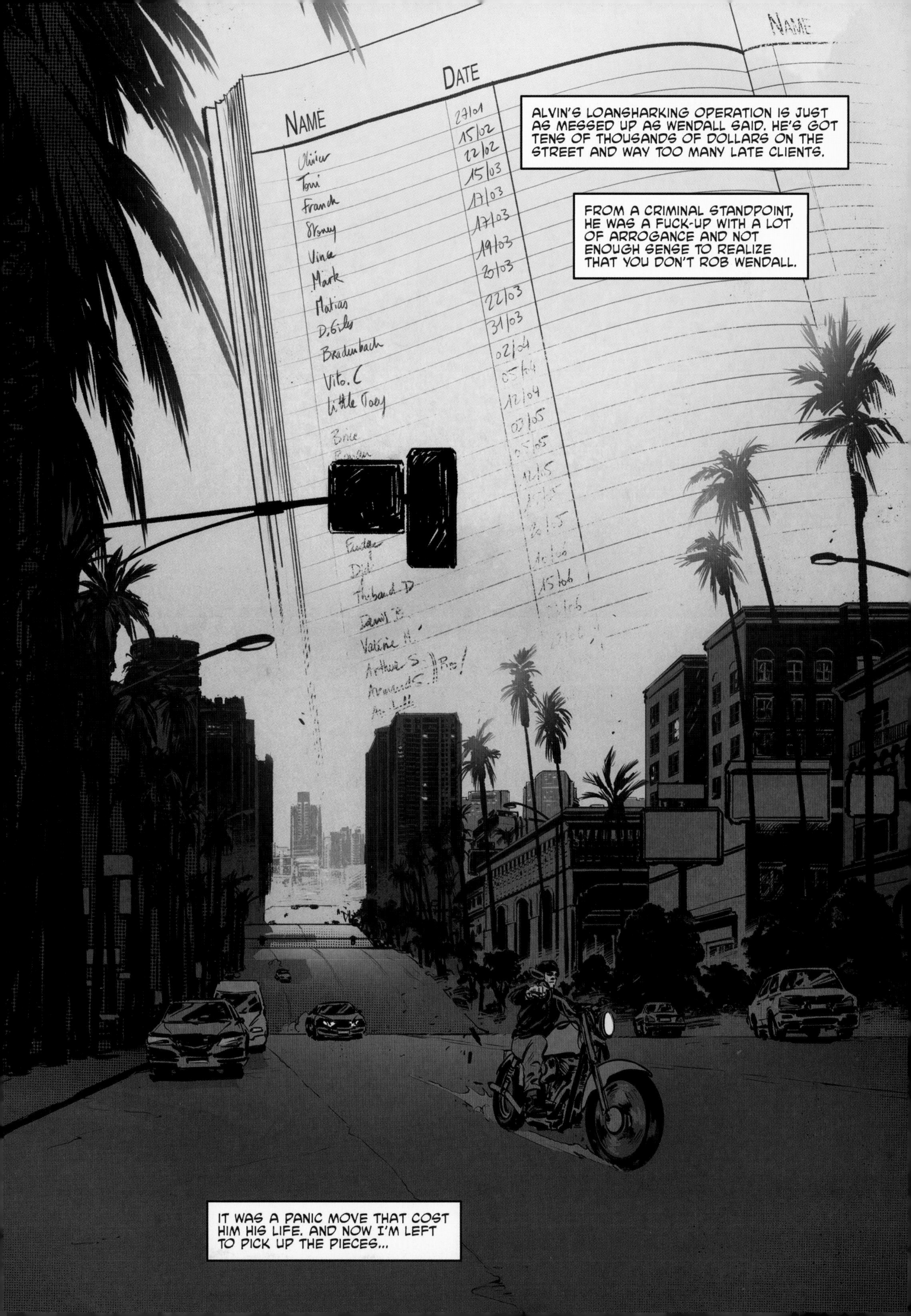
ALVIN'S LOANSHARKING OPERATION IS JUST AS MESSED UP AS WENDALL SAID. HE'S GOT TENS OF THOUSANDS OF DOLLARS ON THE STREET AND WAY TOO MANY LATE CLIENTS.
FROM A CRIMINAL STANDPOINT, HE WAS A FUCK-UP WITH A LOT OF ARROGANCE AND NOT ENOUGH SENSE TO REALIZE THAT YOU DON'T ROB WENDALL.
IT WAS A PANIC MOVE THAT COST HIM HIS LIFE. AND NOW I'M LEFT TO PICK UP THE PIECES...

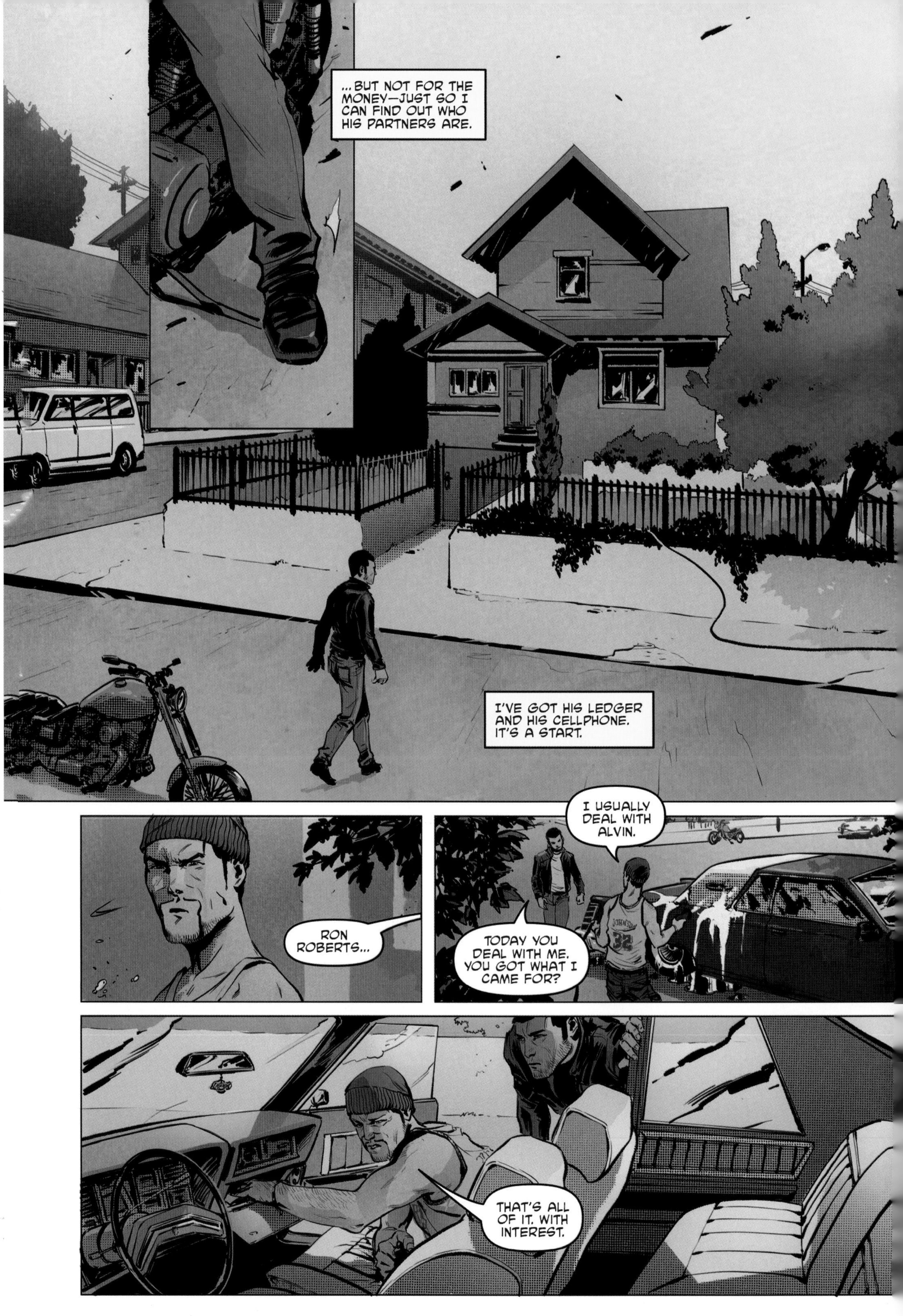
...BUT NOT FOR THE MONEY—JUST SO I CAN FIND OUT WHO HIS PARTNERS ARE.
I'VE GOT HIS LEDGER AND HIS CELLPHONE. IT'S A START.
RON ROBERTS...
I USUALLY DEAL WITH ALVIN.
TODAY YOU DEAL WITH ME. YOU GOT WHAT I CAME FOR?
THAT'S ALL OF IT. WITH INTEREST.

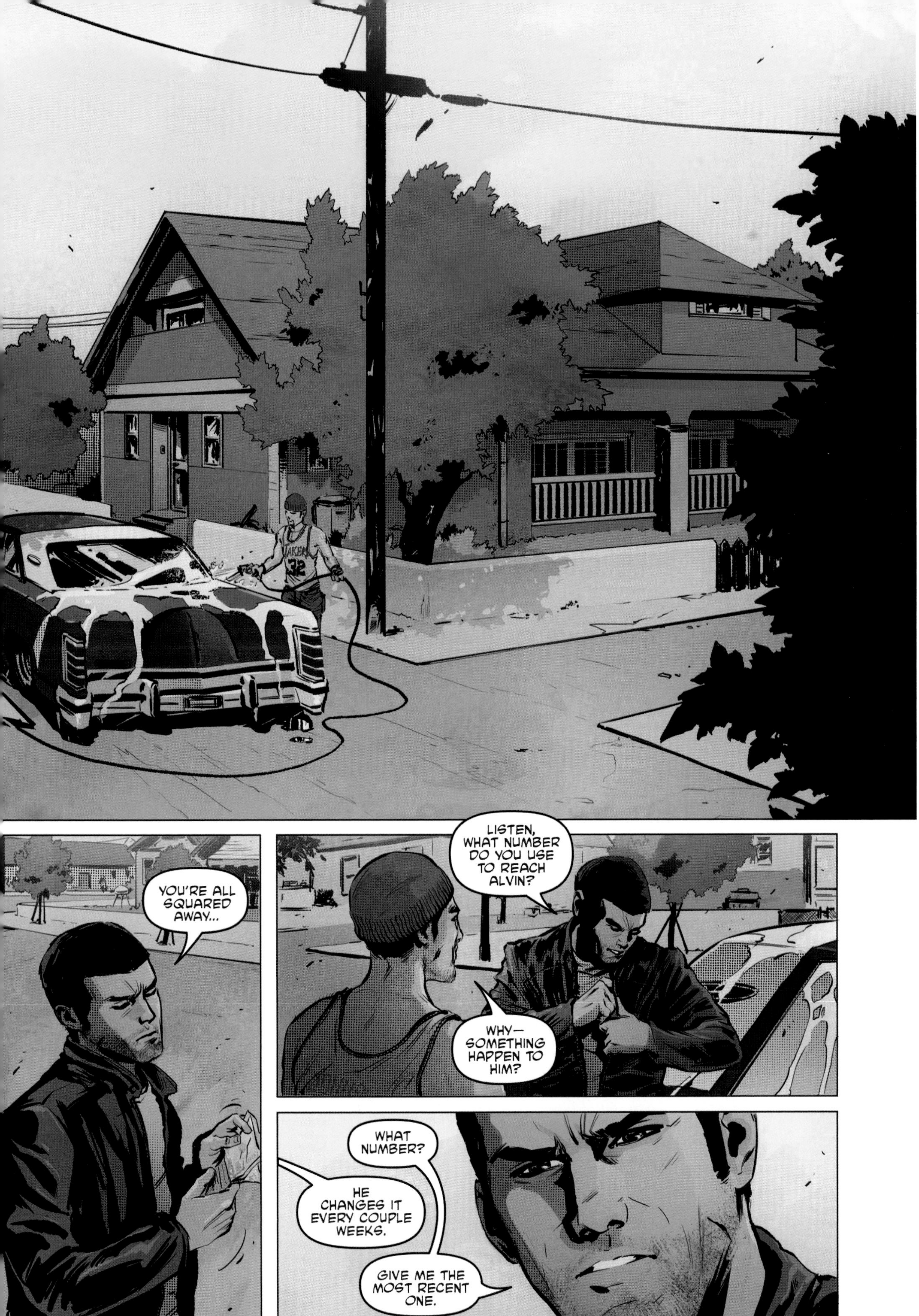
YOU'RE ALL SQUARED AWAY...
LISTEN, WHAT NUMBER DO YOU USE TO REACH ALVIN?
WHY— SOMETHING HAPPEN TO HIM?
WHAT NUMBER?
HE CHANGES IT EVERY COUPLE WEEKS.
GIVE ME THE MOST RECENT ONE.

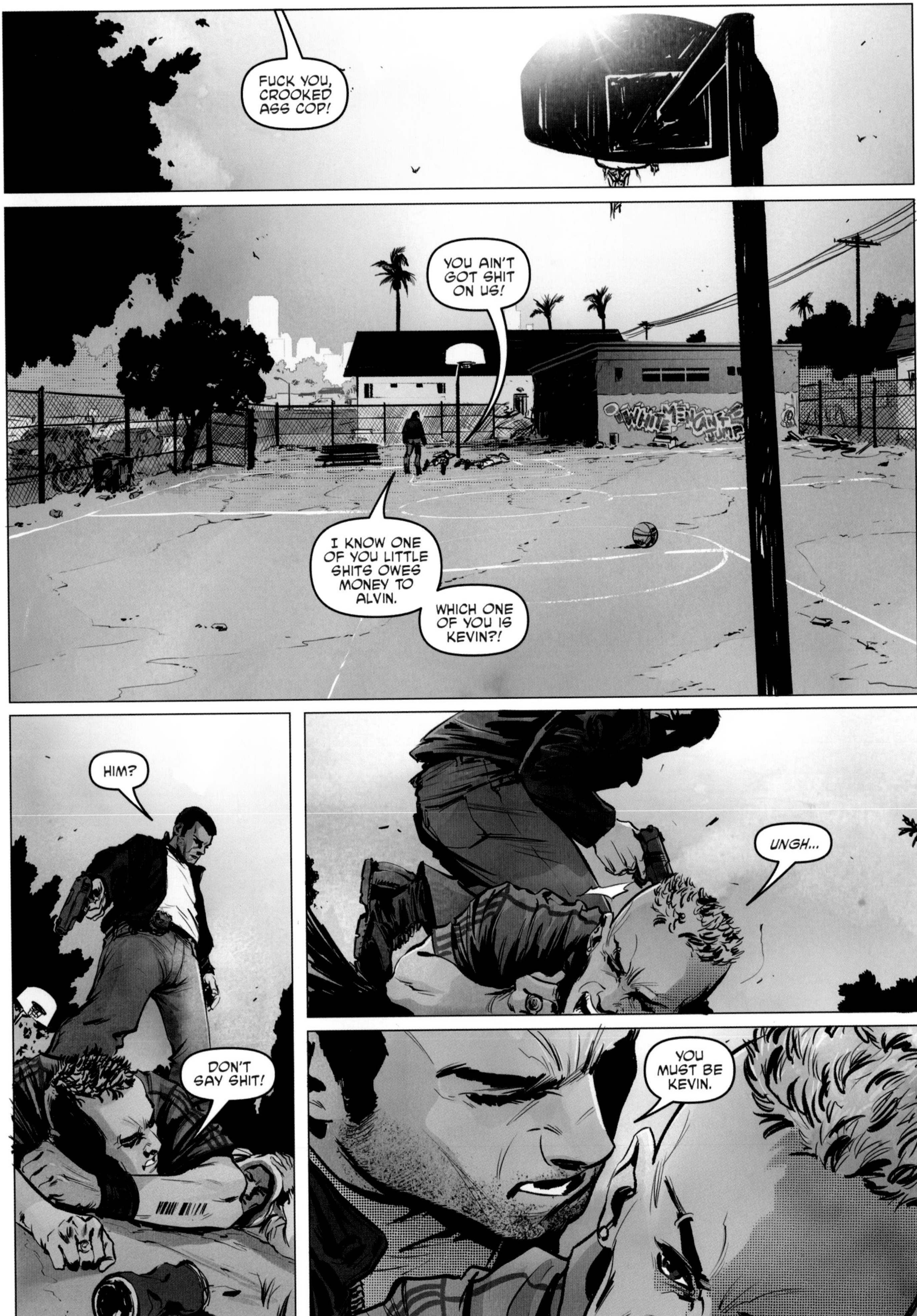
FUCK YOU, CROOKED ASS COP!
YOU AIN'T GOT SHIT ON US!
WHITE MEN CAN'T JUMP
I KNOW ONE OF YOU LITTLE SHITS OWES MONEY TO ALVIN.
WHICH ONE OF YOU IS KEVIN?!
HIM?
DON'T SAY SHIT!
UNGH...
YOU MUST BE KEVIN.

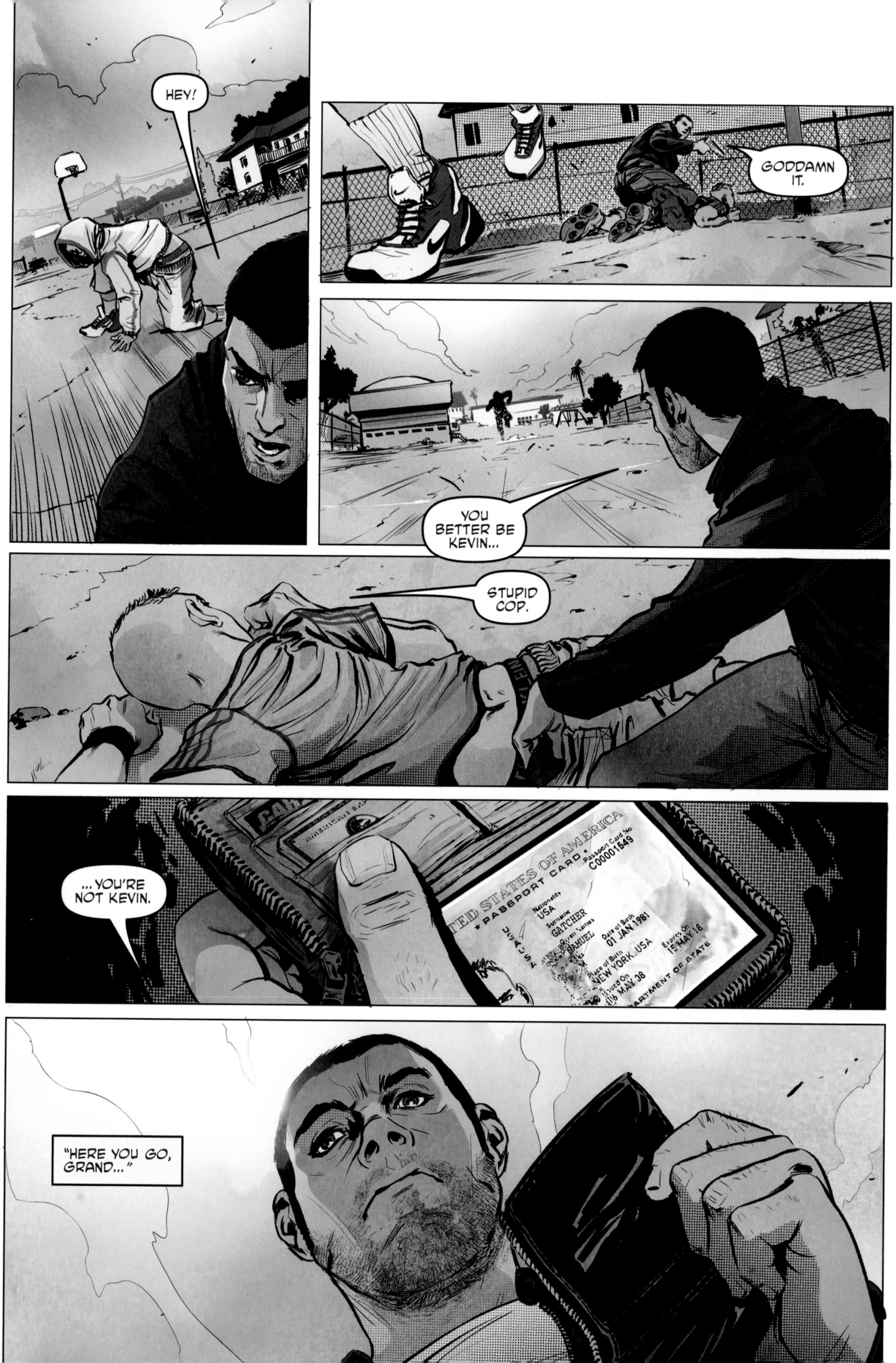
HEY!
GODDAMN IT.
YOU BETTER BE KEVIN...
STUPID COP.
...YOU'RE NOT KEVIN.
"HERE YOU GO, GRAND..."

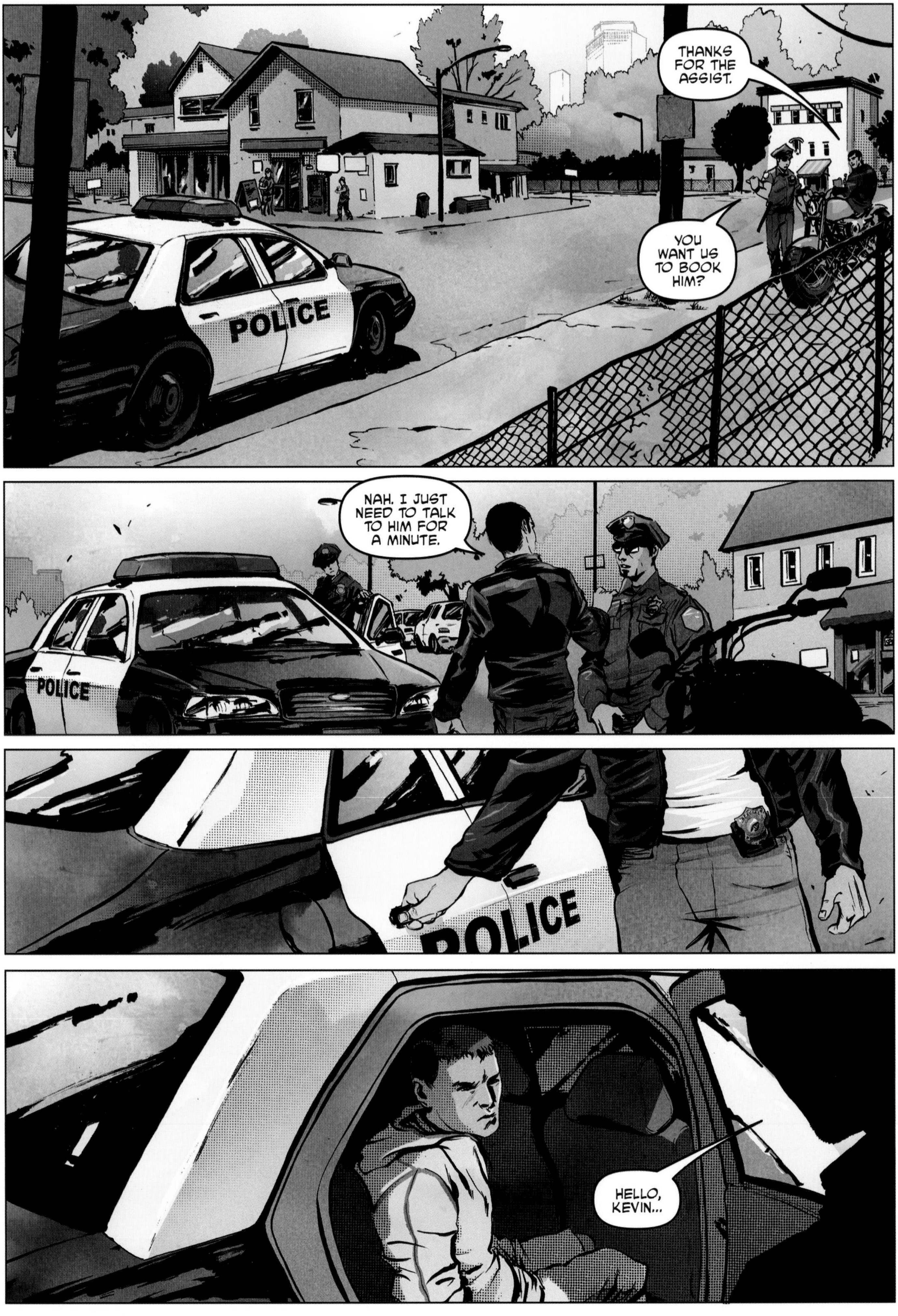
THANKS FOR THE ASSIST.
YOU WANT US TO BOOK HIM?
POLICE
NAH. I JUST NEED TO TALK TO HIM FOR A MINUTE.
POLICE
POLICE
HELLO, KEVIN...

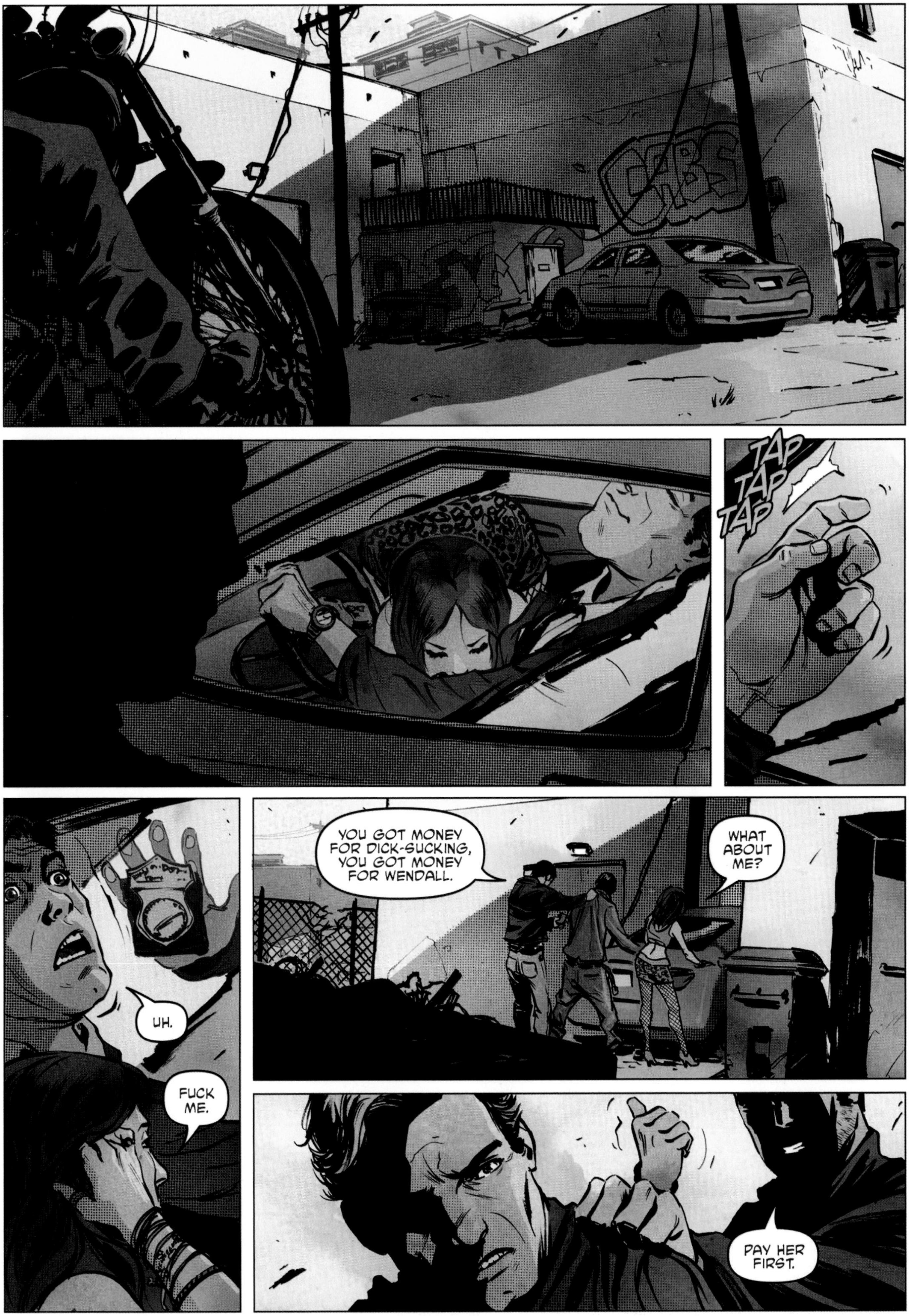
TAP TAP TAP
YOU GOT MONEY FOR DICK-SUCKING, YOU GOT MONEY FOR WENDALL.
WHAT ABOUT ME?
UH.
FUCK ME.
PAY HER FIRST.

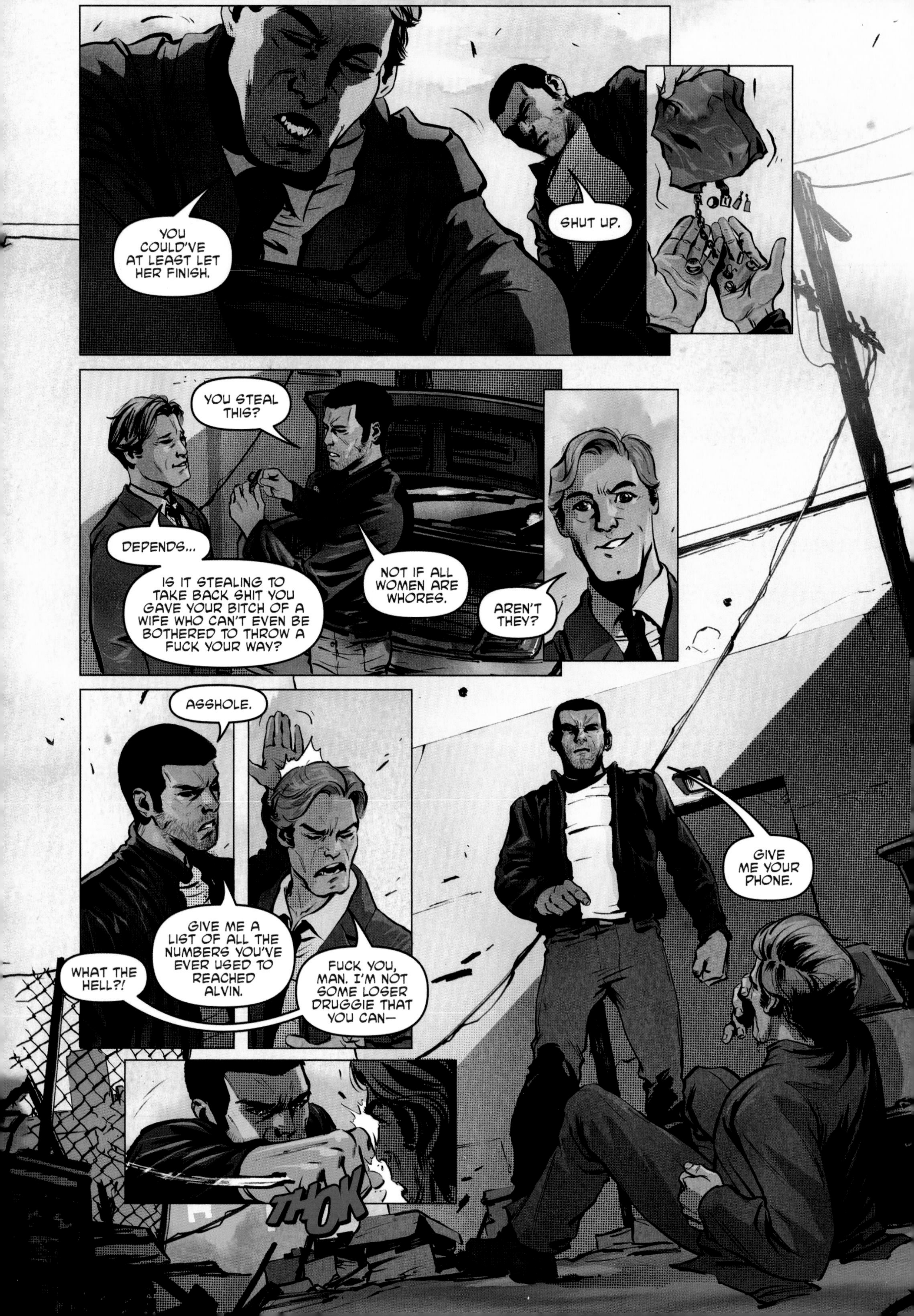
YOU COULD'VE AT LEAST LET HER FINISH.
SHUT UP.
YOU STEAL THIS?
DEPENDS...
IS IT STEALING TO TAKE BACK SHIT YOU GAVE YOUR BITCH OF A WIFE WHO CAN'T EVEN BE BOTHERED TO THROW A FUCK YOUR WAY?
NOT IF ALL WOMEN ARE WHORES.
AREN'T THEY?
ASSHOLE.
GIVE ME A LIST OF ALL THE NUMBERS YOU'VE EVER USED TO REACHED ALVIN.
WHAT THE HELL?!
FUCK YOU, MAN. I'M NOT SOME LOSER DRUGGIE THAT YOU CAN—
THOK
GIVE ME YOUR PHONE.

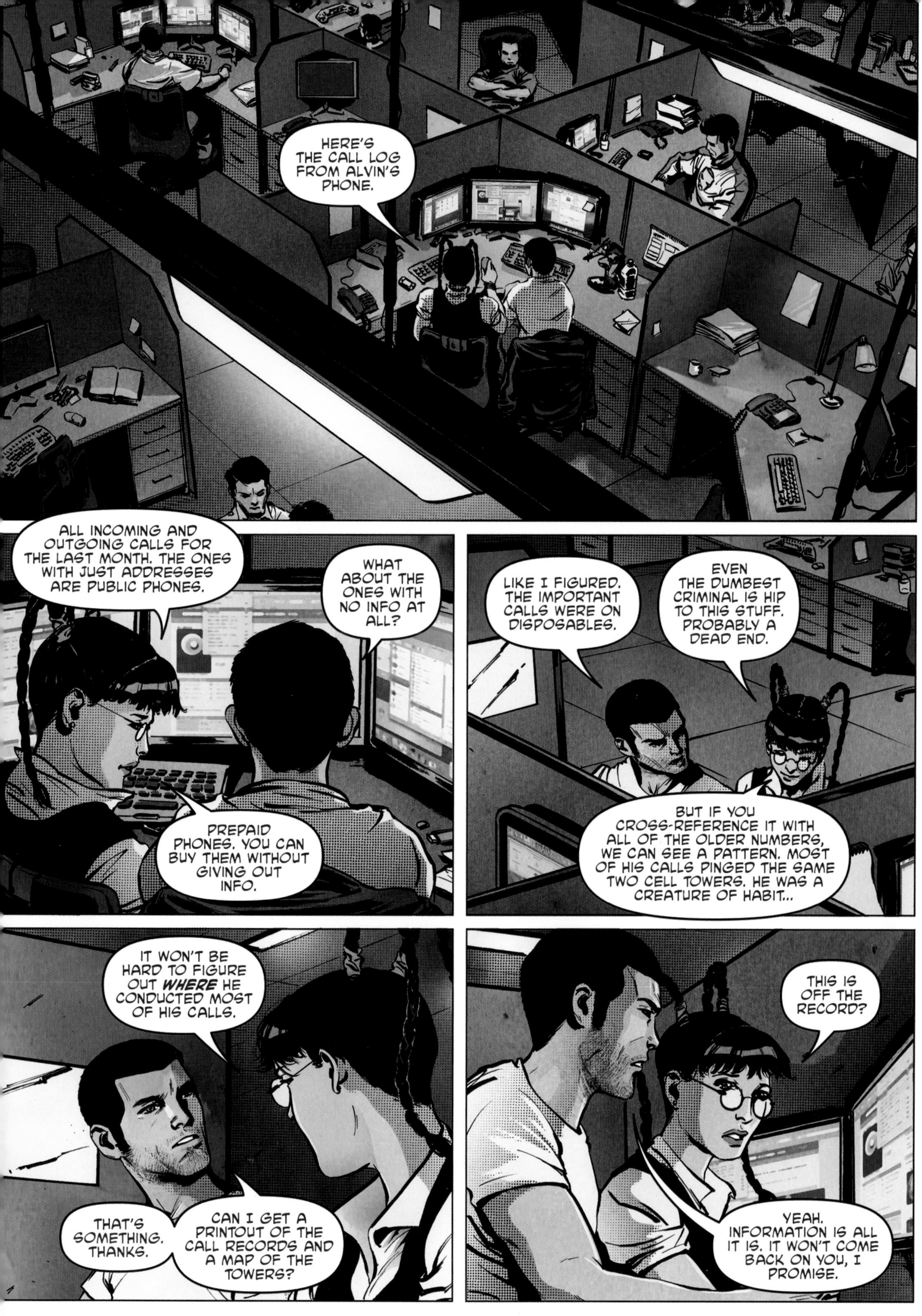
HERE'S THE CALL LOG FROM ALVIN'S PHONE.
ALL INCOMING AND OUTGOING CALLS FOR THE LAST MONTH. THE ONES WITH JUST ADDRESSES ARE PUBLIC PHONES.
WHAT ABOUT THE ONES WITH NO INFO AT ALL?
PREPAID PHONES. YOU CAN BUY THEM WITHOUT GIVING OUT INFO.
LIKE I FIGURED. THE IMPORTANT CALLS WERE ON DISPOSABLES.
EVEN THE DUMBEST CRIMINAL IS HIP TO THIS STUFF. PROBABLY A DEAD END.
BUT IF YOU CROSS-REFERENCE IT WITH ALL OF THE OLDER NUMBERS, WE CAN SEE A PATTERN. MOST OF HIS CALLS PINGED THE SAME TWO CELL TOWERS. HE WAS A CREATURE OF HABIT...
IT WON'T BE HARD TO FIGURE OUT *WHERE* HE CONDUCTED MOST OF HIS CALLS.
THAT'S SOMETHING. THANKS.
CAN I GET A PRINTOUT OF THE CALL RECORDS AND A MAP OF THE TOWERS?
THIS IS OFF THE RECORD?
YEAH. INFORMATION IS ALL IT IS. IT WON'T COME BACK ON YOU, I PROMISE.

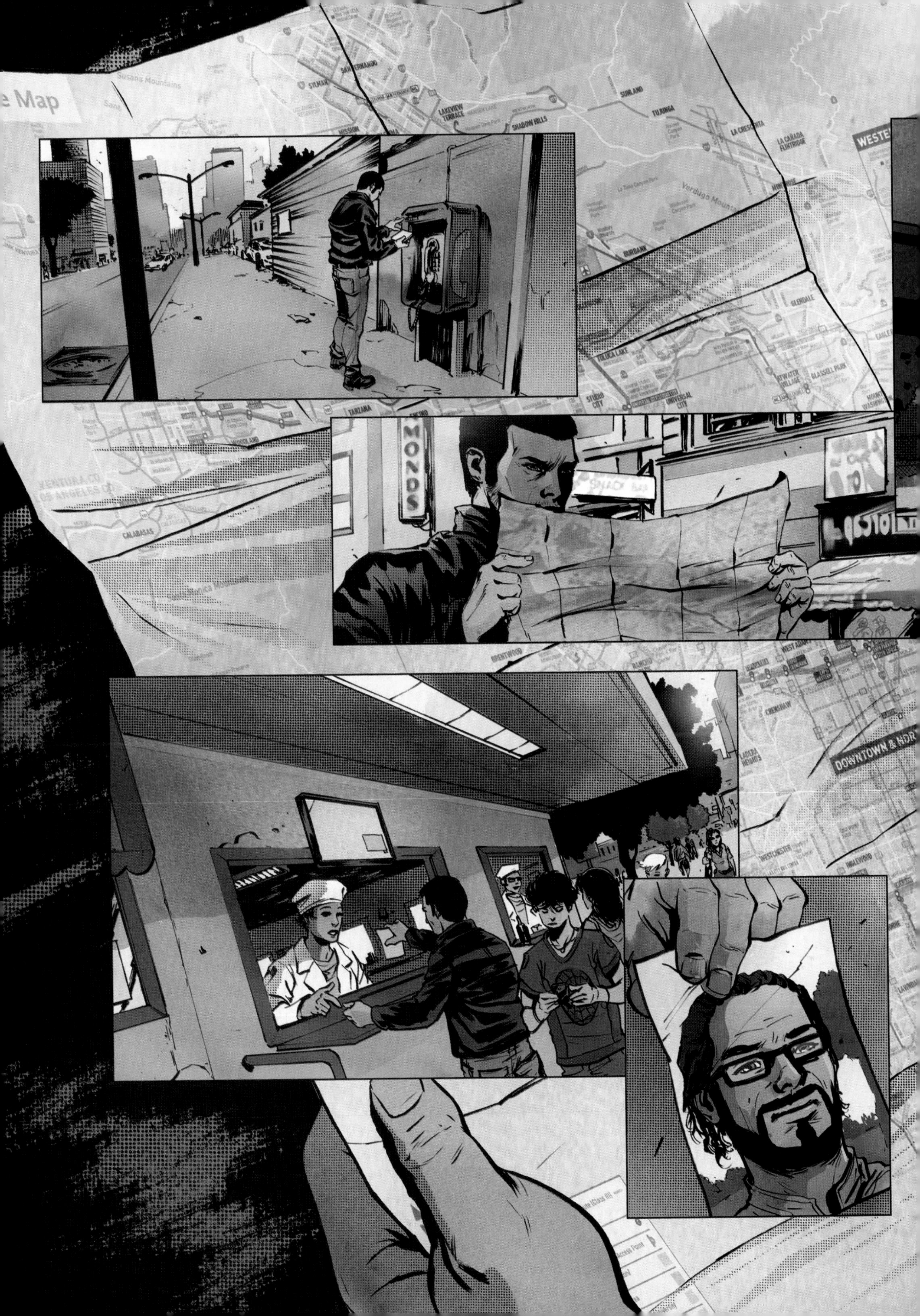
e Map
Susana Mountains
SAN FERNANDO
SYLMAR
LAKEVIEW TERRACE
SHADOW HILLS
SUNLAND
TUJUNGA
LA CRESCENTA
LA CAÑADA FLINTRIDGE
Verdugo Mountains
BURBANK
GLENDALE
TOLUCA LAKE
STUDIO CITY
UNIVERSAL CITY
ATWATER VILLAGE
GLASSELL PARK
TARZANA
VENTURA CO.
LOS ANGELES CO.
CALABASAS
MONDS
BRENTWOOD
CRENSHAW
LADERA HEIGHTS
WESTCHESTER
INGLEWOOD

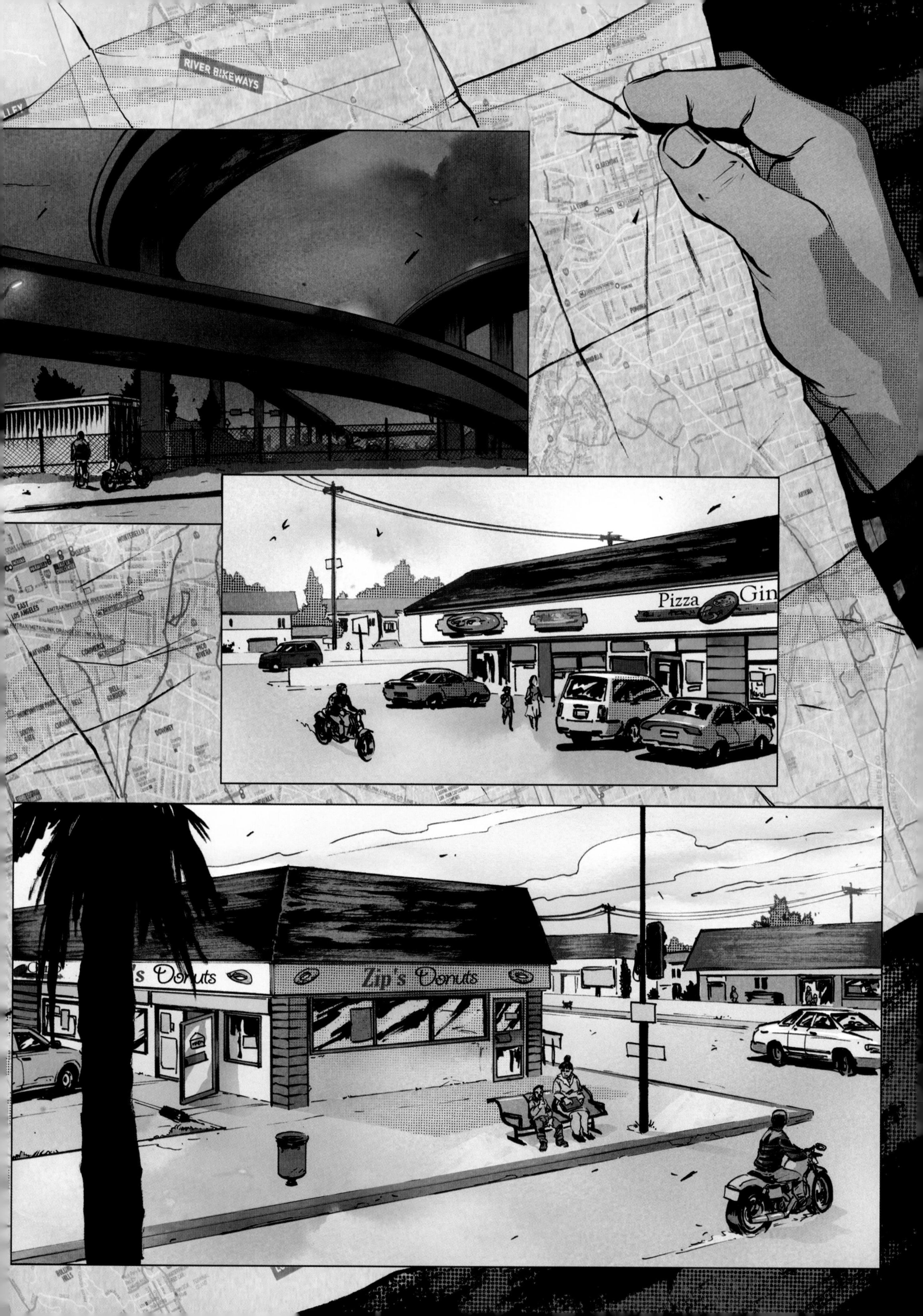
RIVER BIKEWAYS
Pizza
Gin
's Donuts
Zip's Donuts

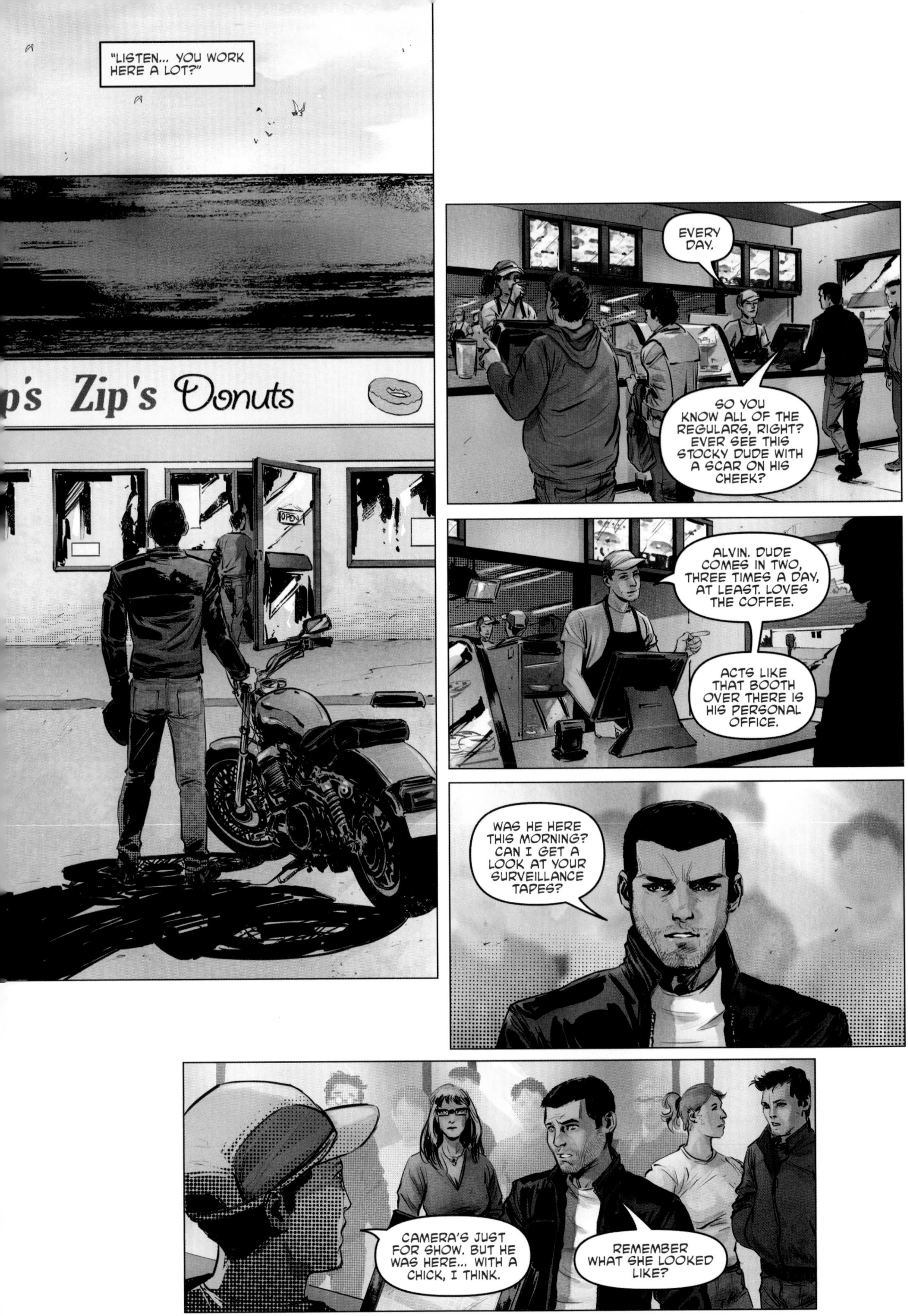
"LISTEN... YOU WORK HERE A LOT?"
p's Zip's Donuts
OPEN
EVERY DAY.
SO YOU KNOW ALL OF THE REGULARS, RIGHT? EVER SEE THIS STOCKY DUDE WITH A SCAR ON HIS CHEEK?
ALVIN. DUDE COMES IN TWO, THREE TIMES A DAY, AT LEAST. LOVES THE COFFEE.
ACTS LIKE THAT BOOTH OVER THERE IS HIS PERSONAL OFFICE.
WAS HE HERE THIS MORNING? CAN I GET A LOOK AT YOUR SURVEILLANCE TAPES?
CAMERA'S JUST FOR SHOW. BUT HE WAS HERE... WITH A CHICK, I THINK.
REMEMBER WHAT SHE LOOKED LIKE?

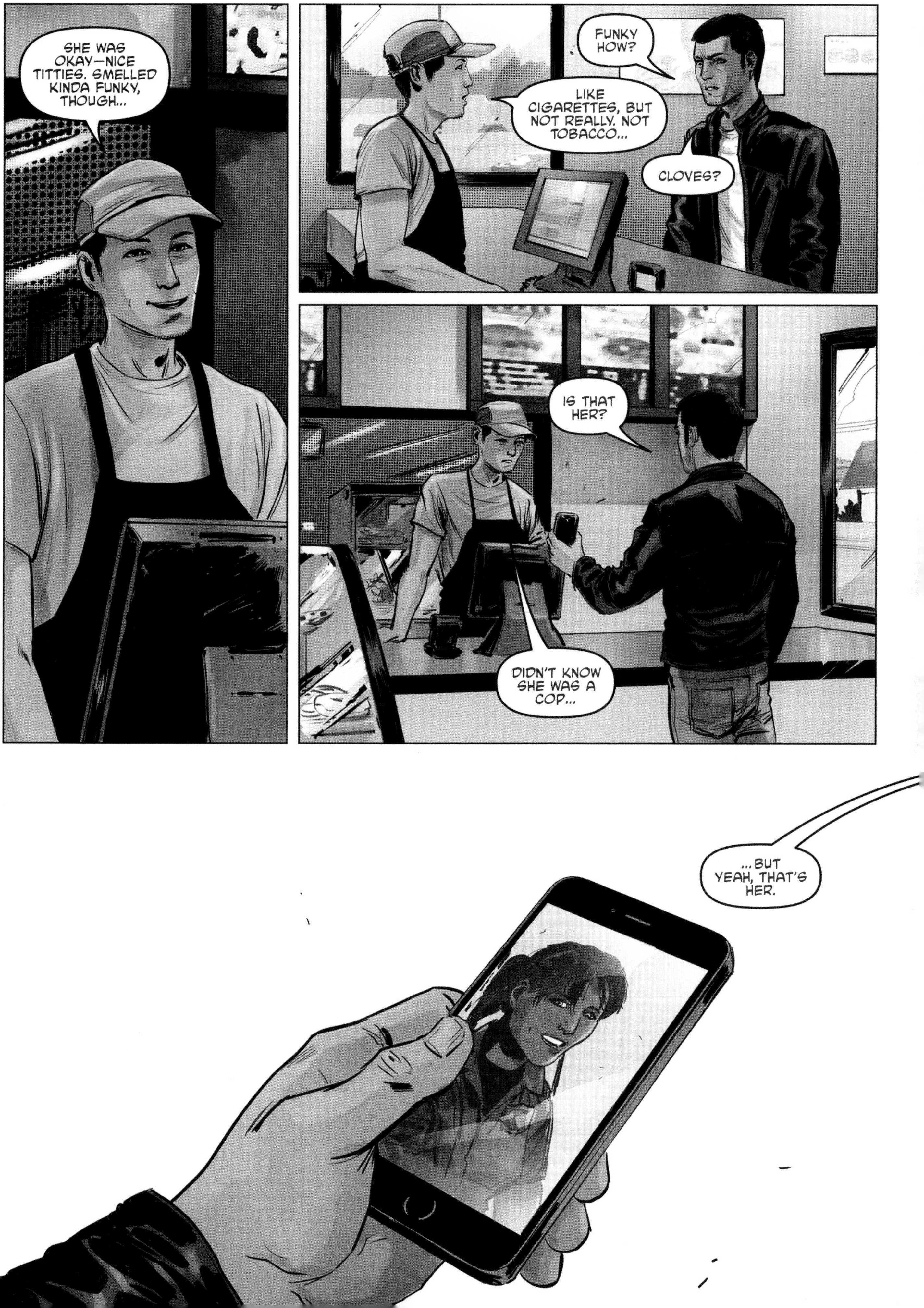
SHE WAS OKAY—NICE TITTIES. SMELLED KINDA FUNKY, THOUGH...
FUNKY HOW?
LIKE CIGARETTES, BUT NOT REALLY. NOT TOBACCO...
CLOVES?
IS THAT HER?
DIDN'T KNOW SHE WAS A COP...
...BUT YEAH, THAT'S HER.

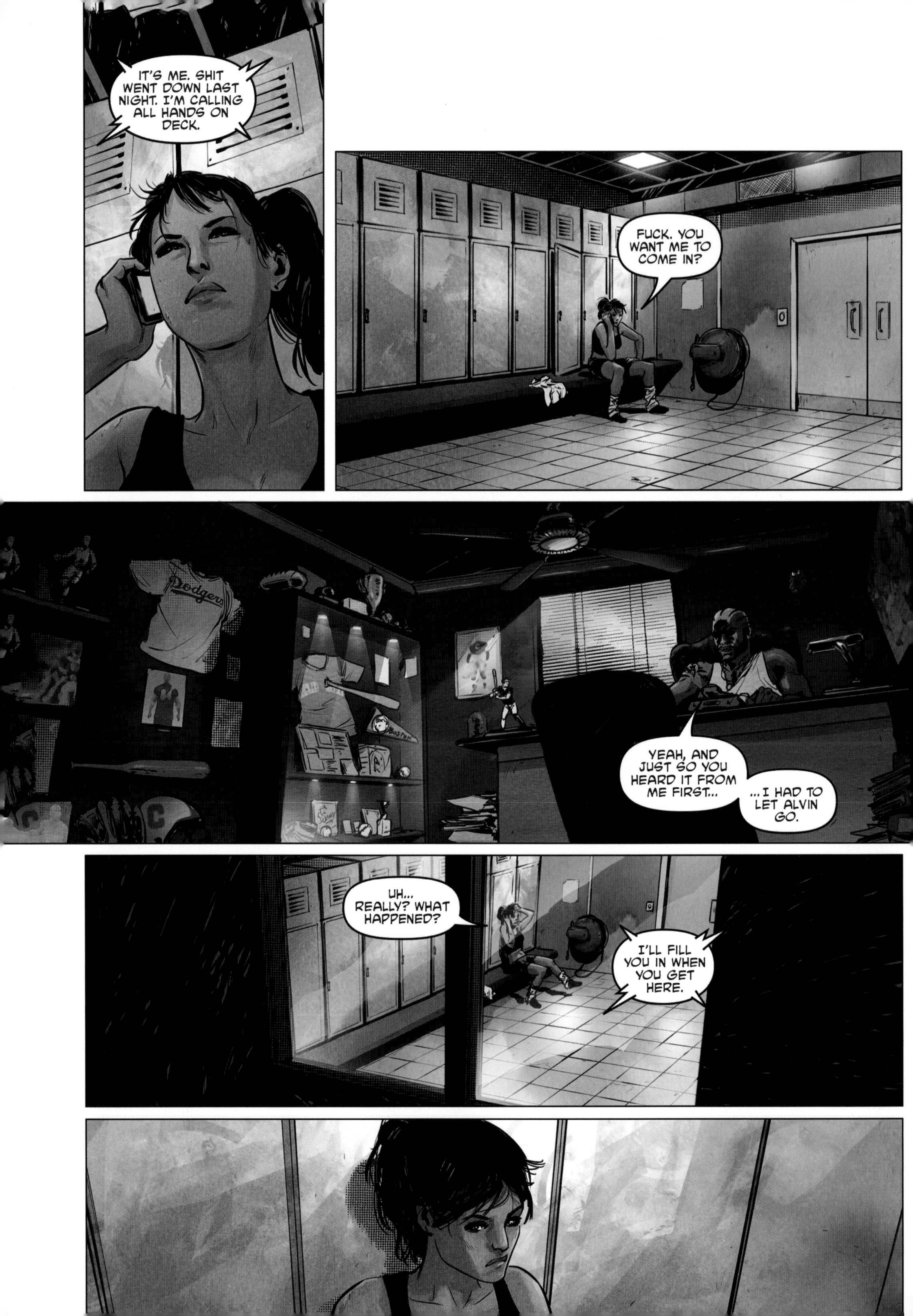
IT'S ME. SHIT WENT DOWN LAST NIGHT. I'M CALLING ALL HANDS ON DECK.
FUCK. YOU WANT ME TO COME IN?
Dodgers
Boston
YEAH, AND JUST SO YOU HEARD IT FROM ME FIRST...
...I HAD TO LET ALVIN GO.
UH... REALLY? WHAT HAPPENED?
I'LL FILL YOU IN WHEN YOU GET HERE.

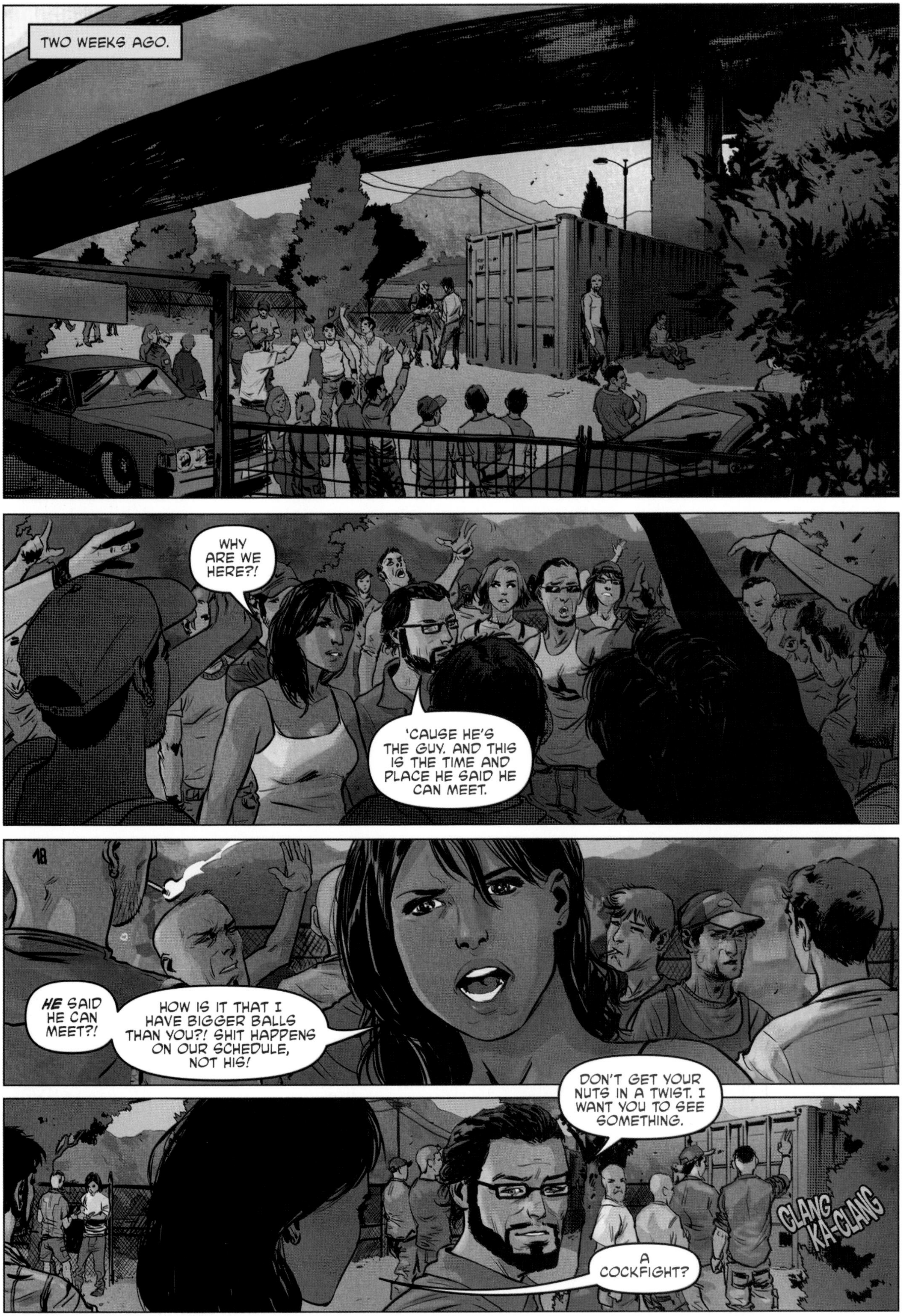
TWO WEEKS AGO.
WHY ARE WE HERE?!
'CAUSE HE'S THE GUY. AND THIS IS THE TIME AND PLACE HE SAID HE CAN MEET.
HE SAID HE CAN MEET?!
HOW IS IT THAT I HAVE BIGGER BALLS THAN YOU?! SHIT HAPPENS ON OUR SCHEDULE, NOT HIS!
DON'T GET YOUR NUTS IN A TWIST. I WANT YOU TO SEE SOMETHING.
CLANG KA-CLANG
A COCKFIGHT?

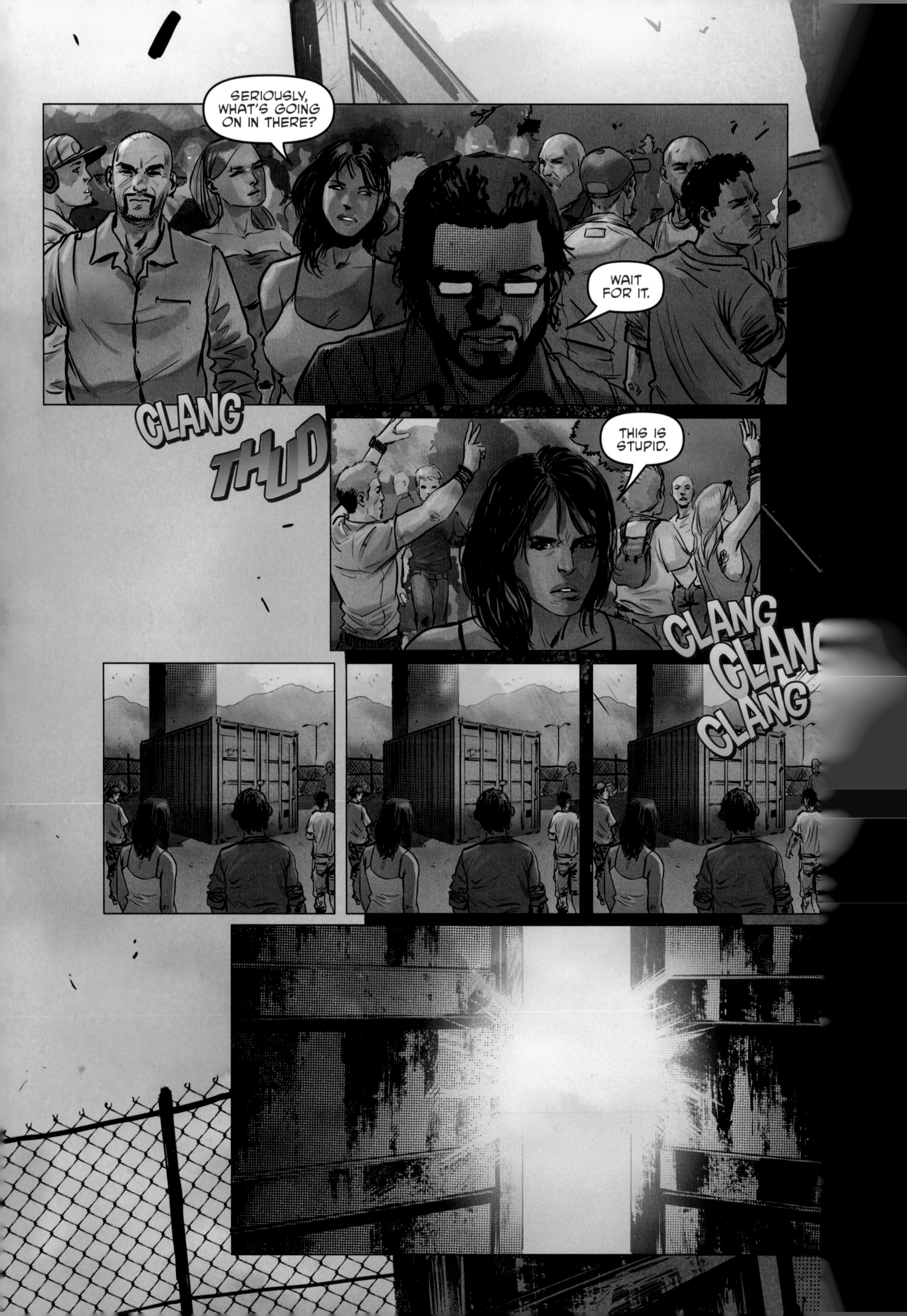
SERIOUSLY, WHAT'S GOING ON IN THERE?
WAIT FOR IT.
CLANG
THUD
THIS IS STUPID.
CLANG
CLANG
CLANG

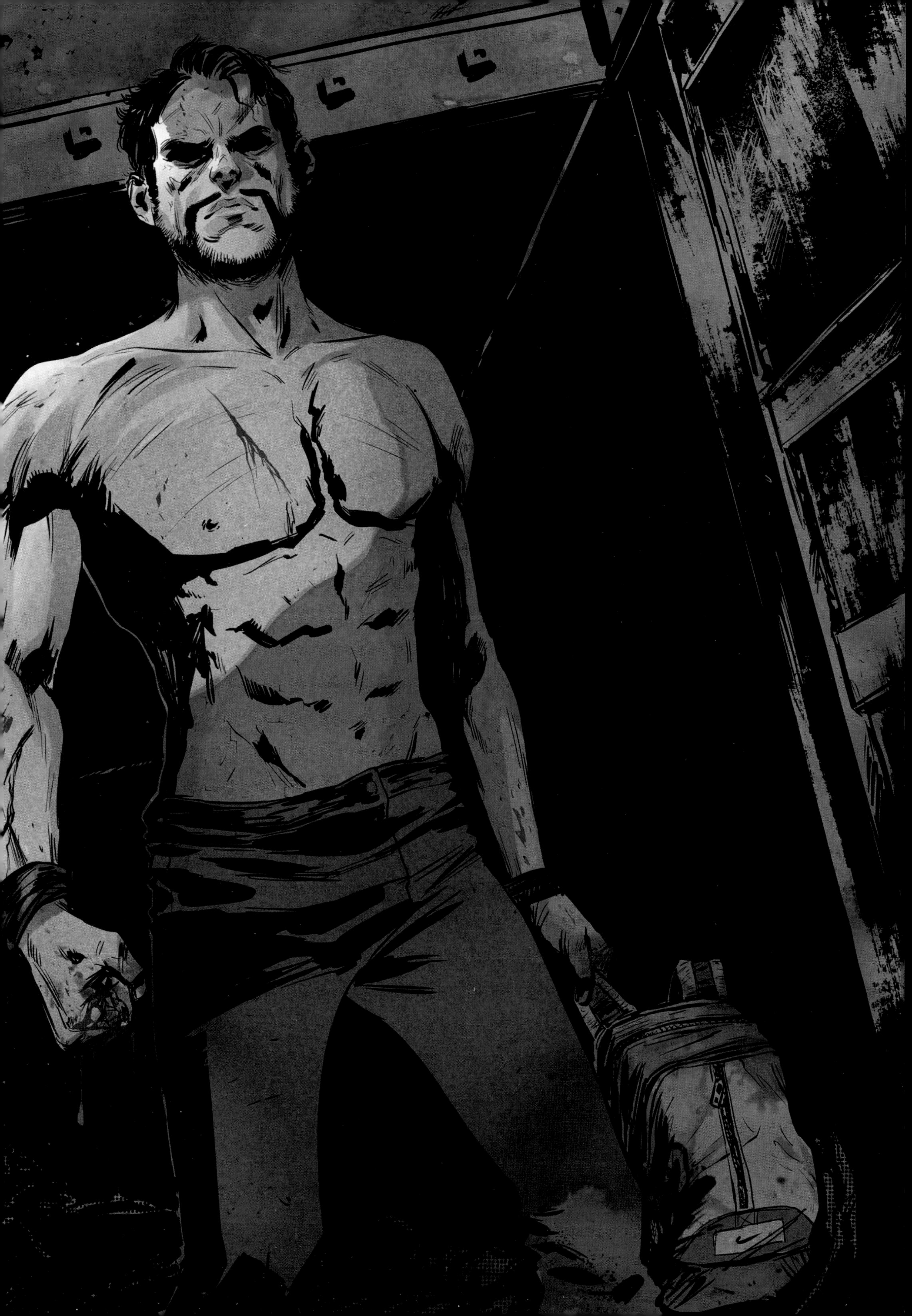

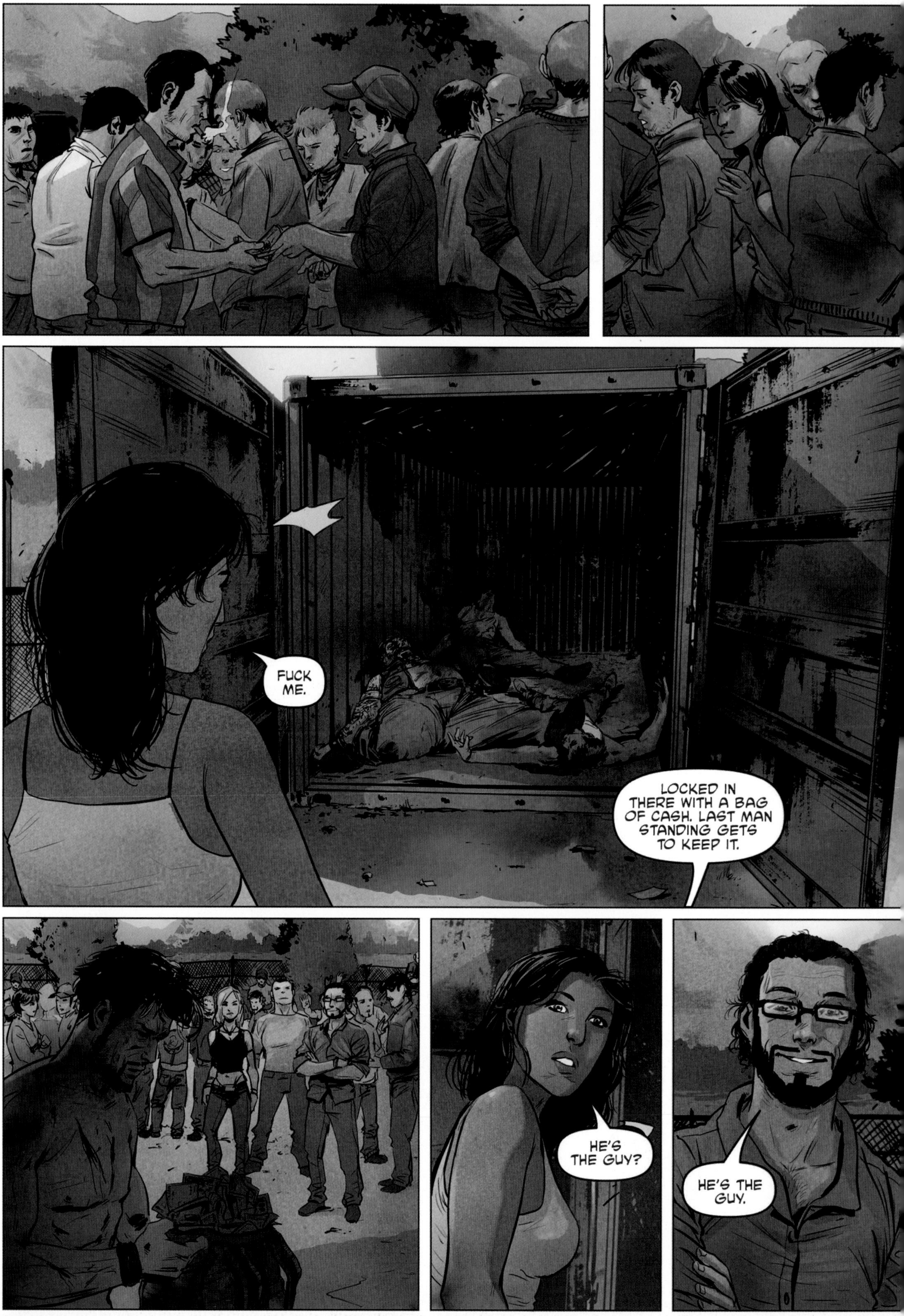
FUCK ME.
LOCKED IN THERE WITH A BAG OF CASH. LAST MAN STANDING GETS TO KEEP IT.
HE'S THE GUY?
HE'S THE GUY.

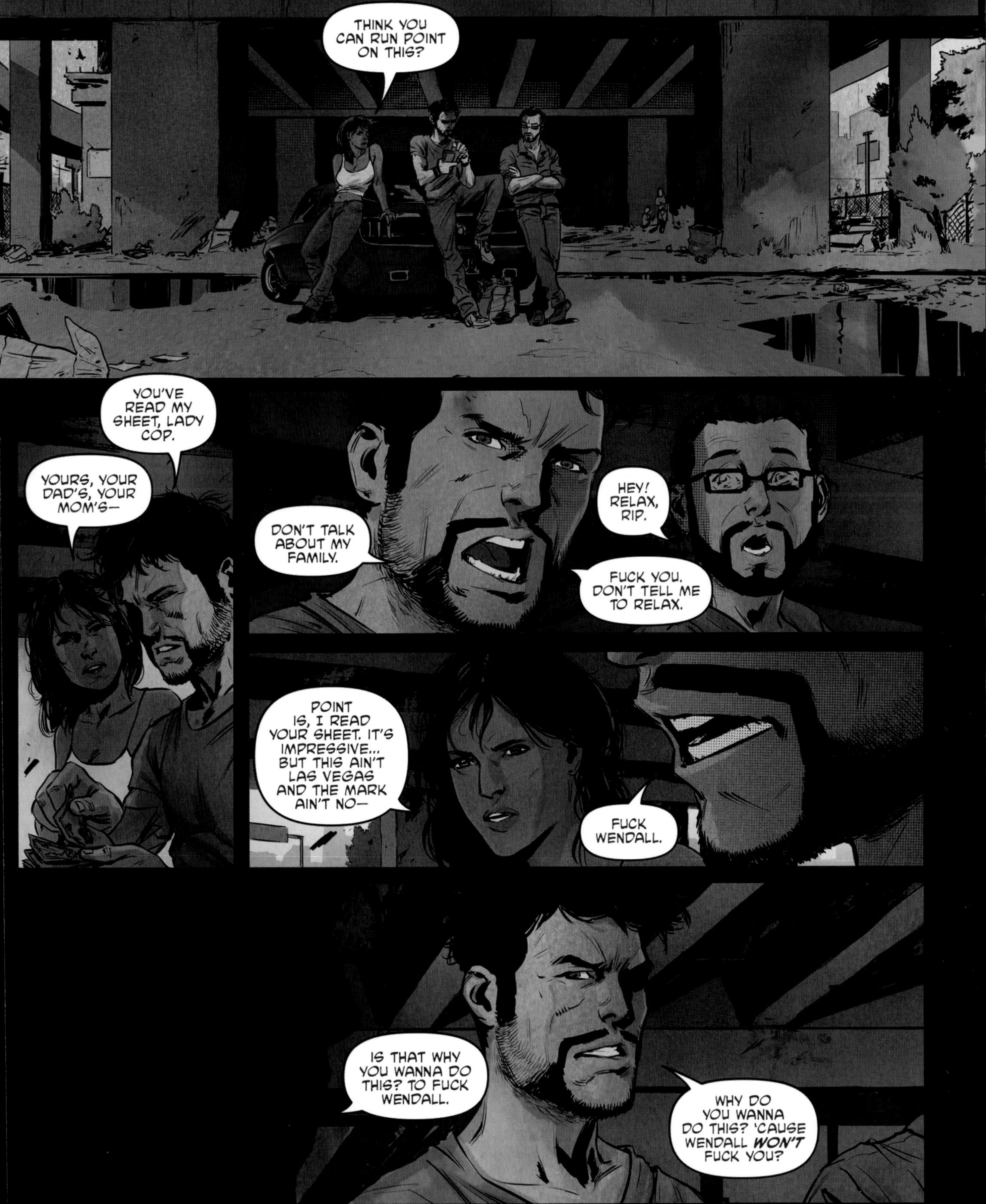
THINK YOU CAN RUN POINT ON THIS?
YOU'VE READ MY SHEET, LADY COP.
YOURS, YOUR DAD'S, YOUR MOM'S—
DON'T TALK ABOUT MY FAMILY.
HEY! RELAX, RIP.
FUCK YOU. DON'T TELL ME TO RELAX.
POINT IS, I READ YOUR SHEET. IT'S IMPRESSIVE... BUT THIS AIN'T LAS VEGAS AND THE MARK AIN'T NO—
FUCK WENDALL.
IS THAT WHY YOU WANNA DO THIS? TO FUCK WENDALL.
WHY DO YOU WANNA DO THIS? 'CAUSE WENDALL *WON'T* FUCK YOU?

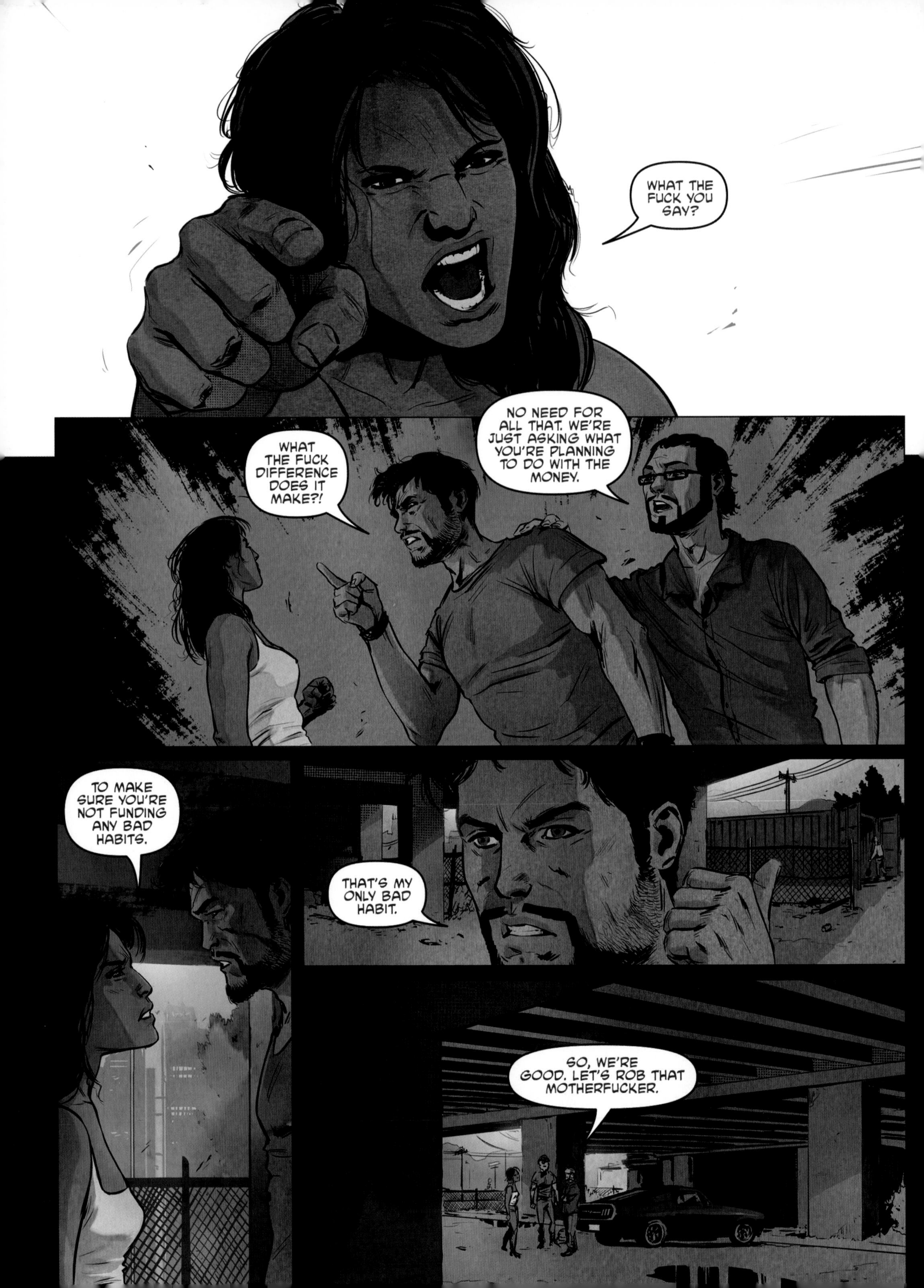
WHAT THE FUCK YOU SAY?
WHAT THE FUCK DIFFERENCE DOES IT MAKE?!
NO NEED FOR ALL THAT. WE'RE JUST ASKING WHAT YOU'RE PLANNING TO DO WITH THE MONEY.
TO MAKE SURE YOU'RE NOT FUNDING ANY BAD HABITS.
THAT'S MY ONLY BAD HABIT.
SO, WE'RE GOOD. LET'S ROB THAT MOTHERFUCKER.

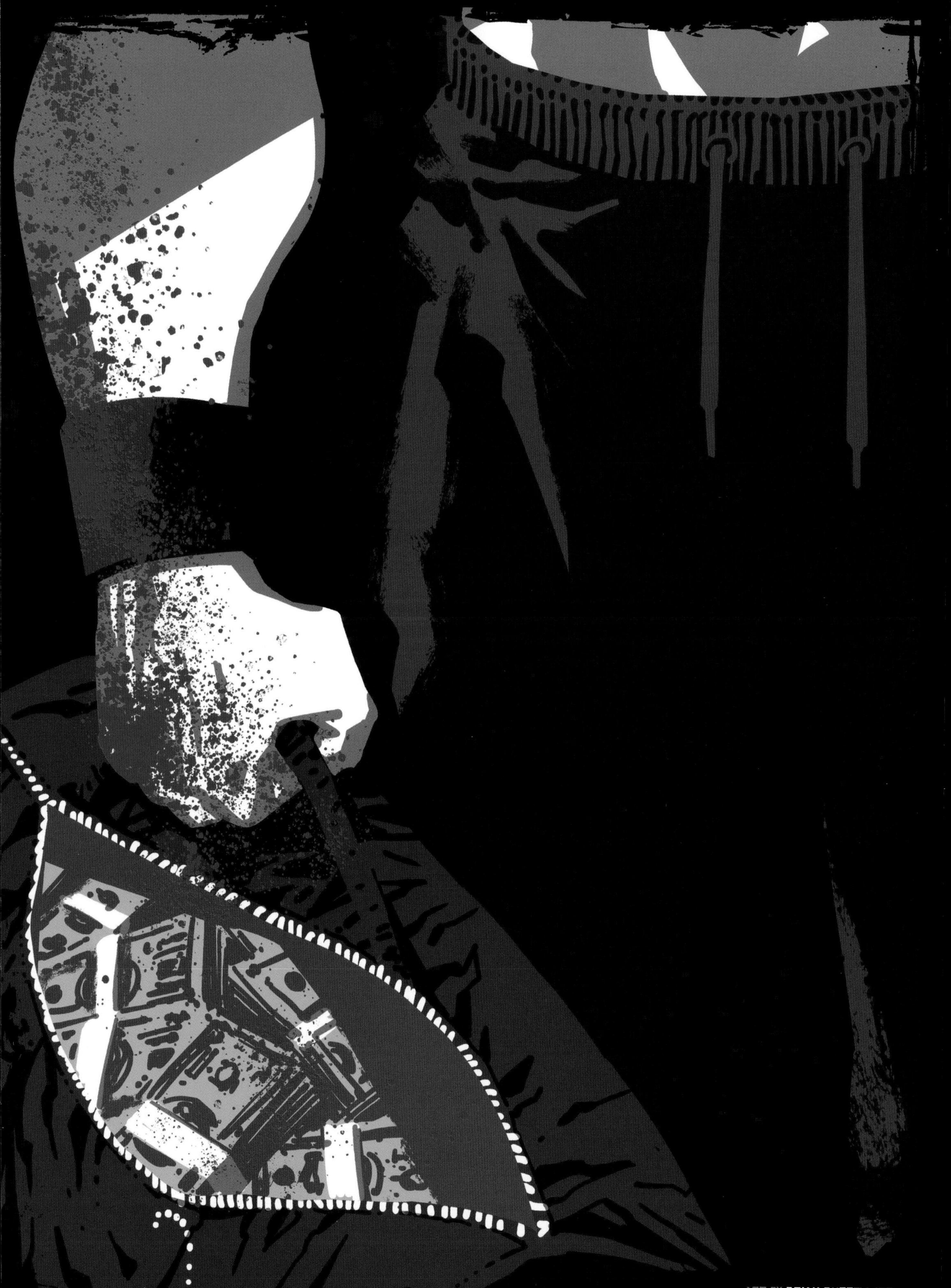

ART BY BRIAN BUCCELLATO

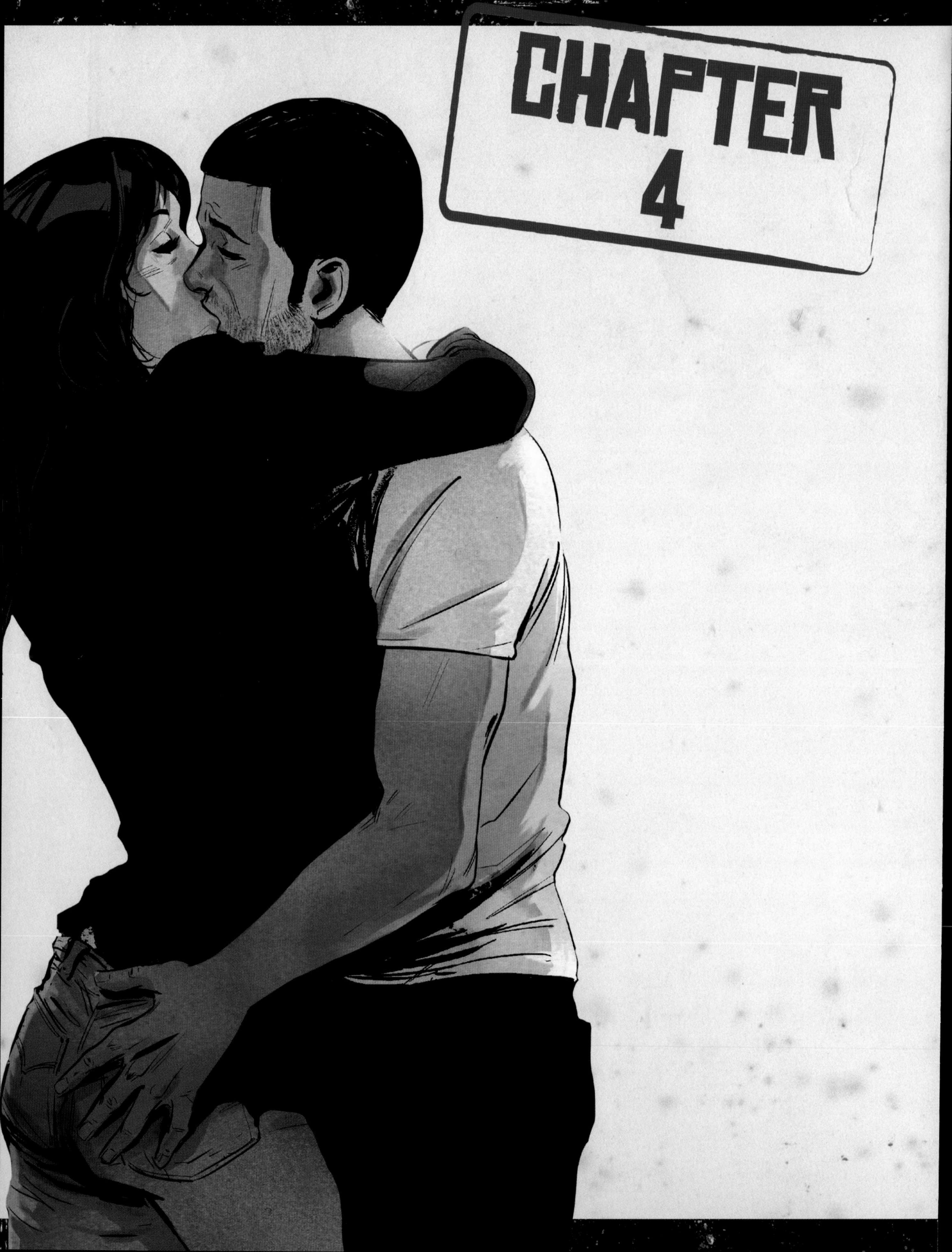
CHAPTER
4

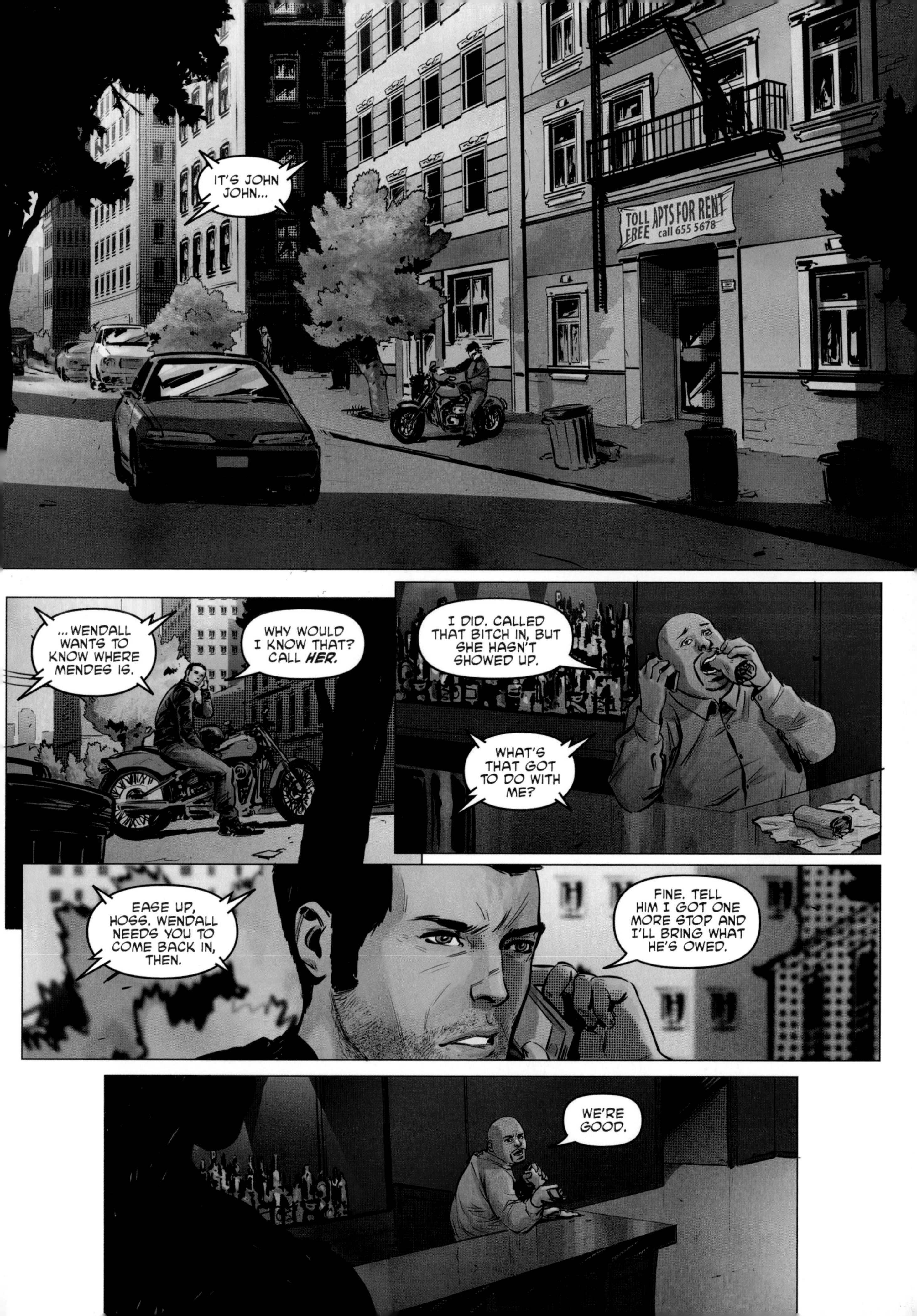
IT'S JOHN JOHN...
TOLL FREE APTS FOR RENT call 655 5678
...WENDALL WANTS TO KNOW WHERE MENDES IS.
WHY WOULD I KNOW THAT? CALL HER.
I DID. CALLED THAT BITCH IN, BUT SHE HASN'T SHOWED UP.
WHAT'S THAT GOT TO DO WITH ME?
EASE UP, HOSS. WENDALL NEEDS YOU TO COME BACK IN, THEN.
FINE. TELL HIM I GOT ONE MORE STOP AND I'LL BRING WHAT HE'S OWED.
WE'RE GOOD.

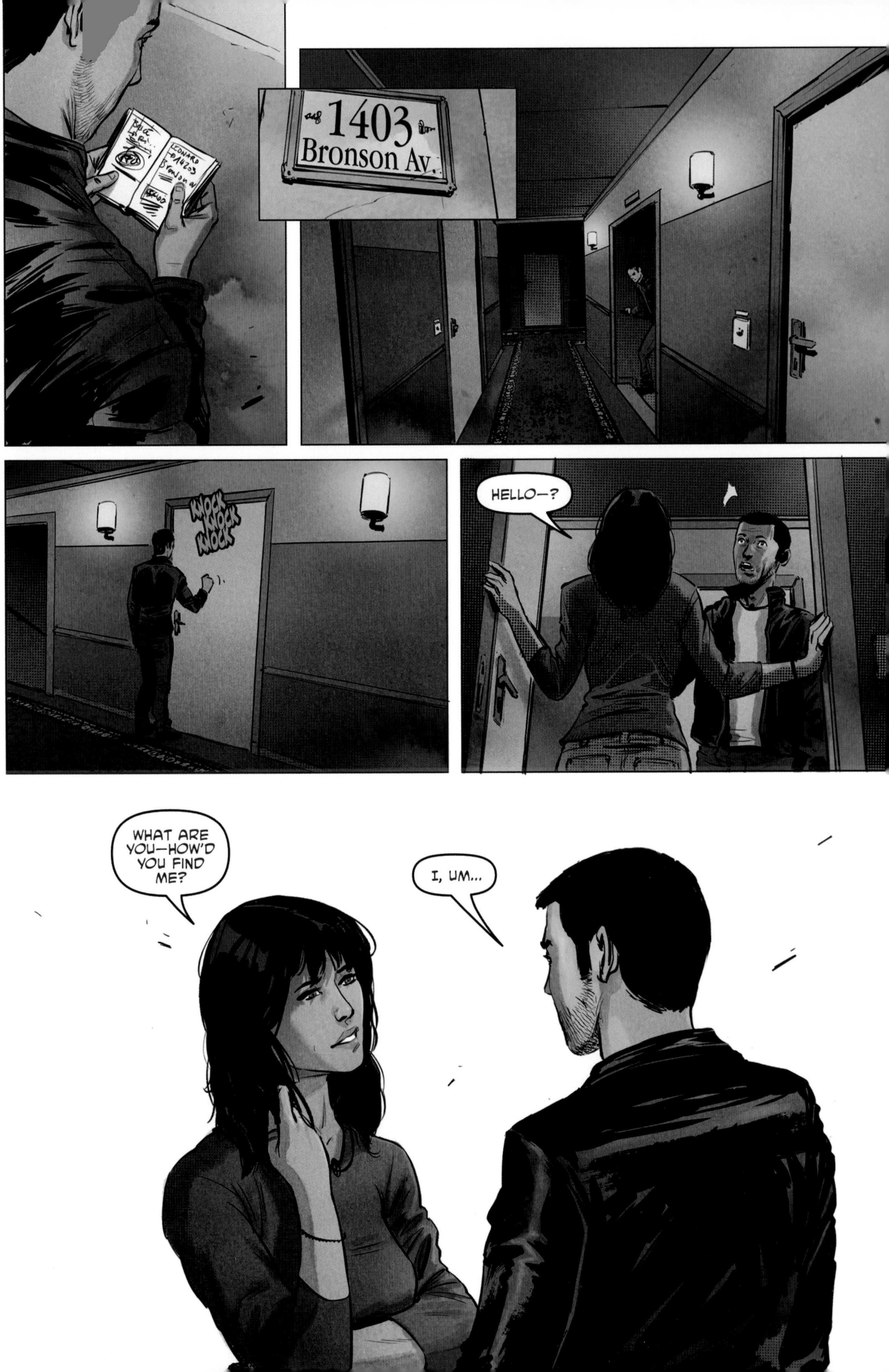
1403
Bronson Av.
KNOCK KNOCK KNOCK
HELLO—?
WHAT ARE YOU—HOW'D YOU FIND ME?
I, UM...

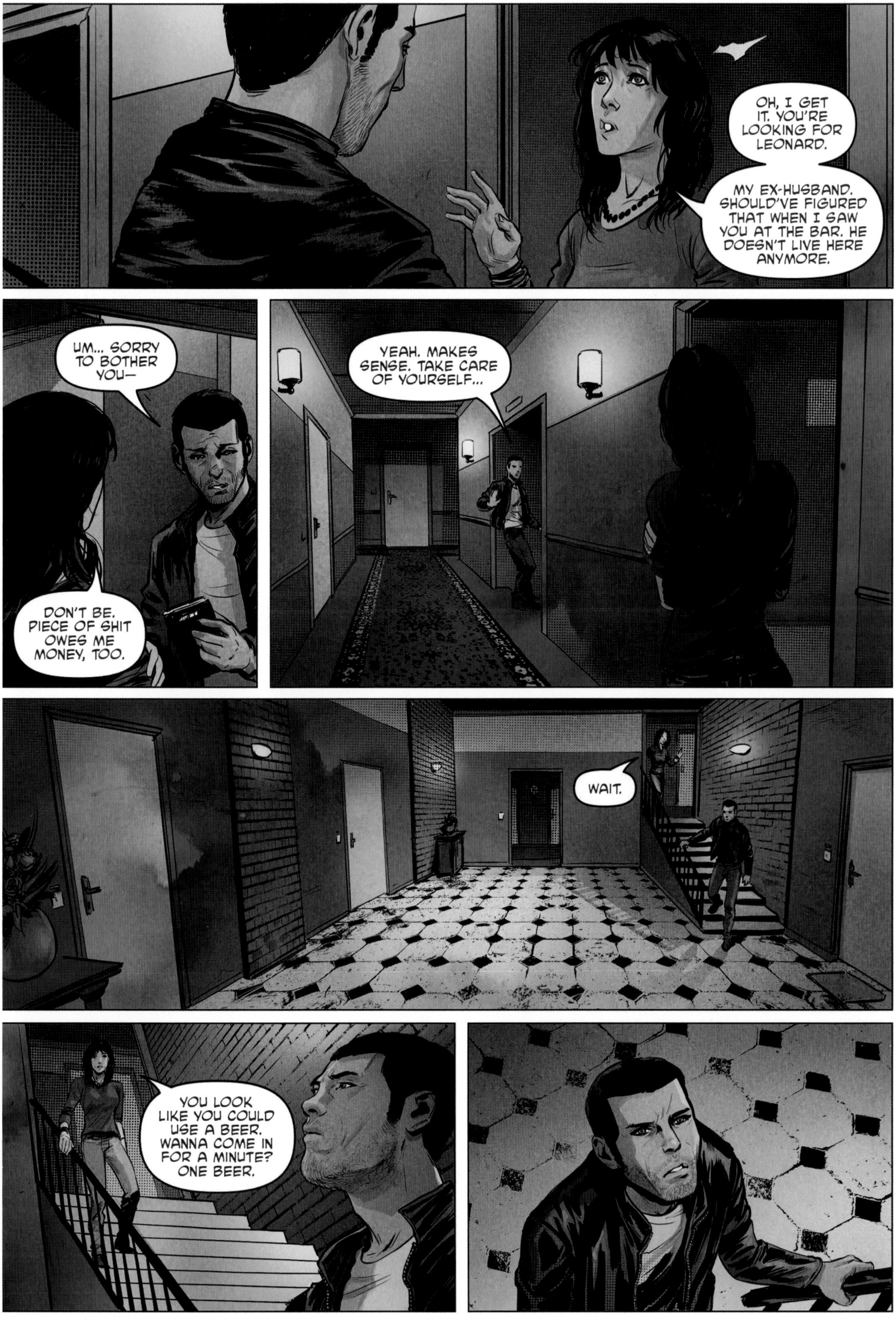
OH, I GET IT. YOU'RE LOOKING FOR LEONARD.
MY EX-HUSBAND. SHOULD'VE FIGURED THAT WHEN I SAW YOU AT THE BAR. HE DOESN'T LIVE HERE ANYMORE.
UM... SORRY TO BOTHER YOU—
DON'T BE. PIECE OF SHIT OWES ME MONEY, TOO.
YEAH. MAKES SENSE. TAKE CARE OF YOURSELF...
WAIT.
YOU LOOK LIKE YOU COULD USE A BEER. WANNA COME IN FOR A MINUTE? ONE BEER.

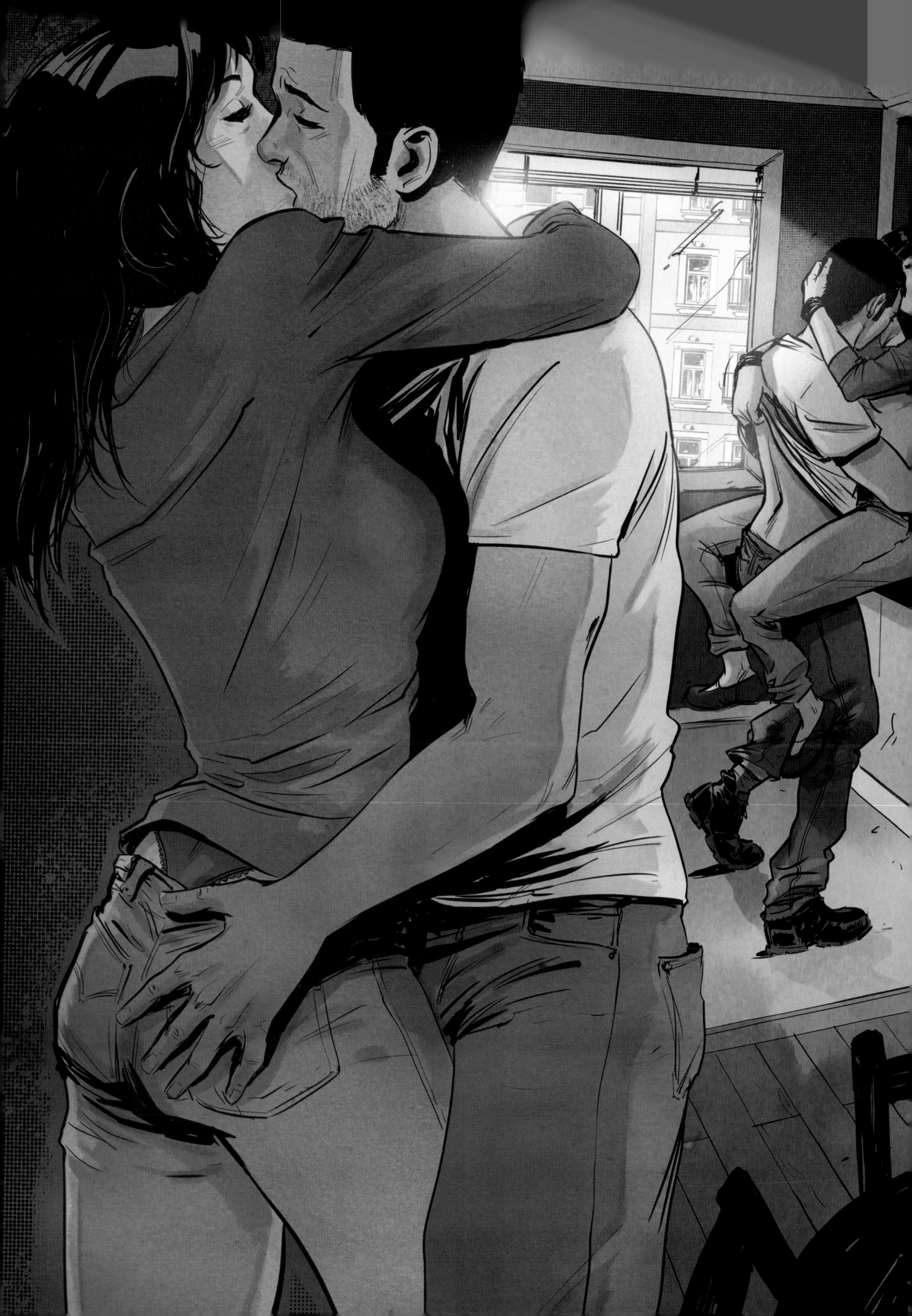

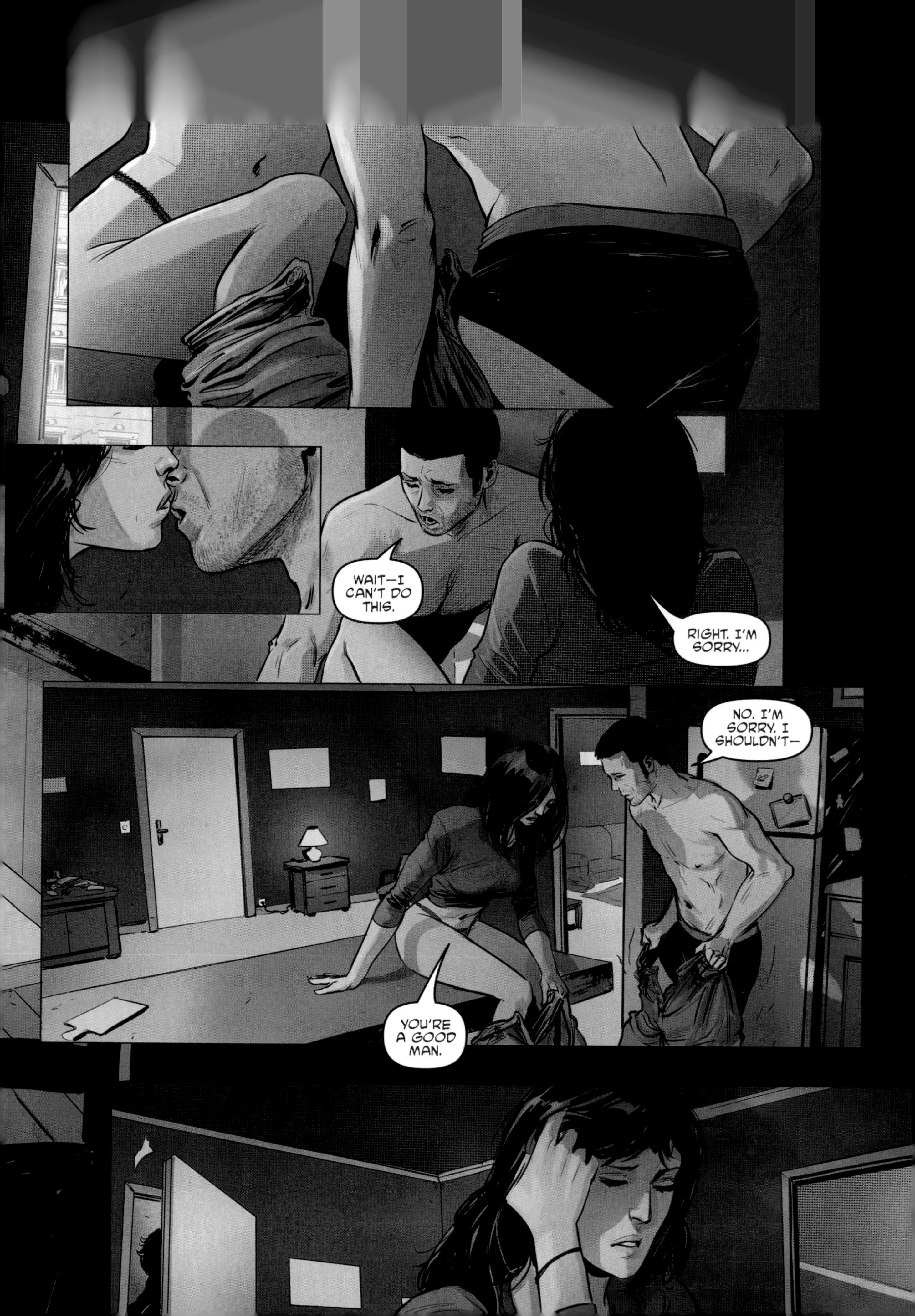
WAIT—I CAN'T DO THIS.
RIGHT. I'M SORRY...
NO. I'M SORRY. I SHOULDN'T—
YOU'RE A GOOD MAN.

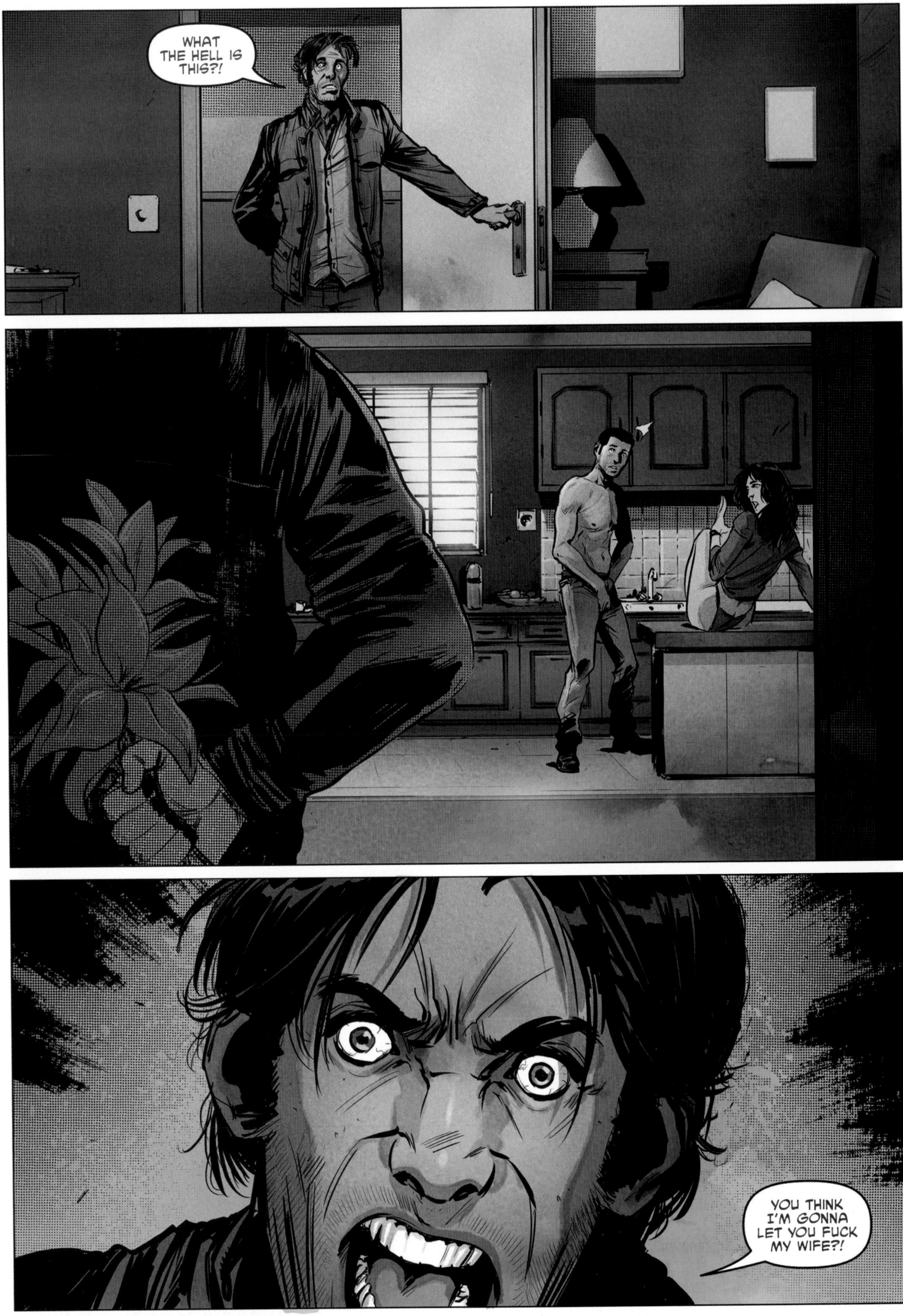
WHAT THE HELL IS THIS?!
YOU THINK I'M GONNA LET YOU FUCK MY WIFE?!

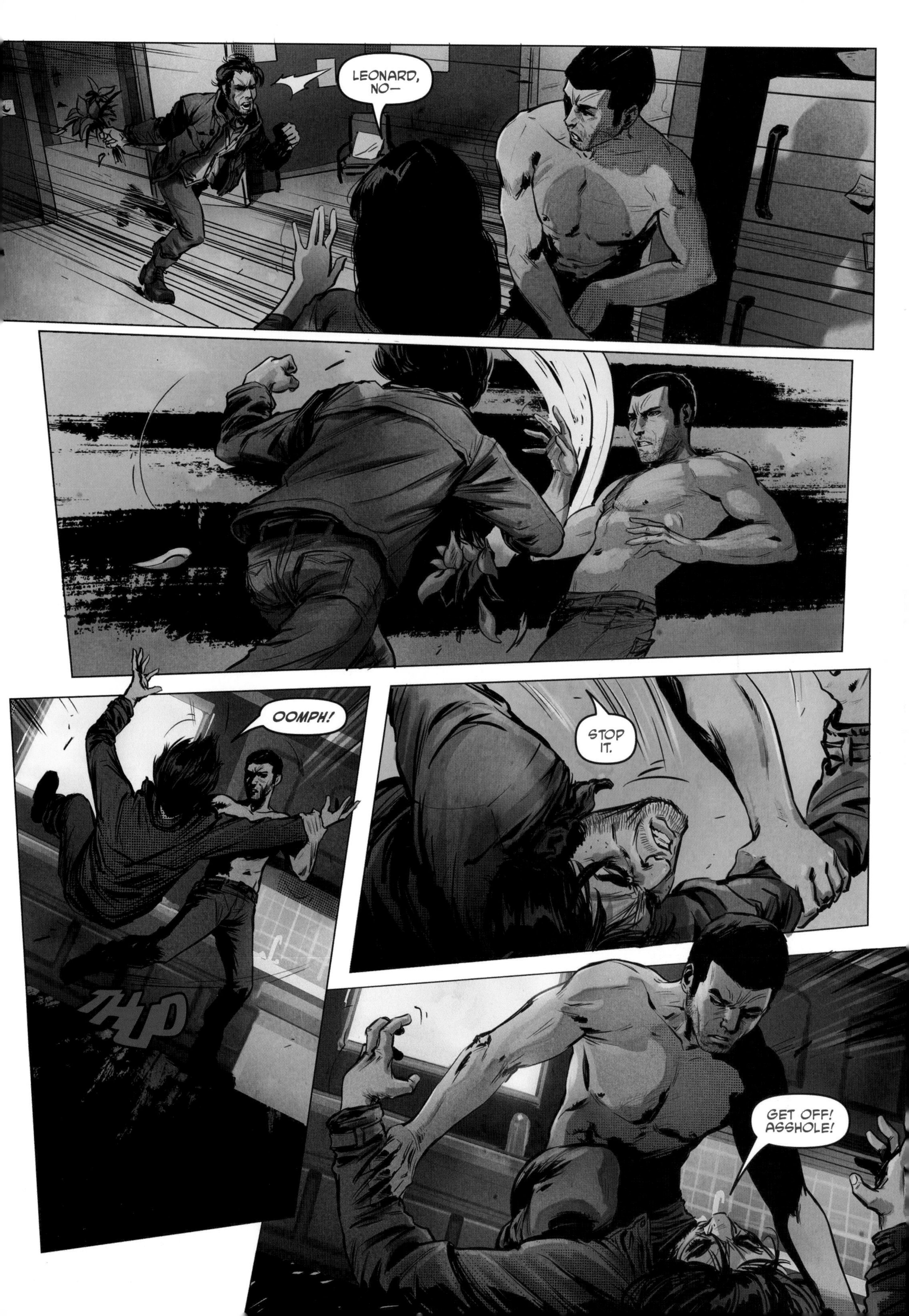
LEONARD, NO—
OOMPH!
THUD
STOP IT.
GET OFF! ASSHOLE!

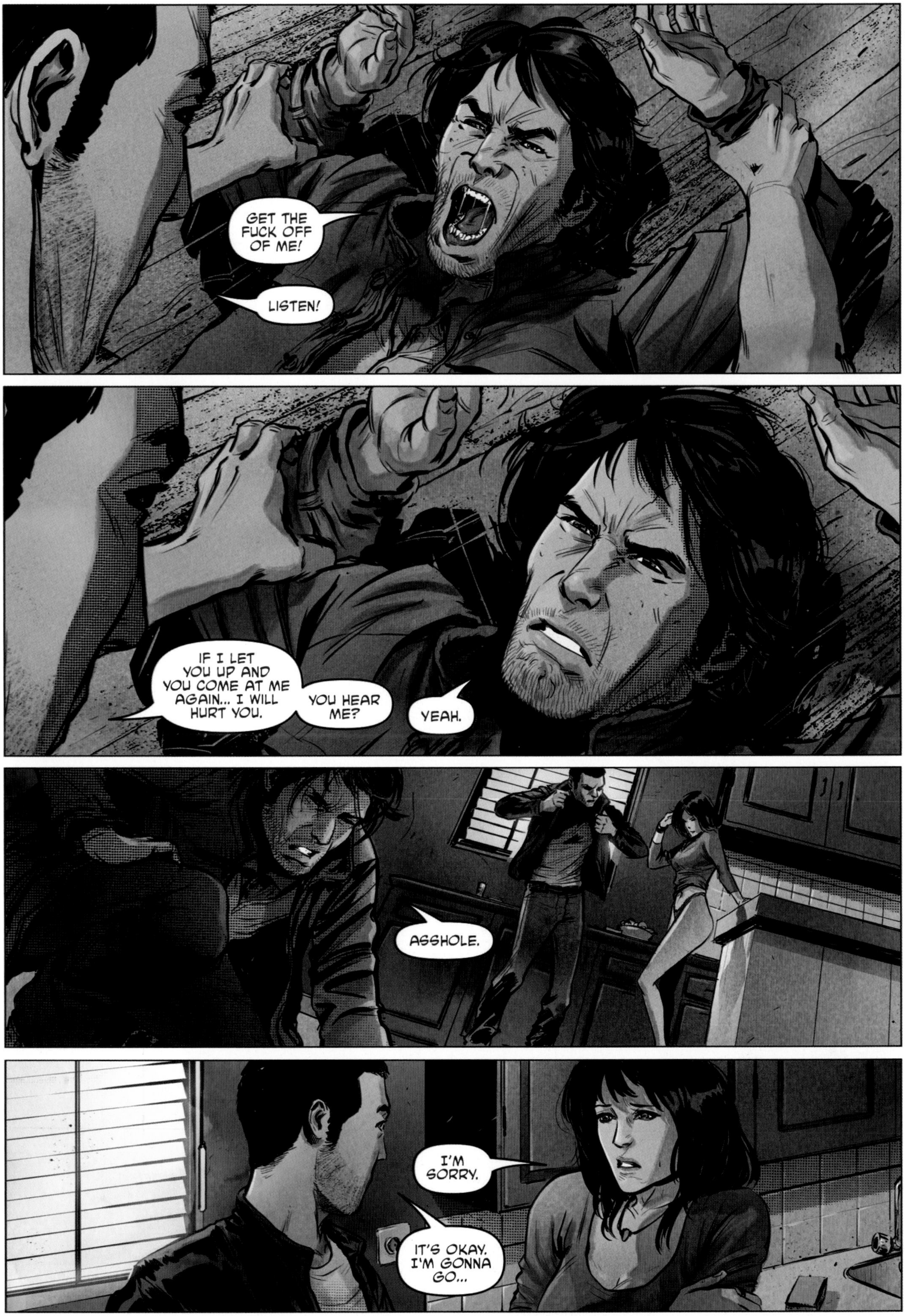
GET THE FUCK OFF OF ME!
LISTEN!
IF I LET YOU UP AND YOU COME AT ME AGAIN... I WILL HURT YOU.
YOU HEAR ME?
YEAH.
ASSHOLE.
I'M SORRY.
IT'S OKAY. I'M GONNA GO...

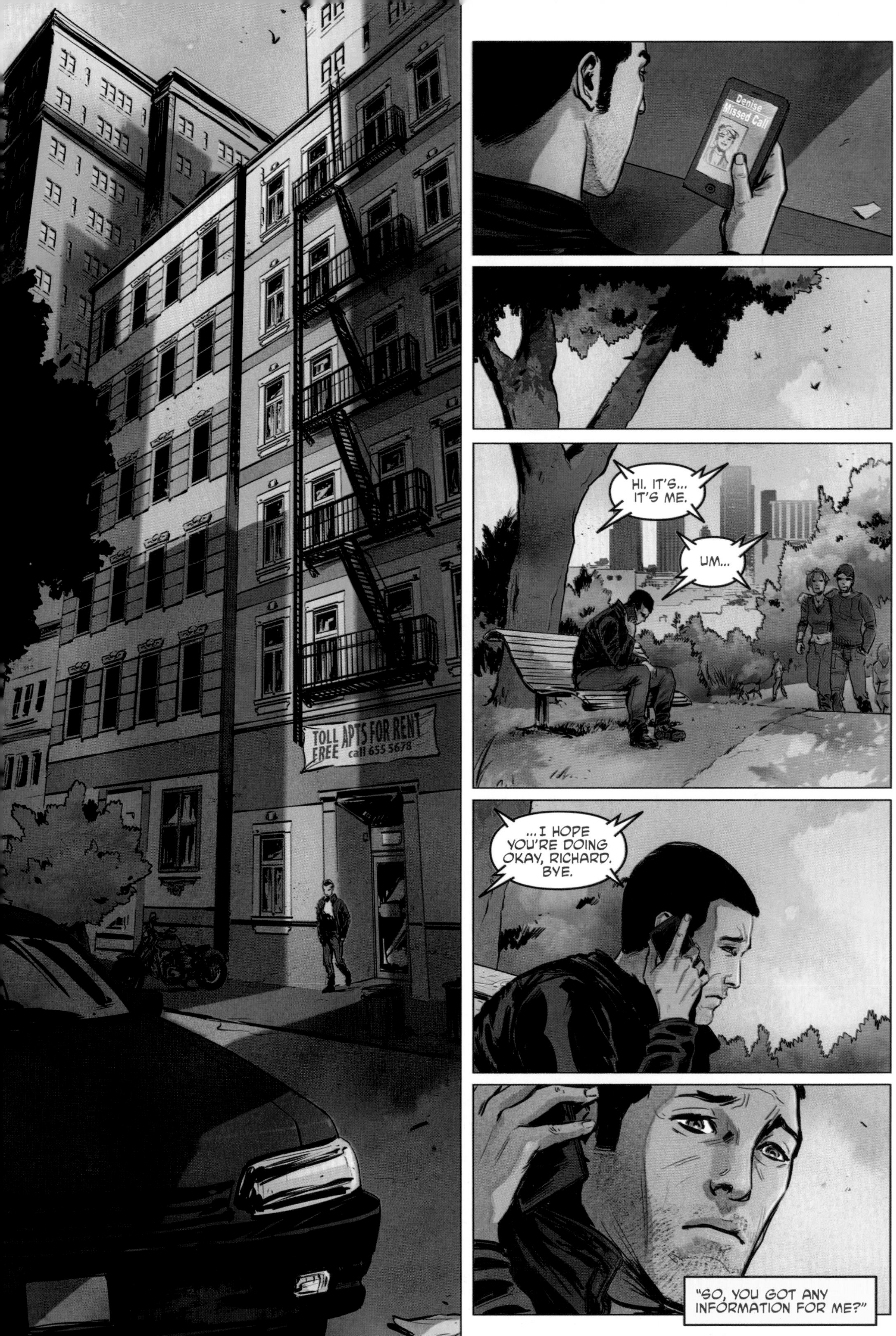
TOLL FREE APTS FOR RENT call 655 5678
Denise Missed Call
HI. IT'S... IT'S ME.
UM...
...I HOPE YOU'RE DOING OKAY, RICHARD. BYE.
"SO, YOU GOT ANY INFORMATION FOR ME?"

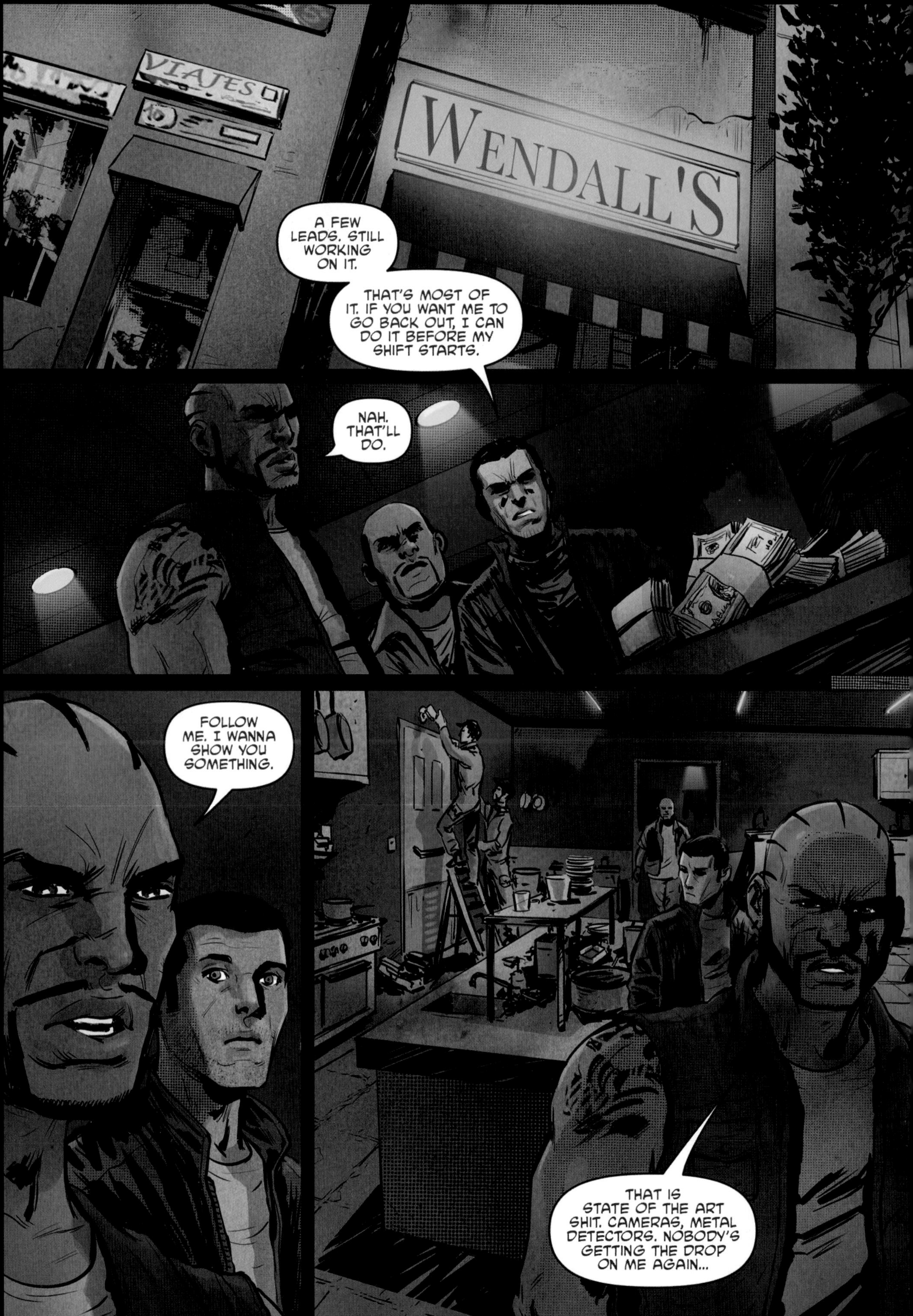
VIAJES
WENDALL'S
A FEW LEADS. STILL WORKING ON IT.
THAT'S MOST OF IT. IF YOU WANT ME TO GO BACK OUT, I CAN DO IT BEFORE MY SHIFT STARTS.
NAH. THAT'LL DO.
FOLLOW ME. I WANNA SHOW YOU SOMETHING.
THAT IS STATE OF THE ART SHIT. CAMERAS, METAL DETECTORS. NOBODY'S GETTING THE DROP ON ME AGAIN...

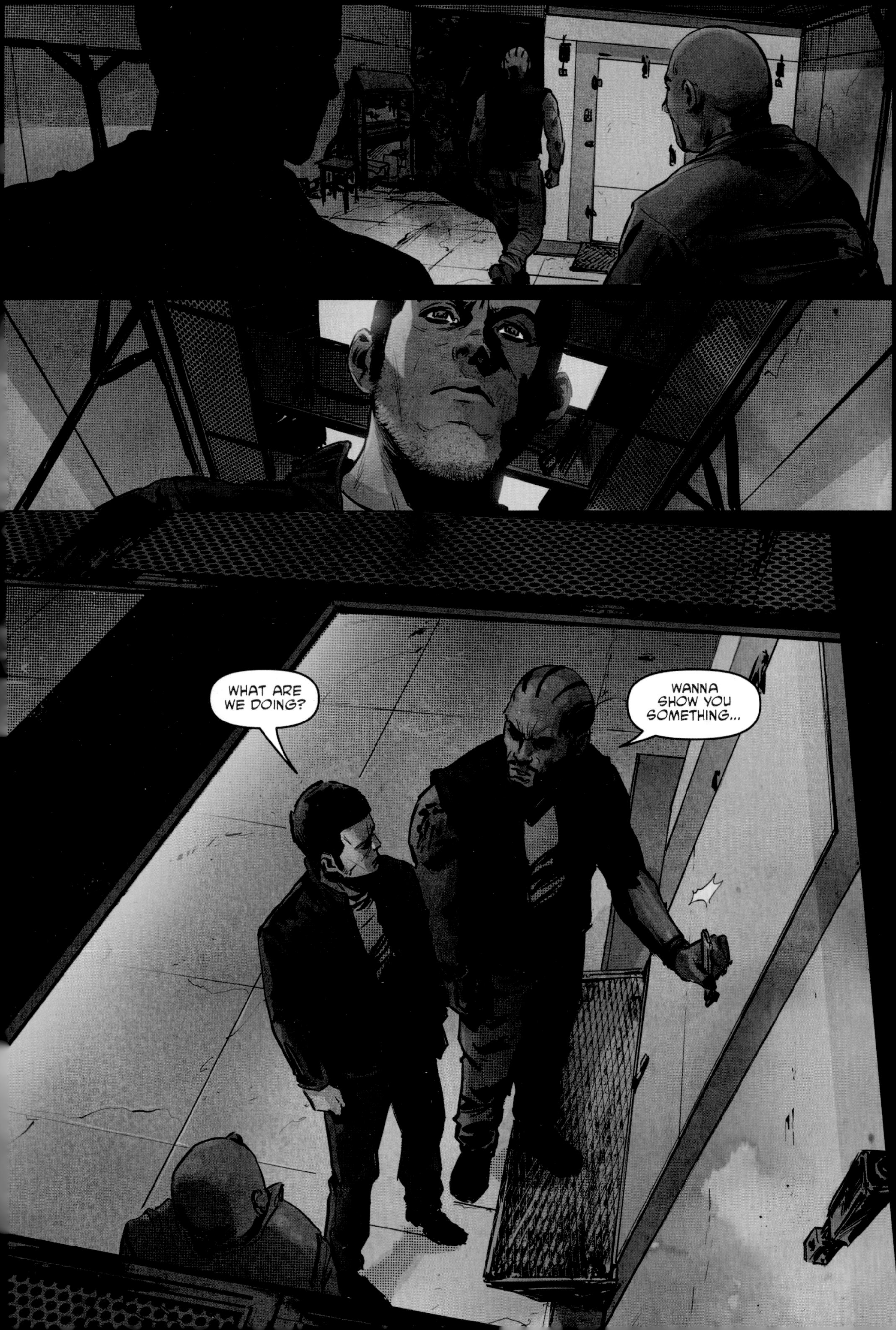
WHAT ARE WE DOING?
WANNA SHOW YOU SOMETHING...

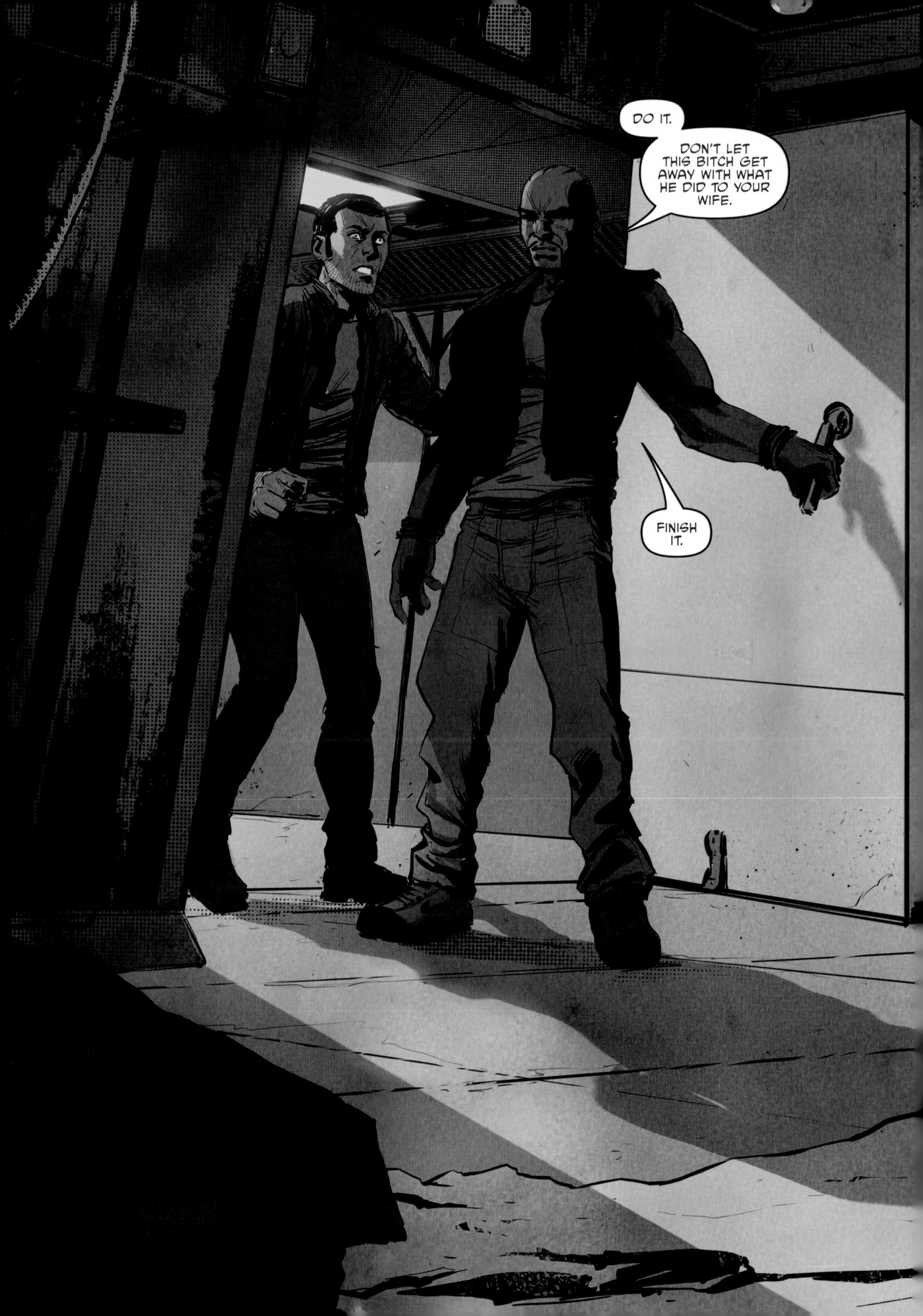
DO IT.
DON'T LET THIS BITCH GET AWAY WITH WHAT HE DID TO YOUR WIFE.
FINISH IT.

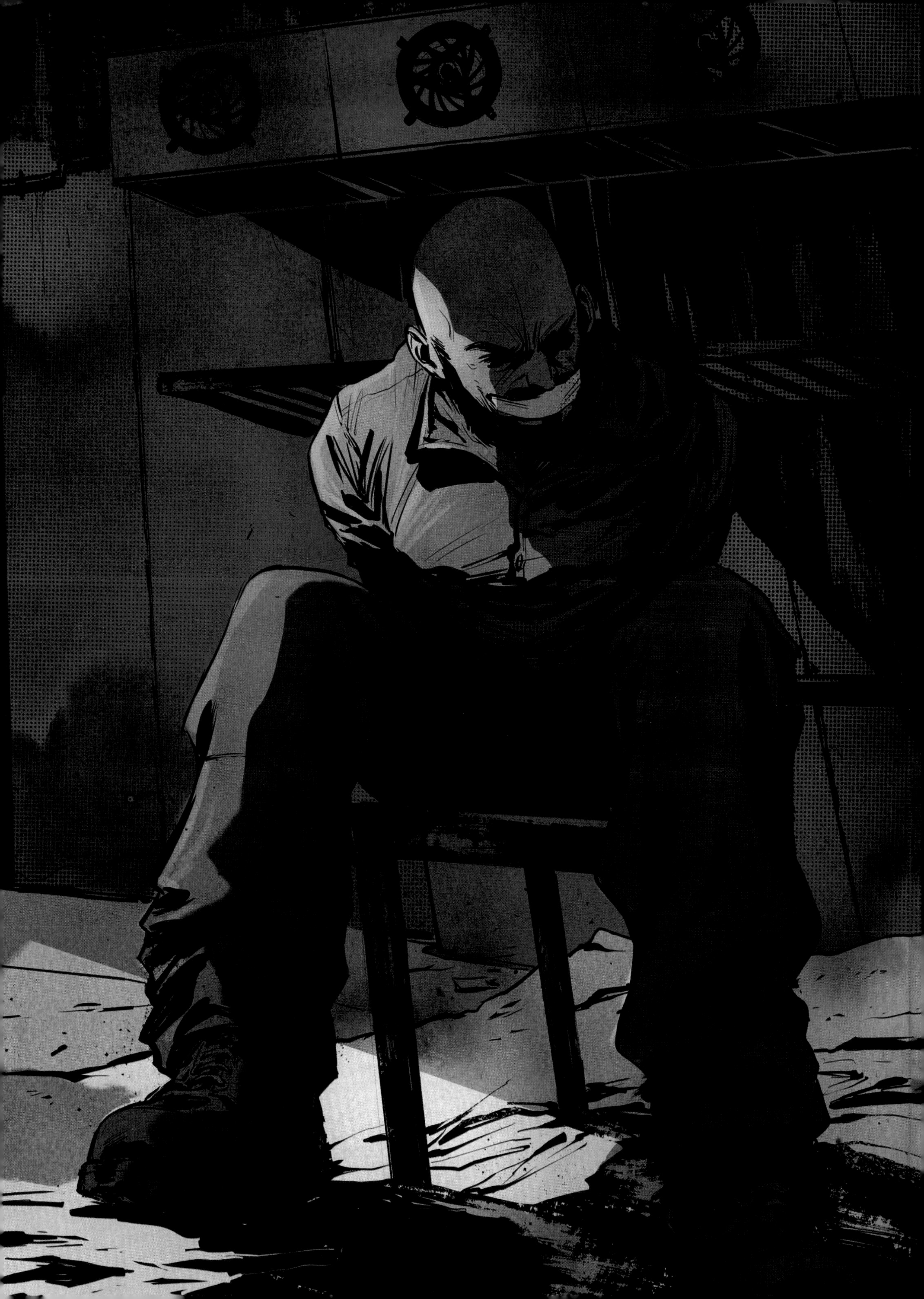

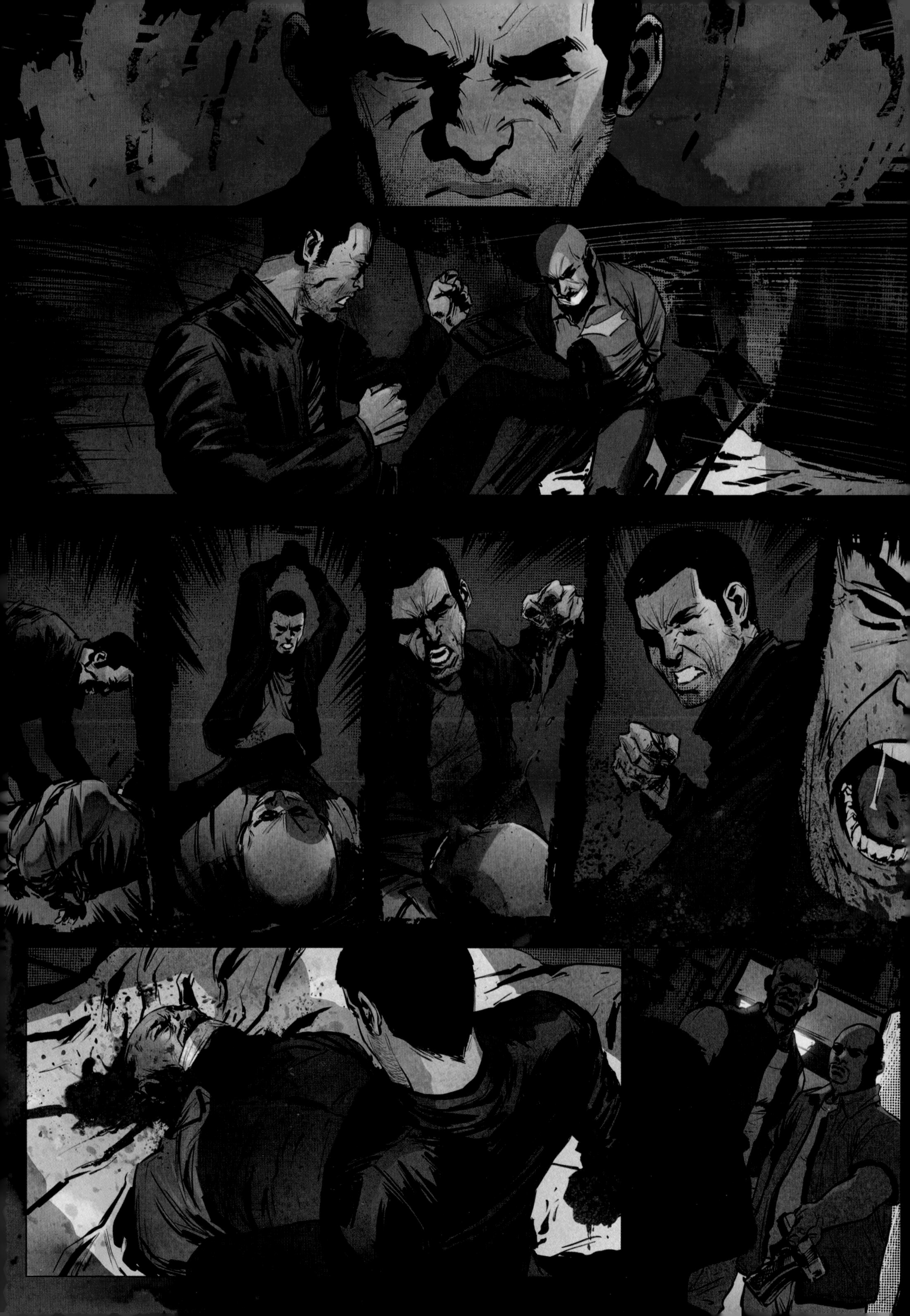

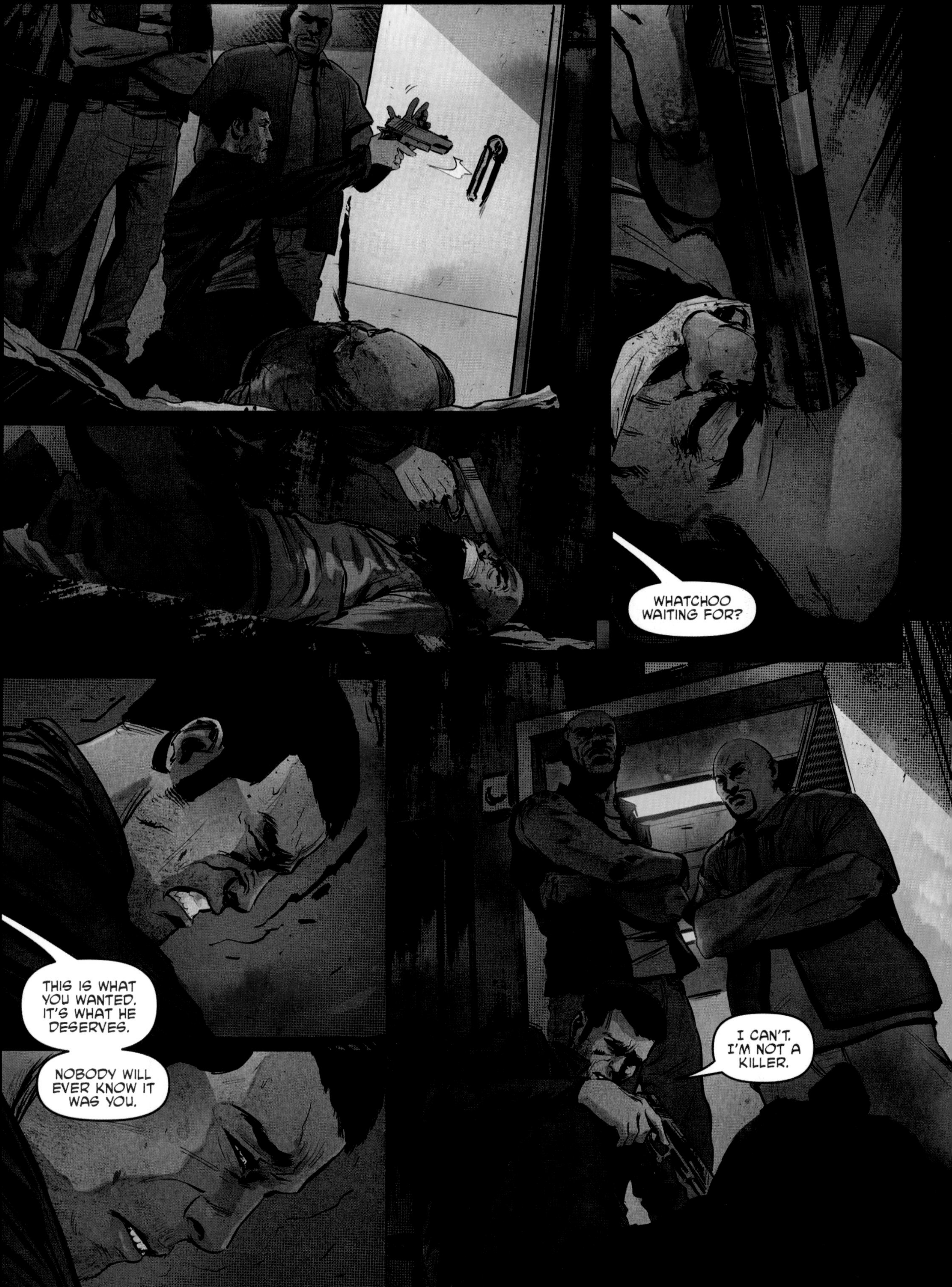
WHATCHOO WAITING FOR?
THIS IS WHAT YOU WANTED. IT'S WHAT HE DESERVES.
NOBODY WILL EVER KNOW IT WAS YOU.
I CAN'T. I'M NOT A KILLER.

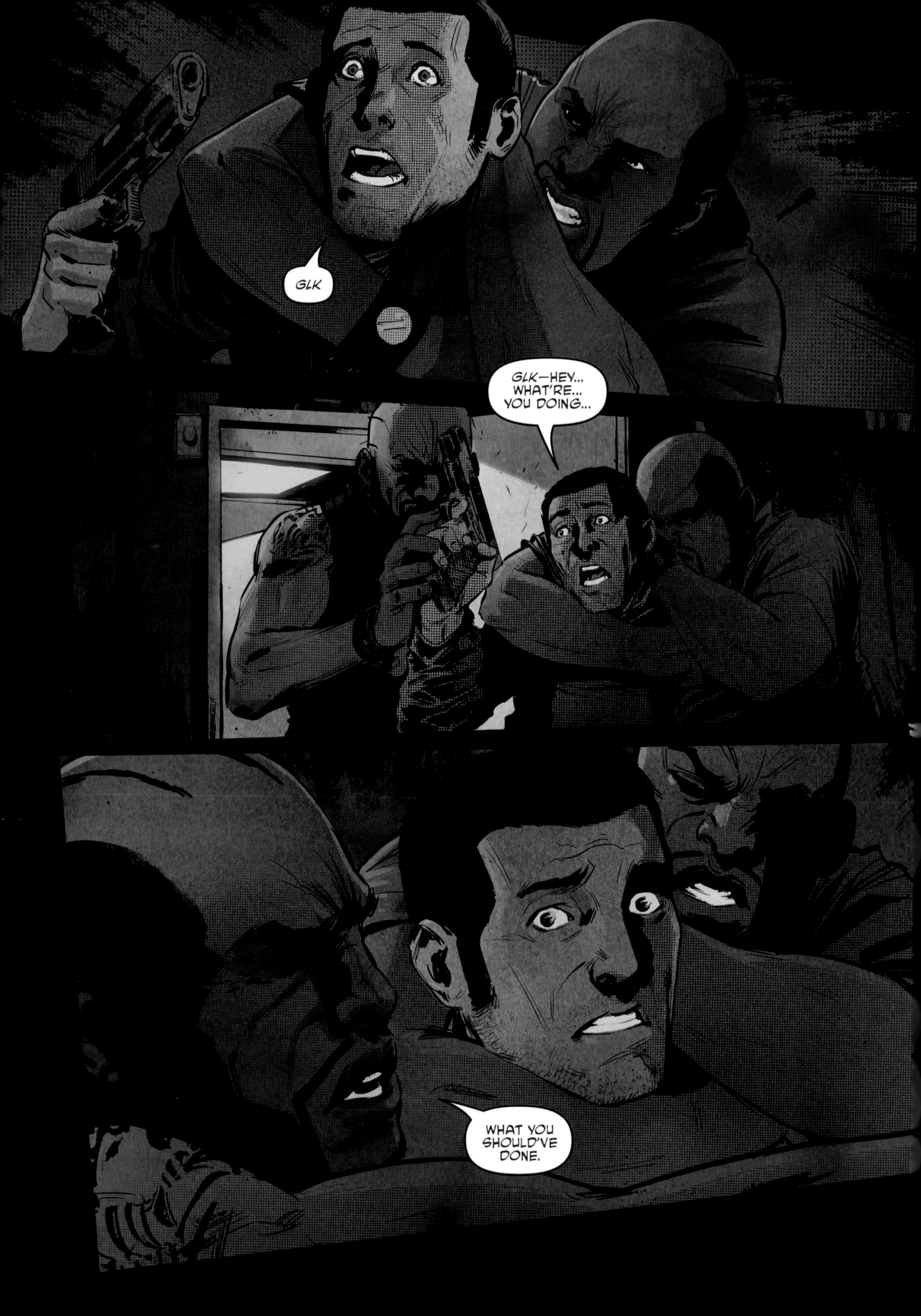
GLK
GLK—HEY... WHAT'RE... YOU DOING...
WHAT YOU SHOULD'VE DONE.

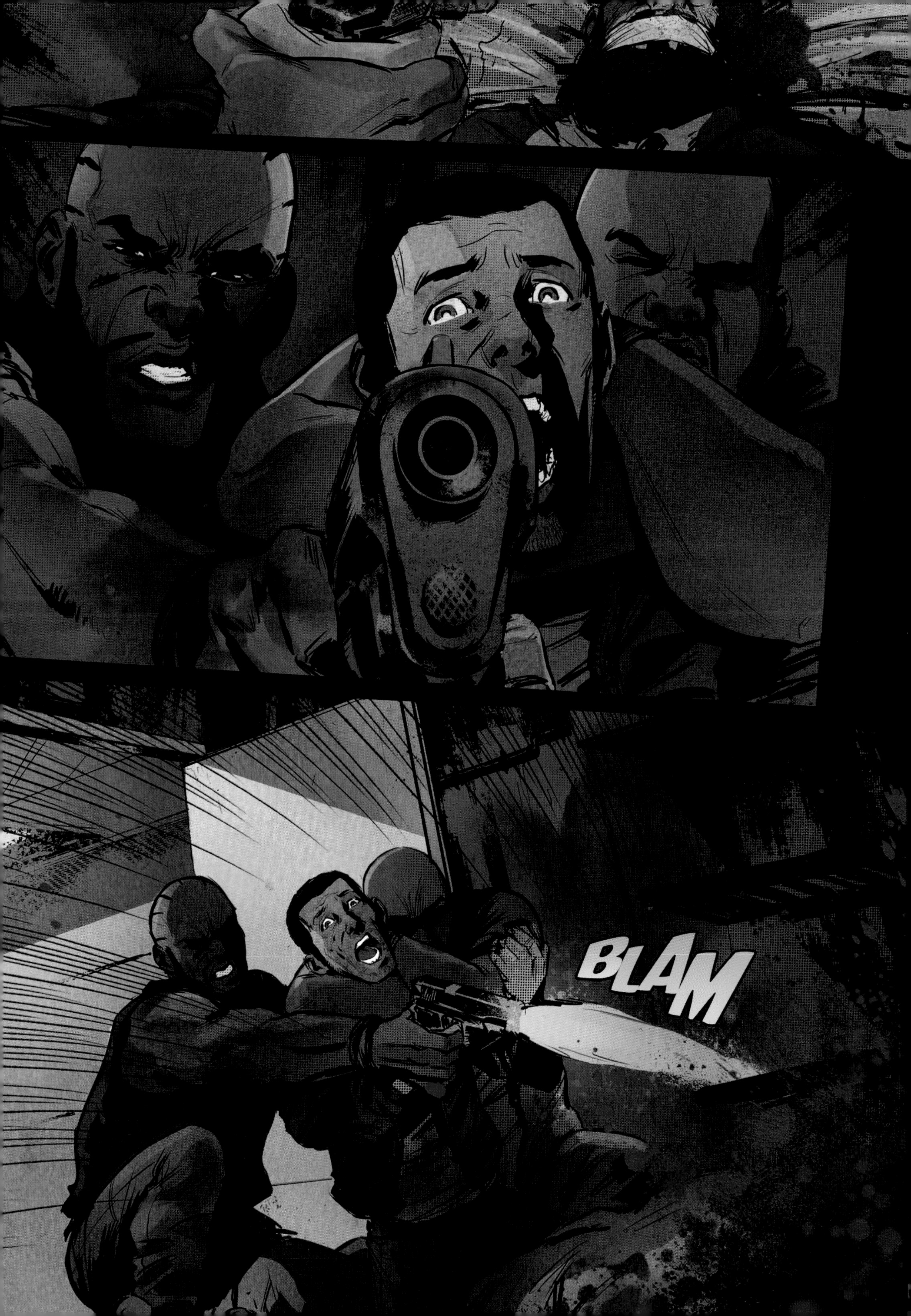
BLAM

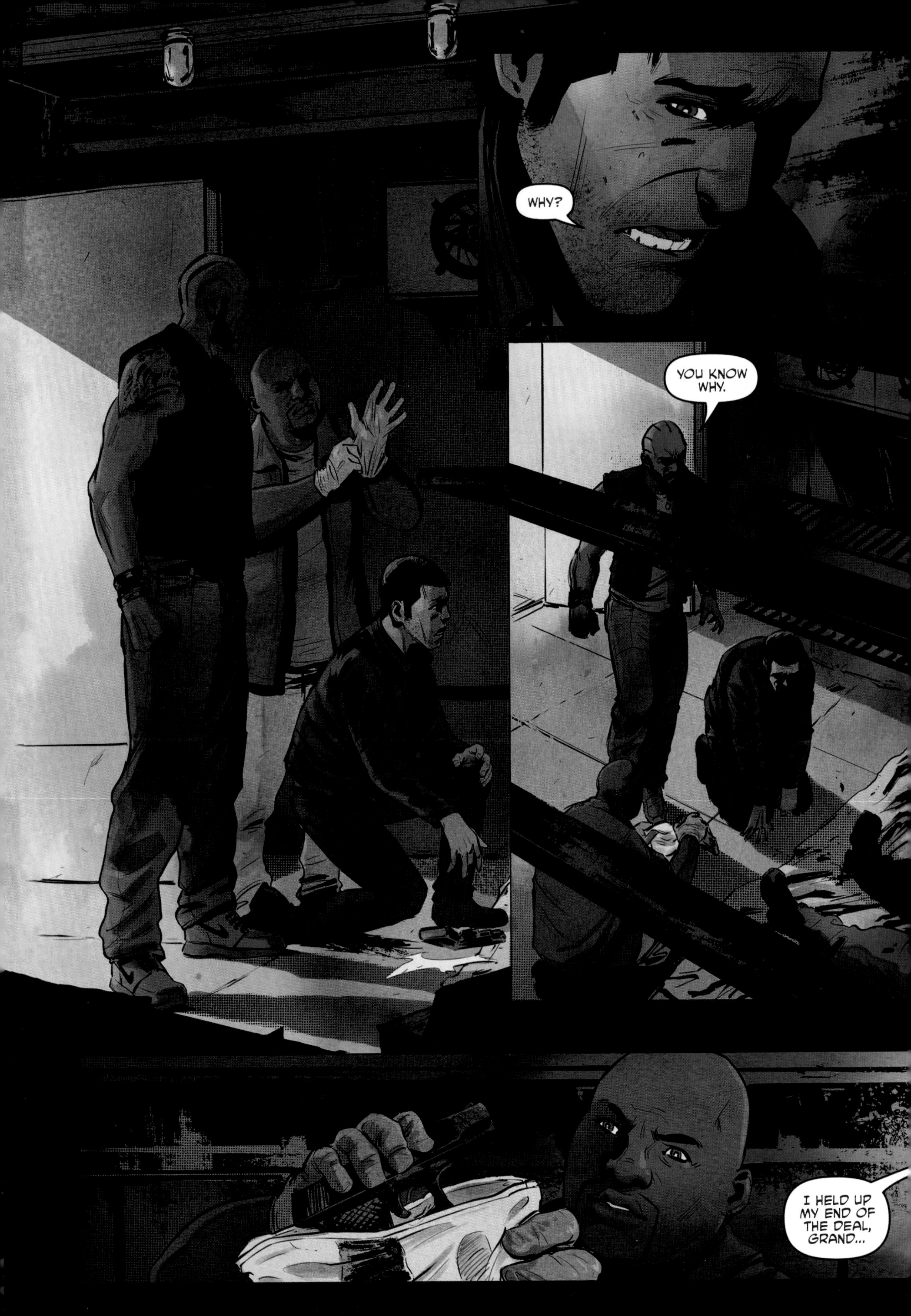
WHY?
YOU KNOW WHY.
I HELD UP MY END OF THE DEAL, GRAND...

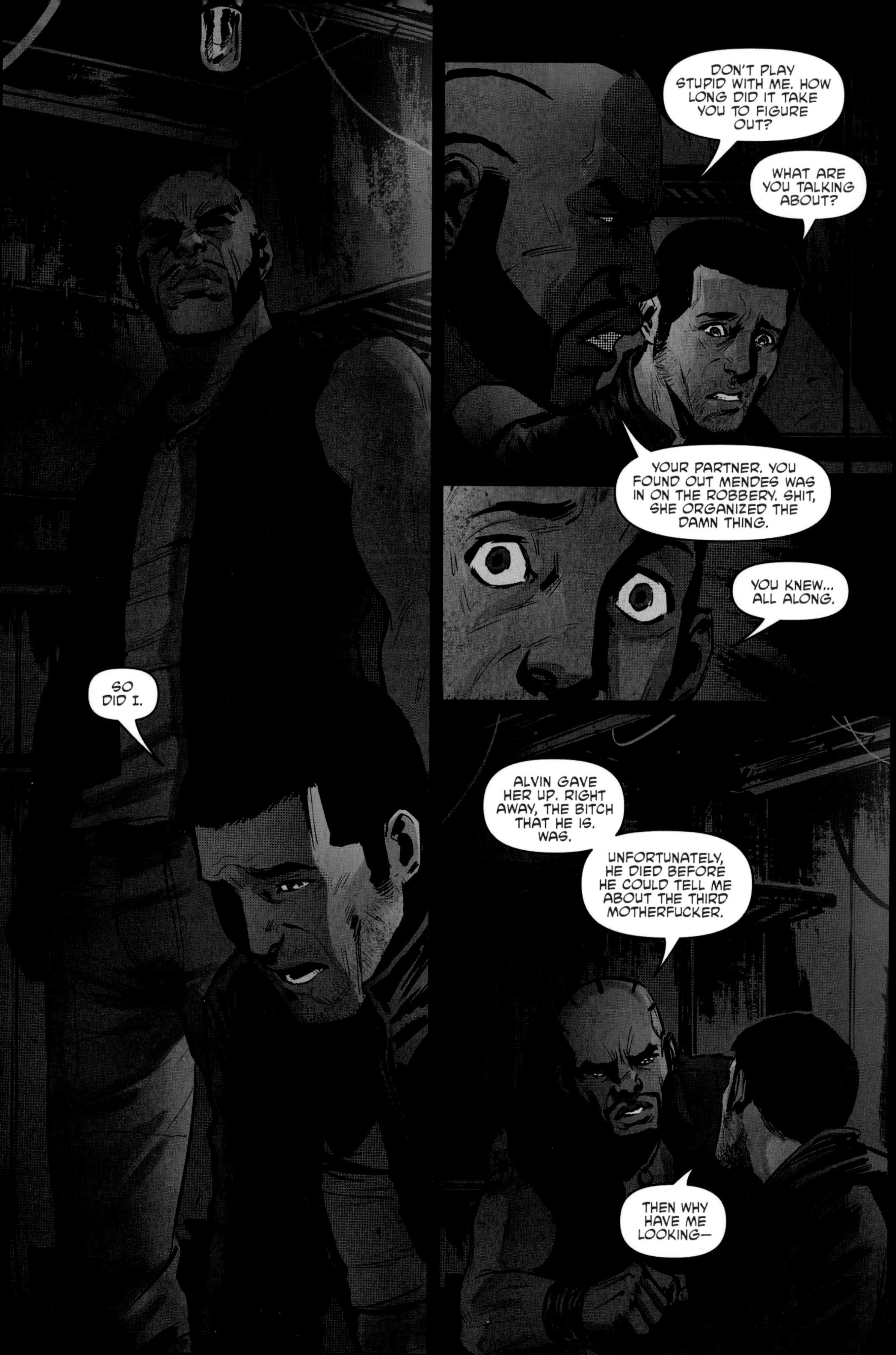
DON'T PLAY STUPID WITH ME. HOW LONG DID IT TAKE YOU TO FIGURE OUT?
WHAT ARE YOU TALKING ABOUT?
YOUR PARTNER. YOU FOUND OUT MENDES WAS IN ON THE ROBBERY. SHIT, SHE ORGANIZED THE DAMN THING.
YOU KNEW... ALL ALONG.
SO DID I.
ALVIN GAVE HER UP. RIGHT AWAY, THE BITCH THAT HE IS. WAS.
UNFORTUNATELY, HE DIED BEFORE HE COULD TELL ME ABOUT THE THIRD MOTHERFUCKER.
THEN WHY HAVE ME LOOKING—

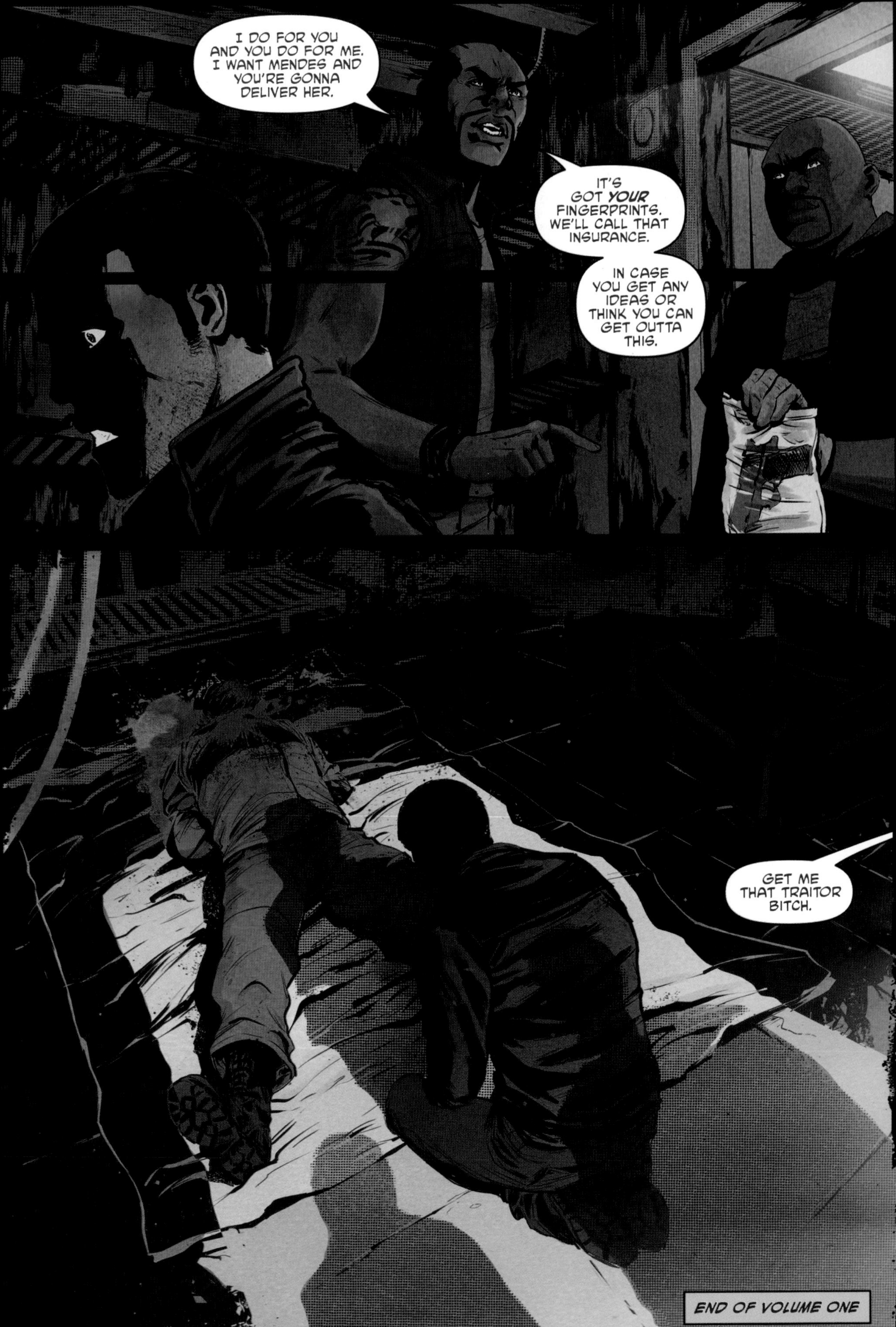
I DO FOR YOU AND YOU DO FOR ME. I WANT MENDES AND YOU'RE GONNA DELIVER HER.
IT'S GOT *YOUR* FINGERPRINTS. WE'LL CALL THAT INSURANCE.
IN CASE YOU GET ANY IDEAS OR THINK YOU CAN GET OUTTA THIS.
GET ME THAT TRAITOR BITCH.
END OF VOLUME ONE

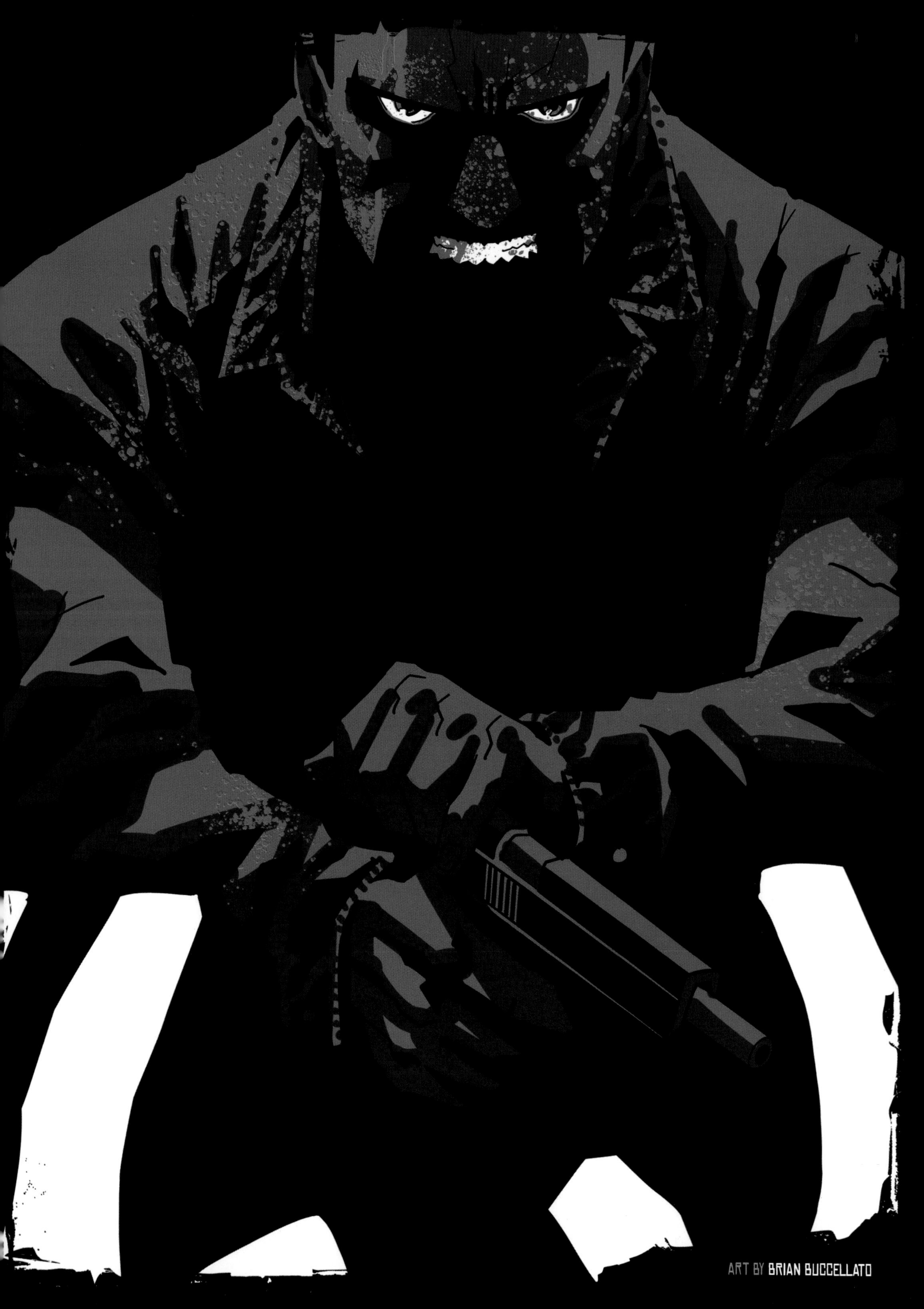

ART BY BRIAN BUCCELLATO

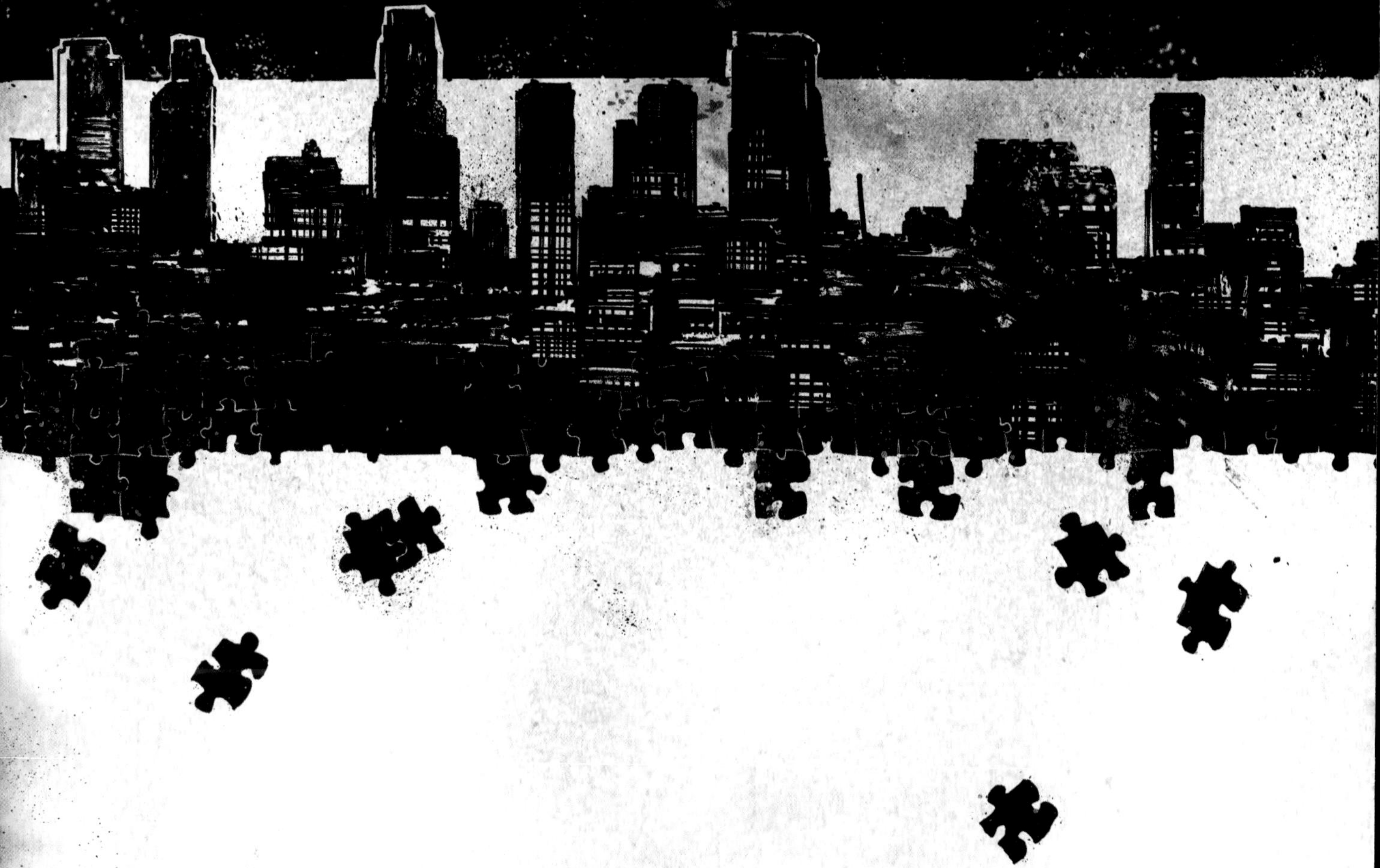

...WELCOME TO THE JUNGLE
WATCH IT BRING YOU TO YOUR
KNEES, KNEES
I WANNA WATCH YOU BLEED...

WELCOME TO THE JUNGLE,
GUNS 'N ROSES
1987

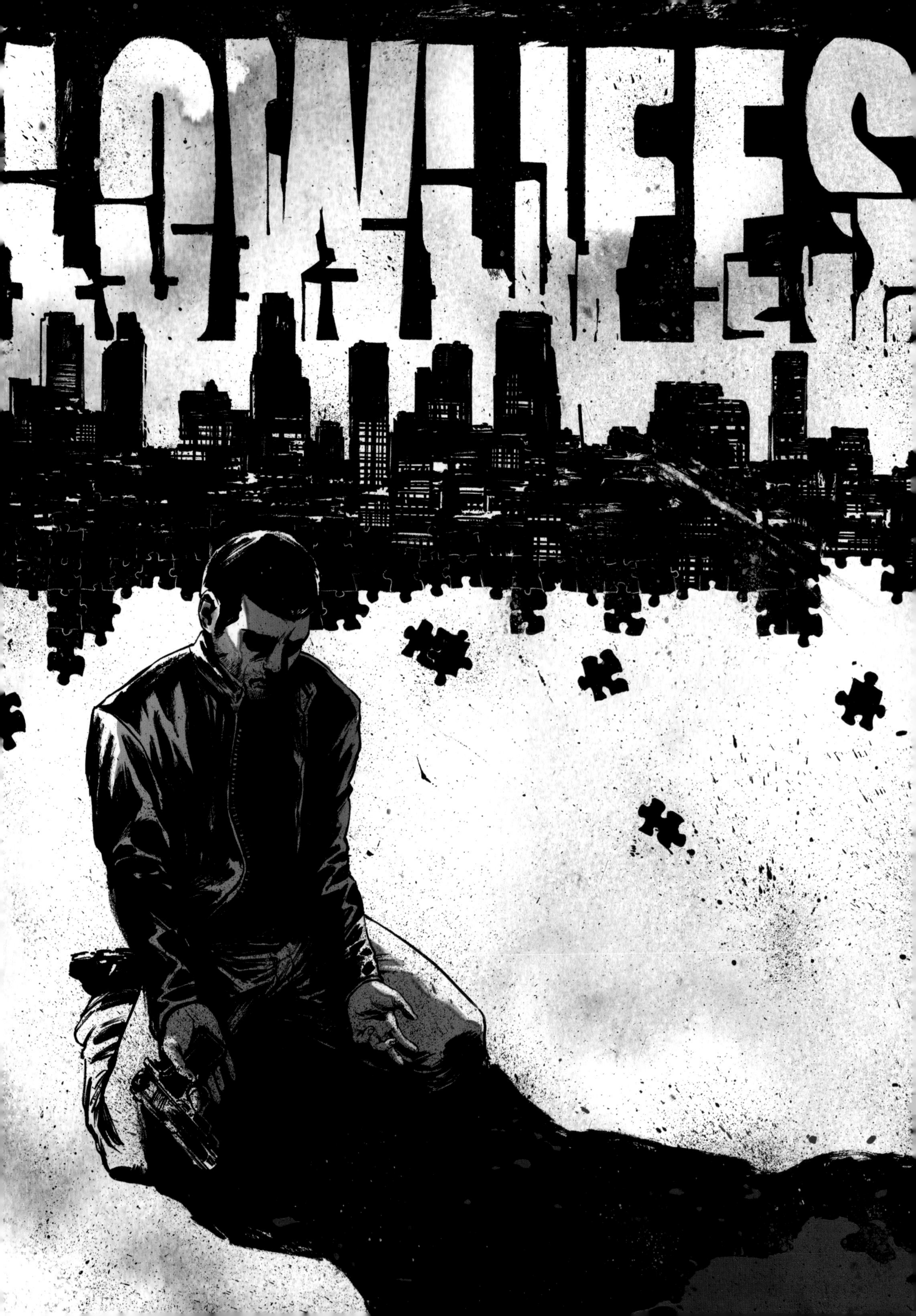

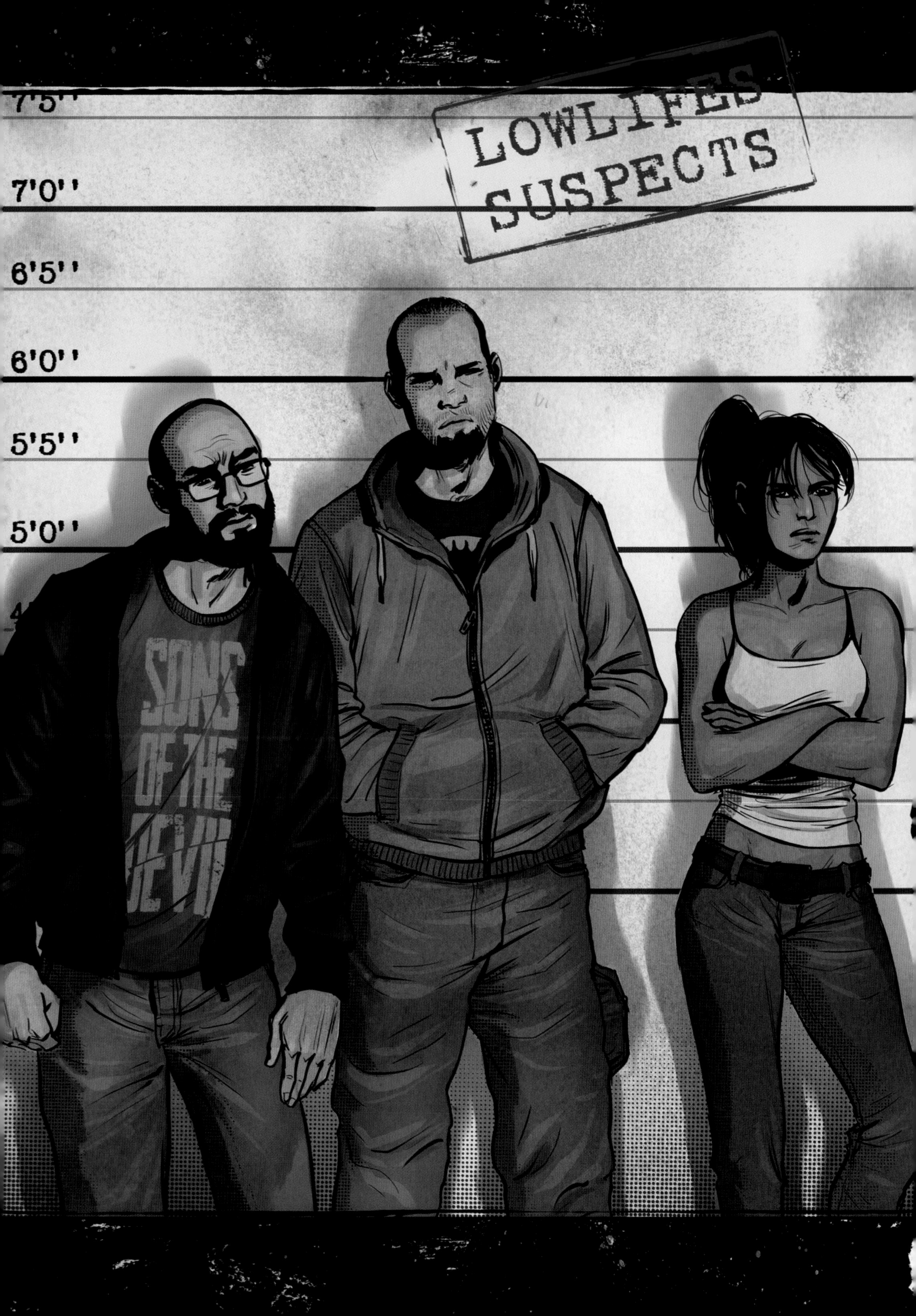

7'5''
LOWLIFES
SUSPECTS
7'0''
6'5''
6'0''
5'5''
5'0''
SONS
OF THE

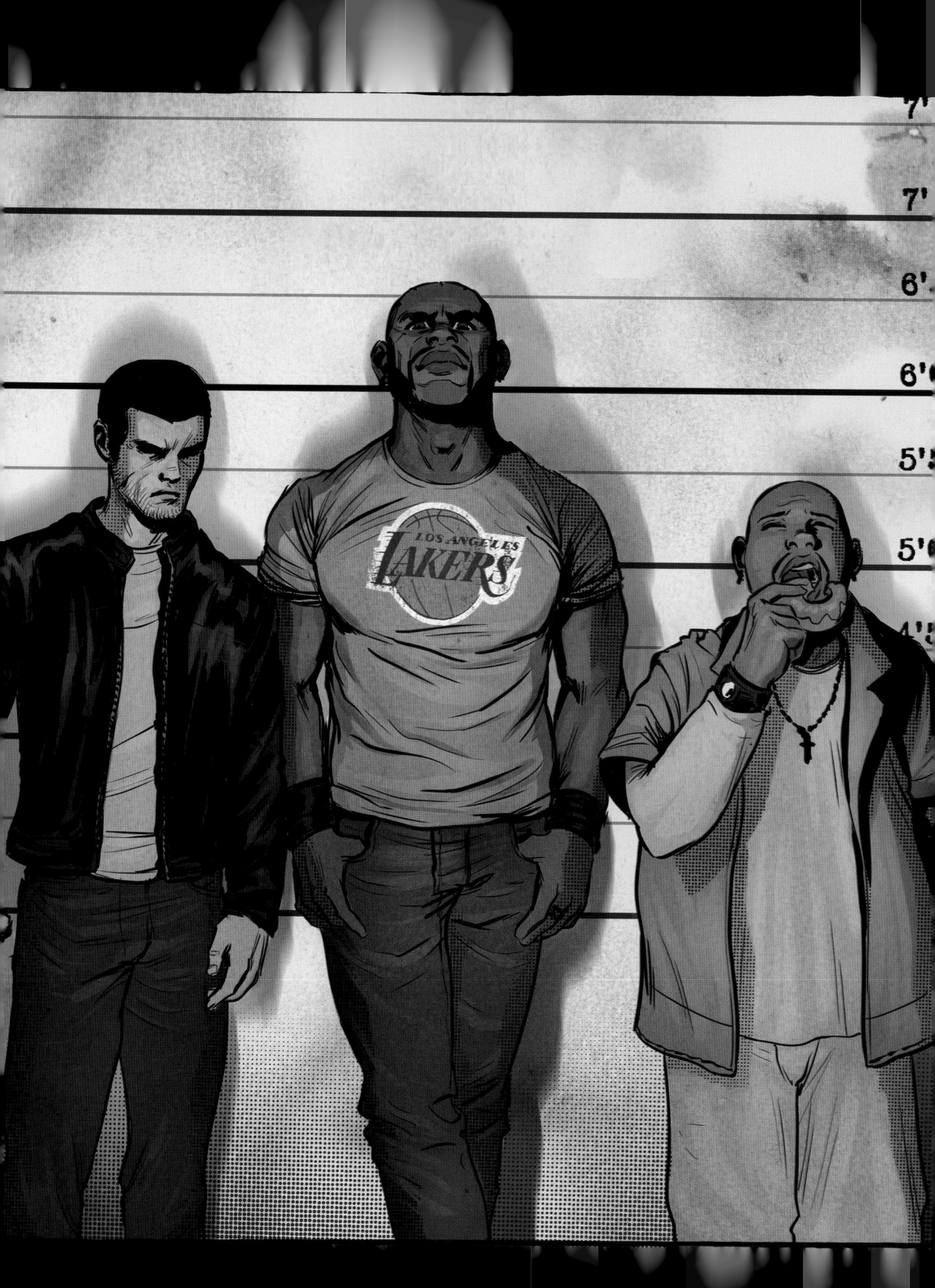
7'
7'
6'
6'
5'
5'
LOS ANGELES
LAKERS

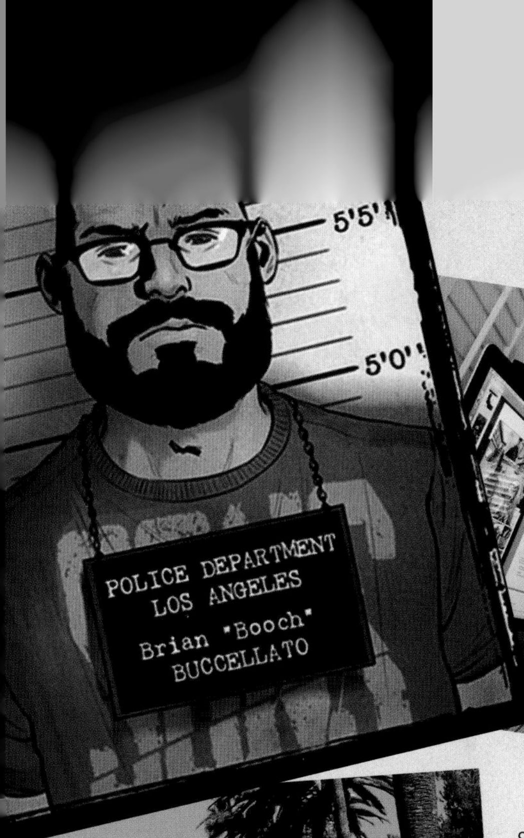
5'5'
5'0'
POLICE DEPARTMENT
LOS ANGELES
Brian "Booch"
BUCCELLATO

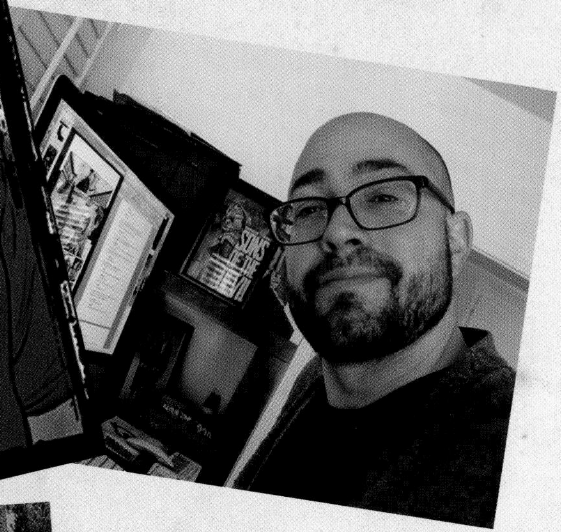

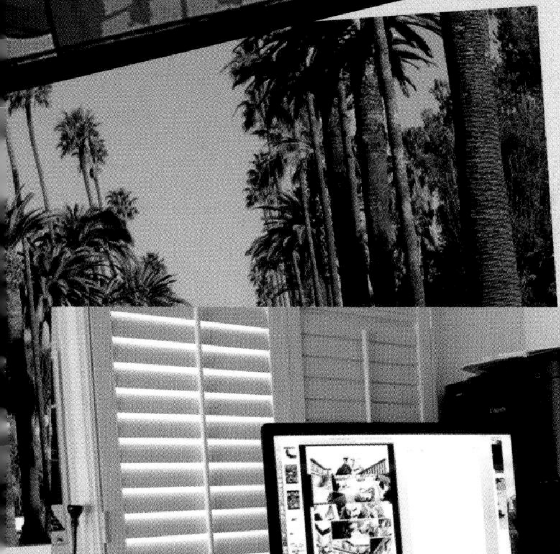

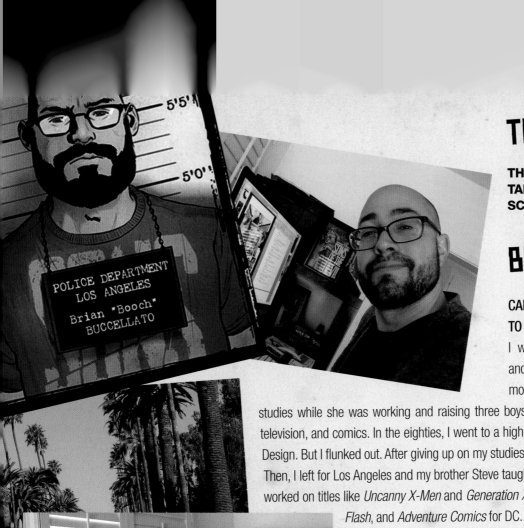

THE BEAT DOWN

THE AUTHORS OF *LOWLIFES* TAKE YOU BEHIND THE SCENES...

BRIAN BUCCELATO

CAN YOU INTRODUCE YOURSELF TO THE READERS?

I was born in Queens, New York, and raised there by my Puerto Rican mother, a divorcee, who did her studies while she was working and raising three boys who all grew up loving movies, television, and comics. In the eighties, I went to a high school in Manhattan called Art & Design. But I flunked out. After giving up on my studies, I worked a series of terrible jobs. Then, I left for Los Angeles and my brother Steve taught me how to color comic books. I worked on titles like *Uncanny X-Men* and *Generation X* for Marvel, as well as *Hellblazer, Flash*, and *Adventure Comics* for DC.

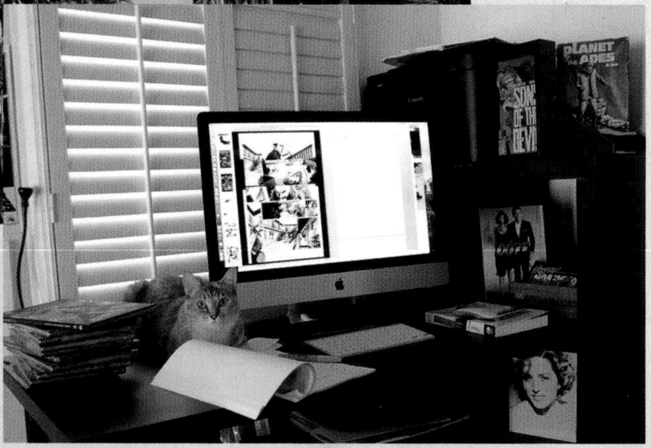

Along the way, I fell in love with writing and decided to pursue it. I taught myself the craft over the course of about ten years and in the end my ability caught up to my passion and I got the opportunity to co-write *The Flash* alongside my friend, artist Francis Manapul. That changed my life.

My most recent solo writing projects include *The Flash, Detective Comics, Injustice* and *DC Comics.* I also have two series I created, published by Image Comics and Glenat, in France: *Sons of the Devil* and *Cannibal.*

DO YOU ALSO READ A LOT OF COMICS?

I did before I got too busy writing. It's hard to keep up with all the great comics being published...

WHAT WERE YOUR BIGGEST INFLUENCES IN CREATING THE CHARACTERS OF *LOWLIFES*? A MIX OF GOOD COPS / BAD BOYS / BAD COPS?

Lowlifes was first written as a screenplay, in the hopes of getting a movie made. My influences for the story came from the movies of Martin Scorsese, Michael Mann, and Quentin Tarantino. I also love the police films from the '70s and '80s. Movies like *French Connection, Taxi Driver, Le Solitaire*, or *The Killing of a Chinese Bookie* were all a major influence on me.

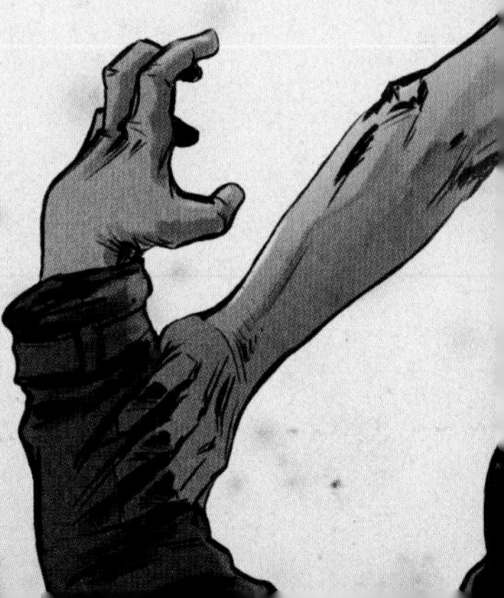

BACKSTAGE

HOW WOULD YOU DESCRIBE THE TONE OF THE SERIES?

It's a dark and realistic police story, with flawed characters who just want to do what they have to for the good of their families.

DO YOU WORK FROM A STUDIO OR FROM HOME? WHY?

I work from home or in cafes. Anywhere, really… I bring my computer with me everywhere and I write ALL THE TIME.

IS THE STORY COMPLETE OR WILL IT HAVE A CONTINUATION?

Lowlifes is meant to be a collection of three stories about three distinct characters whose lives are all connected by violence.

ARE YOU, FIRST AND FOREMOST, A WRITER OF COMICS? WHERE DID YOU LEARN TO WRITE? HOW DID YOU IMPROVE?

I'd say that I started learning writing for movies, first. Movies were my first love, and I bought a few books on writing screenplays and wrote dozens of scripts. Many of them

Rip

Isolated by the trauma
of his childhood abuse
Driven by RAGE and
IDENTITY ISSUES

were terrible, but I got better with each one I wrote. I also took several courses on writing for TV, which helped me A LOT when I started writing comics. The way you tell stories in comics is very similar to the way you tell a story in television.

TALK TO US ABOUT YOUR EXPERIENCES IN THE FILM INDUSTRY.

I owe my first experiences writing for film to my friend Tim Story. He was the director of movies like *Barbershop, Fantastic Four,* and *Ride Along.* I was his assistant for a few years and I wrote for him on a few projects. I also wrote some screenplays for him that were never produced. He was the first person to really treat me like a writer. Actually, I'm part of the emerging writers program at Universal right now. It's a paid writing program that lasts for a year. I just finished writing an action movie, and am working on my second. I hope that once the program's complete I'll have the opportunity to work on projects for them. Wish me luck!

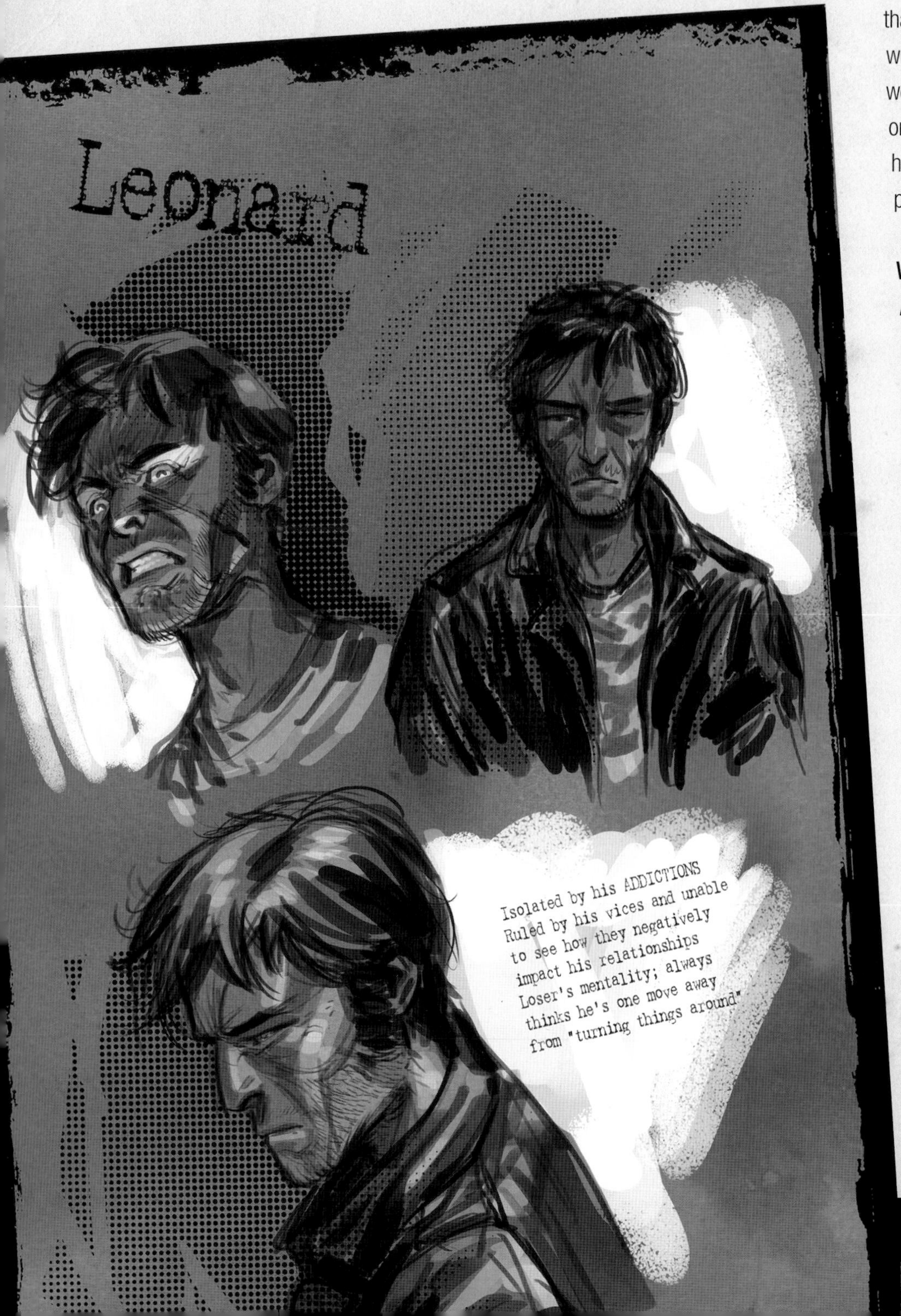
Leonard
Isolated by his ADDICTIONS
Ruled by his vices and unable to see how they negatively impact his relationships
Loser's mentality; always thinks he's one move away from "turning things around"

WHERE DID THE IDEA FOR *LOWLIFES* COME FROM? MOVIES?

Exactly. I wrote a script that I hoped to direct one day. It was a story about redemption, family, and I'm really proud of it.

WHAT HAPPENS IN THIS SERIES?

Lowlifes is a police story about several characters revolving around the robbery of a poker game with extremely high stakes. The main character is Grand. He's a cop in search of revenge who's hanging on to the good person he was before his wife was raped. Tormented by his inability to protect her, which he had sworn to do beforehand, he finds himself, in the aftermath of the tragedy, diving deep into the criminal underworld—a world of gambling, violence, and death. How can he make the world safe for his wife without compromising his morality? Grand ends up on a long and dangerous road of discovery on which he learns that, sometimes, tragic things happen to good people and that perseverance and a willingness to forgive are the keys to being able to move on.

WHAT DO YOU CONSIDER THE GENRE OF THE SERIES? IF YOU HAD TO PRESENT IT TO A PRODUCER IN HOLLYWOOD… ;)

It's a realistic and violent thriller.

HOW DID YOU CHOOSE THE SETTING FOR THE ACTION IN *LOWLIFES*?

I've lived in Los Angeles since the '90s. I love this town and I felt that the area lended itself well to an uncompromising police story.

TALK TO US ABOUT THE DIFFERENT SETTINGS IN THE STORY.

They reflect the varying character of the different parts of Los Angeles. It's a massive town with many different and unique parts. Especially because it's a place where the sun is permanently shining.

ARE THE CHARACTERS FROM *LOWLIFES* BASED ON REAL PEOPLE? WHICH OF THE CHARACTERS IS YOUR FAVORITE?

They're absolutely not based on real people. They were built around the needs of the story. Everyone is the hero of their own story, and these characters each have goals that they consider extremely important. Even if, to others, those goals might seem demented or machiavellian.

HOW WAS THE PROCESS OF WORKING WITH ALEXIS (WHO IS BASED IN FRANCE) DIFFERENT FROM YOUR PAST COLLABORATIVE EXPERIENCES?

I've worked with many artists and have had the opportunity to work with quite a few who don't speak English as a first language. Alexis is a talented professional and had little problem adapting my words. From a stylistic point of view, he's really a French artist, and that made it particularly exciting to see how he would interpret the story.

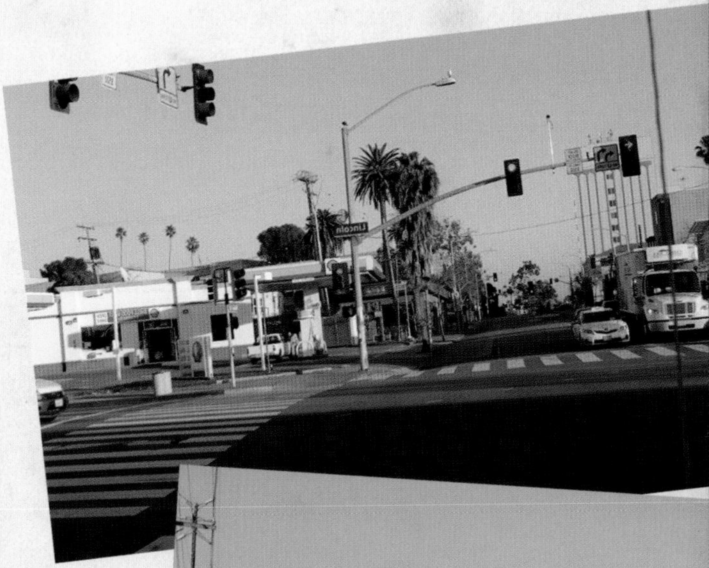

WHAT ABOUT HIS WORK MADE YOU WANT TO COLLABORATE WITH HIM ON *LOWLIFES*?

I think it was his talent for layouts and his ability to convey emotions with his characters—all while drawing in a style that is clearly his own.

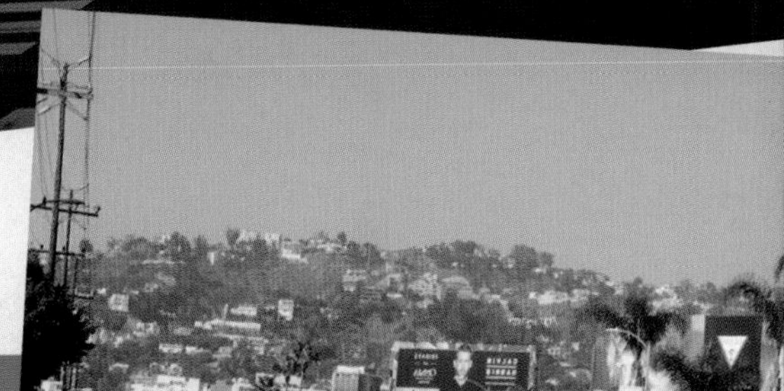

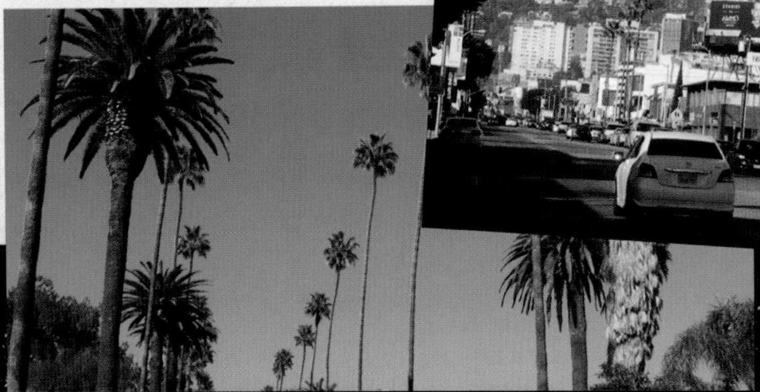

ARE YOU FAMILIAR WITH EUROPEAN *BANDE DESSINEES*? DO YOU READ ANY?

Unfortunately, I haven't read any in a long time. I know the classics like Moebius and Asterix. I'm open to any suggestions you have!

ARE INDEPENDENT, CREATOR-OWNED COMICS, AND SIMILAR SERIES, MORE POPULAR TODAY IN THE UNITED STATES? IF SO, WHY?

I don't know if that's the case. I hope so. If it is, then maybe it's because Americans are finally starting to understand that comics aren't just for kids. It's an incredible medium of artistic expression that deserves wider recognition. It's not just superhero stories meant for kids.

IS AN ADAPTATION OF *LOWLIFES* IN HOLLYWOOD IN THE WORKS?

Jennifer Young and I are actively trying to put together a film project based on this story. You'll have to wait and see!

ALEXIS SENTENAC

CAN YOU INTRODUCE YOURSELF TO THE READERS?

I was born in Le Mans, and that's actually why I had terrible grades in French at school, because I wanted to go Futuroscope (a theme park in France), but apparently that wasn't an acceptable excuse. I passed a "Baccalaureate D" as in "design," but it was actually for math science. :-) Then I got my diploma in graphic design and I worked in offices for ten years before transitioning over to comics!

DO YOU ALSO READ A LOT OF COMICS?

I read a lot of comics, in general. Franco-Belgian comics, American comics, manga—everything! But as far as recently, I don't follow any comics month-to-month. I wait for the trade paperbacks because I don't like following too many different artists, and stories, in a single series. It's too hard to follow. I find it negatively effects the pacing of the story. At the moment, I'm reading *Batman* by Capullo, Snyder, and Glapion. It's great!!!

WHAT WERE YOUR BIGGEST INFLUENCES IN CREATING THE CHARACTERS OF *LOWLIFES*? A MIX OF GOOD COPS / BAD BOYS / BAD COPS?

My influence on the book was Brian ;) In the sense that he had already "cast" the book and I was able to use the "lookbook" he had prepared with actors, as if for a movie, to help me make my choices in designing the characters while bringing my own approach to it. I didn't want to just directly draw the actors he had chosen because that wouldn't be interesting ;)

HOW WOULD YOU DESCRIBE THE TONE OF THE SERIES?

A very dark thriller. I like light-hearted stories. This one combines the poetry of *Reservoir Dogs* with the lightness of *Sin City.*

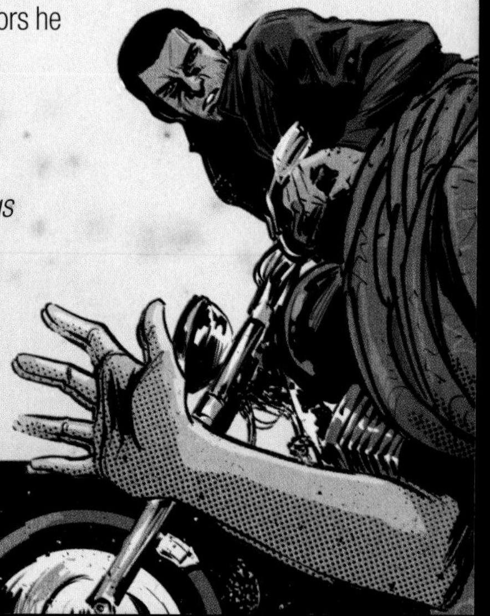

DO YOU WORK FROM A STUDIO OR FROM HOME? WHY?

No I don't work from home, because the less I see my family, the better my mood gets, of course. So, I work from a building I bought not that long ago. I kept a floor for myself and I sublet the rest to a few different bands, haha! Joking aside, I set up a nice studio for myself at home where I work with Brice Cossu (another fantastic French creator) and we have a great time. Virtually, there's more of us, because every day—thanks to some audio-conferencing software, we connect and work as if we're in a virtual studio. If you want to know who with, look at the great pin-ups at the end of the book! ;)

IS THE STORY COMPLETE OR WILL IT HAVE A CONTINUATION?

You'll have to ask Brian! ;)

HOW DID YOU HANDLE THE LAYOUTS AND DESIGN OF LOWLIFES? THE PACING?

Not too poorly, I hope! Regarding the pacing, I stayed true to Brian's script. His dialogue rolls off the tongue and sounds great! When you read it, it sounds natural, and it's a lot of fun. As for the actual layouts, it was easy work, because the images just flowed together. The entire series feels like you're binge-watching a TV show.

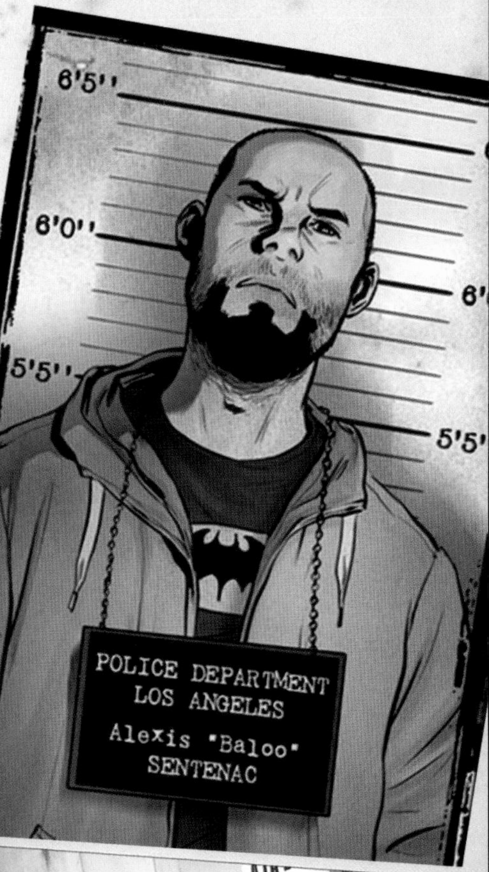
6'5''
6'0''
5'5''
6'
5'5'
POLICE DEPARTMENT
LOS ANGELES
Alexis "Baloo"
SENTENAC

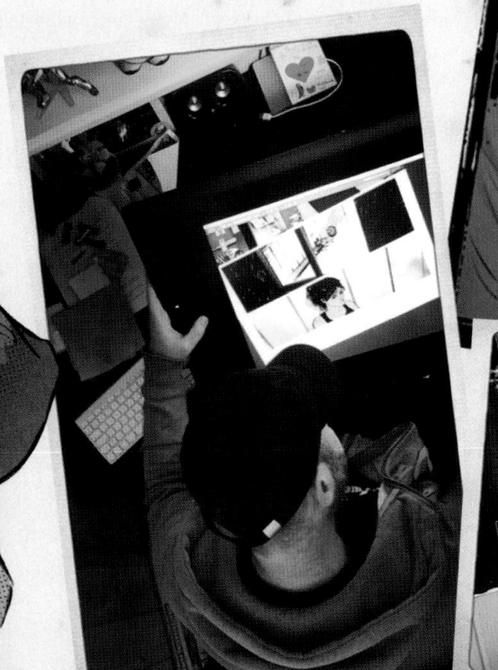

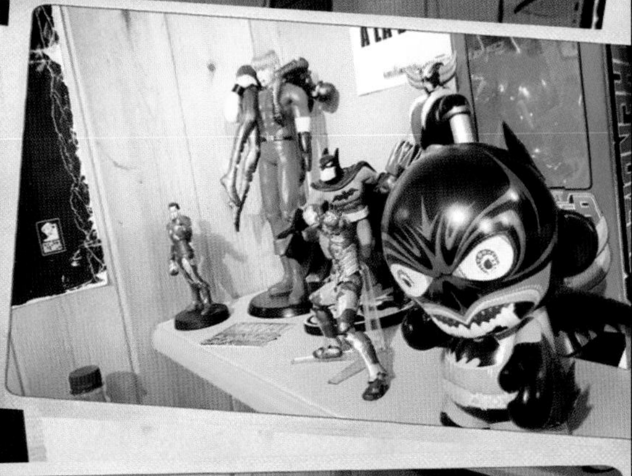

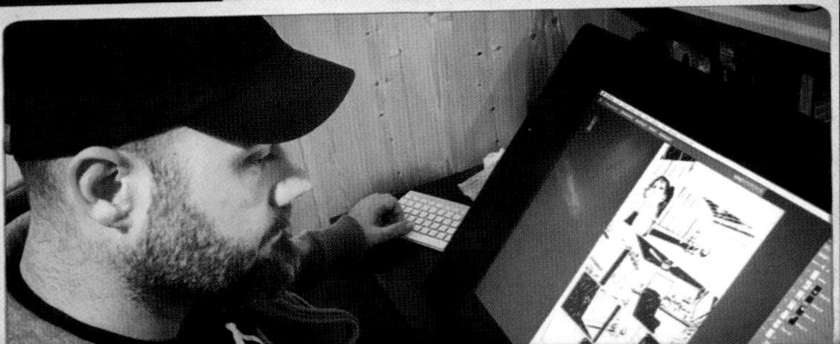

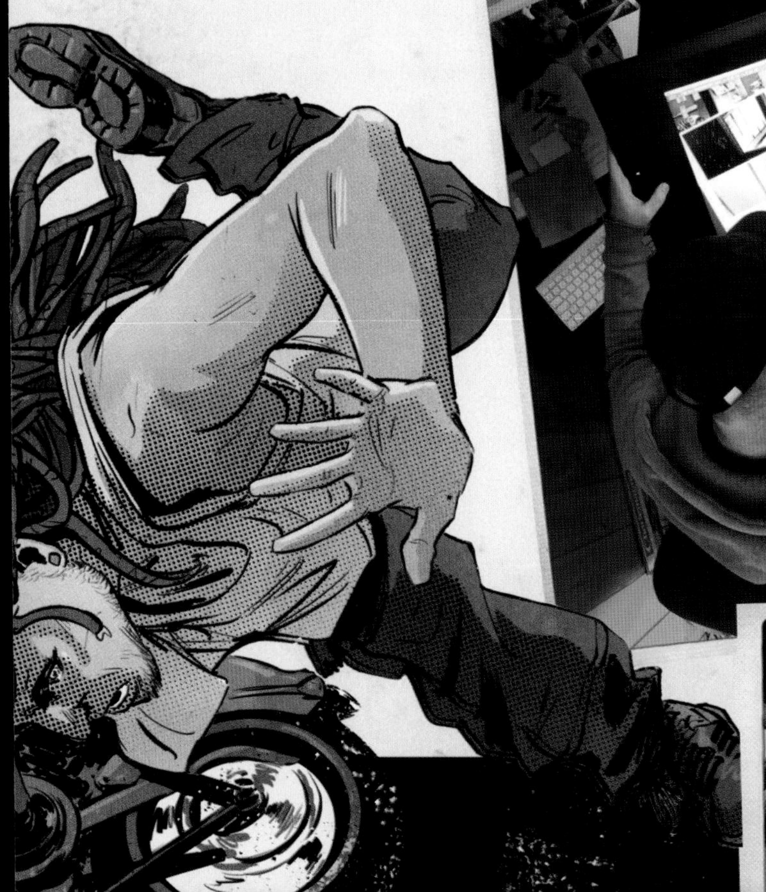

And since I've been immersed in the world of comics for as long as I can remember and now there's this great bridge between American and French comics, I was able to make the story my own using everything that Franco-Belgian comics taught me. Brian's own style is hybrid, too, in its own right, because, for a comic, *Lowlifes* has many pages with more than six panels!

DID YOU TAKE ANY LIBERTIES WITH BRIAN'S SCRIPT?

Yes. I always take liberties with the script. It's important to me, to try to make the story, the word, and the characters my own. To feel close to them. But, freedom isn't treason! I take great care to never lose sight of the writer's initial intent, or else they won't see themselves in it either. I hope I've managed to toe that line here ;)

ARE SCRIPTS BY AMERICAN WRITERS DIFFERENT FROM SCRIPTS BY FRENCH WRITERS?

For the moment, I haven't worked with any other American writers, so I can't really say for certain. What I do know is that, in Brian's script, I found an expert sort of pacing I haven't seen anywhere else.

DO YOU ENJOY THE HARD-BOILED THRILLER GENRE? WHAT DID YOU LIKE ABOUT THE SCRIPT?

Of course I like the genre! I never work on a project that doesn't speak to me ;) I like the uncompromising nature of the story, the characters that lose themselves in their contradictions, who want to find a way out but always end up having karma catch up to them! One bad decision rarely leads to much more than other bad decisions—the serpent keeps eating its own tail.

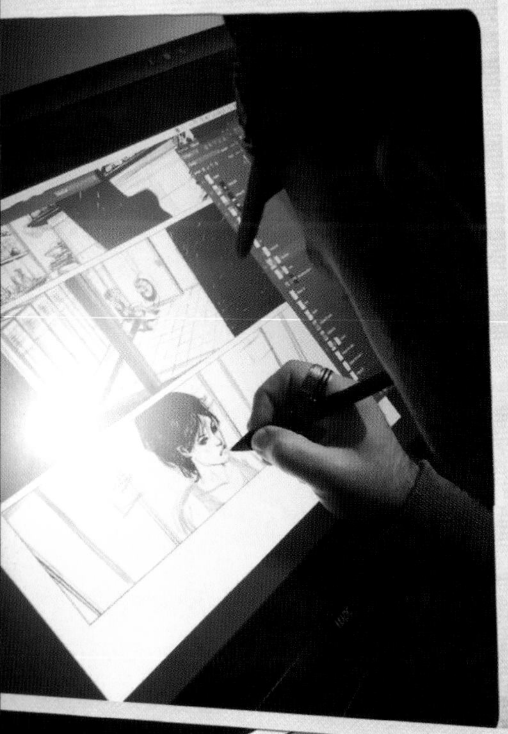

THIS ISN'T YOUR FIRST EXPERIENCE WORKING IN THE AMERICAN COMICS FORMAT. DOES YOUR EXPERIENCE WORKING ON LOWLIFES COMPARE TO *50*?

No, I don't think so, but they are related—like not-too-distant cousins. In *50*, we chase after the bad guy, while in *Lowlifes*, you're trying to run away from him—but you always end up finding your way back.

DO YOU DREAM OF THE USA?

The comics, yes! I hope to go there some day, but I've still got a long way to go. It's not easy!

HOW WOULD YOU DESCRIBE YOUR OWN ARTISTIC STYLE? DO YOU HAVE ANY PLANS TO WORK MORE IN THE U.S. MARKET?

That, I don't know. That's more of a question for my collaborators or readers. As far as whether my style, assuming I do have one, could work in the U.S. market, I think that today, American readers (and others!) are used to an artistic style they didn't even know about ten or fifteen years ago, so maybe there's a chance!

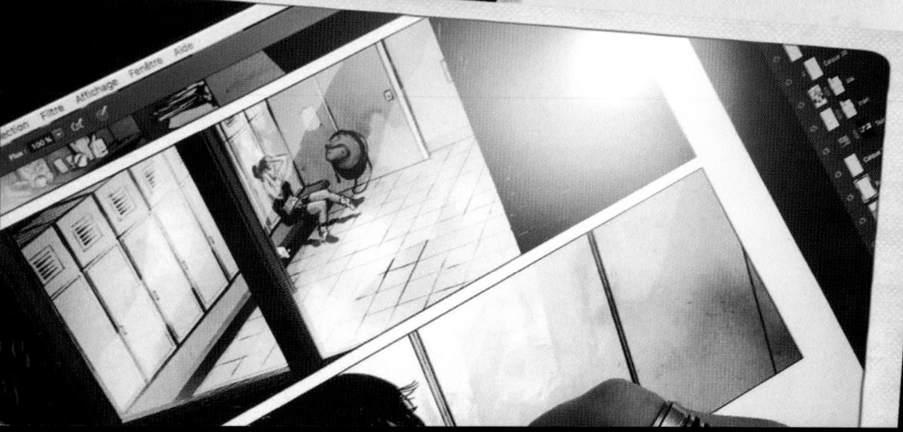

HOW WAS YOUR EXPERIENCE WORKING ON THIS PROJECT SIMILAR TO / DIFFERENT FROM YOUR TYPICAL *B.D.* PROJECTS?

The biggest difference is in the page count (larger than a Franco-Belgian album). With *50*, that was already the case and it leads to a major difference in pacing, both for the story and the work itself. You need to pace yourself!

HAVE YOU PREVIOUSLY DRAWN ANY STORIES WITH LOCATIONS INSPIRED BY REAL PLACES?

I always take inspiration from the real world (even for sci-fi!) but this is the first time I had to get a real sense of the town, of Los Angeles. So I concentrated on getting to know L.A. so that the reader could get the feel of the place even without knowing the exact streets they were on.

HOW DID YOU APPROACH THE COLORING OF THIS COMIC?

I always approach color as lighting, so I referred to Los Angeles' particularly unique lighting. I hope that I succeeded in my intent!

HOW DO YOU MAKE YOUR CHARACTERS LIKABLE? ISN'T IT A DIFFICULT TASK TO MAKE GENERALLY BAD PEOPLE LIKABLE?

That's the hardest part for me, and I have a tough time putting that aspect of my work into words. I'm trying to draw the story in a way that my characters speak to me and touch me, so that, if they affect me, there's bound to be two or three other people that will be affected, too.

DID YOU HAVE ANY FAVORITE CHARACTERS? ANY CHARACTERS YOU MOST ENJOYED DRAWING?

Aaaaah, I always love the villains, so I really liked Wendall, of course. But, I have a soft spot for Rip, who's taking care of his mother and trying to keep a handle on his anger as best as he can.

ARE YOU READY TO CONTINUE THE ADVENTURE?
OR POTENTIALLY WORK DIRECTLY IN THE USA?

I'm always ready for the next adventure, whatever it might be! ;)

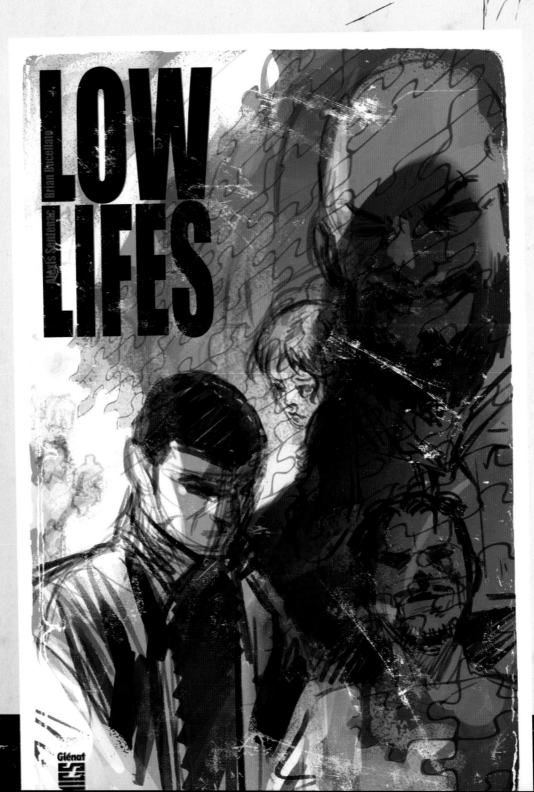

LOW LIFES

Alexis Sentenac · Brian Buccellato

Glénat

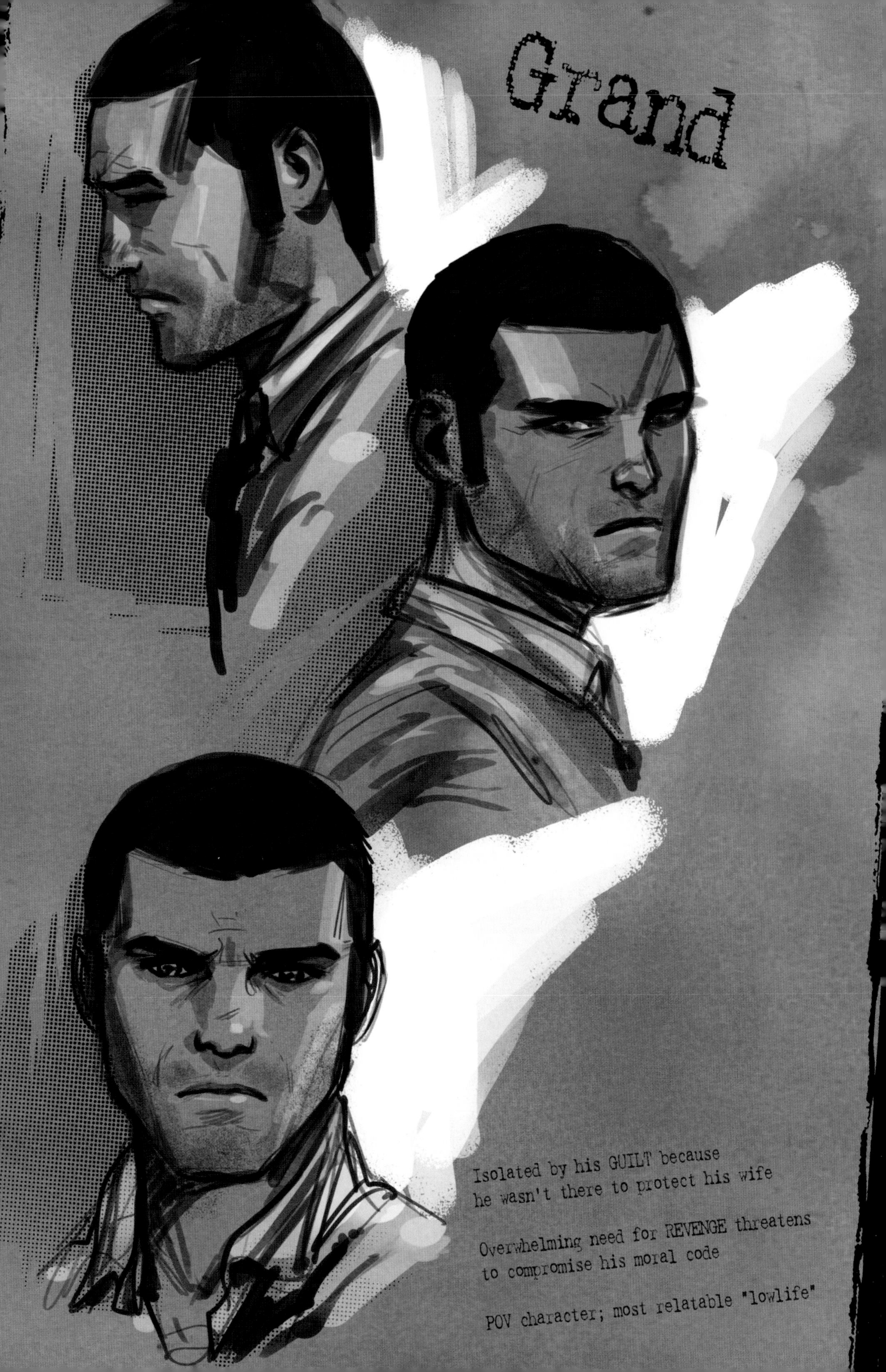
Grand
Isolated by his GUILT because he wasn't there to protect his wife
Overwhelming need for REVENGE threatens to compromise his moral code
POV character; most relatable "lowlife"

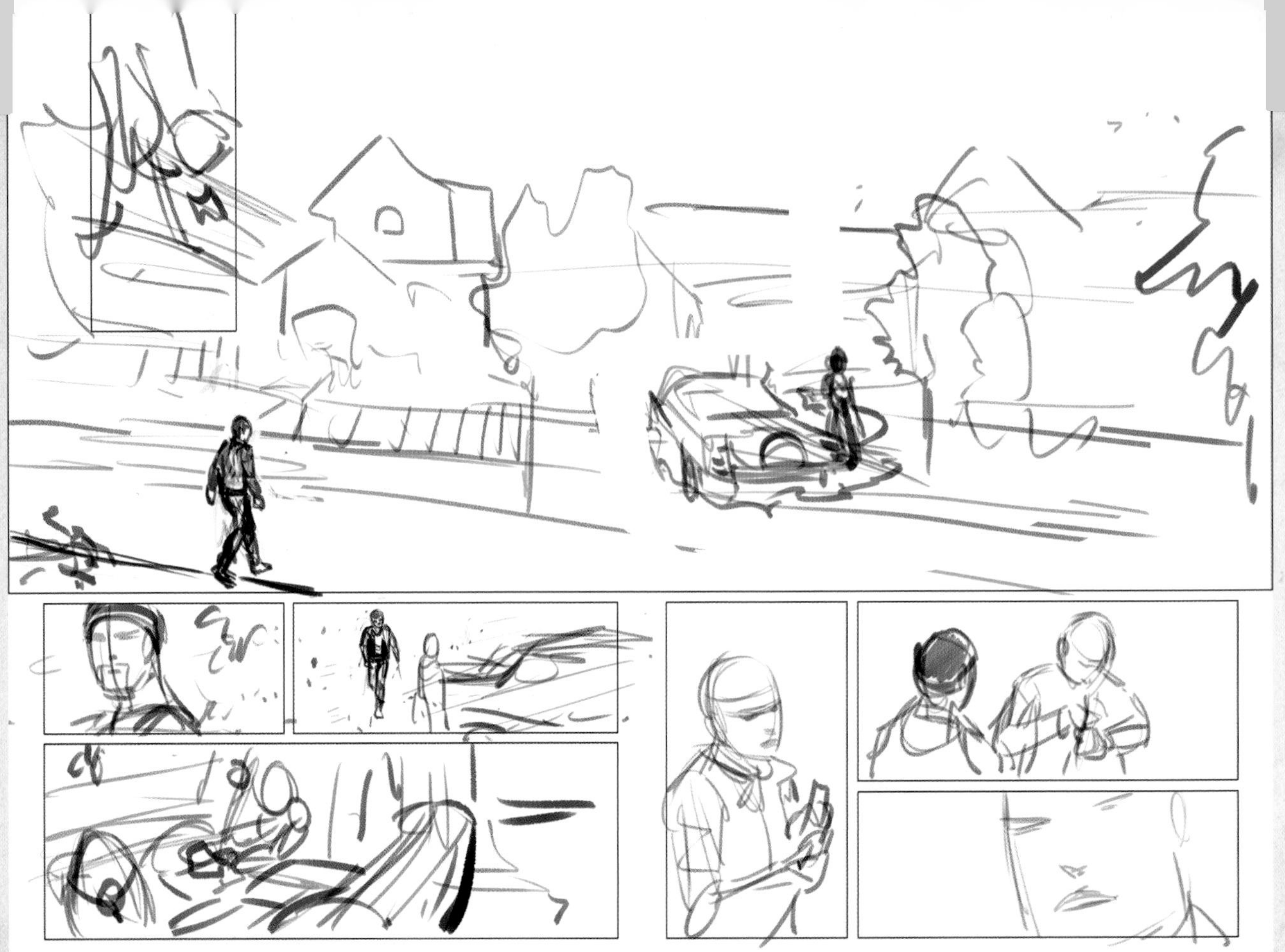

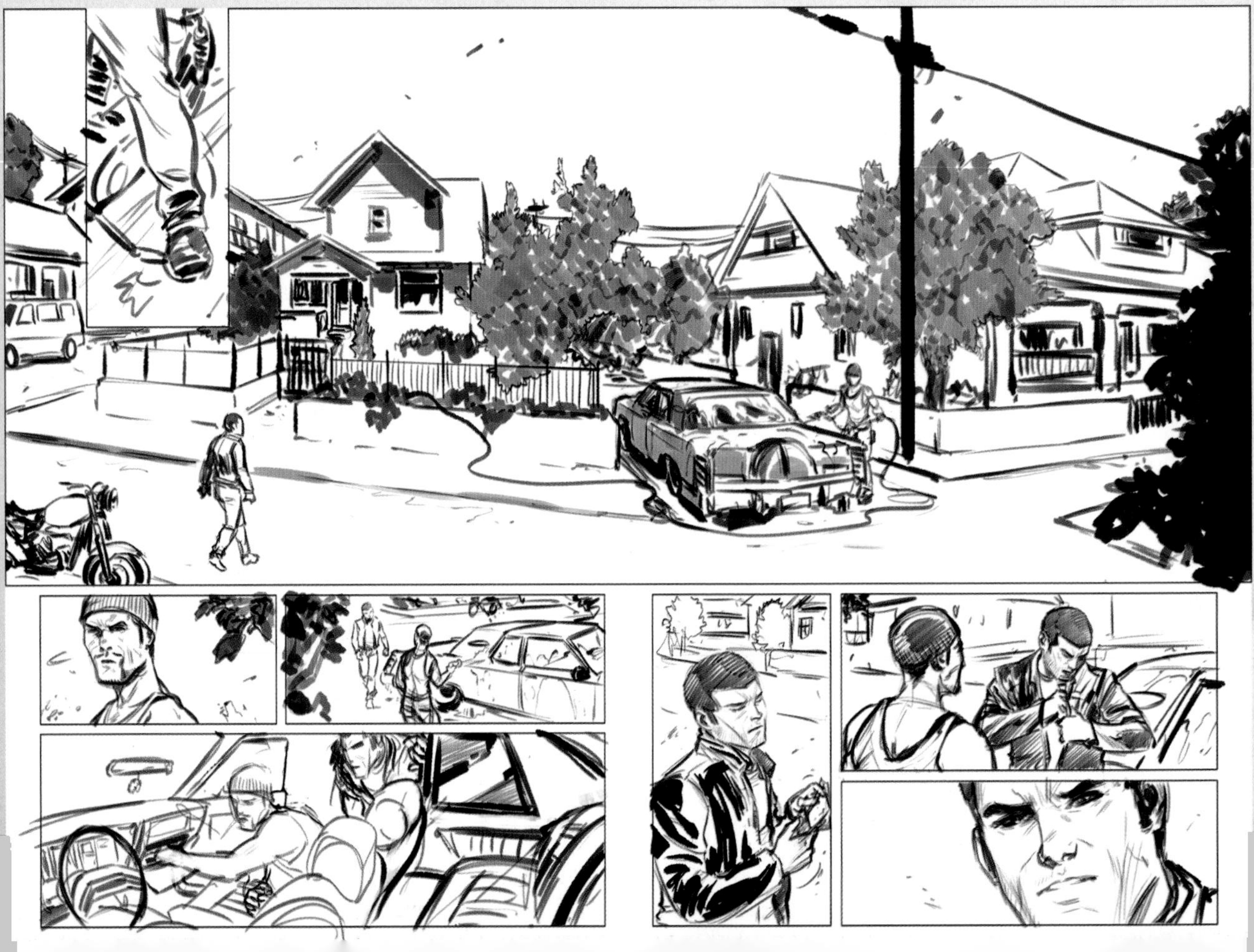

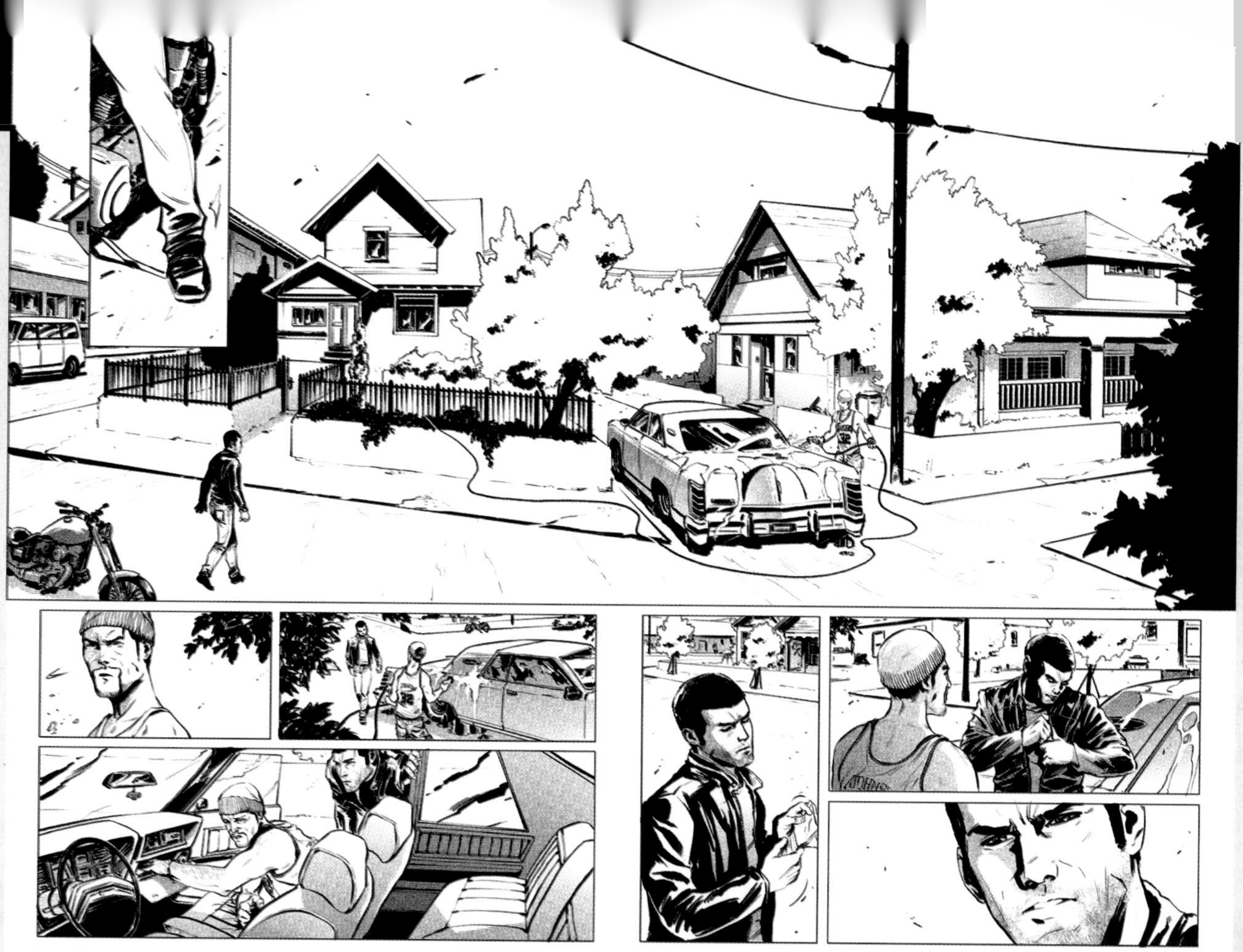

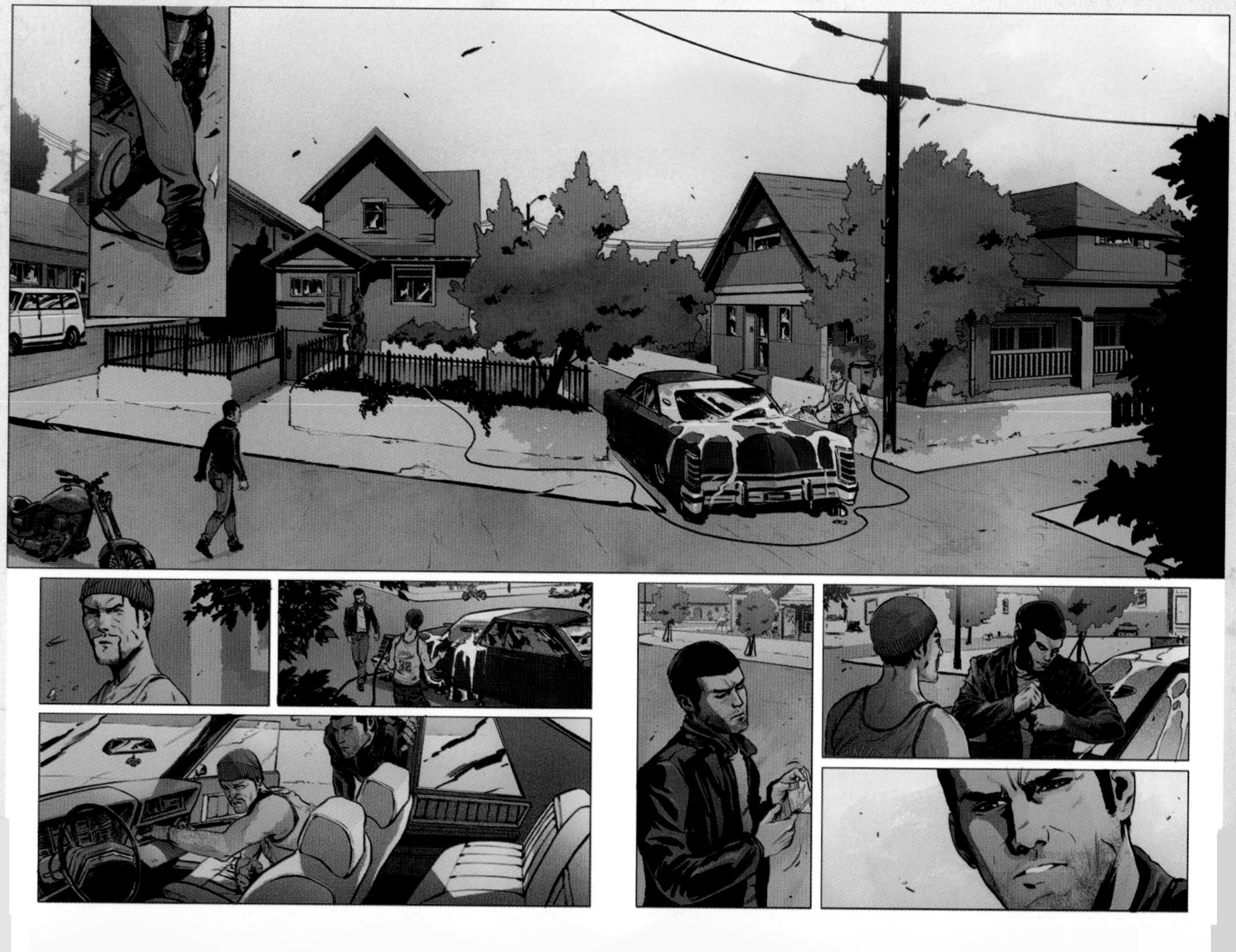

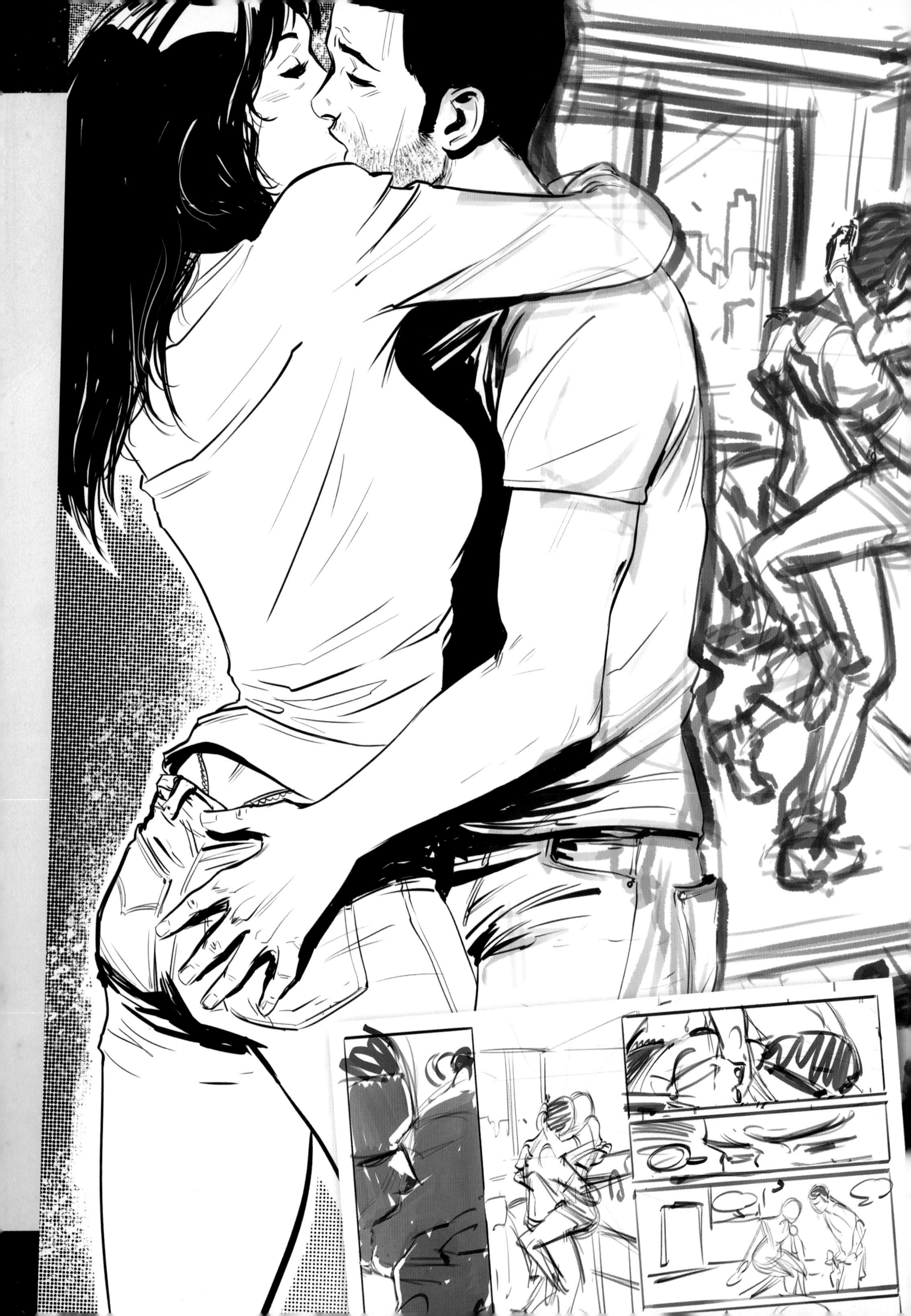

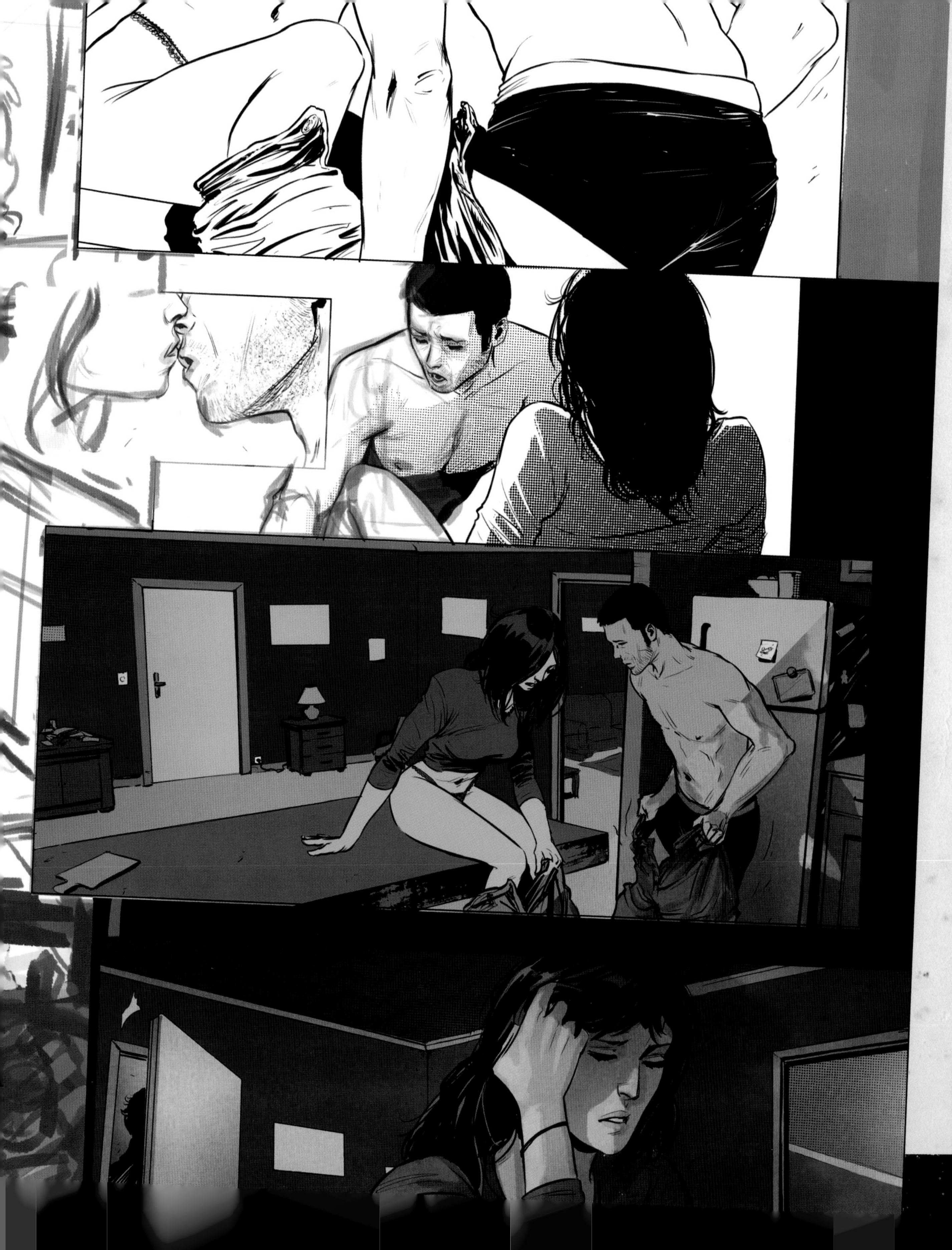

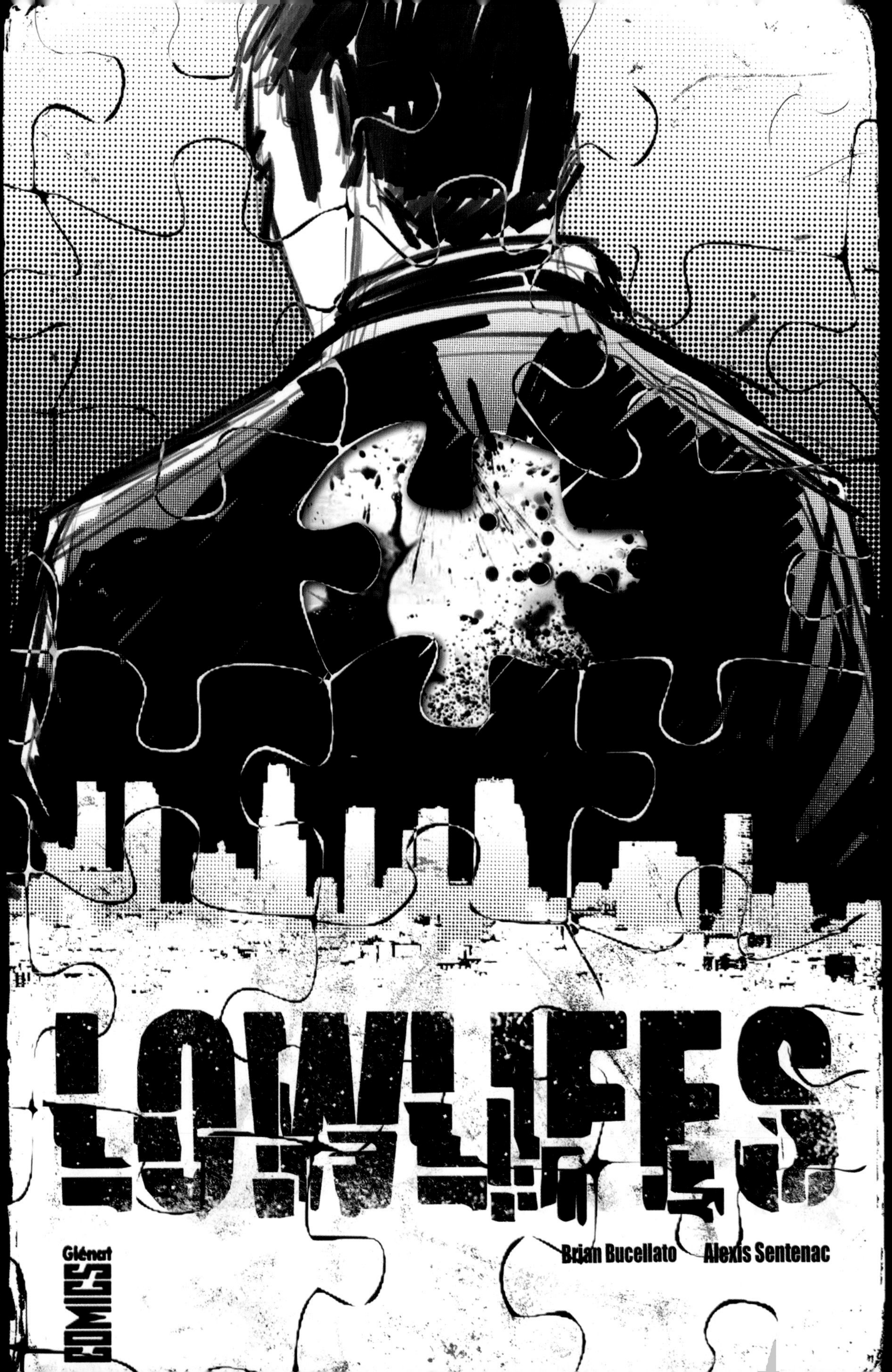
LOWLIFES
Brian Bucellato
Alexis Sentenac
Glénat
COMICS

COVER AND PIN-UP GALLERY

LOWLIFES
Brian Bucellato
Alexis Sentenac
Glénat
COMICS

LOWLIFES
Brian Bucellato
Alexis Sentenac

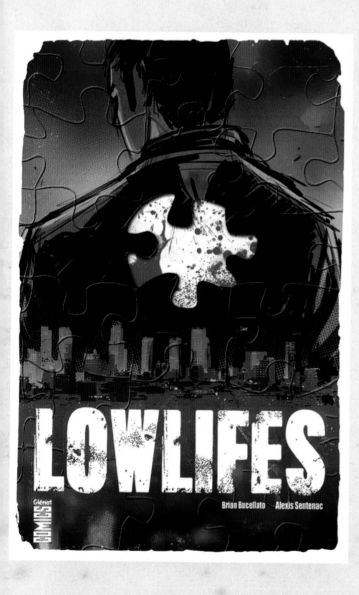

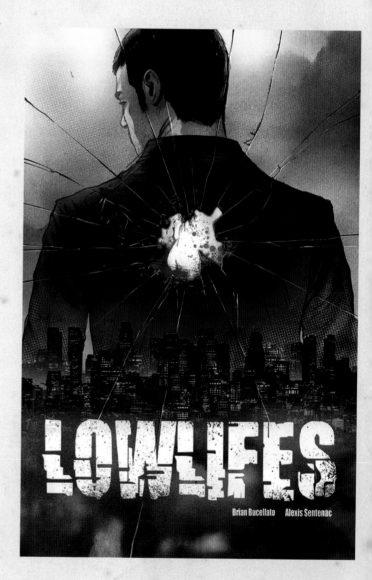

WANTED: A. SENTENAC

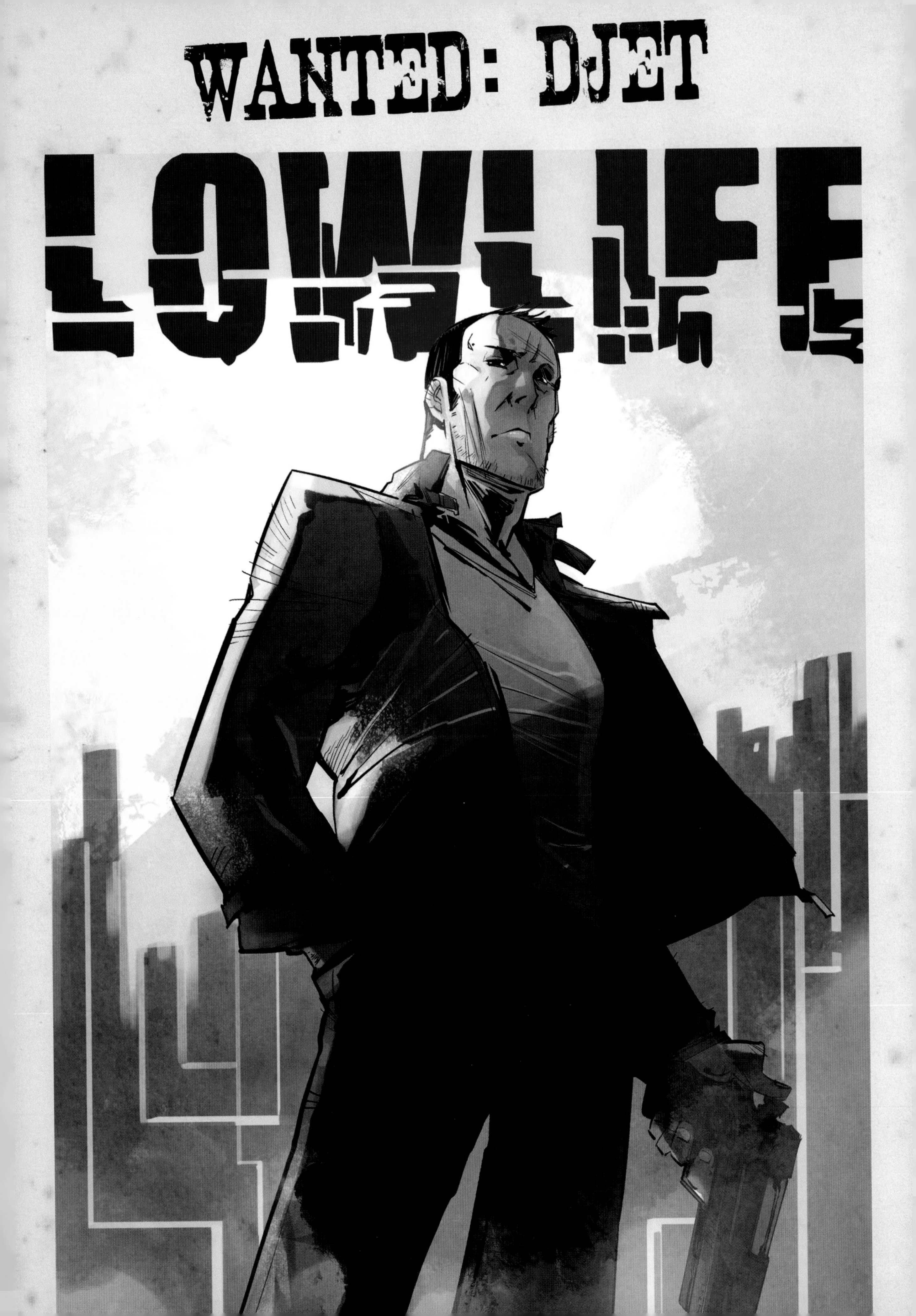
WANTED: DJET
LOWLIFE

WANTED: J. CORGIÉ

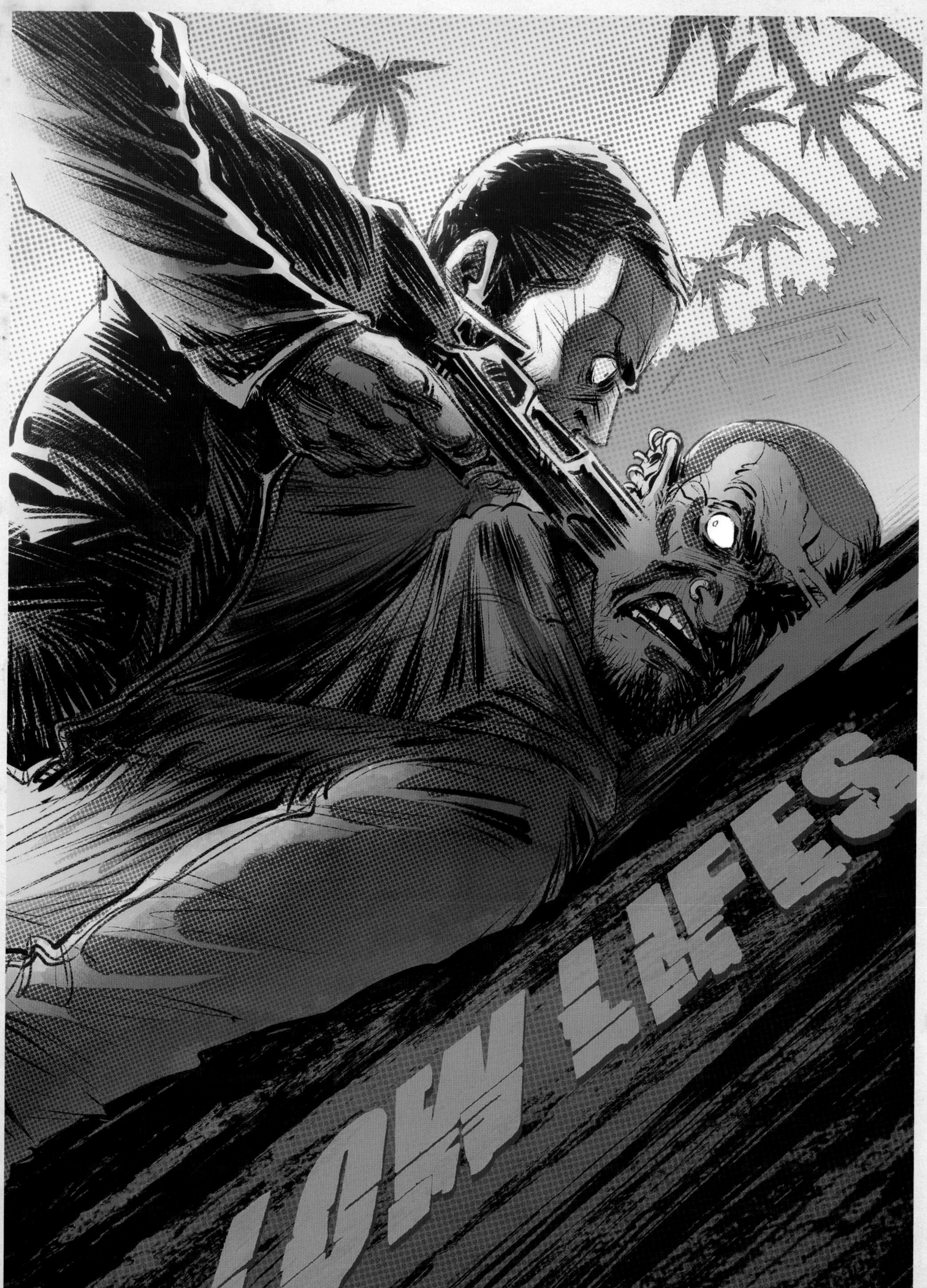
LOW LIFES

WANTED: R. TOULHOAT

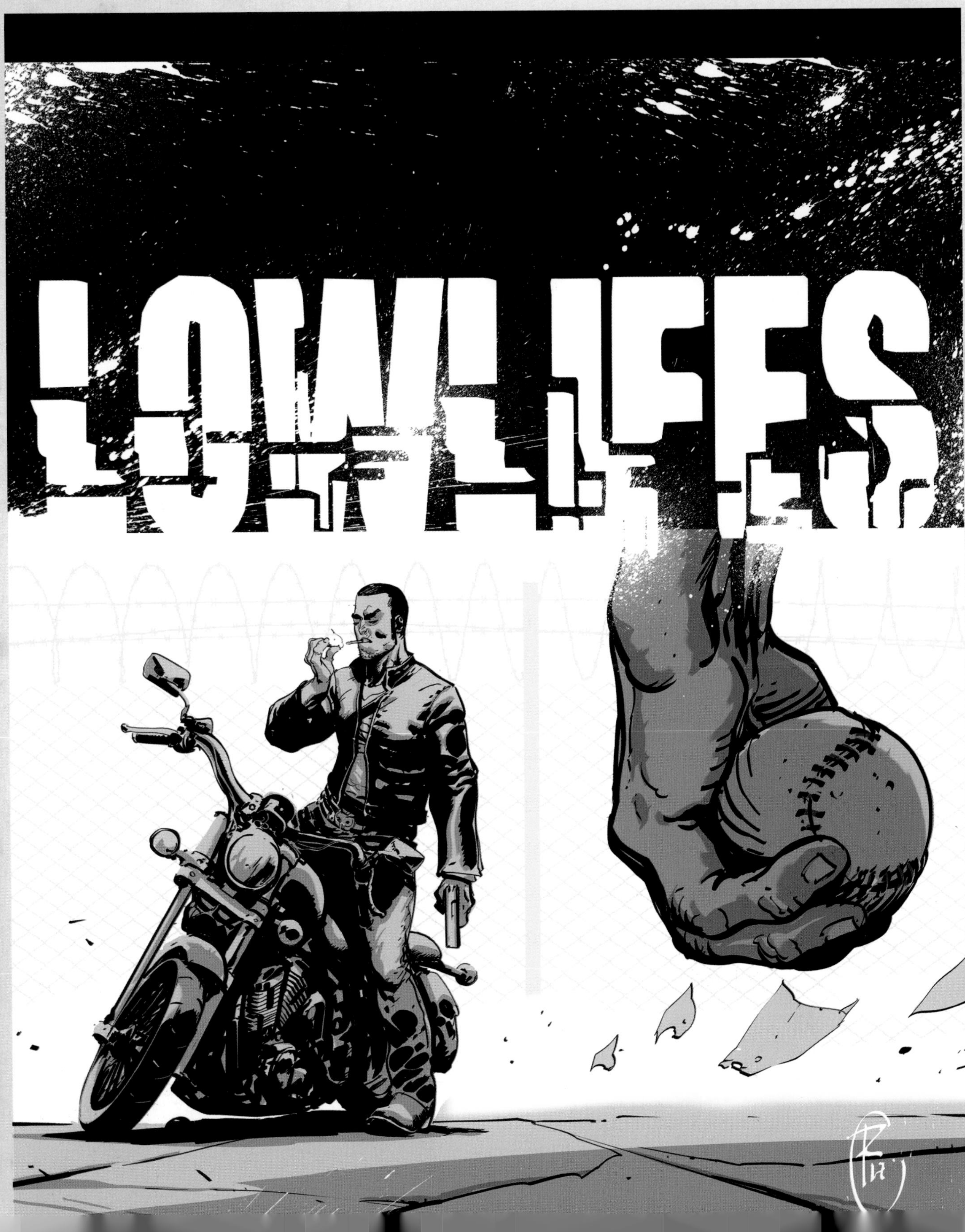
LOWLIFES

WANTED: B. COSSU

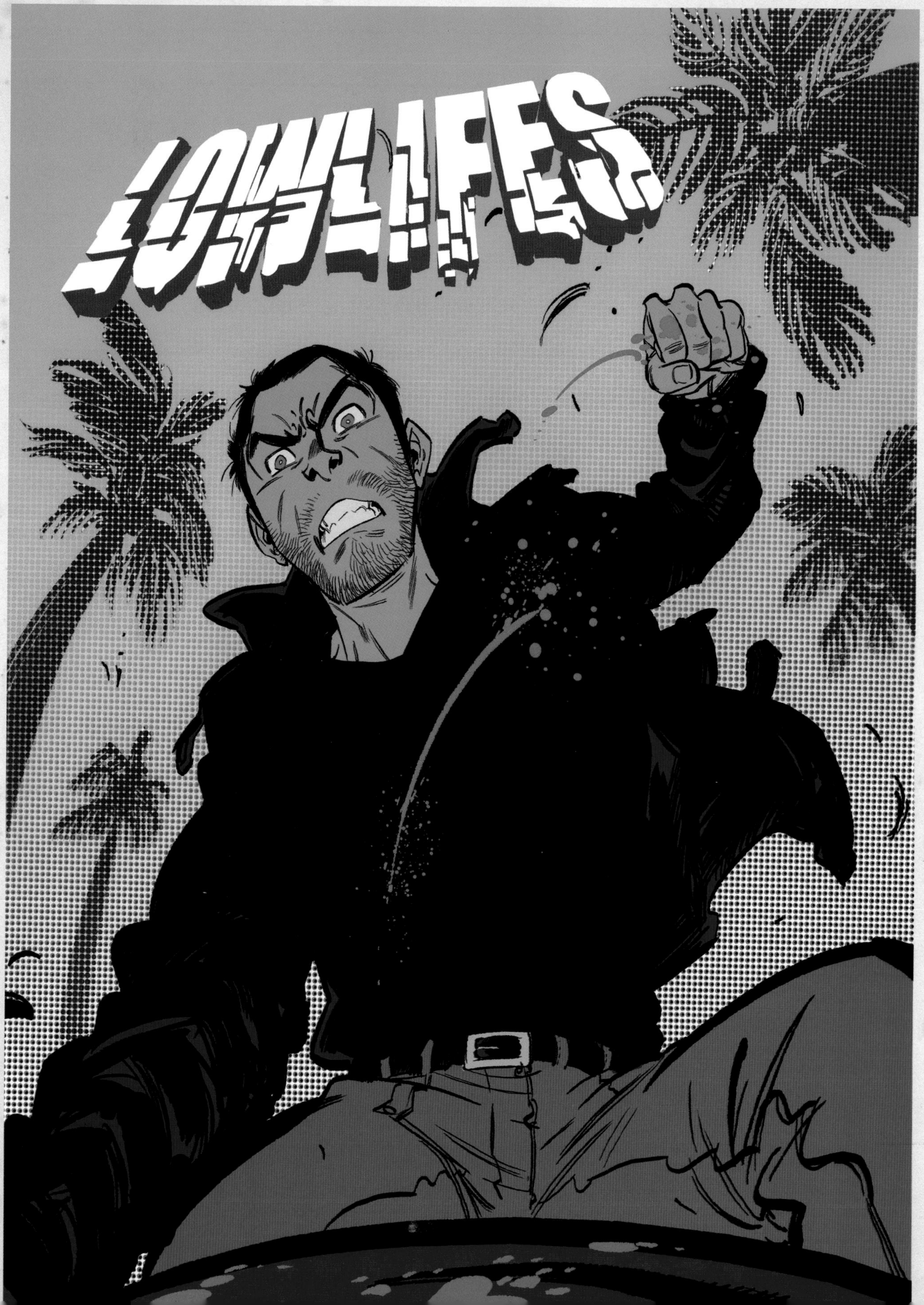
LOWLIFES

WANTED:

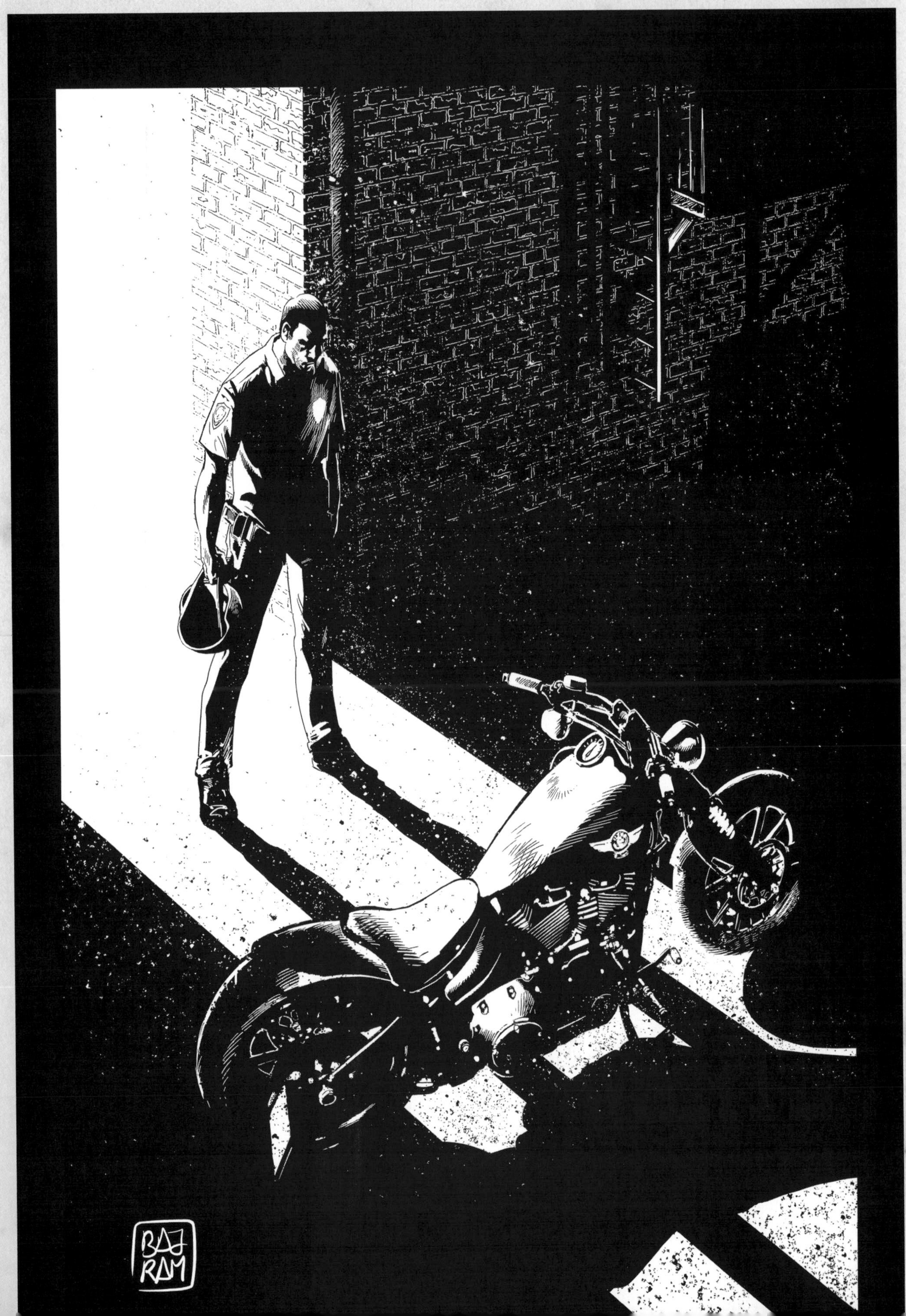
BAJRAM

D. BAJRAM

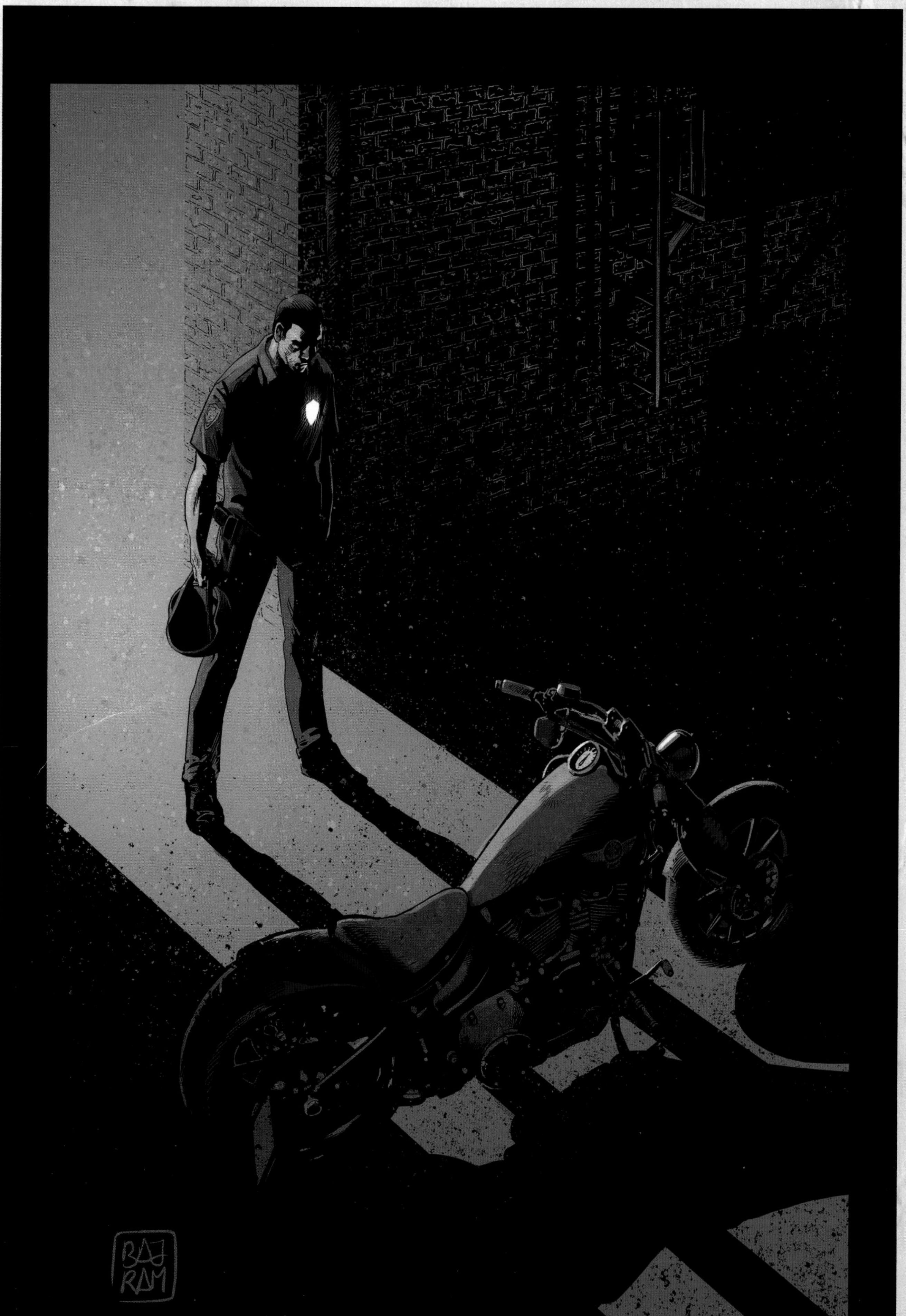
BAJ
RAM

WANTED: T. DE ROCHEBRUNE

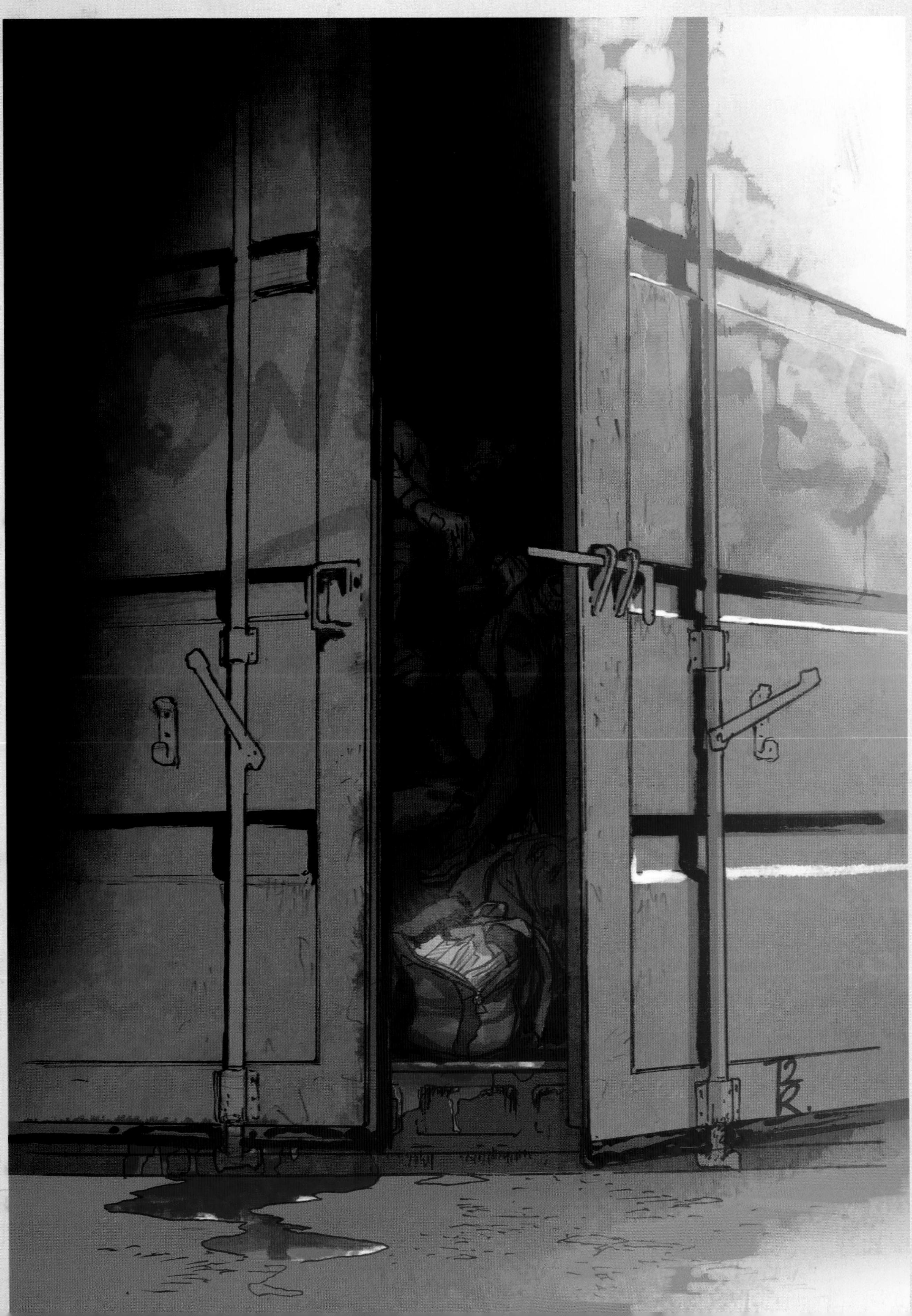

WANTED : A. SENTENAC

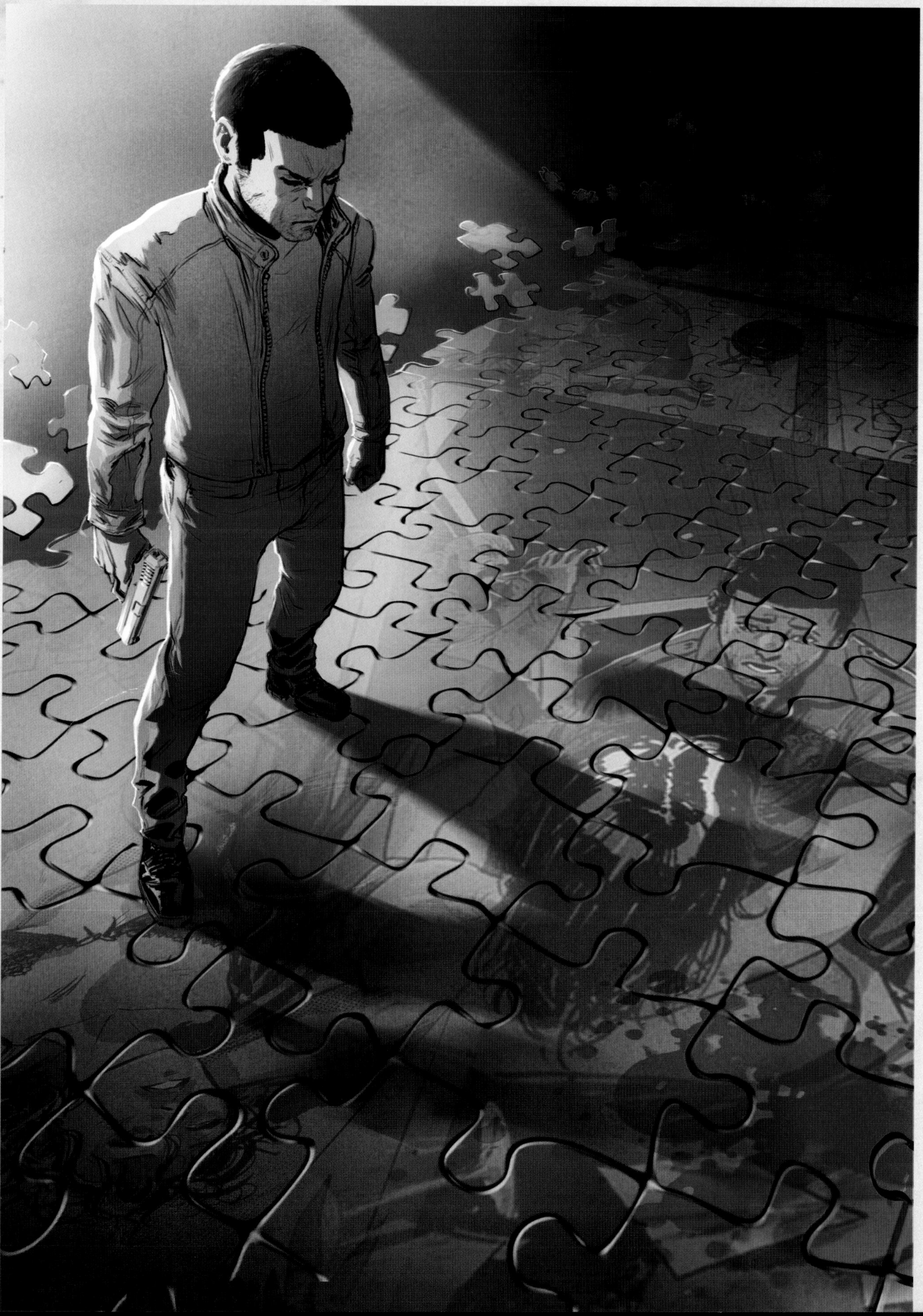

THE AUTHORS

ALEXIS SENTENAC

Born in 1975 in Le Mans, Alexis Sentenac worked as a graphic artist for nine years before getting started in *B.D.* with his first series, *Les Hydres d'Ares* (*Ares' Hydras*), written by Corbeyran and published by Delcourt. After working as a colorist on dozens of graphic albums at different publishers, he has since worked on *La Geste des Chevaliers Dragons* (*Tales of the Dragon Guard*) at Editions Soleil, drew and colored a volume of the series *Carthago Adventures* with Brice Cossu for *Humanoids*, based off a script by Christophe Bec and Dider Alcante. Then, again with Christophe Bec, he published three volumes of the science-fiction series *Siberia 56* at Glenat (which has since been published in the U.S. by Insight Comics!). For the same publisher, he drew, based off a script by Remi Guerin, the comic *50*, a horrific thriller in the *Flesh & Bones* series. He has also scratched his writing itch when he has had time, writing *Nous irons tous au bois* (*We'll All Go To The Woods*), a thriller set in the woods of Bologne, with Alain Austini for the publisher Des ronds dans l'O. He lives in Var with his wife and two kids.

BRIAN BUCCELLATO

Brian Buccellato is an author of comics born in New York who now lives in Los Angeles. He began his career as a colorist in 1994. Then, he continued working as a writer for several large publishers: Marvel (*Spider-Man*), DC (*Batman, Injustice, The Flash,* etc…) Dynamite and Image, where he co-created *Sons of the Devil*. He was the author of *The Flash* and *New 52*, he has also worked on *Batman* and *Superman*.